The Crafter's Sewcial Club

By

J C Williams

Inspired by the wonderful gang at Crafternoon Tea, Isle of Man!

You can subscribe to J C Williams' mailing list and view all his other books at:
www.authorjcwilliams.com

Cover design by Paul Nugent

Interior formatting & design, and proofreading & editing by Dave Scott

ISBN: 9798731709675

Second printing March of 2022

CHAPTER ONE

Stanley Newman, in precisely four minutes and seventeen seconds, we need to be in the car and moving!" Charlotte said, with a half-eaten piece of toast in one hand and a hairbrush in the other.

With no immediate response offered or received, Charlotte set her hairbrush down for a moment and placed her hand on the wooden bannister, peering up the staircase — her favoured position for when she wanted her voice to be heard by little people upstairs. "Stanley!" she shouted, raising her voice to Mum Level Three. "Four minutes and—"

"I heeaaarrrd you, Muuummm," came the immediate and somewhat protracted response from behind Stanley's bedroom door.

"So, you're ready to go? Schoolbag packed, dressed, breakfast eaten, and teeth brushed?" she asked with a hint of scepticism, almost as if she had a sixth sense on matters such as this. Following this reminder — the fourth, so far, this morning — Charlotte heard what sounded like a gaming controller being dropped on the floor, followed by leisurely *I've-got-all-the-time-in-the-world* footsteps. She watched on until his bedroom door opened, and the unhurried figure of Stanley appeared wearing nothing but his white Y-front undies. "Dear Lord," she muttered, taking another bite of her lukewarm toast with a shake of her head. "It's now three minutes and..." she added, looking to her watch, "forty seconds."

Encouraged by the eventual sound of a tap being opened and water gushing out after Stanley had disappeared into the loo, Charlotte returned her attention to her blonde bob, which, in reality, really required more attention than she could bestow in a little over three minutes. "It's a pleasure to meet you, too, Miss Simmonds," Charlotte said to her reflection in the living room mirror, tilting her head just a touch, offering up a closed but sincere smile. "It's an *honour* to meet..." Charlotte added, and then, "It's a *privilege*..." she tried. "No, Charlotte," she said, addressing herself in the third person, "just be yourself, and you'll be fine." And then, in a final attempt, "It's *nice* to meet you, Miss Simmonds," she settled on, applying a subtly-toned lipstick that was sufficient to show she'd made an effort but not too bold to be viewed as overly confident.

She checked her teeth for stray toast fragments, dusted off the shoulders of her navy suit jacket, and offered herself a stern *you've-got-this* expression. "One minute, Stanley!" she shouted, walking to the kitchen. In truth — but in fact known only to her — she'd built in a contingency of five minutes or so to allow for an unforeseen child-related delay, as experience had taught her well. Such as chewing gum in hair, a missing shoe, or, as recently experienced, being advised over breakfast that it was a dress-down day when his only clean and non-half-mast jeans were in a crumpled heap at the bottom of the ironing pile.

It was a little too quiet, though, considering that an obedient nine-year-old boy was hurriedly getting ready as instructed by his mum several times. Instead of relying on her shouty voice, Charlotte this time dashed up the stairs just to ensure things were as they should be and that progress was—

"*Stanley Newman!*" she exclaimed, once inside the bedroom door marked STANLEY'S DUNGEON. She looked on, incredulous, after finding Stanley laid on the floor on his tummy, feet swinging up in the air behind him, still wearing only the grand total of his white Y-fronts.

Startled, Stanley dropped his pen. "Just coming, Mum," he said, looking up.

Charlotte pressed her hand against her forehead. "Stanley, *four* times I've chased you to get ready, and yet you're lying here like a Roman Emperor in only your flipping underpants!"

"I-I-I..." stuttered Emperor Claudius.

"I-I-I," Charlotte repeated, gently teasing him. "Would you like me to fetch you some grapes?" she put forth. "Or, perhaps, a flagon of wine to enjoy while you're looking so comfortable?"

"What's a flagon?" Stanley asked.

"It doesn't matter right now," she said. "Is that homework?" she asked, in reference to the felt-tip pens strewn about, as well as a piece of A4 paper on the floor in front of him, upon which his chin was now presently rested. "You promised me you'd completed it last night, Stanley? Look, never mind... just *please* get dressed so we can go. Stanley, you know how important today is for us both, and all I asked is for you to get ready, so we could leave on time. Is that really too much to expect?"

Stanley pushed himself up onto his knees, pausing there, in that particular position, as if he were saying a prayer (which, perhaps, might not have been such a bad idea right about then, actually). "It's not homework, Mum," he explained, reaching for his sheet of paper. "It's for you," he added, holding it out for her inspection.

Charlotte's eyes fell down on the page, her weariness lifting in an instant at what she saw on it. "Aww, Stanley," she said, pressing her bottom lip out.

Stanley had drawn a giant sheep with the words "EWE CAN DO IT, MUM" written around the fluffy creature in prominent lettering.

"*Ewe* means..." Stanley began to explain, looking up at his mum. "*You*," he said, just in case any further explanation of his brilliant creativity was required.

"This is what you've been doing?"

"Yup."

"Well, Stanley. I love it."

"You see that group of dots? Just there?" Stanley asked, admiring his masterpiece.

"These ones?" Charlotte asked, pointing to what she reckoned he must have been referring to.

"It's sheep poop," Stanley declared with a stifled giggle.

"That's an awful lot of poop, Stanley," she told him. "And, unless we get a wriggle on, then *I'll* be in the poop also, yeah? Right,

I'm going to stick this picture on the fridge. So, I'll see you downstairs in, say, forty-five seconds...?"

"Thirty," Stanley suggested, already standing with one leg inside his school trousers.

Charlotte stopped at the door with the picture held close to her breast. "Thank you, lovely boy," she said, turning around just long enough to blow him a kiss.

Charlotte went downstairs, thinking about the day ahead. It was now five long months since the craft shop closed. It had been her perfect job, working there, combining her two passions: crafting, and helping people to craft. She was absolutely gutted when the owners moved away from the Isle of Man. For a brief period, she'd even harboured the notion of buying the business herself if she could only scrape the money together. Until, that is, the shop's landlord sold the building to a property developer, with the site earmarked to become yet *another* block of overpriced flats.

The local job market was, fortunately, reasonably buoyant. But Charlotte was eager to find a school term-time position to spend the holidays with Stanley and save money on childcare costs. For this reason, such employment opportunities were highly coveted, often by other single parents in a similar situation to her own. With her modest savings shrinking quicker than a woollen jumper on a hot wash, today's job interview had thus arrived at the perfect time.

"Right, short stuff!" Charlotte shouted, grabbing her keys from the kitchen table. "We need to get—"

"*Over here*, Mum," Stanley said, schoolbag in hand, stood next to the door. "Sheesh, Mum. I'm always waiting for you," he declared, with an exaggerated rolling of his eyes. "Oh, wait, hang on, Mum," he added suddenly. "You probably don't want to go to a job interview with your skirt tucked into your knickers, do you?"

"What the...?" Charlotte said, twisting round in an attempt to get a proper look at this purported dressing mishap of hers.

"Gotcha!" Stanley added, giggling away to himself.

Mollie thrust a crisp ten-pound note into the taxi driver's hand. "Keep the change," she said with a cheery smile, sliding across the rear seat.

"Oh, miss!" the driver called out just as the door slammed shut. He opened the passenger side window to continue speaking. "Miss, don't forget your bag!" he said, looking over his shoulder to the footwell.

He turned around in his seat, retrieving said item, its contents clinking against each other in the process as he lifted it from the floor. "Ah! It sounds like you're in for a good night," he suggested, passing the bag through the open window, and taking a guess as to what was inside of it.

"Thanks so much," Mollie said, wiping an imaginary bead of sweat from her forehead. "You're a lifesaver."

With bag in hand and the driver off on his way, Mollie spun around, taking in a generous lungful of seaside air as she did so. She opened the black wrought-iron gate stood before her, offering an appreciative glance at the carpet of wildflower peppering the garden as she passed through. The Manx stone cottage — her imminent destination — may have been modest, but what it lacked in overall size, it more than made up for in nostalgic charm.

Before she'd even lifted the bronze knocker, the front door flew open, giving Mollie a bit of a start.

"Flipping heck, Stanley," she said, clutching her chest. "You frightened the life out of me."

Stanley stood in the doorway, tilting his head first to one side and then the other, looking past her this way and that, and making no attempt to hide the disappointment in his eyes at finding it was only her gracing the doorstep and that there was no one else about.

"Blimey," Mollie said, when no greeting or even a smile was received, "I travel all the way over here for a special visit, and this is the reception I get? Gosh, it's nice to see you, too!"

"Sorry, Auntie Mollie. I heard the gate opening and thought you were the pizza delivery man," Stanley replied. "And then, very sadly, you weren't," he concluded, with a hungry, disappointed sigh.

"Well, what I *can* deliver you is a hug, at least," Mollie offered, leaning down to administer a cuddle that hadn't, as yet, been formally requested.

Once released from her vice-like grip, Stanley peered up at Mollie with a hint of concern present. Being only nine and not yet versed with the social graces, he raised one finger, pointing directly at her face. In particular, in the direction of her eyebrows.

"I think you've been stung by something," Stanley suggested with a grimace, offering an accusing glance over to the flying insects appreciating the wildflower. "Or some type of allergic reaction or other, maybe? My friend Louis gets all blotchy when he eats nuts... or grapes? I forget which. But anyway, yeah, he gets all blotchy, like I said. So maybe it's that."

"Stung...?" Mollie answered, taking a moment to try and work out what on earth the wee one might be talking about. "Oh, you mean my eyebrows?" she asked, with a half-laugh, realisation dawning. "Ah, that. I've just come from the salon," she said to him, by way of explanation.

"Salon?" Stanley asked, still somewhat in the dark as to how this would explain the reddened skin he was seeing.

"Yes, salon. I've just come from there, Stanley. I had my eyebrows waxed."

Stanley chuckled, figuring he was being teased. "You *wax* your eyebrows?"

"Yes," Mollie replied. "Once a month."

Stanley dwelled on this bizarre proposition for a few seconds, taking a long hard look at the irritated skin above her eyes. "But why?" he asked, apparently unable to fathom why someone would take such a drastic course of action, one that would leave them looking like they'd gone six rounds with Mike Tyson. Not to mention *willingly*, and then *every* month.

"Because, young man. It makes your Auntie Mollie look appealing to the men that aren't yet in her life. But soon will be."

"Seriously?" Stanley said, labouring the point. "Men actually like that... that red-skin thing? That's really weird. I don't get it."

"It doesn't stay red *forever*, silly," she said, walking around him in the absence of any invitation to step inside. "And if you don't understand about that, then I won't tell you what *other* thing women have waxed..." she said, though with her voice trailing off to avoid inviting possible additional questions. "Charlotte!" Mollie called out, removing her coat. "Your son Stanley is being mean to me!" she said, giving the young fellow in question a generous hair ruffling. "Be a love, would you?" she added, speaking directly to Stanley again, and handing him her coat.

"Mum, it's Auntie Mollie, not the pizza man!" Stanley shouted up the stairs. "It sounds like she's here for a flagon of wine!" he added. Although he wasn't sure what a flagon was, exactly. But he liked the way the word sounded ever since his mum had mentioned it earlier in the day.

"A flagon, indeed?" Mollie responded with a laugh, although not entirely dismissing the idea. "How'd it go, Charlotte?" she asked, placing the two bottles of red she'd brought along down onto the kitchen table as Charlotte approached. "Did you knock them bandy?"

"I don't know about *bandy,*" Charlotte replied, joining them in the kitchen, where she was much more appreciative of a good cuddle from Mollie, as it should happen, than her son had been only a short time earlier. "I did have two slightly-different-coloured shoes on, however. Not sure how I managed that. One of them navy blue, and the other a sort of deep-sea green."

"I... see. So they were *very nearly* the same colour, then," Mollie replied, trying her best to sound supportive. "A mistake, ehm... a mistake *anyone* could have made, surely?" she said, although not sounding especially convinced of her own words.

"I don't think the lady interviewing me noticed. Either that or she was just too polite to say anything about it."

"Aside from that...?"

"We'll see. I answered all of the questions, and they seemed like a really nice bunch, so fingers crossed. Nice eyebrows, by the way."

"Yes, Stanley was most complimentary about them," Mollie answered, reaching into her handbag to retrieve a white envelope with Charlotte's name written on the front. "I have excellent news," she said, barely able to contain her excitement.

"Excellent, is it?" Charlotte said, taking hold of the envelope being offered to her, interest piqued. "What's this, then?"

"Well, that's the excellent news, Charlotte. You remember my friend Fiona from work…? Well, her grandmother just died."

"Yes, that's *genuinely* jubilant news, Mollie. I think I've a bottle of Taittinger in the fridge, which we could use to formally toast her demise?"

Mollie allowed Charlotte's gentle sarcasm to slide right over her, nodding towards the envelope. "Open it."

"It's a cheque," Charlotte announced as she peered inside of the envelope, although Molly was likely already aware of this fact. "It's for three hundred and twenty pounds?"

"Payable to you," Mollie pointed out.

"I don't understand. This is for me?"

"Yup!" Mollie said, grinning broadly. "Those memory bears you make for people that take you hours and hours, but that you've never got the heart to charge for, even though you should? Well, I accepted a commission on your behalf, and that is your fee."

Charlotte's face lit up in response to the numbers written on the cheque. "I can't take this, Mollie," she said, handing the envelope back, albeit without too much vigour.

"Yes, you can, Charlotte. Fiona had a bag full of her gran's old clothes destined for recycling. I mentioned your crafting talents and showed her a photo of some memory bears you've made from old clothing items, and now she wants four of them made."

"But someone's *died*," Charlotte pointed out, lowering her head in respect. "I can't make money from people dying."

"Nonsense!" Mollie insisted. "Charlotte, Fiona was *delighted* when I explained what you can make with old clothes. She even had a tear in her eye at the thought of it. Trust me on this, Charlotte. You have a talent, for which people are willing and happy to pay. Just think of Fiona and her family cuddling up to their teddy bears, knowing their beloved gran is right there close to their heart every time they pick them up. That's what your talent can do for people!"

"You're going to get me going soon, Mollie."

"I'm serious, though. The items you create for people are about more than money, Charlotte. You give them a physical connection to their loved ones. Something they can take up in their hands and give a little squeeze when they need it the most."

"I suppose," Charlotte agreed, warming to the idea.

"Wonderful. I've given Fiona your address, and she'll be around over the weekend with a bag of clothes for you. I'm sure the extra cash will help until you get this job. Which you totally will, of course, shoe faux pas notwithstanding."

"The money *would* be useful," Charlotte conceded. "And each bear *does* take me hours to make," she added, justifying the cheque she slipped into her bra for safekeeping. "Thank you, Mollie," she said, offering up a grateful wink, and then turning her ear in the direction of the hallway. "Ah. I'm guessing the sound of those feet hammering down the stairs indicates the pizza man's arrival at our front door is imminent. Pepperoni okay?"

"Perfect," Mollie replied, rubbing her grumbling tum. "Wine?"

"Perfect. I'll fetch the flagons."

"Mum…" Stanley began, joining them in the kitchen shortly while holding a large pizza box in his hands, but one other thing besides pizza apparently on his mind. "Other than eyebrows, what else do women wax?" he asked, plonking the box down on the table.

"*What?*" Charlotte asked, flicking her eyes over to Mollie.

"That kid's got some flipping ears on him," Mollie offered, with an emerging grin. "I'll leave that question of his for you, dear Charlotte, and I'll pour the wine," Mollie kindly suggested.

CHAPTER TWO

Charlotte held up a hand, preventing the plate from heading close to her. "No, but thanks, Larry," she said, raising her eyebrows in firm defiance. "Are you trying to make me fatter than I already am?"

Larry's resolve was unwavering, however. He edged forward, plate still in hand, presenting its contents teasingly, just a few inches under Charlotte's nose. "I bought milk chocolate caramel digestives, Lotti. Your favourite biscuits," Larry said, tapping the side of his nose knowingly. "And you are most certainly *not* fat," he admonished.

Charlotte dropped her crochet hook onto her lap, reaching for the freshly poured cup of tea that Larry had placed on the table next to her. "What are you like, Larry?" Charlotte said, but her resistance was minimal at best, and she gratefully lightened his load by reaching for a delicious biscuit despite her previous protestations.

"Take one home for young Sebastian," Larry suggested, smiling broadly. "I'll bet he'd like a caramel biscuit."

"I'll take one when I leave, Larry," Charlotte said, rubbing the back of his hand, and choosing not to correct the minor mistake he'd made with her son's name. "Anyway, moving things away from the lovely biscuits, which I do appreciate, how are you progressing with your blanket?"

"Hmm," Larry replied, caressing his chin. "It's fair to say that I may have veered off course, just slightly, and lost the initial tailwind I'd been enjoying."

"That's okay, Larry," Charlotte assured him. "How far have we veered off course, do you think? Are there troubled waters ahead? Can we at least see land?" she asked, continuing the nautical-themed analogy.

"I've removed the label from the wool," Larry replied, chuffed with his efforts. "So, it's a start, Lotti?"

"That it is, Larry. Tell you what, why don't you see who else would like a biscuit, then I'll come and sit with you again? Just let me finish up with Shirley, and I'll come over and get you started, okay?"

"It's a date," Larry confirmed, heading in the direction of Mabel and Sally, pushing the refreshments trolly with a spring in his step. "I hope you're hungry, ladies!" Larry said, announcing his imminent arrival.

"Larry's quite the charmer," Charlotte said, returning her attention to Shirley, sat beside her. "Okay, so…" she added, admiring the crochet work draped over Shirley's lap. "Right. First off, Shirley, I *love* the colour choice. Why don't we now try a different colour and maybe a different stitch to really mix things up? You could aim to make a striped blanket if you like? All warm and cosy on your bed when it's finished."

Receiving an enthusiastic nod in response, Charlotte took a few sips of her tea. "How about one of these next?" she asked, taking three balls of wool from her bag for Shirley's consideration.

"Orange," Shirley said, with a sparkle in her eye.

"Excellent choice, Shirley. So, now we just need to join the new colour. Do you remember how I showed you?"

Shirley narrowed one eye. "I think so," she said, taking hold of the wool and readying her crochet hook.

Her desire was impressive, but try as she might, Shirley's trembling hand continued to hamper her efforts. Undaunted, she persisted, with an admirable determination.

Charlotte could sense the frustration but resisted the initial urge to steam in and render assistance. "Nearly there, Shirley," Charlotte said, willing her on.

Shirley sighed, throwing her troublesome, unsteady hand a look of contempt before pressing on for another effort. With her crochet hook shaking, she appeared to stop breathing momentarily, such was her intense level of concentration.

"Yep, that's it," Charlotte said, mirroring each and every movement with her own hand, rather like a backseat driver. It was humbling to observe someone trying desperately to accomplish a task that would likely have presented little difficulty a few years earlier. "Oh... go on... yes, *that's it*, Shirley. Blooming good show, girl. That's you all connected up and ready for the next colour."

Shirley looked up, clearly delighted with herself. "I could see it in my mind, Lotti, but it just didn't translate to these blasted hands. But I did it, didn't I?"

"That you did," Charlotte was thrilled to confirm. "That you did."

"Charlotte!" came a sudden, impassioned cry from the knitting brigade congregated around the table directly behind her.

"Yes, Bert?" Charlotte answered, recognising the familiar voice without even needing to turn around to verify. "What's up?"

"I've just dropped another one!" Bert said, with strain in his voice, focussed on his work in progress.

"That'll be those beans you had for lunch, Bert," Charlotte quipped, raising a laugh from the rest of the knitting station.

"Right. I better go and rescue Bert's dropped stitch," Charlotte said to Shirley. "But just shout if you need me, yeah? And Shirley... great work!"

With Bert quickly back on track with a bit of support, Charlotte moved effortlessly through the room, dispensing advice, providing a helping hand, or, perhaps, a few words of encouragement to the enthusiastic residents. Whichever way she turned, there was always a hand raised, eager for assistance, and Charlotte wouldn't have had it any other way.

Charlotte was a firm advocate of crafting's social and mental health benefits, having seen it for herself with her own grandmother and the enjoyment it brought her. For this reason, she'd mooted the idea of hosting a crafting club at the local nursing home — an idea that had been gratefully and immediately accepted by the management.

However, her first visit was slightly underwhelming, with the grand total of two people in attendance, one of whom had slept through most of it. Nevertheless, Charlotte persisted, and numbers steadily increased each week as word of her endeavours quickly spread. So much so, the nursing staff were required to move the venue from the smaller TV room to the larger dining area to accommodate everyone.

Larry, an eager and early adopter of the class, had even taken to choosing a name for their club — MAKE IT SEW — and was actively considering the idea of having club t-shirts printed.

From humble beginnings, Charlotte was thrilled to now boast twenty-seven paid-up members of the club. Well, paid-up, that is, in the sense of a constant supply of tea, biscuits, and entertainment from laughing along with the biggest bunch of lovable kooks that Charlotte had ever had the pleasure to meet.

Emma, the home manager, was delighted by the initiative and elated to see the guys and gals in her care so keen to participate. As for Charlotte, the residents quickly became friends and, collectively, like one big extended family. For Emma to witness the enthusiasm, engagement, and smiling faces all around, it truly warmed her heart.

"Charlotte, we missed you last week," Emma said, reaching down to pick up a stray knitting needle as Charlotte drew near. "Poor Larry even had a joke he'd been saving for you and was fit to burst when you couldn't come," she added, straightening up now. "He eventually told me the same joke. Several times, in fact."

"Oh, he did deliver his joke to me earlier today, actually," Charlotte replied with a groan. "Something about a lion and a hippo? Only he was laughing so much before he'd even reached the punchline that his top teeth fell out. I *still* don't know what happened to the lion," she said. Charlotte then moved a step closer to Emma, leaning in. "I did mean to speak to you today, Emma, actually," she went on, having a cautious glance over her shoulder to the tables nearest.

"That's never a good start to a conversation," Emma said, screwing her face up in apprehension about what was to come. "Are you okay?"

"Oh, I'm fine," Charlotte answered. "You see, I couldn't come last week as I had a job interview that I needed to prepare for."

"Oh, wow. That's excellent news, Charlotte," Emma replied, until the realisation hit. "Ah, no, does that mean...?" she asked, keeping the volume of her voice low.

Charlotte whispered for fear of alarming any ears that might be listening in from the quilting team. "I'm not sure, Emma. If I get the job, then it'll, unfortunately, take up most of the free time I have now," she said, pained by the prospect of possibly not having the opportunity of being there with the group. "I may have the occasional weekend when Stanley's staying with his dad, but—"

Charlotte placed her hand to her cheek, eyes welling up.

"Hey now, Charlotte..."

"I'm sorry, Emma," Charlotte said, dabbing at her eyes with her sleeve. "It's just that I adore coming here to spend time with this lot," she said, throwing her thumb over her shoulder. "But my dwindling bank balance, along with an ex-husband who appears to think child support payments are completely optional in nature, aren't exactly ideal ingredients for a prosperous future."

Emma nodded her head and smiled sympathetically. "Are you not doing the clothing alterations anymore?"

"It's just too unreliable," Charlotte explained. "One minute I'm inundated, and then nothing, for weeks. I'm still doing the memory bears and such, but, again, it's sporadic."

Emma went quiet for a moment, narrowing her eyes, deep in thought. "You know," she said, after due consideration, "we don't have too much spare money left over in the budget, but I could see if—"

"*No*," Charlotte interjected. "I mean no, but thank you, Emma. I couldn't take any money for coming here." Charlotte turned, running her eyes over the room of industrious crafters, each with their heads buried in their individual projects. "I have to confess, Emma," she continued, facing Emma once again. "Coming here each week isn't entirely selfless on my part. You see, I have the pleasure of getting to know you all, and to be a part of your lives. It makes me a happier person, so I couldn't possibly charge for that. Plus, I'm sure there are a thousand other things you could find to spend that money on?"

"Crafting lessons?" Emma suggested, off the top of her head.

"Pardon?"

"Why don't you do crafting lessons? In the broader sense, I mean. Similar to what you've done here, but for others. You could charge a fee. It might be a way to generate some income?"

Charlotte laughed off the suggestion. "Who'd want to pay me?" she asked with a shrug. "You can learn anything you like on YouTube for free these days. Yesterday, in fact, my Stanley took great delight in demonstrating Vinyasa Yoga techniques that he'd picked up online. Why he was watching Vinyasa Yoga videos on YouTube, I haven't the faintest idea. But he was actually rather good at it."

"I know what you're saying," Emma pressed on. "But look at the members of Make It Sew, Charlotte. If it wasn't for you, most of them wouldn't be able to create a crochet blanket, or be able to knit a cardigan, much less anything else, now would they?"

"I suppose not," Charlotte conceded.

"And," Emma added, "don't forget the social element. They're all chatting happily away with each other, having a cuppa, and generally putting the world to rights while doing something they enjoy. For many, this is one of the highlights of their week. It's a formula that's worked amazingly well in here, so something you could replicate elsewhere as well, in general, perhaps?"

"Well, that'll be due to my impeccable sense of humour, no doubt."

"You *should* think about it, Charlotte. You have a, erm…" Emma said, swirling her fingers, searching for the appropriate words. "A rapport with the people here… a definite chemistry… not to mention a lovely personality… a certain, shall we say, *je ne sais quoi*, if you will," she suggested.

Charlotte nodded along, finding nothing at all that Emma was saying the slightest bit disagreeable. "I like this game, Emma. Please, continue," she said with a grin.

"One favour?" Emma asked. "Until you have any solid news on the job front, could I ask you—"

"Don't worry, Emma. I won't mention anything to the gang just yet."

Emma smiled, taking a lingering look around the room, which

was a hive of activity. "You did this. *You*," she told Charlotte. "Be proud of yourself," she said. "Ah. Hold that thought for a moment, you've got Larry incoming," she warned suddenly, glancing over Charlotte's shoulder with a chuckle.

"I've got another joke for you, Lotti!" Larry said, setting out his stall before he'd even arrived.

"I'll leave you to it," Emma said. "I think I've enjoyed his entire repertoire by now," she added, with a warm smile. "Oh, and good luck with you-know-what," she advised.

"What's blue..." Larry began, already laughing at his own comic genius. "What's blue, yellow, and likes to... No, wait, hang on," he said, raising his finger for a moment to aid in his thinking process. "What's *green*, yellow, and likes to..."

CHAPTER THREE

Charlotte sat bolt upright in bed, rubbing her sleepy eyes. For a moment, she wondered if she'd only dreamt the clattering noise that had dared to rouse her from her deep slumber. She twisted her neck, turning her head slowly and listening intently, attempting to triangulate where the noise she thought she'd heard originated. She moved her head this way and that, but the only sound to be had was the beat of her racing heart, pulsing in her ears. Despite her investigation, she could hear nothing untoward presently — only silence.

Once satisfied all was in order and nothing amiss, Charlotte lowered her noggin towards the pillow for a further appointment with the land of nod. It was, after all, Saturday morning and deserving of an extra hour in bed, she reckoned.

"Bloody hell!" Charlotte shouted, before her head had even hit the pillow. "What on earth?" she added, responding to what sounded like a saucepan in a washing machine on a spin cycle. Charlotte leapt out of bed like an Olympic athlete. Instinctively, she bolted first towards Stanley's room, wondering if he'd managed to roll out of bed and somehow triggered a landmine, as that might possibly explain the din.

"Stanley…?" she said, throwing open his door, but the reassuring scene before her of a snoring lump under the duvet indicated he was right where he should be and was not the actual cause of the racket.

Charlotte continued her inspection through the hallway, peering down the staircase, hoping she wouldn't be greeted by a desperate but most probably disappointed burglar owing to the slim pickings on offer.

"*Hello*?" she said firmly, hoping to frighten away any potential intruders with the resolute tone of her voice. With no response received (not that burglars often engaged in small talk), she quickly returned to her bedroom, putting on her dressing gown, and then grabbing the hockey stick which sat behind the door for just such an occasion, just in case.

"*Hello*," she repeated. "I'm *armed*," she said, taking a firm grip of the stick in case its deployment should be required at a moment's notice. Charlotte moved gingerly down the stairs, tensed and ready for action. Once at the foot of the stairs and seeing no one about, she teased open the curtains covering the small portal window near to the front door, for a quick look outside.

"What the...?" she said, in reference to the column of metal rungs in clear view directly outside — a ladder, it would appear, resting up against the exterior wall. *Did I leave that thing there?* she asked herself.

But her question was answered in short order when she caught sight of a pair of boots descending into view, setting off the clattering noise once more. *I'm being burgled!* she thought, panic taking over. *Bloody hell, I was right! I'm actually being burgled!*

Rational thought evaded her. She'd always fancied herself to be calm under pressure and yet, right now, all she could do was hug the hockey stick and mumble to herself.

The occupant of the boots began to whistle a tune that sounded very much like Queen's "Lazing on a Sunday Afternoon," as near as Charlotte could tell, taking Charlotte off guard what with both the odd song choice and the relaxed manner in which it was being offered under the circumstance, and also despite it not yet being Sunday (nor afternoon, for that matter). It was certainly not in any way, shape, form, or fashion a discreet rendition, either. If it was indeed a burglar as Charlotte presumed, they'd evidently missed the portion of their training course concerning stealth.

The whistling ended abruptly, only to be immediately replaced by a deep voice from partway up the ladder now picking up at the point where, it would seem, specific lyrics had suddenly been recalled. Charlotte tuned her ears into the cheerful warbling. She narrowed one eye as a knowing expression suddenly washed over her face — a result of realising that the voice sounded *very* familiar to her.

Charlotte lowered her weapon, suspecting it would no longer be required. She unlocked the front door, swearing under her breath. Once outside and stood in the fresh morning air, she tightened the cord on her dressing gown. Staring up at the "burglar's" wiggling arse above, her suspicions as to the mystery person's identity were soon confirmed.

"Ahem," she said softly, not wanting her sudden presence to result in a nasty fall for the figure overhead. "*Ahem*," she said, once more, followed by, "George, it's seven a.m. on Saturday morning."

"Oh, hey, Lotti," George cheerily replied, bringing his impromptu *Britain's Got Talent* audition to a conclusion. "Lovely day for it!" he added.

"A lovely day for *what*, exactly? George, I thought you were a *burglar*, for goodness' sake. I was all for attacking you with a hockey stick just a moment or two ago! You don't know how close you came to being on the receiving end of a severe beating!"

"Hmm, I should think maybe a cricket bat might be better for that?" George offered cheekily, looking down the ladder. "Or perhaps a croquet mallet?" he added helpfully. "Anyway, I'm here to fix the lead flashing on the chimney stack," George explained. "Like I said I would, Lotti. It's April, after all, and you know what they say about showers in April? I didn't want you to have any problems. You know, with damp and whatnot."

"*George*," she said in a sort of visible disbelief, "*George*, you said you'd fix the flashing, what, two *years* ago? No, thinking about it, we were still married at the time, so that would've been two and a *half* years. At *least*!"

"And so here I am, just as I promised, yeah…?" George ventured gamely. "Better late than never, yes?" he asked, followed very quickly by, "Oi, is that the kettle I hear boiling, Lotti?"

Charlotte returned inside, swearing again under her breath at her unwanted early-morning alarm call, as she was too much of a lady to curse aloud. She suspected there might well be some kind of ulterior motive for the sudden, surprise maintenance project —

thirty-some-odd months late! — but as there was a persistent damp patch on her bedroom ceiling as a result of a leak, she was happy to go with it, for now. She'd worry about any possible hidden motives from George only after a sufficiently caffeine-imbued morning beverage had been imbibed.

As far as ex-husbands went, George was by no means the worst out there. His heart was in the right place, for the most part, and as far as Stanley was concerned, at least, he could do no wrong. George wasn't a bad person, necessarily. He was and remained a wonderful father. They were both peas in a pod, he and Stanley, that's for sure, sharing a childlike outlook on life. Which was perfectly acceptable for Stanley, what with him being an *actual* child, of course.

However, George was devoid of any meaningful sense of responsibility. It was this liberated attitude towards life that Charlotte initially found refreshing when they'd first met. *Carpe diem* was George's motto in regard to pretty much everything. Fancy a holiday, for instance? Why, go right ahead, stick it on the credit card. Work a bit boring, perhaps? Well, simply quit and see what crops up. Fancy a night out with the lads, by chance? Why not? In fact, might as well make an entire weekend of it! And so on and so on. It didn't help matters, either, that when they were married, most of George's mates were still single and eager to party. George was just not ready to give up the bachelor lifestyle to which he was accustomed, even once he was married, a parent, and with a mortgage to pay.

With his shaven head, bushy beard, and hands like shovels, he hadn't been Charlotte's *usual* type. Her friend Mollie had suggested, in fact, that Charlotte must have been going through some sort of lumberjack phase in her choice of men. Living up to that image, you could say, it was George who eventually gave Charlotte the chop, so to speak. The allure of the single lifestyle was evidently too much of a challenge for him to resist. Ironic then — for someone so eager to embrace singledom — that George had shacked up with someone else only a few short weeks after he'd split up with Charlotte.

The separation was far from ideal, especially where the emotions of a then-five-year-old child were concerned. But both George and Charlotte made a firm commitment to remain cordial, and under no circumstances would they allow their relationship status (or lack thereof) to negatively impact Stanley — a vow they continued to try their best to follow to this very day. Fortunately, with her parents acting as guarantors, Charlotte was also able to take over the cottage's mortgage, which at least enabled Stanley and herself to remain in the home they loved, with every other weekend for Stanley spent staying over with his dad.

Of course, Stanley was devastated at seeing his parents living apart. But, over time, he came to realise that there were certain advantages in having two loving and overcompensating parents, including double the number of presents (for both birthdays and Christmas). And although he was likely still too young to realise it, having two separated parents who were on relatively friendly terms with each other was preferable as compared to those parents still cohabitating yet continually bickering.

This morning, Charlotte had left George to his own devices up on the roof as she showered, dressed, and made breakfast and such. Now, Charlotte was impressed to hear hammering from upon high and what sounded like definite progress being made in the repairs. The cynic in her, however, couldn't help but wonder what motivated George's unplanned appearance on this one particular day. It surely couldn't be money he was after, as George knew she didn't have much of that to go around.

"Oh, no," she said, slowly stirring the tea she'd made for George and was about to bring out to him. Charlotte glanced at the calendar on the fridge door to confirm the date. "He wouldn't. Would he?" she asked herself aloud, draining the teabag against the side of the mug. George's monthly child maintenance payment was due this coming Monday, a few days away. Could this be the reason, then, for the early morning maintenance mission? To do this work in lieu of payment? If so, it wasn't ideal timing, as she needed to purchase new shoes for Stanley, who was enjoying something of a growth spurt right at the present moment.

"Here we go!" Charlotte announced once outside a few moments later, with a sunny smile, and looking up the height of the ladder. "Tea break!" she added, to clarify what she was offering.

"Smashing!" responded a voice from up on the roof. "And is that by any chance a bacon sandwich I can smell?" George shouted down, pushing his luck.

"Maybe when you're finished, George," Charlotte answered him, taking his implied request into consideration. "Are you sure it's safe up there?" she added. "Are you not supposed to use scaffolding?"

George made short work descending the ladder. "It's fine so long as you don't fall, Lotti," he told her. "And I don't intend to fall."

George sidled over to the garden gate, cuppa in hand. "You know," he offered, taking an appreciative look over the distant sea view, "there are certainly worse places to live," he suggested, purposefully nodding his head. He held his admiring gaze for a few moments longer, taking the opportunity to blow the steam from his cup before continuing to verbalise his thoughts. "Stanley's fortunate to grow up in a cottage so close to the beach," he added reflectively, and then, "We had some good times here, Lotti, didn't we? I mean, it wasn't a *complete* shipwreck, was it?"

"Oh my god..." Charlotte ventured, joining him by the perimeter stone wall. She looked him up and down, placing her hand to her mouth. "You're not... you're not ill, are you, George...? Is that why you're here? To tell me you're dying, or gravely ill? Oh my goodness, George. Oh, Georgie! Oh, no!"

George narrowed one eye, taking a meaningful slurp of his brew. "Eh?" he said in response. "Don't be daft."

"So you're not dying?"

"I don't think so?" George offered with a shrug. "So long as I don't fall off your roof, that is," he added, looking up.

Charlotte lowered her hand, now that it was no longer required to shield her from any potential terminal illness-related shock. "So if you're not dying, why, *exactly*, if I might ask, are you being so helpful at this time on a Saturday morning?" she asked. "Have you gambled the child allowance, George?" she said, shaking her head from side to side and tut-tutting before she'd even heard the answer. "Is that what you've come to tell me? Is that it...?"

"*One* time, that happened!" George rebuffed. "It was just the one time, I swear, and never again! I've not gambled for, let's see…" he said, bobbing his head as he tried to count out in his mind how long precisely it had been. "Well, a long time!" he eventually settled on.

"Okay," Charlotte replied, inwardly relieved that she could still potentially afford Stanley's new shoes at some point, she hoped, in the very near future. "In that case, I apologise for the inference. But, you can probably understand why I'd be a touch sceptical about your sudden and helpful appearance?"

"I'm deeply offended, Lotti. Deeply," George said with a wry smile. "But…" he added, taking another slurp of his tea, "now you mention it—"

"I *knew* there was something, George! Whatever it is, are you at least going to finish fixing my roof?"

George placed his now-empty mug on top of the stone wall. He turned to face Charlotte, caressing his prodigious beard like a mighty Viking warrior contemplating the battle ahead. "Well, see, there is something I wanted to… That is, there's something that I felt that I *ought* to let you know about…"

Charlotte folded her arms across her chest, staring at George intently. "Which *is*?" she asked, cocking her head, waiting.

"Thing is…" George began. "Thing is," he repeated, sucking in air through his teeth like a car mechanic about to deliver depressing and expensive news, "I've asked Vanessa to marry me. And I didn't want you to hear about it from Stanley, or, you know, like, through the grapevine." George winced, uncertain as to what reaction he'd receive to his matrimonial announcement.

"Oh," Charlotte said simply, looking away for a moment to collect her thoughts. She walked over and rested her hands on the gate with a faraway expression.

"Ehm, you okay?" George asked, keeping a safe and respectable distance.

"Yes," Charlotte advised. "Quite okay," she quickly added, but said in a tone that women had mastered such that it was understood that this meant, in actual fact, that she was *not* completely okay.

It was a type of delivery George was well accustomed to, it would appear, what with him discreetly taking a side-step in order to somewhat increase the distance between them.

"Are you sure?" he asked. "It's just that with me getting engaged, we might need to, you know, uh... finalise the divorce."

"Yes. Great," Charlotte said, looking to her feet. "Of course we do. We should."

George sensed it was an excellent time to return up the rungs of the ladder and continue on with his chimney repairs. He felt that to remain where he was would be akin to poking a sleeping lion with a very sharp stick. "I'll just..." he explained, pointing upward, in the general direction of where the roof was, and where he would soon be headed.

"I'm absolutely fine," Charlotte said, referring back to George's initial question. Again, not ordinarily a sign that she was taking it as well as she initially indicated.

George quickened his pace, eager, it would appear, to return to the job at hand.

"A bachelor lifestyle," Charlotte said, turning to face the cottage, staring at the grass.

"What's that?" George said, foot hovering above the first rung on the ladder.

"A bachelor lifestyle," Charlotte repeated. "When you left me, that was your reason. You said something about feeling like you couldn't breathe and that you were more suited to a bachelor lifestyle. You remember?"

George nodded in confirmation. "I do," he said solemnly.

"And yet by some miracle," Charlotte went on, raising her head, holding her palms to the heavens like she was delivering a sermon to her flock, "not two months after we'd split up, and you were already shacked up with Carrie. And then a year after that, you'd moved on to Vanessa. Is Vanessa the lucky lady, or have you moved on yet again since then? Who exactly *is* the lucky lady here in question?"

"No. It's Vanessa, as I said," George interjected. "Lotti..."

"I was humiliated, George. Yes, couples break up. That's life. But, to tell people, our *friends*, that you wanted some space, only to jump straight back into another relationship almost immediately, that was a bitter pill to swallow. And now, *Mr-I-Want-to-Be-Single* is heading down the aisle for a second attempt at marriage."

"I'm sorry," George said sincerely. "The last thing I wanted to do was humiliate you, Lotti. You know that, right?"

"Are you happy?" she asked flatly.

A flicker of a smile emerged on George's face, along with a glimmer in his eye. "Very much so," he replied, as the grin overtook his bearded face.

Charlotte's frosty demeanour thawed. She puffed out her cheeks, "Well," she said, exhaling. "In that case, I'm pleased for you, George. And, I do mean it, George. I wish you both happiness, whoever the girl might be. Do I get an invite to the wedding?"

George shuffled his feet for a moment, and now it was his turn to look down at the grass. "Eh, well, thing is… it's just that, erm… you know…"

"I'm kidding, George, don't worry. And, yes, I guess this means we'll need to finalise the divorce papers, then, as you said," she told him. "Ah, a divorcée at the age of thirty-two…" she said. She chewed over that statement for a few seconds, releasing an audible sigh. "Oh, and George," she added, "just so you know, for what it's worth, it wasn't always a complete train wreck, you know. Or shipwreck, or what have you."

George winked. "You're not wrong, Lotti," he offered, and then, changing the subject entirely, his eyes widening, "Oh, something else," he said. "Now, I don't mean to pry, Lotti…"

"Which means you're going to?" Charlotte suggested.

"Pretty much, yes," George answered. "Stan-the-Man mentioned about these Crafternoon sessions, I think he called them, that you were thinking of starting up?"

"He did? Wow, I guess he *was* listening to me after all," Charlotte said, impressed and taking a mental note to commend her son when he woke up. "Yes, I was mulling over the idea of organising sewing and crafting lessons," she continued. "It's something I'd like to do, but there's the cost of hiring somewhere, and I don't think I'd squeeze too many people into my little kitchen as an alternative."

"Ah!" George offered, finger raised up into the air and appearing rather pleased with himself. "Well, you see, I might have a solution for you. One that will potentially get you up and running, and also, hopefully, buy me some brownie points in view of the whole divorce situation."

"Go on," Charlotte said, interest piqued.

"Well, I've been asked to carry out some repairs down at the Laxey church hall," George said, pointing in the vague direction of where the hall was located, far off in the distance. "A few new tiles, replacing some flooring, touching up some paintwork, and such."

"It's nice that you've plenty of work on, George. But, I'm—"

"I thought you might not react particularly well about, you know, the whole divorce situation thingy. In fact I was worried you'd pop your cork about it, even," George explained. "So, I wanted to have something nice to offer up in my back pocket in addition to the chimney repairs. I would've probably offered it anyway, mind you. It's just that by mentioning it today, in particular, I thought I'd—"

"You're waffling, George."

"Yes. Yes, I am," George conceded. "Anyway, what I've done is, I've offered to complete all of the repair work in return for two hours of hall hire once a week for the next three months."

"What?" Charlotte replied. "Why do you want to hire the church hall?"

"*Derr*," George offered playfully. "I *don't* want to use the hall, but I know *someone* who *might*, Lotti." George waited for a couple of seconds, as he could hear the cogs whirring inside her head. "You can now start your Crafternoon club up without having to worry about paying the rental costs for a while."

Charlotte stood there, mouth agape, allowing George's words to sink in. Once they'd registered, she walked over to George, stood up on her tippy toes, and planted a kiss right on his furry cheek. "I'm actually tearing up, George," she told him. "That's such a wonderful, thoughtful gesture, George. Thank you."

"S'nothing," George said with a sniff, polishing the imaginary medals on his chest. "Also, it sounds like a great initiative, Lotti. I think you'll do well with it."

Charlotte gratefully accepted the encouragement. "You can be the guest of honour, George. You'd look wonderful with a pair of knitting needles in hand," she suggested. "The gang up at the nursing home have a blast each week, so, hopefully, it'll be more of the same, but to a broader audience," she offered with a cheerful smile. "You know, George," she added, "I think you've now properly earned that bacon sarnie you were pining for earlier, yeah? As well as another cuppa, if you'd like? I'll wake up the kiddo, and he can join us."

"Hell, yeah!" George said, starting the climb up his ladder. "Oh…" he offered as an afterthought, coming to a halt halfway up, "if and when you meet Vanessa, it's probably best if we don't mention about me working for free to get the hall rental paid for my soon-to-be ex-wife, okay? I'm sure she'd be okay about it, but…"

George looked down from his elevated position to see Charlotte pressing her thumb to her forehead, teasing that he was, perhaps, under her thumb.

"Of course," Charlotte said with a laugh, walking over to the foot of the ladder. Charlotte placed her hands on the cold metal, looking up at George. "Now, then. What were you saying about me popping a cork?" she asked, giving the appearance she was about to yank the ladder right from under him and send him tumbling to the ground.

"*Moi?*" George asked, with feigned shock. "Nonsense, Lotti, you're as sane as they come. Calm, cool, and collected!"

"Seriously, though, George. Thank you," Charlotte said, releasing her gentle grip on the sides of the ladder. She felt a wave of excitement wash over her, clapping her hands together, and then dancing a happy little jig as the giddy realisation hit her: "It's happening, George!" she cried. "The Crafternoon Social Club is really happening!"

CHAPTER FOUR

Charlotte sat hunched over, elbows resting on the kitchen table, offcuts of fabric covering every available centimetre of the wooden surface. The casual observer, had there been one present, could easily have been forgiven for believing this to be organised — or very possibly disorganised — chaos. However, that observation would have been wide of the mark, as Charlotte had a tried and tested system, with each section of fabric strategically placed and ready for deployment when the need should arise. At least that was her story, if asked, and by golly she was sticking to it.

Sat on the nearby oak sideboard watching events unfold was an adorable elephant calf. It sported what appeared to be a grateful smile offered, perhaps, in gratitude to its creator across the kitchen, who sat with her needle in hand. Either side of the large-eared little fellow, flanking it like two bookends, were a pair of jolly orangutans with oversized heads squeezed into a bucket hat apiece. They were both unable to watch on like their tusker friend, however, as the two of them were still waiting patiently, at present, for their eyes to be affixed.

Charlotte often bit down on her bottom lip when concentrating. So, after making intricate memory bears for four days straight, the skin there was now a bit raw from being nibbled. Her neck ached, her fingers felt arthritic, and her bum cheeks had fallen asleep hours earlier. Still, she was completely delighted with the results of her current industrious endeavours. She just hoped that Mollie's friend, Fiona, would be equally as pleased when she came to collect them later that day, and the aches and pains would soon be forgotten when the fruits of her labour were finally handed safely to their new owner. She felt it a privilege to take on the task of turning a bagful of surplus clothing into items that would be loved for years to come. It was an enormous responsibility to be entrusted with such personal things, and one that wasn't lost on her. Often, the shirt, jumper, or even trousers that she'd just cut to pieces were someone's only remaining physical connection to a loved one no longer with them — one of the reasons, then, that Charlotte poured so much passion into any of her creations.

Suddenly, the tabletop vibrated, breaking Charlotte's concentration. She patted her hand down on the fabric layers, feeling for a lump that would be her phone and the most probable cause of the rumbling. "Hang on, I'll be right with you!" she said, although, of course, any potential caller wouldn't have been able to hear her at this point.

With her mobile quickly recovered, and verified as indeed being the source of the mystery vibrations, Charlotte dutifully placed the phone to her ear. "Hello! Charlotte Newman, crafting goddess!" she announced brightly. "Ehm, yes. Yes, this is she," Charlotte confirmed, changing tack and adopting a more formal tone now, as she felt the occasion required. "Oh, hello. Yes, lovely to speak to you again," she said.

Charlotte pushed her chair back, listening intently as she rose, and then paced slowly around the kitchen table, circling round it like a sailing ship mapping an island coastline. She made the occasional encouraging noise for the benefit of the caller, who was doing most of the talking. "Well that's splendid news," Charlotte declared as the conversation drew to a close. "Bye, now," she concluded, ending the call, and then placing the phone next to the handcrafted menagerie sat on the sideboard.

"Splendid news?" she said to the baby elephant. "Why on earth did I say *splendid*?"

But, of course, the wee tusker, along with the two orangutans, remained mum on the subject. After all, who were they to judge? Plus, as the orangutans didn't yet have eyes, they were left somewhat in the dark as to what was going on at this point anyway.

Taking her phone back and leaving the animals to ponder her words on their own, Charlotte began to swivel her hips rhythmically — despite the absence of any music to dance to other than what may have been playing inside her head. Her lips parted to reveal a toothy grin as her arms swung side to side above her head. "Yes! I've got a job!" she yelled to nobody in particular, what with her being home alone and all. "I don't believe it," she said, not believing it. "I've got a job!"

After an impressive and energetic performance across the length and breadth of the kitchen floor, she came to a halt, appearing dazed and in a state of shock. She sat back down at the kitchen table, her hands trembling, nervous but excited. "I've got a job," she said once more, desperately wanting to share the news of her good fortune with someone other than the row of stuffed toys. She then took up her phone, dialling a number consigned to memory.

"Come on," she said, urging the call to connect, and then, "Mollie, I have amazing news!" she blurted out, without so much as a hello, as soon as her best friend was on the line. "No," she offered to Mollie's initial response, "I don't have a date," she replied. "No, it's even *better* than that," she teased. "Mollie… Mollie, I've been offered the job!" she said, followed by a squeal of delight so high in pitch at its tail end that only the ears of the neighbourhood's beloved pet canines would likely have been able to register it. "I *know*," she added, nodding in agreement into the phone, "I absolutely *do* rock!"

No one could fault Charlotte for having something of a spring in her step as she walked towards Laxey Primary School for the afternoon pick-up. The memory bear handover had resulted in tears of appreciation from their recipient, always a good indicator of a well-satisfied customer. Further raising Charlotte's spirits was the occasion of the damp patch on her bedroom ceiling drying out nicely. In addition, the inaugural meeting of the official CRAFTER-NOON SOCIAL CLUB was scheduled for later that week. And now, to top it all off, she also had a job offer on the table. Yes, Charlotte had something of a John Travolta strut about her, and there wasn't much, right about now, that could diminish her mood. Nossir, not even being greeted by the appalling half-smiling/half-sneering face of Amelia Sugden stood at the foot of the steps leading down to the school playground area...

"Oh, Charlotte!" Amelia called up, offering a friendly wave that Charlotte felt rather confident was insincere.

"Just wonderful," Charlotte muttered under her breath, more as an observation made to herself than an answer to the person hailing her. She offered the woman a half-hearted nod in return, wondering what she could possibly have done to warrant this current, unwanted attention from Amelia.

Amelia, by way of introductions, was the self-appointed head of an intimate clique of school mothers, of which Charlotte was quite happy to possess no membership card. For this group, the outward perception of leading perfect lives, and the flaunting of such, was what they lived for and thrived upon. For them, social standing was everything. Or at least that's certainly how it appeared. They all had flawless makeup, regardless of the time of day, wore designer clothes, drove posh cars, and typically spent their evenings gathered round a large grand piano singing fancy songs with their academically gifted offspring, all while sipping expensive champagne. Okay, granted, the last part was only surmised by Charlotte, being only envisioned in her mind. But, still, one gets the idea.

Charlotte and Amelia also shared some personal history. A good few years earlier, back during their own school days, the object of Amelia's yearning, Thomas Pinkerton, turned out to only, as it should happen, have eyes for Charlotte. Charlotte did date him for a bit, but it wasn't exactly in any way the romance of the year as far as she was concerned, that's for sure, peaking, as it did, with a visit to the cinema and then a quick smooch around the back of the roller disco. Charlotte hadn't even been aware of the matter of this unrequited love on Amelia's part until Amelia — fuelled by ample amounts of prosecco consumed, fifteen years afterwards, at a mutual friend's Christmas party — accused Charlotte of viciously stealing away her heart's desire.

Since then, Amelia had developed an innate ability to condescend and insult both Charlotte and others with consummate ease. Her comments, often barbed, were delivered to offend; of this fact, most were in no doubt. But when the offence was inevitably taken, Amelia would feign innocence, attempting to persuade the offended party to feel stupid and foolish for taking offence when no offence was ever supposedly meant. Her act was that polished that Charlotte had been left, on previous occasions, to wonder if she'd actually maybe taken the wrong end of the stick after all and was, perhaps, merely being overly sensitive in allowing herself to become offended when she ought not to be. However, her suspicions regarding Amelia's intent were confirmed following discussions with plenty of other parents who'd similarly found themselves on the receiving end of Amelia's sharp tongue, as well as a fair handful of teachers at their local school, not to mention even the bloody lollipop man for that matter. All were able to readily attest that, sadly and most unfortunately, Amelia's apparent mean-spirited nature was not merely a product of Charlotte's imagination.

"Charlotte!" Amelia called out once more, presently inviting her closer with a firm wave of her hand.

Charlotte glanced at her watch and, as it was still five minutes until kicking-out time for the kids, considered it a little too long to be able to politely avoid Amelia's solicitations. Charlotte offered up a forced smile, trudging down the small set of steps towards the pit of the viper's den, as it were.

"Ladies," Charlotte said by way of greeting, once she was stood before Amelia and the other members of Amelia's clique also present.

"I love that jumper," Amelia said, her hand stroking Charlotte's upper arm. "I always think to myself it looks terribly comfortable. I imagine that's why you wear it so very often? If it's as comfortable as it looks, I mean?"

"It is," Charlotte confirmed. "I knitted it myself. I don't suppose you knit?"

"Oh, you can *tell*," Amelia cooed, looking over to the other two women there with her, and then back again to Charlotte. "It looks homemade, Charlotte. Rustic, I guess you could say?" she went on. "And no, I don't knit. Not really my thing, of course. But you should be *super* proud of yourself for being so creative."

"Thanks," Charlotte said. "So...?" she added, raising her eyebrows, inviting an explanation as to why she'd been summonsed into the presence of their coven.

"Ah, yes!" Amelia replied, as if the thought of what she'd wanted to say initially, temporarily mislaid, had suddenly reappeared in her head. "Well, you see, I was out walking my little Terrance, my precious little fur baby, last weekend, and I nearly had cause to call the police!" she said, setting off an audible gasp from her pair of associates hanging on her every word.

"Oh?" said a bored Charlotte, her attention not nearly as rapt as that of Amelia's two friends.

Amelia furrowed her brow, clearly wracked with concern about whatever it was she may have witnessed. "Well, I was heading back about seven a.m., from taking wee Terrance for walkies," she said. "And I strolled by your quaint little cottage on the way home, as I always do, and my goodness, what should I see...?"

"I don't know. What *did* you see?" Charlotte replied, figuring that her participation would expedite the story's delivery and allow her to be on her way sooner.

"Well..." Amelia began, a smirk emerging as she was about to recount precisely what she'd been a witness to. "Only a man climbing out of your bedroom window!" she said, flicking her eyes over to her friends. "His haste in moving down the ladder naturally had me wondering if he'd maybe been caught in a compromising position of one kind or another — some carnal act, say? — by some other suitor, and thus, he was perhaps making good his escape...?" Amelia offered, enjoying her moment. "Or maybe he'd woken up from the night before, regretted where he'd suddenly found himself, and wished to make a swift exit?" she added, snorting at her own comic genius.

Charlotte let Amelia's words hang in the air for a second or two, wondering what on earth this woman could possibly be wittering on about. And then of course she recalled George's early-morning foray. "Ah, you mean on Saturday?" she said. "Well, the chance would be a fine thing," Charlotte quipped, trying to remain calm and not stoke the flames of any potential gossip. "That was just my ex, George," Charlotte explained. "He'd simply come round to help me out with something."

Amelia raised one eyebrow in response.

"Not like *that*," Charlotte replied, shaking her head and giving an exasperated sigh. "He was helping me fix my roof."

"I see," Amelia said, one eyebrow still arched.

"Anyway, is that all you called me over for?" Charlotte asked. She then glanced down to her watch in a manner indicating that she had somewhere else to be — *anywhere*, in fact, than where she was presently stood.

"I'm just teasing," Amelia professed, although she really didn't sound like she was. "Anyway, we'd heard about your Crafternoon Social Club idea," Amelia said, moving the conversation forward with a nod, mirrored by her two compatriots taking note of this and nodding along as well.

"Oh," Charlotte said, half expecting to receive a verbal pat on the back for her initiative. "Yes, it's—"

"You knew about our coffee morning, I presume?" Amelia asked, arms folded across her chest.

"Excuse me?"

"Our *coffee morning*, Charlotte," Amelia answered, stressing the words to impress upon Charlotte the importance of what she was saying. "The Laxey school parents' committee, only last week, announced our coffee morning. You must have heard us mention it at the monthly meeting?"

Charlotte hadn't been to that particular meeting, or any of the previous ones, either, for that matter. As Amelia undoubtedly knew.

"Coffee morning? Sorry. Can't say that I have."

"That's right," Amelia said. "You may not have been bothered to come along to the meeting. But, you're most welcome to attend the next one if you're not too busy. Anyway, we've arranged a coffee morning each week. The idea is to invite elderly people who are stuck at home to come along and mingle."

"Mingle? Oh...kay," Charlotte said, still no closer to knowing the point of the current conversation or where it might be headed. Nor did she understand how the elderly were meant to "come along and mingle" if, as Amelia indicated, they were *stuck at home.*

"Ah. It sounds great," Charlotte relented, offering a raised fist of encouragement, trying to speed the convo along in hopes of it ending soon.

"Oh, it is," Amelia affirmed. "So, you can imagine our surprise and disappointment, then, when we heard that you'd gone and set up a club in direct opposition to ours."

Charlotte laughed. She wasn't sure if this was a joke that she just wasn't getting. "Opposition?" she said. "You're serious?"

"Quite."

"I'm not the *competition*," Charlotte answered her, offended by the implication. "Crafternoon is a social club for people who want to meet fellow crafters, both young and old, and work on their current projects over a cup of tea. The clue's in the name, Crafternoon. As in, *afternoon*," she said. "I've absolutely no intention of getting in the way of your morning coffee group, Amelia. No, if anything, I think having two new social clubs for the village can only be a *good* thing. And surely both can happily coexist, separate but equal? One merely complementing the other?"

However, any further discussion on the subject was cut short with the school bell announcing it was kicking-out time. Mere seconds later, the playground was filled with giddy youngsters, delighted that their educational shackles were cast aside for at least another day. Through the red school jumper-wearing throng, Stanley cleaved a swathe straight through, like a seasoned explorer chopping his way through the forest undergrowth, offering a wave for his mum as he approached.

"Have you got them?" Stanley asked, before he'd even arrived at his mum's feet.

"Hello to you, too," Charlotte said with a laugh. "How was school?"

"Yeah, great," Stanley said — the stock response from any child, anywhere, when asked this same question after school. "Have you got them?" Stanley asked again, looking to his mum's bag hanging over her shoulder.

"I sure have," she replied, wetting her thumb to wipe away some ink from his cheek. "I'm not sure we needed a whole hundred of them printed, though?" she added, sagging her shoulder as if her bag were filled with a pile of heavy rocks.

"Come on," Stanley suggested, taking his mum by the hand and leading the way with gusto, "those flyers aren't exactly going to hand *themselves* out, Mum!"

Charlotte, as Stanley was aware, had spent the previous evening designing an eye-catching advert for the CRAFTERNOON SOCIAL CLUB — with Stanley's considerable input. Charlotte suggested at the time that they were perhaps going a touch overboard, what with bobbins, sewing needles, wool, sheep, cake, crochet hooks, and anything else even remotely linked to crafting having made it into their final artwork. Still, she didn't want to dampen the creative enthusiasm on display. Also, there could be no doubting, with everything included in the design, what the club was all about, they both agreed.

For his part, Stanley was more than happy to help in distributing the finished flyers around and about Laxey's houses and shops. It wasn't just that he was showing support for Mum, however. The fee of five pence that he'd negotiated for each delivery no doubt also played some small part in his enthusiasm.

A village on the east coast of the island, Laxey was a thoroughly pleasant area to live in and for Stanley to grow up in. A former mining and fishing village, it has the honour of being home to the world's largest working waterwheel. Many of the stone cottages, including Charlotte's, were built to house the once-thriving mining industry workers. The village was built around a wooded glen, with its steep winding paths and streets eventually leading out onto a promenade and popular beach. It was quite the spot to take a load off and secure a delicious ice cream, listen to the gentle waves, relax, and idly watch the world go by.

One negative result of the array of sloping streets, however, was soon becoming apparent to young Stanley, heading through another garden gate, flyer in hand...

"How many's that, Mum?" he asked over his shoulder, pushing

the folded paper through the brass letterbox.

Charlotte looked down at the two-inch-thick pile in her hand. "Dunno, my love. Eight, maybe nine?"

"*Nine?*" Stanley moaned, rolling his eyes, and stomping his feet as he walked back over to her. "I've not even earned enough to buy a Twix yet! And my legs are flippin' killing me as well."

"Well," Charlotte said, figuring a bit of encouragement wouldn't go amiss right at the moment, "how about we divide and conquer? That way, we'll get them all delivered twice as quick, yeah?"

Charlotte crouched down until her head was level with Stanley's.

"Tell you what, kiddo," she said to him, "I'll even let you have my share of the wages," she offered, much to Stanley's delight. "Just don't tell the boss," she added with a wink, "as I hear she's a bit of a dragon!"

"Agreed," Stanley said, holding out his hand to shake on it and seal the deal before Mum could change her mind.

Three hours and change later, Stanley lay sprawled out on the sofa, watching cartoons with an empty Twix wrapper lying on his chest. The poor lad's knuckles were red raw from jamming his hand into so many letterboxes, and he'd warned his mum — several times — that his feet were in danger of falling clean off due to excess use. Stanley had certainly earned his wages in addition to the sumptuous mug of hot chocolate that Charlotte was, at present, preparing in the kitchen (with marshmallows and cream).

"Mum!" Stanley shouted. "Your phone's in here and it's buzzing! I'd get up and bring it in for you, but remember what I said about my feet nearly falling off?"

"That wouldn't do at all," Charlotte said, appearing with Stanley's drink, placing it on the end table right next to him so that he'd barely have to move to reach it. "You'll need those feet of yours for football practice tomorrow," she observed.

"I expect so," Stanley replied, reaching out lazily for his mug of hot chocolate, and then taking a tentative sip.

"Right, now what's Auntie Mollie saying for herself?" Charlotte added, attending to the message on her phone.

She read the text to herself:

> The poster was on my doormat when I came home. Looks fab...very creative 😊 Oh, thank Stanley for the love heart he'd drawn on it...Cute xx
> By the way, you may already know this, but you only put the time on it and not the day?
> Coffee tomorrow?
> Molls x

Charlotte lowered her phone, looking dead ahead, resisting the urge to curse aloud.

"Stanley, where's that one poster we kept for your scrapbook?"

"That depends, Mum. Are you going to claim it was undelivered and take five pence off my wages?"

"No, you're good. I promise."

"It's stuck on the front of the fridge," Stanley advised, with him busy right at the moment admiring the whipped cream tower rising skyward from his drink, and trying to work out how he was going to take another sip without destroying said creamy tower just yet. "I put it there for safekeeping," he said absently, in reference to the flyer.

Charlotte headed to the kitchen, wondering how she'd missed seeing the artwork there earlier, and sincerely hoping that this was one of those moments of jest from Mollie that her friend did so enjoy performing at Charlotte's expense. After all, Stanley and herself had spent that long designing and titivating the poster in question that surely they wouldn't have missed something as important as including the actual *date* on it...?

She winced, closing one eye, removing the flyer from the fridge, hesitantly, and without looking directly at the details printed on it. Taking a deep breath, Charlotte allowed her eyes to fall down to the page gripped in her hands.

"Stanley!" she shouted, slowly raising her head.

"Yes, Mum?"

"Stanley, you're not going to bloody believe what we've gone and done...!"

CHAPTER FIVE

Sausage, bacon, two fried eggs, mushrooms, and a piece of black pudding," Bonnie announced, producing the plate and its various contents for consideration. "Whaddya think about that, then?" she teased, pausing for just a moment, directing the feast under her dad's nose, allowing the delicious fried aroma to waft invitingly, circulating in and around his nostrils, before placing the plate down onto the table in front of him. "And," she added, finger raised, "I'm just about to squeeze you a fresh glass of orange juice as well." Bonnie headed back to the kitchen, glancing over her shoulder on the way there. "None of that shop-bought juice today, Dad," she advised.

Benjamin stared down at his plate, smiling. He couldn't fail to be impressed by the inventiveness of the chef in the way the food was creatively presented: two eggs for eyes, two rashers of bacon forming a pair of eyebrows, black pudding for an oversized nose, and then the sausage forming the shape of a smiling mouth.

"Excellent!" Benjamin shouted, loud enough to be heard by its intended recipient in the kitchen. "You've done a cracking job!" he quipped, a well-used dad-style egg joke being offered up. "But... what are the mushrooms doing...?" he asked the soon returning Bonnie, uncertain as to what form or function they served in her otherwise splendid artistic composition.

"It's a *moustache*," she replied, in a manner suggesting that this should have been perfectly obvious.

"A moustache?"

"Yes. And in fact I was going to make the moustache larger..." she added, pausing for dramatic effect. "Only there wasn't *mush *room* left on the plate."

Benjamin shook his head, releasing a groan. "You're laughing at your own joke. You are, aren't you?"

"Absolutely, Dad. After all, I learned all of my cheesy jokes from the best," Bonnie replied, handing over a sun-kissed glass of orange juice adorned with a pretty pink umbrella resting casually against the rim. With both hands now free and stood behind him, Bonnie draped her arms around his neck like a scarf, offering up a kiss to his cheek. "I love you, Pops. Happy birthday."

"Love you too, Bonn," Benjamin said, stroking the back of her hand. "And thank you," he said, giving her hand a gentle squeeze.

Bonnie took her seat opposite her dad, where her own sumptuous feast awaited. "Smells good," she remarked, jabbing her egg with her fork, setting the yellow yolk loose to run free like a river of sunshine all over her rasher of bacon. "You like your jumper, then?" she asked, looking him up and down.

"Yes, indeed," Benjamin replied, giving himself a once-over. "Very trendy," he suggested. "And so it suits me to a T, I'd say," he added, "what with me being the young, hip, trendy thing that I am, of course."

"Of course," Bonnie confirmed.

Bonnie tucked into her breakfast, providing furtive glances to her dad so often that she was in danger of developing a crick in her neck. She went to speak, but the words didn't arrive; instead, she offered up a smile whenever her dad should happen to look back.

Benjamin, for his part, was shuffling his food around his plate, with little if anything ending up anywhere near his mouth.

"You're doing what I used to do when Mum made us mince and potatoes," Bonnie said eventually, releasing a sigh. "She'd load my plate up, and all I'd do is shift the contents around my plate to appear as if I were eating it. I'd then pop the fork into my mouth with a minuscule amount on it," she told her father. "I never did care much for mince and potatoes."

Benjamin nodded along, in neither agreement nor disagreement, and then said, "I'm sure I remember telling you to eat the vegetables as well, Bonn?"

"Ah, but you only did that in order to take the heat off *yourself* for not eating *yours*," Bonnie replied, throwing him an accusing stare which thawed into a smile.

"It's a fair cop," he said with a shrug.

"You need to open your cards," she suggested, pointing her fork over to the small pile of envelopes sat on the sideboard. "Dad..." she said, after a moment or two, when no response was forthcoming.

Benjamin continued to nudge his food around his plate, eyes fixed towards the table, trancelike.

"You do need to eat, Dad," Bonnie said softly. But, again, her words went unanswered. "Dad!" she said once more, only this time with some frustration evident in her voice.

Benjamin lifted his head, startled. "What? Oh, sorry, honey," he said. "I was miles away." He lowered his fork, placing it down onto his plate next to the uneaten food. "I do very much appreciate it, Bonn. Honestly I do. But I'm afraid I'm not feeling too hungry just now."

Bonnie considered a reply, poised to deliver something of a lecture on the virtues of eating your breakfast, perhaps. But before the words came, she stopped herself, choosing instead to offer a further smile across the table. It broke her heart to see her dad like this. His happy-go-lucky approach to life was, at present, a distant memory. He looked tired, with dark rims under each eye. And despite his best efforts at stealth, she often heard him heading downstairs in the middle of the night, where he'd sit looking through old photographs for hours. The absence of a good night's sleep in weeks was doing nothing for his physical or mental health, she reasoned. But it was difficult to tell a grown man what to do, especially when that man was also her dad.

"What about opening those birthday cards, Dad?" Bonnie said after a bit, eventually clearing away the plates and choosing to make no further comment about his untouched meal. "You can pretend to not look disappointed when you discover there's no cash inside them, eh? What do you think? If you like, I can pop a fiver inside mine, and then—"

But Bonnie's casual birthday card commentary was interrupted when Benjamin placed his elbows on the table, lowering his face into the palms of his hands. "I'm sorry, Bonnie," he said, a moment before his shoulders began to heave. He sobbed, head held down, gripping his fringe between his fingers.

Bonnie set the plates back down, closing her eyes for a moment and taking a deep breath. "It's okay, Dad," she said. She moved around the table, cuddling into her dad, biting her bottom lip in order to stem her own flow of tears. "It's all right, Dad," she said gently, rubbing his shoulder. "Today was always going to be a challenge, Dad."

Benjamin lifted his head, wiping his eyes on the back of his hand. "It'll get easier, Bonn, won't it?" he asked, looking up at her.

Bonnie immediately nodded, giving him a caring, sympathetic smile. "It absolutely will, Dad."

"You know, Bonn..." Benjamin said, wrapping his fingers around her hand. "On the subject of cards. Your mum would spend bloody ages in the card shop, choosing just the right one. She'd read the verse inside, check the picture, read the verse again, and then shortlist it along with several others. She'd then repeat this process, at least five times, and then, and only then, would she make her final decision once completely happy. I have to admit, I used to get fidgety and impatient, wondering how somebody can take that long to select just one bloody card, you know? For me, I'd be in the shop for ten seconds, at most, selecting a card. The only criteria I worried about was if it was the correct greeting for the right gender, and how much it cost. I don't think I ever looked inside at the verse. A couple of times, I didn't even manage to get the gender selection correct, as your gran would happily attest to."

"Mum always did buy the nicest cards," Bonnie entered in, her eyes drifting away for a moment in fond recollection. "Sadly, I don't think I ever paid too much attention to the words written inside, back when I was younger," she confessed. "It's all about the cash inside when you're a kid," she added, with a wistful sigh.

"I'm not sure I ever meaningfully took in the words in her cards either, Bonn," Benjamin admitted, welling up once again. "I mean... sure, I read the card and everything. But I don't think I ever took the time to appreciate just how much thought and consideration had gone into the selection, making sure it was the most perfect card she could find."

Benjamin reflected on this for a moment, casting a glance over to the family portrait of the three of them hanging next to the door, taken the summer before. "Bonnie," Benjamin said, his voice breaking with emotion, "Bonnie, I'd happily give up everything I own for the opportunity to open just one more birthday card from your mum."

"I know, Dad," Bonnie said, also struggling through the tears. "But we'll get through this, Dad. We're here for each other, the two of us."

Benjamin stood, taking Bonnie in his arms. "We sure will," he said. "We're the dream team, Bonn."

The two of them held each other, silent, caught up in their own thoughts. Bonnie also glanced over at the same portrait, a smile emerging on her face. "Do you remember the day of the photoshoot, Dad?" she said, breaking into a laugh.

"I couldn't forget it, Bonn. I suppose you're talking about when my trousers split open?" Benjamin suggested, answering her question. "I did think it was a bit drafty, as I recall," he added. "It was lucky your mum had her sewing kit with her. Otherwise, that photographer could well have ended up seeing more than she'd bargained for."

"Mum did a wonderful on-the-spot repair job, as you can't even see your tartan underpants anymore," Bonnie joked, scrutinising the framed photograph even though she'd seen it countless times before. "Now, back to cards… do you fancy opening yours, or will I put them away until later?" Bonnie asked, before adding with a wry smile, "I should probably confess to not really reading the verse inside your card too carefully when I bought it, Dad."

Bonnie prodded her dad in the ribs, raising a giggle.

"But, I will from now on, I promise," she told him. "I *am* pretty confident, though, that I've at least managed to choose the correct gender. Unlike some I could mention!"

"Let's do it, Bonn," Benjamin answered. "Open the cards, I mean. But first…"

"Yes?"

"I think maybe I'll have another go at that sumptuous breakfast you went to all the trouble to make me, yeah? While it's still on the table? Mushroom moustache and all…"

Bonnie never liked the idea of leaving her dad alone during the day, not of late, at any rate. But at least in attending school and being with friends, it meant she had something of a distraction, something to take her mind off matters. For her father, though, working as he did from home as a web developer, he could and did spend days without even needing to leave the house, let alone speak to another human being. Some days Bonnie would even find him sat working in his pyjamas. Bonnie could see her dad beginning to slowly withdraw, and it concerned her. Previously, her father had always been the bright light at any party or in any situation, always armed with an impossibly abundant array of awful puns and terrible jokes, an overly eager singing voice always at the ready, happy to implement at a moment's notice, and he was also the self-proclaimed king of board games. He was like the boy who never really grew up, such was his infectious zeal for life. Her father did seem grateful for how friends and family rallied around in support, this much was true. Still, his preference, currently, appeared to be staying indoors, primarily with himself for company, and alone with his thoughts.

At Bonnie's school, everyone had also been supportive, teachers and fellow students alike. But it'd been a terrible struggle for her, too, and her grades, inevitably, began to slip. She had her own grief to deal with, of course, along with trying her best to provide comfort and support to her dad during the occasion of his suffering as well. It'd only been three months since her mum had lost the courageous battle with her illness, but the acute pain Bonnie felt had hardly eased any.

Presently, Bonnie was walking down the school corridor on her way to class. "Bonnie!" Mrs Lacey, the school secretary, called after her. "Bonnie!" Mrs Lacey said once more, weaving her way through the muddle of schoolchildren milling about in the corridor before their next lesson. Fortunately, it wasn't difficult to spot Bonnie in a crowd, on account of her stunning, flame-red hair — an enviable trait inherited from her mother's side. "Bonnie!" Mrs Lacey called again, upon approaching the small group of girls Bonnie was walking with. But the ambient noise inside the corridor was akin to that of a jet fighter taking flight, making it something of a challenge to be heard over the din.

"Oh, hi, Sue," Bonnie said, looking up after feeling a hand placed on her shoulder.

Mrs Lacey, as well as knowing Bonnie through school, was also a friend of the family, having grown up with Bonnie's mum.

"I'll catch you up," Bonnie suggested to her friends, turning her attention to Sue, who now stood before her. "Oh, fudge," Bonnie said, snapping her fingers. "Sorry. I meant *Mrs Lacey*, not *Sue*, a moment ago," she added, correcting herself as they were, at present, on school premises, after all.

"Don't worry, it's fine," Sue told her. "Just call me 'Mrs Lacey' if you see the headmaster kicking about."

Bonnie offered a friendly salute in the affirmative. "It was lovely to see you last night, Sue. And that birthday cake you made for Dad was absolutely gorgeous. And delicious as well," she said, patting her belly to illustrate that last point. "I just *may* have even had another slice after you left."

"Wait and see what I've made us all for dessert on Friday," Sue said teasingly, rubbing her hands together like she was starting a fire. "Anyway, the reason for stopping you is this," she said, handing over a large, colourful printed page.

"What's this?" Bonnie asked, looking down and running her eyes across the text. "The Crafternoon Social Club," she said, reading the main heading on the page aloud. "I'm *fifteen*, Sue. Not sixty?" she said with a smile and a confused furrowing of the brow.

"It was dropped through my letterbox just the other day," Sue explained. "And I know you're only fifteen, but..." she said, building up to the big reveal. "But it does say in the advert that the club is for both experienced crafters *and* for novices eager to learn new skills. Anyhow, I remembered you saying you wanted to finish making your mum's quilt that she'd been working on, and I thought—"

"Oh, Sue," Bonnie said, eyes twinkling at the prospect. "Sue, that's a brilliant idea. I've been browsing YouTube tutorials for help, but I don't really have a clue what I'm doing. Certainly not enough to let loose on Mum's precious quilt anyway."

Bonnie clutched the flyer to her chest. "Thank you, Sue," she said, fidgeting like she was eager to administer a hug, but being on school grounds uncertain if that was a good idea.

Sue took the decision away from her, doling out a brief but much-appreciated embrace. "You know," Sue added, upon releasing her grip and taking a step back, "I had a thought. It might be a daft one..."

"Oh?"

"What about your dad, Bonnie?"

"Dad? I'm not sure I understand. What about him?"

"A new social club, and practically on your doorstep by the looks of it. It could be a great way of getting him out of the house, I reckon," Sue explained. "He could learn a new skill? It might help him take his mind off of things and, who knows, get him out of his pyjamas. He could go along and even learn how to make his own socks!"

"Hmm, I suppose," Bonnie said, supposing. "Mum *did* try teaching him how to knit once, as I recall. Although I'm pretty sure one of the needles ended up bent in half, which I don't think was an accident, actually."

Sue glanced down at her watch. "I'm keeping you from your next lesson, Bonn. Anyway, I'll come along to Crafternoon with you if you like? Keep you company, yeah? Plus, it'd be nice to spend some time with you and meet a few more folks from the neighbourhood."

"I'd love that, Sue. I really would."

"It's a date, then," Sue said, turning around in order to head in the direction from whence she'd come. "Oh," Sue added, wheeling about, and extending her finger towards the piece of paper still in Bonnie's hand. "There was a time detailed on there," she explained. "But I couldn't see an actual date for when it's on?"

"Oh, you're right," Bonnie said. "I'll have a look to see if they've got a Facebook page or something?" she offered. "And I'll be sure to drop the knitting suggestion on dad tonight," she added, with a hopeful smile. "I'll not hold my breath that he says yes, mind you, but one never knows? Anyway, thank you for thinking of me, Sue."

"Anything for a sewing buddy," Sue replied, and then, lowering her voice so as not to be heard by those students walking by, "Bonnie," she said sincerely, "you know I'm always here for you, don't you? If you ever need to talk…"

Bonnie smiled, nodding in response. "I do, Sue, thanks. And I really appreciate it," she replied, flicking her eyes over Sue's shoulder for a moment. "That is… I do, *Mrs Lacey*," she added, correcting herself as the towering, imposing figure of Mr Nelson, the school headmaster, appeared nearby, having come round a corner and now headed in their general direction.

Sue and Bonnie parted ways, with Bonnie continuing her journey to her English class and arriving through the door just as the school bell chimed. She looked down at the flyer in her hand, with a broad smile and spring in her step as she made her way to her seat. She was surprised that the idea of attending the CRAFTERNOON SOCIAL CLUB would make her as enlivened as it did. The quilt Sue mentioned — presently draped over a wingback chair in the living room — was a project her mum had begun, but had never finished, about a year or so earlier. Neither Bonnie nor her dad had either the heart or the inclination to move it from where her mum had last laid it. So there it sat. For Bonnie, it was a constant and bleak visual reminder that her mum was no longer there to finish it. The suggestion had come up of perhaps storing the unfinished blanket in the loft, but again, neither Bonnie nor her dad had the heart to carry through. Recently, Bonnie had harboured the notion of finishing the project herself. But she was worried she simply didn't possess the required skill set to do so, and was concerned that any attempt to try could potentially ruin what her mum had started. Which of course was not what she wanted at all.

"I can *do* this!" Bonnie said to herself, aloud, as she took her seat, resulting in a few quizzical stares from her classmates. "I'm going to finish the quilt!" she continued. "It can't be *that* hard... can it?"

CHAPTER SIX

Charlotte eyed Stanley with suspicion. He'd just turned his back on her, and for the first time in at least twenty minutes, not a word was being spoken. Only silence.

Charlotte crept from her location stood next to the oven, walking surreptitiously around the kitchen table, and eventually standing directly behind him. "Hey! Whatcha doing!" she said, loud enough to send poor Stanley at least several inches into the air.

"Mum!" Stanley protested, turning around, whisk held firmly in hand. "I was, ehm… just about to ask if I could lick this…?" he told her, pointing a finger from his spare hand towards the chocolate-covered implement in the other.

Charlotte slowly bent down until her head was at the same height as Stanley's. She looked deep into his eyes, then gave a quick glance over to the whisk in his hand. "Lick *that* whisk?" she asked, meeting his eyes once again. "Even though you've already licked each and every baking-related implement we've used so far? And even though you'll now soon collapse into a sugar-induced diabetic coma?"

"Yup! That's my plan!" Stanley replied, looking transfixed at the deliciously indulgent chocolate mix slithering invitingly down the wire loops.

Charlotte looked at the whisk again, and couldn't help but notice that large portions of it had chocolate already liberated from it. She moved her nose closer to Stanley's own, running her eyes over him intently, searching his face for clues. "Hmm," she said, like a lawyer cross-examining a stubborn witness before a judge.

"So what you're saying is that you've not *already* administered a severe tongue-lashing, in the most literal sense, on the whisk already, young man? Is that what you're telling me? So, when you had your back to me, just now, and you weren't speaking for those long, unusually quiet few moments, you're telling me that wasn't you *already* having a go at that whisk?"

Stanley thought carefully, chewing on the inside of his cheek, weighing his response. "Nope," he declared eventually. "No, I never touched it, Your Honour." And then, "Some of it..." he continued tentatively, throwing it out there as a possible defence, "Some of it... came off? When you startled me, and I jumped...?"

"Hmm," Charlotte said, appearing not overly convinced by this claim of innocence. "Stick your tongue out, then," she instructed, not unlike the school nurse.

Stanley did, reluctantly, as instructed, although only the tip of his tongue appeared through his pursed lips.

"Right. And the rest, mister," Charlotte demanded, though unable to entirely contain the grin emerging on her face. "A-ha!" Charlotte exclaimed, as the remaining section of tongue meat appeared from within the confines of Stanley's gob.

In a rapid strike action that a king cobra would have been most satisfied with, Charlotte quickly grabbed Stanley's tongue, pinching it between her thumb and forefinger before Stanley had the chance to retract it.

"Just as I suspected. You've already licked half the whisk, as your mouth is full of chocolate," she observed. "The evidence is clear," she said, releasing her grip, and then moving her wiggling fingers in the direction of his midriff, where a severe tummy tickling was soon administered (although perhaps not the wisest course of action given the amount of cake mix he'd just ingested).

"That's... from... the... *last*... cake..." Stanley insisted, in between bouts of giggles. "The... one... *before*..."

"Oh, is that right?" Charlotte countered, moving her tickle-based interrogation now to his armpits. "As it so happens, this is the *very first* chocolate cake we've made today. So how is it you've already got fresh chocolate all over the inside of your mouth, *and* on the tip of your nose, if you didn't *already* lick the whisk, hmm?

Explain *that*."

In the face of this present verbal and physical onslaught, Stanley opted to come clean at this point. "All right, all right!" he said, eager, it would appear, to bring the torturous tickling session to a conclusion. "Okay, I licked the whisk!" he admitted, almost breathless with laughter. "I licked the chocolate from off of the whisk!" he added, lest there be any doubt as to what precisely was being licked and by whom.

"Case closed," Charlotte replied, clapping her hands together in satisfaction, and returning to normal height with her investigation concluded. "Oh," she added, almost as an afterthought on her way back over to the oven, "and you didn't *actually* have any chocolate on your nose. That part I made up," she confessed, followed by a sinister laugh. "But yes. Yes, you can lick the rest of the—" she said, turning around to find young Stanley with most of the whisk, all that he could fit, already safely ensconced in his mouth.

Charlotte, ably assisted by her willing sous-chef with an insatiable sweet tooth, had been baking since school had kicked out. Already, two banana cakes, a fruit loaf, and a lemon drizzle cake were sat cooling on the sideboard (soon to be accompanied by the chocolate cake). The only thing more impressive than the magnificent aroma gloriously permeating the kitchen was the size of the pile of used dishes stacked precariously in the sink.

The baking of the sweet treats had taken more time than Charlotte had anticipated but was, she felt, well worth the effort involved. With the inaugural session of the official CRAFTERNOON SOCIAL CLUB less than twenty-four hours away, what better way was there, she reckoned, to welcome her new members than with a slice of lovely homemade cake to accompany their cuppa?

Charlotte had been inundated with enquiries as to the club on social media, despite her faux pas in omitting the actual date on the flyer. By her estimate, she was hopeful of around fifteen to twenty people attending, and possibly even more. From messages exchanged during the course of the week, she was expecting, as well, a nice mix of complete novices and seasoned crafters, all with a diverse range of ages. So far, the positive reaction she'd received in response to her advert was an endorsement that what she was doing was a good idea. For days, at the start, she'd been wracked with self-doubt, concerned that the take-up for her new initiative would be a big fat zero. The thought of sitting in an empty church hall, embarrassed for even having tried, nearly put paid to her efforts before they'd even had opportunity to bear fruit.

Fortunately, again, her concerns were allayed by the enthusiastic response she'd received. And likely, her most significant stress on the day would be about whether she had made enough cake to satisfy the hungry masses. Yes, Charlotte could see it now — a packed church hall, full of industrious crafters, each engrossed in their own special project, all happy, and part of a new community initiative that would only go from strength to strength. Well, that was certainly the plan, at least, in Charlotte's head.

"Yay! Dad's here!" Stanley announced abruptly, waving excitedly towards the kitchen window, and rousing his mum from her various crafting-themed musings.

"Your father?" Charlotte asked, wondering for a moment if she'd mixed her days up. "What? But you're not due at your father's today, Stanley…"

"I told you, Mum! He's bought me a new pair of football boots!" Stanley explained, darting over to the front door.

"Ah," Charlotte replied, "I thought he must have smelt the cake. Well, tell him to come in if he likes."

A moment later, George filled the kitchen doorframe, nostrils flaring, taking in through his beak a portion of the cake molecules wafting his way through the air. "That smells bloody amazing!" he said, tilting his head back in appreciation.

"What's in there, Dad?" Stanley asked, tugging at the carrier bag in George's hand.

"What? In *here*, you mean?" George replied with a casual shrug. "Oh, nothing terribly exciting," he added nonchalantly, moving the bag a few inches away every time Stanley attempted to peek inside.

"*Daaaad,*" Stanley pleaded. "Did you *get* them?"

"Hmm? What? The ones with the pink stripes?" George asked,

eventually relinquishing his grip on the bag. "That's what you said you wanted, right?"

"*Pink* stripes?" Stanley replied, upon taking possession of the bag. He smiled, running his eyes over his dad's face, hoping for any signs of mirth to be had there, which he was relieved to ultimately see.

"*Yellow* stripes," George announced, confirming what Stanley could now already see, as Stanley bolted away to try them on.

"So," George said, turning his attention to Charlotte. "Do you have any dishes you *haven't* used?" he asked with a smile, taking a glance at the sink. "Not that I'm volunteering to help you wash, mind you."

Charlotte offered him a smirk in response as she attended to her current enterprise, scooping out the chocolate mix into a baking tin. "I may have gone a little overboard in making cakes for tomorrow," she confessed. "But I'm sure they'll all be eaten," she said. "And if not by the new social club members, then Stanley will have school lunch sorted for a least the next month."

"They do look good," George suggested hopefully, moving over to the collection of already finished cakes and taking an appreciative, protracted sniff. "Ah. Stanley showed me the flyer you'd both made," George said, changing subject slightly. "It was impressive," he added, taking one last lingering, admiring sniff of the cakes, before finally pulling himself away lest he drool all over the fruit loaf. "I did have one suggestion, however."

"You did?" Charlotte said.

George puffed out his chest, preparing to deliver his brilliant idea. "Well," he began, raising his hand like he was about to write on the school blackboard. "So... Crafternoon Social Club, it's called, yes?" he asked, somewhat rhetorically, seeking verification of what he appeared to already know.

"Yes, that's correct," Charlotte confirmed, unsure where George was headed with this.

"Well, what about..." George said, arm still raised. "What about calling it the Crafternoon *Sewcial* Club."

"Eh?" Charlotte said, distinctly underwhelmed. "I don't understand. That's what it's *already* called."

"No, no," George explained, "I mean, as in, *S-E-W*," George told her, spelling the letters out so that Charlotte could see what he was getting at. "Instead of S-O-C, you see?" he added further, smiling, and entirely pleased with his creative genius. "*SEWcial*, rather than *Social*, yeah?"

"You came up with that? By yourself?" Charlotte asked.

"Yeah! It's like a play on words. As you'll be sewing and such."

"Yes, I get it," Charlotte said, getting it. "You know, George, that's actually pretty good, I have to say. I might use it, if you don't mind?"

"Go nuts!" George answered. And then, "Wait..." he added, his expression hardening just a bit, "you said you're making cakes for *tomorrow*?"

"Yes... Yes, I am," Charlotte replied, lowering her rubber spatula. "Why?" she asked, concerned at the tone by which George's question was delivered.

George ran the palm of his hand over the top of his shaven head, looking as if he didn't want to be there anymore. "You did read the text I sent you at lunchtime...?"

"No," Charlotte replied, wiping her hands on her apron.

"Ah, okay," George said. "You just need to know that I *did* send you a text, Charlotte."

Charlotte patted her pockets, looking for her phone. "I've been going nonstop all day," she said, continuing the search for her mobile by scanning her eyes around the kitchen.

"Here," George offered, spotting the phone resting up against a tin of Oxo cubes on the wooden sideboard. "Just out of curiosity, how long does cake stay fresh for?" he asked. "You know, just in case you don't end up actually needing them for tomorrow, for example?"

"This isn't going to be good news, is it, George?" Charlotte asked, before she'd even unlocked her phone in order to read his message from earlier, and taking a guess that she might not like what she'd find once she did.

George stood behind her, looking over her shoulder to the phone in her hand. "I just wanted to make sure I did actually send it," George told her, peering down. "Yes, okay, I can see that I did."

There on the screen for the both of them to see — clear as day — was an unread message from among Charlotte's list of contacts, with the particular contact in question having been given the designation *Knobhead Nick.*

"Here, what's this?" George protested, pleased to see that, yes, he'd successfully sent the text earlier, but not so much about his new apparent moniker. "I'm offended, as my name's not even Nick!" he joked, not contesting the other portion.

"I renamed you that shortly after you left me," Charlotte explained with a chuckle. "Sorry, I never did get round to changing it."

Charlotte opened George's message, then went quiet as she read the contents to herself.

Knobhead Nick:

> Hey! Be around later with Stanley's boots. Oh, the woman from the church phoned. She says she's double-booked. The yoga class are in from 4 till 6. You'll need to arrange for something in the next week or so.

"So, to confirm, you didn't receive my message?" George asked, stepping back, concerned by the sound of Charlotte's grinding teeth.

"Why, yes, of *course* I received the message," Charlotte replied, her voice dripping in sarcasm. "That's precisely why I've gone ahead and spent money I couldn't really spare on loads of ingredients, and then proceeded to spend *four hours* of my time, so far, baking cakes for an event that's *not even happening.*"

"Oh," George said, sidling over to the relative safety of the kitchen door. "I *did* tell you," he said, pointing in the direction of the phone in her hand.

Charlotte pulled a chair out from under the table. "Oh, George, this is a nightmare," she said, taking a seat. "It's not just the cake," she said with a heavy sigh. "How am I supposed to let everybody know that it's cancelled, and what are they going to think of me letting them down, already?"

"Email?" George suggested, not really sure what else to say in the situation.

"I don't have all of their contact details," Charlotte said, talking more to herself than to George. She looked up. "Are you absolutely certain they can't fit me in tomorrow?" she asked him.

"That's what she said," George answered with a shrug. "How about I help you get in touch with people?" he offered. "Those you can't get in touch with... well, perhaps you could wait outside the hall and tell them tomorrow? You could even give them a slice of cake for their trouble, for the journey home?"

"I appreciate that, George," Charlotte said. "It's very kind of you to offer."

Charlotte stared at the wooden surface of the table, running all available options through her mind.

"Well, I should probably..." George suggested, motioning towards the door. "Maybe leave you to it, yeah? Give me a shout if you need anything?"

"I might give her a call..." Charlotte said, in the absence of any other available options. "Maybe she could see her way clear to moving things around to accommodate us..."

George reached for his phone. "It's the same woman who hired me to carry out the hall repairs," he explained, scrolling through his phone to find her number. "I think she's on the church committee or something?" George went on, filling the silence as he continued his search. "She actually said she knew both of us, though I couldn't say I recognised the name or the face."

"Hold on," Charlotte said, getting up and taking the pen from the magnetic whiteboard hanging on the front of the fridge. "Go on," she said, pen at the ready.

"It's... Amelia something-or-other," George said, still searching. "Amelia Smudgen... or Smidgeon... or, hang on..."

"Sugden?" Charlotte entered in. "Amelia Sugden?"

"Ah. Here we are," George replied, finally locating her. "Right. Amelia Sugden."

"Yes, it would *have* to be Amelia Sugden, *wouldn't* it?" she said, shoulders drooping. "I might have bloody well known."

"You want her number?" George asked, confused by the adverse reaction to the name.

Charlotte shook her head in the negative, sticking the pen back on the fridge. "There's no point," she said, appearing resigned to her fate. "Let's just say that I'm not exactly Amelia's favourite person, and it wouldn't surprise me if there wasn't even a yoga class on tomorrow, either."

"Ah," George said. "Now you mention it, I think I do recall you talking about her."

George could see what this meant to Charlotte, and the fact that she appeared on the verge of tears. "Stick with this, Lotti," he said. "It's a good thing you're doing," he told her, "and I'm sure it's not going to be the end of the world if you delay things by a week or so. You might just need to make some more cake."

"Thanks, George," Charlotte replied, taking a roll of clingfilm over to the row of cakes. "You may as well take this with you," she added, wrapping one up. "It's your favourite. Banana cake. You can call it payment for the Sewcial Club idea, I suppose."

"You're welcome," George offered with a bow, feasting his eyes on the cake soon to be in his possession. "Hey, I was thinking of taking Stanley over to the park for an hour, if you don't mind? Test his new footie boots out? You could come, if you like."

"Sure," Charlotte replied, turning the oven off. "We could both do with a run-around ahead of eating that lot," she said, nodding her head in indication of the remaining cakes.

Charlotte sat on the low stone wall outside the Laxey church hall, swinging her legs back and forth to keep the blood flowing to her feet. She'd been sat there for that long that her bum cheeks were starting to tingle. Fortunately, Charlotte had managed to respond to each and every crafting-related message she'd received, explaining how there'd been some confusion regarding the booking time, and that she would revert with the new details once available. Her concern remained that not all potential attendees would necessarily have contacted her initially, and could therefore possibly still turn up, being none the wiser. The last thing she wanted was for prospective new members having a wasted trip with no explanation. And so she sat there on the wall, like a garden gnome, waiting patiently to clarify the situation, if required.

The issue of the hall double-booking played heavily on Charlotte's mind. Was it a genuine mistake? She certainly hoped so. Amelia was often frosty with her, but to deliberately scupper her club seemed rather vindictive and somewhat extreme, especially considering it was a social club for the community they both called home.

"Keen to get started, are we?" an affable woman in vibrant green Lycra leggings suggested, walking up the pavement towards the church. "Always nice to see a new face," she added, extending her hand in Charlotte's direction.

"Oh, hiya," Charlotte answered amiably, jumping down from the wall to meet the cordial greeting, taking the proffered hand and giving it a shake. "I presume you're the yoga lady?" Charlotte asked, eyes falling on the tightly rolled-up mat held securely under this new arrival's left arm.

"I'm Helen," said Helen. "The Yoga Lady," Helen added, repeating Charlotte's own words. "Come on inside, and we'll get you warmed up in no time," she said, marching with impressive purpose and vigour up the path, front door key in hand.

"No, no…" Charlotte replied, following after Helen. "I'm not…" she started to say, but Helen had by this point already disappeared into the building.

"I noticed you didn't have a mat with you," Helen said, flicking on the hall lights as Charlotte joined her inside. "Not to worry. That's not a problem, as I always bring a spare."

Helen looked Charlotte up and down, no doubt noticing that Charlotte wasn't exactly dressed for yoga in her dungarees and Timberland boots. "Some of the girls get dressed behind the curtain," Helen advised, pointing over to the raised stage at the rear of the hall. "Or, you can change in the women's lav, if you prefer," she added, indicating where that could be found.

"Oh. No," Charlotte entered in. "No, no, I don't have a change of clothes, I—"

"You don't…?" Helen said, looking Charlotte up and down once more, quizzically. "But you look more like you're off to the pub than a yoga class," she observed with a laugh. "Still, that's fine. Just be aware that we do work up something of a sweat here during the class, and you might end up a touch warm in those dungarees. Plus, they'll no doubt limit your range of movement to some degree. But as long as you're comfortable, I suppose, that's the only important—"

"I'm not here for the yoga class," Charlotte interrupted firmly, but politely as possible, lest she soon end up in a Downward Dog position or some other such yoga pose. Although, Charlotte couldn't help but appreciate Helen's toned physique, wondering if a yoga class might not be something she ought to consider for herself after all.

"Oh," Helen replied flatly, casting Charlotte the sort of look that might well translate as something like *so-why-exactly-are-you-inside-a-yoga-class?*

Charlotte began to chuckle, waving her hand through the air. "There's been something of a mistake," Charlotte began to explain. "You see, I'm not here for yoga at all. I was with the *other* class."

Helen smiled politely. "I see," she said, when it was pretty evident from her bemused expression that she didn't, in fact, see. And then, in a moment of realisation, Helen bit her bottom lip, her expression turning to one of sympathy. "Oh, I'm sorry," Helen said, placing her hand to her forehead in consternation. "I'm so *sorry.* My *goodness*, whatever must you think of me?" she added, shaking her head, appearing frustrated with herself. "You're with the other *class*?" she asked, lowering her voice to a whisper, yet her whispered voice still echoing around the empty hall nonetheless.

"Ehm... yes?" Charlotte answered, more than a little confused, feeling Helen's reaction to be slightly over-egged, not to mention a bit unnerving. Charlotte looked behind her, back towards the front door. "I might just..." she said, beginning to turn in that direction.

"No," Helen said, grabbing hold of Charlotte's arm, preventing her exit. "I know they've moved some classes around, but don't give up now, dear. Not after you've come so far!"

"Oh...kay...?" Charlotte said in reply, glancing down at the fingers gripping tightly onto her arm. She thought about knocking the hand away, but Helen, being as fit as she was, appeared like she could handle herself, so Charlotte thought better of it.

"Oh, no," Helen said, releasing a pained groan. "I can't believe I was so insensitive just now! Can you *forgive* me?"

"Yeah, sure," Charlotte said, absolving Helen of all sins whatever they might be. "If I could just…" she said, patting Helen's hand. "Go?"

"You're not going to the pub, are you…?" suggested a horrified Helen. "Oh, god. Oh, god, I can't believe I even mentioned the pub earlier! I'm sorry. Tell me you're not going to the pub…?"

"I'm not going to the pub," Charlotte was pleased to report, even though a stiff drink, right about now, would certainly have gone down a treat, she reckoned.

"Greeeaaat, greeeaaat," Helen replied, speaking very slowly, as if Charlotte were somehow intellectually disadvantaged. "But your meeting isn't on until *seven this evening*, dear," Helen said, pointing over to the large corkboard with the community notices pinned to it. "You can even come in through the rear door, if you like?" she offered helpfully, drawing Charlotte's attention over to the rear entrance. "Nobody will even see you."

"*What*? Why would…?" Charlotte began. "Wait," she said, training her eyes on the notice board.

With the grip on her arm released, Charlotte headed over there, and then pressed her nose closer to the notices. The church hall was a popular meeting place, it would appear, with a host of assorted clubs posting various notices on the board, all advertising different get-togethers to be held therein. But, by using her considerable powers of deduction, and by process of elimination, there was only one club that could possibly, Charlotte reasoned, produce such an unusual conversational exchange from Helen.

Charlotte held her hand up to the rather plain, understated notice in question, partially obscured by another that advertised the local youth club. "Do you think I'm an alcoholic…?" Charlotte asked.

"I'm not here to judge," Helen replied simply, lowering her head in respect.

"You think that I'm here for an AA meeting?" Charlotte asked incredulously, and just loudly enough for the members of the yoga class arriving to overhear. "I'm not here for a bloody *AA meeting*. I'm here for the *Crafternoon Sewcial Club*," she told Helen. "But you've nicked our four-p.m. slot!" Charlotte said, crossing her arms over her chest.

"Wait, what?" Helen replied, moving closer to where Charlotte was stood. "But I didn't nick the four-p.m. slot at all," she said. "I was *asked* to move my class," Helen explained. "At *very* short notice, and great personal inconvenience, I might add," she added, "due to some apparent mix-up or other."

"Let me guess," Charlotte guessed. "Did this request come from Amelia?"

"Yes," came the succinct reply.

Charlotte rolled her eyes. "Then it seems our Amelia has gone out of her way to disrupt *both* of our weeks, I regret to say," she said to Helen. "I'll leave you to your class," Charlotte told her. "My apologies for disturbing you, Helen. Again, I'm *not* in AA. I was supposed to be here for a crafting club that I'm hosting. And I'm just going to hang around outside to see if any of my class mistakenly turn up, all right?"

Charlotte felt that now was as good a time as any to leave, so she uncrossed her arms and headed for the front door. "By the way, Helen..." she said, turning back on her heel momentarily, and feeling much more gracious now, "you look absolutely fantastic. So I just might be back next week to join in, dressed accordingly!"

Over towards the door, Charlotte's immediate path to the exit was obstructed by several people filtering into the hall simultaneously, chatting merrily away to each other. "You're not here to craft, are you?" Charlotte asked them, her eyes darting between them.

"What's that? Ehm... no," one surprised voice replied on behalf of the group. "Yoga," she added, holding up her well-used mat.

After that, Charlotte retook her position outside, sat upon the exterior perimeter wall. Fortunately, due to the brief interlude inside, the blood supply had returned to her buttocks, at least. Not too terribly long later, a glance at her watch revealed that it was now three minutes past four, and, as such, it appeared by this point that her cancellation message must have filtered through to the people who had needed to know. "What a horror show," Charlotte remarked, shaking her head upon reflection of the events of the afternoon, and genuinely astonished that anyone should be quite so rotten and devious as Amelia apparently was.

Charlotte still had an hour or so to spare before she was due to pick Stanley up from his afterschool playdate, so she figured she'd use that time to phone around and see if she couldn't secure an alternate venue for her club, and one, especially, that didn't involve Amelia's undue influence. With one final glance up and down the street to confirm there were no last-minute stragglers, she pushed herself down from her resting place and started away from the church, muttering what may or may not have been a few choice expletives under her breath as she went along.

She hadn't made it more than fifty metres, however, when her progress was impeded by a stout fellow, facing away, with his back to her, filling most of the narrow pavement where Charlotte was presently walking with his generous frame. Charlotte quickly deduced this chap to be a bus driver on account of the idling bus parked up on the road next to him with an empty driver's seat. Oh, that and the fact that he was wearing a bus driver's uniform, also.

"Come on, then," the laughing driver was saying through fits of giggles, offering up a supportive, steady hand to one of his passengers making their way off his bus. "I hope you're on my route next week, Joyce. Honestly, I can't remember the last time I laughed so much!"

Charlotte hadn't been paying too much attention to the events up ahead, caught up in her own thoughts and staring at her feet until the path was clear. Not, that is, until the driver's raucous belly laugh cut through the air like a lighthouse foghorn.

"I hope the crowdfunding goes well, Joyce!" the driver boomed. "And I'll be sure to contribute to your dreams of becoming an exotic dancer!" he added merrily, heading back to his seat to commence the next stage of his journey.

Charlotte looked up surreptitiously, trying not to appear overly obvious, but at the same time intrigued as to the source of the driver's excitement and mirth. She fully anticipated finding some nubile young slip of a girl, one who'd been perhaps flirting with the driver and discussing with him her future career options in pursuit of a life as a, shall we say, burlesque queen.

But, no. With the driver no longer obscuring her view, Charlotte caught sight of the lady in question, smiling and waving as the bus pulled away, and receiving generous waves in return from both the driver and those remaining passengers aboard. She was a delicate-looking thing, modest of stature and rather more mature — *much* more mature, in fact — than Charlotte had certainly been expecting, stood there with a cloud of sea-spray white hair, an umbrella in one hand and a red bag in the other. She shuffled up the pavement, slow but steady, with a steely look of determination about her.

Charlotte smiled, staying where she was but allowing the elderly woman plenty of room in which to pass.

"Thank you," the woman said, easing past Charlotte and returning Charlotte's smile.

"Oh!" Charlotte said, her eyes falling down to the vibrant red bag in the lady's hand. "Excuse me, madam," Charlotte called after her, gently, so as not to startle her. "I couldn't help but notice that you knit," she said, gesturing to the ball of yellow wool peeking out the top of the woman's bag. "Are you, by any chance, heading to the Crafternoon meeting…?" she ventured.

"Yes. Yes, indeed I am," the lady said. "Are you the welcoming committee?" she asked, coming to a halt and turning round to face Charlotte.

"No," Charlotte answered, shaking her head. "Well, yes, actually. Sort of, I suppose. I'm really sorry about this, but the session has been cancelled today due to a double-booking. I let as many people know as I could, but I wanted to be on hand, just in case…"

"Oh," the woman replied, looking skyward, and perhaps weighing her options in light of this news. "Hrmm. Double-booked, you say?"

"Yes, by a yoga class. I'm so sorry. Have you come far?"

"Andreas," the woman answered.

Charlotte put her hand to her mouth. "Oh, no!" she said. After all, the village of Andreas was a fair distance away, up the north end of the island, and so not exactly right around the corner.

"It's fine, dear. There's a bus home at six."

"What?" Charlotte said, checking her watch even though she knew roughly what time it was. "That's nearly two hours from now!"

The lady offered a shrug like this was only a minor setback in an otherwise wonderful day. "Oh, it's fine. I'll just park myself up on a bench somewhere with my knitting," she suggested, unbothered.

"Did I hear the bus driver say your name was Joyce?" Charlotte asked Joyce. "Sorry, I wasn't being nosey," Charlotte added, which, although more often than not, meant she was doing precisely that.

Joyce nodded. "You heard correctly," she said. "And I think that cheeky devil was hoping for a special, private performance!" she added, apropos of nothing, with a knowing wink, and rotating her hips illustratively as well for good measure.

"Oh," Charlotte replied simply, darting her eyes back and forth nervously, uncertain as to how she ought to respond. Joyce was, after all, by Charlotte's estimate, well into her eighties. Charlotte had just assumed that what she'd heard earlier was only a joke, or some sort of miscommunication or misunderstanding. But now she wasn't so sure.

"I'm Charlotte," Charlotte said finally, by way of introduction, determined not to judge. "I'm the leader of the Crafternoon Sewcial Club," she explained. "Or at least I *will* be, once we've had our first session."

"Oh, I see," Joyce said brightly.

Charlotte pondered a moment. "Look, I only live right nearby, Joyce," she said after a tick. "I've an idea. How about we have the very first club meeting at my house? I'm working on a new jumper at present. So we can both knit, and have a chat. At least until your bus comes? We can have a nice cuppa if you like, and we also have quite a lot of cake to get through at my house, as it should happen."

"Cake, you say?" replied Joyce, taking this bit of information into consideration. "Hmm. Well, I *was* thinking of gate-crashing that yoga class," Joyce remarked. "But, then again, I was at my own regular yoga class only just yesterday. And, on reflection, a cup of tea *does* sound rather pleasant, I suppose," she said. "But... only if you're not some sort of weirdo...?"

"Weirdo? *Me*?" Charlotte asked, nonplussed, in response to the eighty-something-year-old aspiring exotic dancer.

"Yes. Some weirdo who lures old ladies in off the street with the promise of tea, knitting, and cake?"

Charlotte laughed, sensing she was the object of a gentle ribbing. "I can assure you I'm no weirdo," Charlotte promised. "Though some people may at times disagree. And the offer of cake is very real."

"Well, in that case, then," Joyce said, extending her arm, inviting Charlotte to lead the way. "Let's get that kettle on, and the needles out!"

"Were you teasing me about going to a yoga class just then?" Charlotte asked, by way of conversation, escorting Joyce along towards their destination.

"No, not at all," Joyce answered. "Once a week!" she announced proudly. "I can sometimes wrap my leg around my neck, you know," Joyce added, deadly serious. "If we have time, I'll show you if you like," she offered.

"Ehm... yeah," Charlotte replied. "Maybe... maybe we'll just stick to the knitting this time around...?"

CHAPTER SEVEN

Those related to, friends with, or perhaps married to, a habitual crafter would no doubt be familiar with their crafter associate's peculiar little character traits. If you were brave enough to speak to the individual whilst they were, say, knitting, for instance, you would often receive a raised finger as a temporary placeholder each time. This roughly translated for you to absolutely shut the hell up until further notice. The following well-worn phrase would then often be uttered: *"I'm just counting."* (With this made as a stitch-related reference, rather than in regard to some mathematical equation). This explanation, or one very much like it, would be spat back at you, delivered in a passive-aggressive tone that would likely startle you upon the first time of hearing it. Indeed, the crafter in question wouldn't dream of moving their arse up from their chair without the declaration first that they were *"just finishing this row."* That is if they were deep in the crafting zone, of course. Like the falling tree in the empty forest scenario, many have wondered if a crafter would still regurgitate that line if they were home, alone, with nobody to hear said declaration.

To their loved ones, helpless passengers along for the ride on the crafter's crafting journey, these endearing little foibles were to be expected, and even embraced. You simply grew, or evolved, if you will, to recognise when it was permitted, recommended, or even safe to interrupt them whilst they were busting themselves crafting — the same sort of cautious approach adopted by, say, a zookeeper entering the big cats' enclosure.

Days out, holidays, or absolutely any reason to visit another town or village could and would often result in a detour to the lo-cal crafting shop, researched and identified by the afflicted in ad-vance of the journey, but then explained away by them as merely the happiest of coincidences when approaching the shop. If you were one of those long-suffering, non-crafting loved ones accom-panying the stricken, you'd stand there smiling patiently, won-dering how on earth this particular new shop was going to differ appreciably from the sixteen or so you'd already been forced into visiting recently.

Still, as far as habits or preoccupations went, it could easily be worse. The afflicted, for instance, were unlikely to find them-selves in a position where they'd be required to sell a stolen TV or similarly valuable electronic devices in order to fund their addic-tion (unlikely, that is, though certainly not impossible, depending upon the severity of the addiction). So there was that, at least.

However, with this type of addiction, what you *could* expect was to forgo cupboard, drawer, and floor space, as every available inch of storage would be requisitioned for crafting-related sup-plies. Which, as it should happen, was precisely the situation Charlotte presently found herself in...

"Just me!" Mollie announced, opening the front door, and tak-ing a step inside. "I hope you're not pretending to be out?" she sug-gested, when no immediate response was received. Mollie waited for another moment, taking a bite of the apple in her hand. "Are you decent, Charlotte? It's only—"

"In the kitchen!" Charlotte replied.

Mollie walked through the hall, taking up a position stood in the kitchen doorway. She took another bite of her apple, shaking her head slowly.

"Don't judge me..." Charlotte whimpered, wrapping her arms around the balls of wool on the table, gathering them a little closer, like a protective parent.

Mollie didn't initially offer an opinion one way or the other. She was, perhaps, a little overwhelmed, running her eyes over the stacked boxes covering a large section of the tiled floor. "Are they *also* all full of—?"

"Yes," Charlotte confirmed, lowering her head, allowing her

cheek to come to rest on her makeshift pillow fashioned from woollen balls. "I think I've died and gone to heaven," Charlotte added, closing her eyes, content, like she'd… well, died and gone to heaven.

"Is all this…" Mollie entered in, sweeping her hand around the kitchen, "the reason you didn't meet me for our run?" she asked, before throwing her apple core into the bin.

"Yes," Charlotte replied. "Yes, it is. You see, if it's a mistake, then I wanted to spend as much time as I could with them. Before they're taken away from me."

Mollie knelt down, easing open the flap of a cardboard box for a glimpse inside. "Bloody hell," she said, before moving onto the next box, where she repeated the process. "There must be, what, twenty boxes here…?" Mollie said.

"Seventeen," Charlotte immediately responded, and then added, "With three hundred and forty balls of wool in total. I've counted them all."

"Isn't this why you'd ripped up your credit card, Charlotte? To keep this kind of situation from happening?"

Charlotte lifted her head from her sumptuous pillow. "No, no, that's just what I'm telling you. I didn't buy this lot!" she said, now holding up one of the balls she'd been resting her head on. "Do you know how much all of this would cost?" Charlotte asked rhetorically, lovingly caressing the wool in her hand against her cheek.

"Dunno," Mollie replied with a shrug. "But, if you didn't buy it, then have you been sleeping with that guy who owns one of the local crafting shops? You *did* say you'd do anything for a discount card."

"Ha! That fellow knows I was joking when I'd suggested that!" Charlotte countered. "At least I hope he does…?" she added with a cheeky smile. "Anyway, this lot didn't come from his shop. They're from Joan's Wools and Crafts."

"And you've no idea why?" Mollie pressed on.

"No, they just turned up about an hour ago," Charlotte explained. "I must confess, I felt like a little girl on Christmas morning when I looked inside the first box. I thought the deliveryman had come to the wrong address at first."

"You're absolutely sure he didn't?"

Charlotte shook her head in the negative. "No, not at all!" she was delighted to affirm. "No, see, there was a letter attached to one of the boxes," she added, rummaging underneath the one particular box sat beside her. "Hang on…"

"Right, I'm hanging on," Mollie advised, patiently hanging on, as requested.

"Ah, here it is," Charlotte said, finally locating the letter, and then removing the handwritten note from within its white envelope.

Charlotte proceeded to unfold the letter, cleared her throat, and then read aloud:

Dear Crafternoon Sewcial Club,

Keep up the amazing work. Hopefully, this modest donation will help you on your way.
I wish you well with your new venture!

Best wishes

"Best wishes, *and*…?" Mollie entered in, swirling her fingers in the air, inviting further detail.

"That's it. There's nothing else," Charlotte said, turning the page over to look for additional information even though she'd already performed that very same task earlier. "I did phone the wool shop to ask, but they were sworn to secrecy, so…"

"A mystery benefactor," Mollie remarked. "How very interesting."

"I know, right?" Charlotte said, giving the wool another adoring glance.

"So, I'm guessing our run is on hold?" Mollie put forth, reaching for and then filling the kettle. However, there was little need to ask about the run, as it was eminently clear that Charlotte was at present entirely consumed by matters of the woollen variety and would likely continue to be for some good while.

"Would you mind?" Charlotte asked, raising and wiggling a ball of wool with a daft grin etched on her face. "You can help me decide what we're going to do with this lot," she said, opening her arms like she was inviting them all closer, into her bosom.

In truth, Mollie appeared just as pleased to see Charlotte smiling again, and was quite willing to forgo their jog in the rain and settle on a cuppa and a biscuit as a suitable alternative.

In point of fact, after the initial disappointment caused by the church hall double-booking, Charlotte had been despondent for most of the week. For a time, there was even talk of writing the club off as a bad idea. Fortunately, a rousing well-timed pep talk arrived via Stanley, affirming that the club was fantastic and worthwhile. His motivational speech concluded with his desire for his mum to firmly "snap the heck out of it," which proved to be the catalyst for her to do precisely that. And snap the heck out of it she did.

In the following days, with renewed determination, she'd set up a Facebook page for the crafting group and already had nearly fifty people click 'Like' on the group's page. Her request for any crafting donations had already borne fruit, and she'd even managed to secure a new home for the club in the form of Union Mills Methodist Church, in Union Mills, on the outskirts of Douglas. It was a twenty-minute-or-so drive from the previous location but offered the benefit of a larger capacity (which Charlotte was hopeful would soon be required), as well as the added bonus of onsite parking.

The diverse age range of those signing up had taken her by surprise, yet pleasantly so. So far, the swing in ages was extreme, with the youngest member being a sprightly fifteen-year-old named Bonnie, and her oldest being the also-sprightly ninety-two-year-old Joyce (the aspiring exotic dancer, whose age Charlotte had estimated a few years short).

As an extra added benefit, with Charlotte being flexible about her timings, the church secretary had generously offered the hall without charge for the first three months. The church committee was impressed with the club's mission, and was willing to allow it time to establish itself before taking a fee for the hall hire. It probably didn't hurt any that the secretary was also an avid crocheter, and now a signed-up member of the new club.

Securing a new home for the club also meant that Charlotte's subsequent interaction with Amelia was not quite as unpleasant as it ordinarily was. The next time Charlotte saw her, Amelia was there in the schoolyard again, flanked by the same pair of perfectly (though some might say gaudily) made-up friends as usual, and with Amelia offering up a less-than-sincere explanation for the unfortunate double-booking error. At one point in the conversation, Amelia had even inexplicably laid the blame for the confusion at Charlotte's feet. However, Amelia then ever-so-kindly offered to drop everything in order to rearrange her bookings at great personal inconvenience to rectify the situation, hero to the people that she was. There was no apology offered, of course, and Amelia stood, arms folded across her chest with a smug grin, likely awaiting a grovelling acceptance to her kind and generous offer. Charlotte did so enjoy the opportunity, then, to rebuff Amelia's overture, waving the issue away, and insisting the whole affair had been nothing more than a minor nuisance and one which Amelia needn't concern herself with any longer. Charlotte was delighted to further elaborate that the mix-up had, in fact, spurred her on to secure even more spacious premises, costing her the grand total of nothing. This was, of course, not the sort of reaction Amelia was possibly hoping for.

Yes, as far as her new venture went, things were currently coming along quite swimmingly, Charlotte reckoned. And now, this new, welcome donation of a large volume of wool was only the perfect icing on the cake, so to speak. The only grey cloud possibly circling overhead, at present, was the absence of a formal contract for her new job. But this was, she could only hope, merely a minor oversight on the part of her prospective new employer, as her latest bank statement didn't exactly make for the most enjoyable of reading material.

Later in the day, Charlotte managed to drag herself away from her new woollen arrivals long enough for an appointment with the gang at MAKE IT SEW, with Stanley in tow.

She did so enjoy her time spent at the nursing home, and had now resolved to continue volunteering there, whatever her future work commitments might entail. Visiting the group was a tonic for her soul. No matter what trials and tribulations she happened to be facing at the time, they would always be forgotten in an instant as soon as she stepped through the nursing home's front door. Charlotte adored being with them all, listening to their tales, and absorbing their zest for life — it was thoroughly invigorating. And if she could give a little back in helping them learn a new skill or hone an existing one, well, that was the least she could do in return, she reckoned.

"Come on, slowcoach!" Charlotte said, giving the hand enclosed in her own a gentle tug. "That bag's not too heavy for you?" she asked, though not serious, as she knew Stanley's bag contained only a pair of knitting needles and the beginning of a blanket she'd been working on.

"You think Larry will be there tonight?" Stanley asked, picking up the pace a touch as they approached their destination. "Only he said he'd teach me to juggle the next time I came."

"He did, did he?"

"Yeah," Stanley confirmed. "He told me he was the greatest juggler the circus had ever known. I think he even said he'd won some kind of world record for juggling!"

Charlotte slowed for a moment, looking down at Stanley. "The circus?" she asked, tilting her head, as Larry possibly having been in the circus was certainly news to her.

"Yeah. Didn't you know?" Stanley asked, happy, it would appear, to know something his mum didn't.

"No. No, I didn't, Stanley," Charlotte replied. "But I'll certainly look forward to your demonstration, later, once Larry has coached you," she said, smiling warmly.

Stanley nodded. "I popped three oranges in the bag," he said, half to himself, deep in thought. "Just in case Larry couldn't find anything to juggle."

"Super idea, Stanley," Charlotte answered. "Hmm, I wonder if he's ever tamed the lions, as well?" she added. "I mean, if he's been in the circus, as he says…?"

"I could ask!" Stanley suggested, eager to explore this option, it would seem, judging by the fact that he was now up ahead of mum and pulling *her* along.

The two of them walked the short distance from the carpark and into the nursing home's memorial garden. They both enjoyed the meticulously tended gardens, which were, just now, an explosion of colour and a paradise for the local bee population. Charlotte would often stop for a moment while passing by, pressing her nose into the roses, which always managed to lift her spirits. Benches were situated sporadically, so that visitors might rest awhile, appreciate the tranquillity, and perhaps take a moment to remember those friends who were no longer with them. However, it never felt sombre sitting in the garden as it was so vibrant and teeming with life, with a chorus of birdsong often accompanying the busy buzzing of the bees and the gentle flapping of butterfly wings and such.

"Come on, my lovely," Charlotte said, once she'd filled her nostrils with the glorious floral scent of the garden. "Stanley...?" she said, running her eyes around, trying to locate her crafting assistant for the evening. She'd let go his hand only a moment or two before, it seemed. Where could he have gone off to so quickly? "Hmm," she said, when there was no immediate sign of him. It wasn't the largest of gardens like, say, Kew, for example, so there weren't an awful lot of places he could hide. Wait, she thought, maybe he *was* hiding?

"Stanley, we haven't got time for hide-and-seek!" she called out, checking her watch.

But then she had a hunch. Charlotte headed in the direction of the fruit trees, located to form a guard of honour on either side of the winding path. Off to one side, a little way in, at the base of a lovely apple tree, she caught sight of a distinctly Stanley-shaped pair of buttocks sat resting on his heels as he knelt before the tree in a sort of praying position. He was leant forward, head bowed, and he appeared to be doing something with his hands though Charlotte couldn't see exactly what.

"There you are, Stanley. I thought you might be here. Honey, we need to—"

"One minute, Mum!" Stanley replied, still busying himself with whatever it was he was currently busying himself with.

"Dolly's tree?" Charlotte asked, kneeling down beside him. There was a ringed border around the base of the tree, set into the earth, with this area being filled in with decorative white stone chippings — stone chippings through which Stanley's fingers were presently foraging, Charlotte could now see.

"Uh-huh," Stanley confirmed, in answer to his mother's question. "She never did like weeds," he remarked, ripping another of the little green devils up by the root from its hiding place and, in the process, freeing the stone chippings of the presence of one more unwelcome interloper.

Charlotte gently rubbed Stanley's back. She watched, smiling, as he collected the pile of weeds he was gathering into a small bundle as he went along, putting all the little stones meticulously back into place when he was done, taking care to ensure everything was as it should be.

"Dolly would be very proud of you, Stanley," Charlotte told him, giving his back another rub as he finished up. "You know," she suggested, "we could bring a bunch of flowers for her the next time we come?"

"They'll need to be lilies," Stanley commented, getting to his feet. "They were her favourite," he added, stretching his arms above his head like he'd just woken from a nap.

"Then lilies it will be," Charlotte answered, giving him a nod of assurance. "Come on, we can pop those weeds in the compost bin," she said, pushing herself upright as well.

Dolly's passing earlier in the year was the first time Stanley had been exposed to grief. She was described by many of her fellow nursing home residents as being somewhat cantankerous, but with a gentle layer if you were willing to dig deep enough to uncover it. A keen gardener, she'd often be found with dirt-covered knees and a pair of secateurs in hand. The two of them, Stanley and Dolly, just seemed to gel, with him often following her around the grounds like a hungry duckling. At first, she would often shoo him away, as if he were a pest. But those observing the blossoming of their charming friendship suspected the frosty initial response on Dolly's part was merely a ploy to maintain her well-practised façade of irascibility. One has a reputation to uphold, after all.

However, soon enough, she warmed to the little tike, and many a green-fingered hour was spent educating Stanley on the ways of cultivation. Indeed, at the tender age of only seven, Stanley had been able to successfully recite the names of nearly two dozen lily species at school show & tell one day, a presentation at which Dolly was happily in attendance as a special guest. Dolly would surely have been most impressed that Stanley's appreciation of the blooms remained with him after she'd moved on.

Following a quick wash of his hands in the gents' loo after to-day's bit of gardening, Stanley led the way into the nursing home with at least a minute to spare, coming to rest at the door of the dining room, in which the club's session would be held.

"Door's closed," Stanley announced over his shoulder to his mum. "It's never usually closed," he added with a shrug. He pushed open the heavy door just a wee bit, enough so he could have a little peek inside. "There's no lights on, Mum," he told her. "Have we come on the wrong day?"

Charlotte took a step closer, moving her head towards the gap in the door. "How curious," she remarked, upon confirming Stanley's observation for herself that the lights were indeed off. She raised her hand, helping Stanley push the door fully open, and then took the lead as they both took a single step in. The dining room before them was in complete darkness, with not only all the lights off but all the window curtains drawn closed as well.

"How very strange," Charlotte said, as an executive summary of the situation. "Hmm," she considered, "perhaps we should pop back over to the reception desk, and see what—"

"SURPRISE!" came a collective roar as the lights suddenly came on, revealing those people inside, previously hidden, and congregated in the far corner of the room.

"Aaagh!" Charlotte cried, jumping back a pace and nearly sending poor Stanley for a tumble in the process. "What the...?" she added, trying to get her bearings, and trying to figure out what the dickens was happening.

The members of MAKE IT SEW were all stood, hands in the air, with broad smiles across their faces. "Gotcha!" Larry said, jumping forward with his party hat resting at a jaunty angle. "Happy birthday, Lotti!" he shouted, pulling the cord on the party popper that had been held in his hands at the ready.

"Happy birthday, Lotti!" the remaining residents there in the room shouted in unison.

"Ehm…" Charlotte said in reply, this being all she could muster in response, "I don't really know what…"

"We made vol-au-vents and sandwiches!" Larry announced, turning with an extended hand, introducing the buffet table.

"Yes, I can see that," Charlotte said, seeing just that. "How wonderful," she added, surveying the scene. "Only it's not… It's just, ehm… The thing is… Don't think I don't appreciate this. Truly, I do… It's just, well… Larry, it's *not* my birthday today."

Larry's arms dropped slowly to his waist, the party popper still in his hands but with no more pop left to be had.

All eyes turned to Larry, accompanied by a collective groan. From the others' reaction, it appeared highly probable that Larry had been the lead instigator in the day's proceedings. There were many frowns directed towards Larry's general location, and Larry, for his part, looked absolutely crestfallen.

Charlotte placed her hand to her mouth. She didn't know what to do or say. The gang had even gone to the effort of fashioning a birthday banner with the letters of her name made from fabric offcuts. It was evident that a considerable amount of time and effort had been expended, and Larry looked as if he were hoping the floor would open up to swallow him whole.

"Gotcha!" Charlotte shouted, lowering her hand from her mouth, and then extending an outstretched finger in Larry's direction. "You should have seen your face, Larry!" she said with a snort. "That's payback for all those practical jokes you've played on me this year!" she added, slapping her thigh for good measure.

Larry's sad expression changed, turning instantly into a toothy grin (false teeth, but still). "You had me there!" he said, hopping from one foot to the other in giddy delight. "Oh, you had me there! It's just as well, too, as this lot would have had my guts for garters if I'd got the date wrong!"

The throng behind him seemed likewise relieved, and Larry motioned for Charlotte to follow him to a nearby table. "Come on,

Lotti, let's go and see the cake we've made you!" he said, a spring in his step as he walked over.

Stanley was impressed with the group's baking skills, polishing off two slices of birthday cake in short order, and then hovering about, appearing for all the world as if he were eager to secure a third. Meanwhile, his mum made the rounds, chatting with everyone and accepting all the well-wishings coming her way. Periodically, Stanley attempted to get a word in himself. He stood on the periphery, patiently waiting his turn, hoping to jump through a gap as soon as one presented itself, like a thirsty gazelle eager for a drink at a desert waterhole.

"Mum!" Stanley said, when an opportunity finally arose. "Mum!" he said again, tapping her arm.

"No more cake for you, mister!" Charlotte gently admonished, although delivered with a smile, and completely misreading his intentions.

"No, no. That's not what I wanted," Stanley answered, pulling her aside.

"What is it, honey?" Charlotte asked, once they were out of earshot of the others.

"I'm a little confused," Stanley said, looking a little confused. "I mean, any chance to eat cake is good…" he said, looking around to make sure the coast was still clear. "But, um…"

"But it's not actually my birthday today," Charlotte said, finishing Stanley's thought for him.

"Lying is bad, though. Right?" Stanley asked, just wanting to make sure lying was still bad, because, if that was no longer the case, then that would change his understanding of the world considerably.

"It's still bad," Charlotte confirmed. "And you know it's not my birthday for another few months yet, but…"

"But sometimes a little white lie is okay, if it means not hurting people's feelings?" Stanley answered, finishing his mum's thought for *her* this time around.

"How did I raise such a thoughtful little boy?" Charlotte asked.

"Erm… I don't know?" Stanley replied, uncertain if this was a question he was supposed to answer, or if it was one of those other types of questions adults sometimes asked, the kind you weren't really meant to give an answer to.

"I feel awful," Charlotte confessed. "I was going to tell them, really I was, but you can see just how much effort they've gone to. Plus, they would have strung poor Larry up by his shoelaces if they knew he'd got the wrong date. Stanley, am I a terrible person?"

Stanley shook his head firmly in the negative. "No," he said. "No, I don't think so, or else what would we do with the cake? Cake is made for eating."

"Ah. Thoughtful *and* logical," Charlotte said, pulling him in for a quick cuddle. "Cake is made for eating," she agreed.

Stanley was happy they were in complete alignment, and got the impression he'd said something profound although he wasn't sure quite what. "Let's keep the confusion to ourselves for the time being, yeah?" his mum advised, to which Stanley snapped his lips together and locked them with an imaginary key, and then tossing the key away.

Charlotte and Stanley were just about to make their way back over to the others when Emma, the nursing home manager, appeared through the dining room door. "Ah, Charlotte. Happy birthday," she said in greeting. "I hope you enjoyed your surprise party?" she asked with a sunny smile. "And hello to you too, Stanley," Emma added brightly.

"Yes, yes. A wonderful surprise," Charlotte said, giving nothing immediately away. "There is something I should probably mention, actually. But I think I'll save it until another time."

"No problem," Emma replied. "I am glad I caught you here, though, as I wanted to show you this," she went on, handing a glossy flyer over for Charlotte's inspection.

"Oh? And what's this?" Charlotte asked, starting to look it over.

"The team from Oxfam dropped it off earlier," Emma explained. "They're running a charity campaign to collect knitted or crocheted squares," she said. "They then send the completed squares to communities who can make use of them, with the squares getting sewn together once they've arrived at their destination."

"Yes, I see. They make them into blankets and such," Charlotte answered, reading through the flyer, interest piqued. "What a lovely idea."

"Anyway," Emma continued, "I just wondered if you'd like to get the gang here to make a number of squares, and we could drop them off at the charity? I'm sure they'd like to get involved," she said, adding, with a wink, "And I know an excellent teacher who could show them what to do." Emma waited for Charlotte to read through the contents of the flyer. "So you're up for it, then?" she asked after a moment or two, already suspecting the answer and encouraged by Charlotte's broad smile.

"Very much," Charlotte confirmed, eyes drifting away dreamily as she imagined her group beavering away after responding to the rallying cry.

"Brilliant!" Emma said. "And, of course, I'm looking forward to making some myself," she added, turning to get back to her duties. "Speak soon!" she said, calling over her shoulder as she left.

"I can help too, Mum," Stanley suggested, the lock on his mouth having been released.

"Absolutely!" Charlotte said, leading them both back over to the buffet table. "You know," Charlotte added, "I've been trying to think of a suitable project for my new Crafternoon Sewcial Club to sink their teeth into as well," she said, glancing down to the flyer once more. "And you know what, Stanley, my boy? This could be the very thing."

"Well, you've got enough wool at the house to make thousands of them squares!" Stanley offered jokingly, though he was not actually that far off the mark.

"That I do, Stanley," Charlotte agreed, smiling at the thought of the stash waiting for her when they returned home. "Oh, anyway," she said, snapping herself back into the present, "don't forget, Stanley, you need to ask Larry the circus juggler to give you a demonstration!" She raised her hands in the air as she said this to mimic juggling, although looking more like she was weighing two objects on a scale.

"Oh, and should I also ask about the lion taming?" Stanley asked excitedly.

"You *definitely* should, Stanley," Charlotte answered with a sly, crooked grin. "Yes, definitely. This, I'm rather looking forward to…"

CHAPTER EIGHT

S orry I'm late, Dad!" Bonnie called out, breathless, and plonking her schoolbag down onto the kitchen table. "I left on time," she went on, filling a glass of water from the tap. "But I saw Mrs Beattie struggling up the hill with her shopping, and you know what she's like once she gets you talking. So, at least that's my good deed done for the day!"

"Dad?" she said, leaving the kitchen, and popping her head around the living room door. "Wakey-wakey!" she joked, breaking her dad's attention away from his computer screen.

"Heya, Bonn," Benjamin said, leaning back in his chair, and rubbing his eyes with the back of his hand. "I didn't realise it was that time already. The day's just run away from me."

Bonnie walked over, placing a kiss on his cheek. "I'll bet you've been glued to that chair all day, haven't you?" she asked. "Did you get out and stretch your legs like you said you would, Dad?"

Benjamin rolled his eyes playfully. "I walked to the kitchen for some of that chocolate cake about an hour ago. Does that count?"

Bonnie returned the playful eye-rolling. "Right. Just give me five minutes so I can change out of my uniform," she advised. "And then we can get going," she said.

She progressed no further than the stairs in the hallway, however, before realising there'd been no response or confirmation to her last statement. Knowing her dad as well as she did, she suspected what this likely meant.

"Dad..." she said, returning to the living room. "Dad, did you, perhaps, forget where we were going today?"

"What? No!" Benjamin replied immediately, swinging around

in his chair, fixing his eyes to hers. "No, of course not!" he reiterated, appearing quite sure of himself.

To be fair, he was offering a pretty decent performance, although clearly not convincing enough, as Bonnie could see right through it. "Oh?" she said, leaning against the doorframe, casually examining her nails. "So where are we going, then? Freshen my memory, will you?"

Benjamin locked his fingers behind his head, staring out the window, looking for, perhaps, some divine inspiration. "We're... going... to..." he said slowly, clicking his tongue against the roof of his mouth between each word.

"You're driving me to the crafting club I told you about," Bonnie interjected, saving him. "You said you'd take me, remember?"

"Of *course* I remember," Benjamin insisted. "Wait, hang on, Bonn," he added, a thought occurring. "I thought Sue was going with you, and the two of you were walking, as it's only around the corner?"

"Hah! Now I *know* you weren't listening," Bonnie said, pointing an accusatory finger. "That was the old plan. But Sue now has something on at school tonight, so can't go. Plus, the location is now in Union Mills rather than Laxey."

"Oh, yes," Benjamin said, nodding in agreement. "Yes, yes, yes. It's all coming back to me now."

"Fabulous. Well, I'll go get changed," Bonnie answered. "Oh, and Dad," she said, wishing to include one minor point. "There's no sense in you dropping me off, only to have to drive all the way home and then come pick me up later, now is there?"

"There isn't?" Benjamin asked, worried about where exactly this was headed.

"There isn't," Bonnie cheerfully declared. "So you may as well just come in and join me."

"Fine," Benjamin conceded with a sigh. "Fine, I suppose so," he said, as he knew this was a battle he wasn't going to win. "It's just going to be all women, though, is it?"

Bonnie shook her head. "Of *course* not, Dad! *You're* going to be there, as well!"

"Where *are* you?" Charlotte said, shifting her attention to the row of bungalows on the right-hand side of the road. She slowed her speed even more than she'd done already, driving along now at the leisurely pace of a kerb crawler hoping for a 'date.'

She glanced in her rear-view mirror, catching a glimpse of a rather excited-looking chap gesticulating wildly, the front of his vehicle, at present, positioned less than a millimetre or so from her rear bumper. "Sorry!" Charlotte said, even though her apology could not have been heard by the other motorist. She switched on her indicator, pulling over and allowing the fellow to pass, with him offering a spirited two-finger salute as he did so.

"I *did* say I was sorry," Charlotte remarked as she gave a cheerful wave in return, although, again, the chap wouldn't have been able to hear her.

Andreas, a semi-rural town in the north of the island, was not an area Charlotte often visited. As such, locating Joyce's house was proving somewhat difficult. She'd been up and down the same street several times, certain this was the area she should be in. That is, of course, if her interpretation of the provided directions was accurate. "Aww, fiddlesticks," she said, reviewing the handwritten notes she'd scribbled onto the back of a used envelope. She'd even drawn a lovely illustration to represent Joyce's neighbourhood and house, but her pretty diagram didn't appear to have helped any because she seemed no closer to completing her quest.

Just then, Charlotte's mobile sounded. Her phone was, quite helpfully, linked to her car speakers via Bluetooth. "Hello," she said, pressing the 'connect' button on the steering wheel. "Hello?" she said again, uncertain if the call had, in fact, connected.

"Charlotte…?" Joyce's voice rang out, coming through the car speakers.

"Yes. Hello, Joyce. I can hear you loud and clear," Charlotte replied. "How are you?"

"Are you in a red car, by any chance?" Joyce enquired. "I do hope so," she added, "otherwise, we might have ourselves a burglar staking out the neighbourhood!"

Charlotte could hear Joyce laughing, so had to assume that Joyce knew she was not a burglar. "I do have a red car, and I'm not here to burgle!" Charlotte answered. "It'nly me!" she said, laughing along.

Charlotte waved in all directions, not knowing where Joyce's call was originating from, but certain Joyce must have eyes clapped on her as they spoke.

"You can see me, right?" Charlotte asked, still waving this way and that.

"Hmm? Oh, no, not at all," Joyce responded.

"Oh," Charlotte said, bringing her waving session to an abrupt conclusion as there no longer seemed to be any point to it. "Em... then how did you know I was in a red car...?" Charlotte asked, somewhat puzzled.

"Well, I saw a red car drive past quite a number of times," Joyce explained. "I figured it must be you, and that you were either lost or you just really enjoyed driving!"

"Ah, yes! That's me. A driving enthusiast!" Charlotte said with a laugh. "Uh, in all seriousness, though. Could you maybe walk out to the edge of the road, and I'll see if I can see you? Would you mind?"

"Righto," Joyce answered. "I'm walking outside now... bringing my phone with me... Okay. Right. Here I am."

Charlotte turned her head, twisting her neck like an owl, running her eyes up and down the street. "I can't seem to..." she began, worried she was still in the wrong place, or had veered too far off course. And, then, "Ah!" she said, her eyes drawn towards a pair of cerise-pink tracksuit bottoms. "Is that you, pretty in pink?"

"That's me! Pretty in pink!" came the immediate and jovial confirmation.

"Okay. I see you. Let me swing the car around, and I'll be with you shortly," Charlotte said, taking an admiring glance, before setting off, at her most splendid hand-drawn map, the accuracy of which should never have been in doubt.

There was just something about Joyce that made people instantly warm to her. Perhaps it was her lively personality, crazy sense of humour, or the fact that age presented no obstacle for her. Whatever it was, Charlotte connected with Joyce the moment she'd seen her that day outside the yoga class. There was a sense that they'd known each other for years even though they'd only just met. Since that first meeting, they'd exchanged several phone calls resulting in Charlotte ending up in tears of laughter each time they spoke. Joyce may have had more candles on her birthday cake than most, but she didn't seem to allow age to dampen her thirst for new adventures. Only the week before, Charlotte learned, Joyce had been on a kayaking-for-beginners course. She enjoyed the experience so much, she told Charlotte, that she was due to return to the same location for an afternoon of coasteering. She was a breath of fresh air, was Joyce. "Impossible" was simply a word that didn't appear to exist in her vocabulary.

So, when Charlotte secured the new meeting place for the crafting club, the first person she called was Joyce. Concerned that the new venue, even further afield from where Joyce lived, might present a problem for her, Charlotte had extended the offer of a ride. However, she needn't have worried as Joyce promptly brushed off the issue of the increased distance, declaring it an opportunity to spend longer on the bus, meeting new people. As Joyce explained over the phone, the journey was as much a part of the adventure for her as the eventual destination. There was always somebody new to talk to on each trip, Joyce suggested. And, if she didn't care for the person she was sat next to, well, she'd simply get up, swop seats, and find somebody that she did.

Still, Joyce wasn't overly familiar with the area of Union Mills, their destination, and as such, accepted Charlotte's offer of a ride for at least this first time. And so…

"I did what you suggested," Joyce announced, once they were loaded up in the car and off on their way.

"Oh?" Charlotte replied absently, paying more attention to the upcoming roundabout just ahead than she was to her passenger right at that one particular moment.

"Tinder, it's called," Joyce went on, nodding her head, appearing pleased she'd remembered the name. "There are a few oddballs on there, if I'm honest," she confided, glancing through the passenger window thoughtfully as she watched the Manx country-side go by. "Do you know what a threesome is?" Joyce asked abruptly, now looking across to Charlotte.

"Firstly..." Charlotte began. And then, after a long pause, and once she'd safely navigated the busy roundabout, she asked, "Wait, did you just say *Tinder*?"

"Yes!" Joyce confirmed. "And there were plenty of hunks on there about your age, just so you know," Joyce added with a playful wink. "You could really fill your boots!"

"My...?"

"Boots," Joyce reiterated.

"Okay...? Um..." Charlotte said, unsure where to even start with this. "All right, so when, exactly, did I suggest that you join an online dating app, Joyce?" she asked, taking the plunge.

"You indicated that it'd be nice for me to have a gentleman to share a meal with once in a while," Joyce replied, reminding Charlotte of the details of a previous conversation they'd had.

Charlotte reached over, turning the volume down on the radio. "Yes, but I never imagined you'd sign up on *Tinder* as a result of our small talk, Joyce," Charlotte answered.

Joyce waved away the concern heard in Charlotte's voice. "You planted the seed in my head, dear. Then one of the girls told me about Tinder, so I thought I'd see if there were any suitors out there looking for a good time!"

"A good...?"

"A good time!" Joyce happily confirmed.

"Joyce," Charlotte said, panicked. "*Please* tell me you didn't write that part down, in your profile? The bit about you looking for a good time...?"

"Yes, I did!" Joyce replied. "And my profile is proving to be quite popular!"

"I'm not surprised," Charlotte answered. "Still. How about I have a quick review of your profile," she suggested, "and make sure you're not going to get yourself into any—"

"You couldn't pull over, could you?" Joyce interrupted. "Just up ahead," Joyce added, pointing to where she wanted Charlotte to come to a halt.

"What? Sure, of course," Charlotte said, turning on her indicator, and then pulling over and coming to a stop. "Everything okay?" she asked worriedly, looking Joyce up and down.

"Yes, fine," Joyce replied, reaching for and pressing the button to open the passenger-side window. "Hello, Beryl!" Joyce called out, through the opened window.

There was a lady sat in the bus stop adjacent to where they'd stopped. The woman leaned forward, unsure who it was calling her name. She pushed her glasses up her nose, staring directly at Joyce, but without a flicker of recognition apparent.

"It's me!" Joyce added, audibly identifying herself.

"Oh!" Beryl said, her face erupting into a smile as recognition dawned, and offering up a generous wave to Joyce. "Sorry, Joyce, I didn't know it was you at first. I've only brought my reading glasses, not my looking-further-away glasses."

"Are you off to your life drawing class, then?" Joyce enquired, apparently well aware of Beryl's social schedule.

Beryl shook her head. "That's tomorrow, Joyce. Today, I'm going to pick up my good shoes," she began. "Remember I was telling you about my good shoes? Right, well I'm going to the cobblers in town, of course, because the last time I used that chap who lives at the bottom of the street… Remember I mentioned him before? … Well, you'll never believe what happened, which is a very funny story, but slightly disturbing at the same time, and—"

"Do you want to come to the crafting club with us?" Joyce cut in, likely suspecting Beryl would prattle on at least until the next bus arrived if allowed.

Beryl smacked her lips together, allowing the idea to bounce around in her head for a moment. "Hmm," she said, raising her eyes skyward. "Hmm," she said again, considering Joyce's suggestion, and weighing up her options.

"There's going to be cake!" Joyce added.

But before Joyce had even finished saying the *ake* in cake, Beryl was reaching for her handbag, and the CRAFTERNOON SEWCIAL CLUB had successfully recruited another member, (even if it did require pulling them in off the street, quite literally). The cobblers, it would appear, would have to hold on to Beryl's "good" shoes for at least one more day.

Soon, Charlotte's cheeks began to ache from continually grinning, listening to her two passengers chatting away incessantly and barely stopping to take a breath. It certainly made the journey towards the island's capital, Douglas, fly by in a blur. It also transpired that Joyce wasn't the only pensioner in the car who'd signed up to the services of an online dating agency. It didn't sound like they were looking for love, necessarily. Just hopeful, perhaps, of snagging a distinguished gentleman apiece to stamp their dance card on a Saturday night.

"I think I need to get in on this dating website action," Charlotte entered in, during a brief lull in their conversation, "as you two are getting more attention in a week than I've had all year!"

"It's all about the selection of the profile picture," Beryl replied, with an experienced, sage-like tone.

"It *is*," Joyce was quick to agree. "Just don't show them too much flesh, however," she cautioned, finger raised. "Keep them keen for more!" she advised, resulting in the two of them erupting into a bout of laughter.

"I'll make a mental note," Charlotte promised, making a mental note. "So, do you post a headshot of yourselves, or maybe an action shot like from when you're out kayaking?" Charlotte asked by way of conversation.

"Oh, we don't use photographs of *ourselves*," Joyce told her, as if this should have been obvious.

Charlotte looked over to Joyce, expecting there to be some form of follow-up explanation. "You don't?" she asked after a moment or two, when there was nothing further offered.

"No, of course not," Beryl chipped in. "I use a picture of Linda Gray. You know, that one from Dynasty?"

"*Dallas*," Joyce said, gently correcting Beryl. "And I use a picture of Farrah Fawcett," she told Charlotte. "After her Charlie's Angels days, but before she died of cancer, of course."

"Of course," Charlotte answered, unable to stifle a chuckle. "It's no wonder the both of you have proved so popular with the boys, then," she remarked.

Joyce adjusted her position, turning so she could look back to

Beryl sat in the car's rear. "Speaking of which. Perhaps you could help me with something?" Joyce suggested, gazing at her friend, eyes filled with hope.

"Oh? With what?" Beryl asked, appearing happy to comply.

"Well, as I was just beginning to tell Charlotte a bit earlier," Joyce explained, "I've had a message on my phone from this chap named Barry. And this Barry fellow asked if I had a friend who might like to participate in a threesome. So naturally I thought of you, Beryl."

"It sounds perfectly lovely!" Beryl replied. "And what do I need to do, exactly? What's involved in performing this threesome type of affair that he's proposing?"

"Ah. Well I'll have to find out the particulars from Barry," Joyce advised.

"Do that," Beryl answered. "It sounds like loads of fun."

"I expect it will be," Joyce agreed.

"No threesomes! Threesomes bad!" Charlotte told them, almost shouting. She wanted to nip this worrisome threesome thing in the bud before plans could possibly be set in motion. Unless they were having her on, of course. Surely they knew what a threesome was??

"We're here," Charlotte announced shortly thereafter, blessedly relieved, and turning off the main road and into the carpark at Union Mills Methodist Church. She pulled up next to Mollie's car, who'd already arrived with Stanley, as planned, bringing along with them the assorted cakes they'd baked for the no doubt hungry crafters.

"Look, ladies…" Charlotte began, unfastening her seatbelt and turning to face the others before they got out of the car. "If you *really* don't know what a threesome is," she said, on the off chance that the old girls genuinely didn't know what a threesome was, "I'll clarify to you, yeah?"

What followed was an extremely awkward and uncomfortable (on Charlotte's part, at least) elucidation regarding the birds & the bees in general and threesomes in particular, to which Joyce and Beryl sat listening in wide-eyed wonderment along with the occasional giggle. As to whether the two of them truly needed this explanation or not, Charlotte couldn't tell, but by the end of it, Joyce had promised to block Barry on her Tinder profile, and both ladies also assured Charlotte that they would seek her advice on similar matters in the future should such a need arise.

With that bit of business sorted, the three of them exited the vehicle and walked across the carpark in the direction of the church hall. Charlotte slowed her pace as they approached the entrance, taking in a deep breath. She felt slightly apprehensive, as there was no one else about. There were still ten minutes before the scheduled start time, but it would have been encouraging to see some early arrivals streaming in eager to get started, she thought to herself.

Once inside, Charlotte saw only Mollie and Stanley in the hall, positioning chairs under the tables they'd arranged across the floor.

"Look, I made a pyramid from all the balls of wool!" Stanley announced, face lit up as he saw his mum. He rushed over to stand beside his impressive handiwork, showing off the masterpiece he'd constructed atop one of the tables. "We brought along every box delivered to the house!" he explained.

"I love it!" Charlotte said, walking over and running her eyes over the meticulously arranged multi-coloured pile. "Hmm, do you think we have enough wool?" she joked, pressing a finger to her lips.

The wool stack was as wide at the base as a washing machine and nearly as tall, so it was unlikely they'd run short anytime in the near future, much less the next century.

"Sorry about that," Mollie said with a laugh, joining her friend. "I suggested bringing only a *few* of the boxes, but Stanley was quite insistent that it was better to have too much than not enough. So I deferred to his judgement."

Charlotte glanced down to her watch, and then over to the door. "I'm starting to suspect one lonely ball of wool might have been enough, actually," she said with a sigh.

"Chin up," Mollie said, extending an index finger, placing it under Charlotte's chin, and giving it a gentle lift upwards. "It's only the first day of the club, mind you, and you've already got two members," she offered, presenting a positive spin on the situation. "So, what say I get us all a cup of tea, and I'll slice up that delicious fruit loaf you made?"

"Sounds good," Charlotte agreed. "And, Moll," she said, "thank you so much for helping out."

"I wouldn't miss it for the world," Mollie answered, then suddenly, directing her ear towards the door, "A-ha! That sounds like voices!"

And sure enough it was, with their ranks about to be swelled a bit further.

"Oh, hiya," a bright-eyed young lady with flaming-red hair said, appearing in the doorway. "Crafternoon Sewcial Club?" she enquired, half in and half out the door.

"Sure is," Charlotte replied, inviting her in with a friendly wave. "And, you're just in time for cake!"

The girl in the doorway looked behind her for a moment. "We're in the right place," she said, opening the door fully. "I'm Bonnie," she offered, once stood inside. "And this is my dad, Ben," she added, introducing the rather reluctant-looking chap following her in.

"Welcome, welcome!" Charlotte said, bounding over to the two of them like Winnie-the-Pooh's Tigger, hand extended. "Sewing, knitting, crocheting, or…?"

Bonnie held up the canvas bag in her hand. "Ehm, a quilt," she replied, opening the top of the bag for Charlotte's inspection. "I was hoping to finish what my mum had started?" she explained. "Only I don't really know *how*, exactly."

"Ah!" Charlotte said, peering at the rolled-up quilt inside.

Charlotte didn't ask where Mum was at present. She could hear the emotion in Bonnie's voice, and worked out what this likely meant.

"It looks absolutely lovely," Charlotte continued. "And I think you've certainly come to the right place, Bonnie, as I'm happy to help. And Joyce, over there, is quite the quilter as it should happen. So if I somehow come up short, I feel confident that she'd be delighted to offer a helping hand as well, if asked."

"That would be brilliant," Bonnie answered. "I really appreciate it."

"Ah. And, Ben...?" Charlotte said, now shifting her attention over to Bonnie's father.

Benjamin tilted his head, unsure what the question was. "Em... Hi?" he said, giving a little wave.

"Sewing, knitting, crochet, or...?" Charlotte asked, repeating the same question she'd presented to Bonnie a few moments before.

"Oh, I see," Benjamin answered, fidgeting. "I... well, that is... erm... I suppose I'd have to say..." he said, waffling. "Knitting...?" he proposed tentatively, looking over at Stanley's impressive woollen pyramid.

"Ah! I've just the project for you, then!" Charlotte told him, rubbing her hands together in anticipation.

"Uh... okay," Benjamin said, having no idea what he'd just got himself into.

"Knitted squares," Charlotte explained a bit further to Benjamin, escorting both new arrivals over to the table where Joyce and Beryl were sat. "Ben, we'll have you knitting like a professional in no time!"

"Uh... okay?" Benjamin said again, *still* having no idea at all what he'd just got himself into.

It may only have been humble beginnings, and there weren't as many in attendance as Charlotte had hoped for. But as she walked around the hall once everyone had settled in, listening to the sound of needles clacking, she allowed herself a moment of satisfaction, watching the small group at the inaugural gathering engrossed in their respective projects. Beryl had quickly taken Stanley under her wing, offering an experienced hand as he progressed with his own knitted square. It may only have been two or three rows deep, but the delight derived from his fledgeling creation was written all over his little face. "Look, Mum!" he said, holding it up and showing it off proudly, before immediately plunging head-first back into the job at hand, tongue hanging out such was his fierce concentration.

Seated further along the table, Joyce was happily imparting her own knowledge, talking Bonnie through the process of applying additional fabric squares to her partially completed quilt. Seeing this interaction made Charlotte immensely happy. She could stand at the front of the classroom, so to speak, instructing people as to what to do, but that wasn't the vision she'd had for the club. She wanted and hoped for the club members to interact, sharing their collective talents and experience whilst making new friends over a cup of tea. She didn't want age or ability to impede or deter people, and you only had to look at Stanley learning from Beryl, or Joyce patiently guiding Bonnie, to see that this was precisely what was happening.

"Here you are," Mollie said, handing Charlotte a cuppa as Charlotte stood surveying the scene. "You know, I don't think you've stopped smiling since we got started," Mollie remarked.

"The Crafternoon Sewcial Club," Charlotte observed, running her eyes around the hall admiringly. "This is exactly how I imagined it, Moll," she said. "Although, granted, there were a few more members in my head when I'd pictured it..."

"It's only the first week," Mollie reminded her. "Word will spread, keep in mind, and..." she said, trailing off, suddenly distracted.

"What is it?" Charlotte asked. "Is something wrong?"

Mollie cocked her head to the side, first one way, and then the other. "Can you hear that? Can you hear singing?" she asked. "I can hear singing," she said. "And I might be going mad, but it sounds like it's getting closer."

"Maybe a car radio outside?" Charlotte suggested, now hearing it too but uncertain as to its source.

"No, I mean *really* getting closer," Mollie remarked.

As if on cue, the iron latch on the door lifted off its cradle, resulting in the mystery singing voice becoming suddenly louder and much more apparent as the door eased open.

"There you go," Mollie said, satisfied she hadn't imagined things.

The brim of a hat was first to appear into view, accompanied by a man's head underneath it. "Just us!" a cheery voice announced, with the chapeaued fellow then stepping inside.

"Larry!" Charlotte said, now she could see his face. It was Larry the Lion Tamer. "What are you doing here, Larry?" she asked, though fully delighted to see him of course.

"Well, we wanted to come along to support our friend with her new initiative!" he explained, now inside and stood before her.

"We?" Charlotte asked, accepting the kiss he placed on her cheek.

"Yes, *we*," Larry replied, tipping his hat to Joyce, Beryl, and the other seated club members. "The rest are just hanging their coats up in the foyer," he told Charlotte. "You see, I'd suggested the idea yesterday, over lunch, of coming along. I said I'd organise a taxi if anybody else was interested."

"Aww, Larry," Charlotte said. "That's perfectly lovely of you. I would've picked you up if I'd known, and saved you the taxi fare."

"Ah, it's fine," Larry said, returning the wave that Stanley was presently offering up. "Anyway, we didn't get a taxi in the end," he informed Charlotte.

"Oh my goodness, you didn't walk all the way here, did you?" Charlotte asked, her smile switching to a look of concern, knowing that anything was possible where Larry & co were concerned.

"No, I hired us a minibus!" Larry clarified, turning to see if his friends had joined them as yet, which they hadn't. "We wouldn't, all of us, have fit into a taxi."

"What? Just how many of you *are* there?" Charlotte asked, open-mouthed.

"Including me? Em, let's see..." Larry replied, running his finger through the air as he crunched the numbers. "Fourteen," he finally declared, once calculations had been completed.

"*Fourteen?*" Charlotte asked, wondering if this was perhaps just another one of Larry's jokes, and looking past him to see if these other people he mentioned actually existed. "Oh, hi, guys," she said, just as the others began to file in, revealing that Larry hadn't been telling porkies after all.

Pleasantries were exchanged, and Charlotte looked back over to the tables to make sure they had enough chairs in place to seat their new group of guests. "Not a problem!" Mollie called over, reading her best friend's mind. "We've got plenty of chairs and plenty of cake!" she assured Charlotte.

"You know…" Charlotte began, turning her attention back to Larry. "You know, Larry, you've made an already lovely day even lovelier," she said, her face beaming. "Thank you."

"It was the least we could do, Lotti," he answered, removing his hat and clutching it to his chest. "Besides, I needed somewhere to work on my blanket, didn't I?" he added, looking down to the bag held in his other hand. "I may have been a little bit slack at our weekly class, so I needed to play catch-up!"

"Yes, you do. Otherwise, that teacher of yours will be very cross!" Charlotte offered playfully.

"She's a tyrant," Larry remarked, pointing his hat in her direction and giving her a cheeky wink. "But we wouldn't be without her," he added with a grin.

"Well, welcome, everyone," Charlotte announced, addressing the group as a whole. "Welcome, one and all," she said, sweeping her arm through the air around her, "to the Crafternoon Sewcial Club!"

CHAPTER NINE

The residents of the Isle of Man were, on the whole, a fairly charitable bunch. And competitive, too. As such, the local Oxfam volunteers weren't at all daft when they added an element of competition into the latest initiative, that they had named *SQUARE IF YOU CARE*.

The charity was proposing a stretch target of twenty thousand completed squares (knitted or crocheted) for the Isle of Man to strive for. Demanding, but not impossible, they suggested. To help reach this, the charity had thrown down the gauntlet to local organisations and community groups to get involved. They'd even devised a league table to spice things up and promote a little healthy competition amongst those participating. Each completed square would equate to one point, and the group with the most points at the end of the campaign would be rewarded with a handsome trophy and, of course, bragging rights amongst one's crafting peers.

Additionally, a local businessman — impressed with the initiative and anxious to get involved — had stepped in with a generous offer of financial sponsorship. As well as covering any associated costs — such as Oxfam's postage and advertising — the sponsor also offered an incentive for the community groups involved. The community group topping the leaderboard at the competition's conclusion would receive a donation of two pounds for each square they'd submitted — so, potentially a welcome cash injection for the winning group to put to good use.

As such, SQUARE IF YOU CARE was creating quite the buzz on this sleepy little island in the middle of the Irish Sea, as one might well imagine. However, it was all entered into in the spirit of friendship, charity, and community...

"I'll force the guys at the nursing home to pull a double shift!" Charlotte declared, rubbing her hands together in glee — although the hint of a smile spread across her face revealing she wasn't *entirely* serious. "If each completed square takes a couple of hours or so..." she said. "And I multiply that by..." she went on. "Hmm, I think I'm going to need a paper and pencil, actually, and maybe a calculator..."

"Yeah, Charlotte," Mollie entered in, sucking air through her teeth, "what you're describing sounds a bit like a backstreet sweatshop. In fact, no, strike that, it sounds a *lot* like a backstreet sweatshop."

Mollie received their coffees from the cheery barista, along with the two slices of carrot cake, generous in proportion, that they'd both ordered.

"There's a spot free by the window," Mollie advised, motioning to Charlotte with a nod of her head. "Charlotte...?" she said, noticing her friend's attention was still elsewhere. "Over there," she said, pointing with a coffee-laden hand, and leading the way.

Friday afternoon was typically Charlotte & Mollie time, with this time usually consisting of a brisk, scenic walk to burn off some calories, followed immediately by a visit to their favourite coffee shop in town to put said calories straight back on. Being both the manager and one of the few employees working at a busy farm shop, Mollie was often required to work weekends. So Friday was, for them, the perfect day for her and Charlotte to catch up. Or catch up in person, that is, as they *did* of course speak most days on the phone. Several times a day, in fact. This was much to Stanley's bafflement, as he wondered what two people could possibly find to talk about on such a regular basis. This was something peculiar to the female of the species, his father had suggested when questioned on the subject. It was also a phenomenon, his father hastened to add, that menfolk, in general, were unfortunately no closer to understanding.

"Why do I let Amelia get to me so much?" Charlotte asked Mollie, falling into the well-worn rouge leather sofa, and changing the topic of conversation away from any potential senior-citizen slave labour. "This whole coffee morning club she's set up, conjuring it out of thin air straight after I announce Crafternoon..." she went on. "And now they're somehow entering this crafting competition as well? How is that even possible? They're a *coffee morning*, for Pete's sake. The clue should be in the name."

Mollie sat opposite, across the reclaimed oakwood coffee table, listening diligently, the good friend that she was. "Maybe Amelia's, I don't know, just wanting to do her bit for charity?" she suggested, dipping her complementary biscotti biscuit into her latte. "Besides, the more people involved, the better, no?"

Charlotte looked out through the window thoughtfully, her face reflected back to her on the glass. "I don't know, you could be right," Charlotte answered. "Perhaps I'm being too negative and focussing on the wrong thing. Instead of patting her on the back for doing a good thing, I default to wondering what her angle is..."

"Well," Mollie conceded, "Amelia *is* Amelia. She did orchestrate the issue with the double-booking at the hall, after all, amongst other things."

Charlotte looked to her friend now, sensing mixed messages being delivered from across the table. "You're like a little devil fellow on one shoulder and an angel on the other!" Charlotte said with a laugh.

"Just keeping an open mind, Lotti," Mollie said with a sniff, fork raised and readied to attack her carrot cake. "I'm guessing you'd like to beat Amelia's group in this competition?" she ventured.

"That would not be in any way an unwelcome outcome," Charlotte confessed. "Not at all."

Charlotte enjoyed a bit of a challenge. It wasn't that she was all-consumingly competitive, but she did want to make a good account of herself if she entered into something. After all, who didn't want the glorious feeling of finishing first?

Charlotte thought back to the time she'd entered the parents' egg-and-spoon race at Stanley's school sports day. She'd only just made it in time for the race, having forgotten her trainers and needing to run back home to fetch them, and when she finally did arrive to the start line, she was stressed and out of breath. But she was no slouch when running a sixty-metre distance, she knew, and so her confidence level remained high. Astonishingly, the mum stood next to her wasn't even facing in the right direction, she noticed, and neither were some of the others! With this group of numpties, she reckoned, she would have been almost certain to win, the odds tilted overwhelmingly in her favour.

Charlotte had given Stanley a smile and a wave, placed her apportioned egg confidently on her spoon, and then the instant the starter's pistol was fired, so to speak — as, in this case, a tambourine secured from the music department was being shaken to start the race in lieu of a gun — Charlotte was out of the blocks like a shot. She gave it all she had, Stanley's face spurring her on to victory. When she crossed that finish line in first place not long after, she knew the decision to go back and collect her trainers had been the correct one. Like a great warrior raising her broadsword aloft after a heroic, glorious victory, Charlotte held up her unbroken and intact egg for all to witness. The success was hers. Turning to offer a magnanimous smile to her fellow competitors soon to cross the finish line behind her, her eyes were met with something she'd not expected to see...

The other six parents in the race *hadn't even reached the halfway point*. Moreover, the other parents *weren't actually running*. Rather, they were *walking*. And not only that, but they were walking *backwards*, and seemed to be travelling at *quite a leisurely pace* to boot, even as far as walking went. Charlotte's jubilant smile drifted away, and was replaced by a look of confusion. It was at this point that Stanley's teacher, and adjudicator for the day, Mr Robinson, rushed over to inform Charlotte that the race was 1) walking only, and 2) walking backwards (as an exciting twist) — points apparently explained in the pre-race brief that Charlotte had missed due to her dashing home to fetch her trainers. Faced with this explanation, Charlotte had lowered both her egg and her head, burying her chin into her chest.

At Stanley's insistence, she'd not entered any other parent-related races since. But the point of this whole sordid walk down memory lane was that, dash it all, she always tried her best.

"She just made me feel really terribly stupid," Charlotte, back in the present once again, informed Mollie. "Making out that I was trying to upstage her or some rubbish. I didn't even know about her dumb coffee morning group!"

"We're still on that Amelia, I take it?" Mollie asked, smiling wryly.

"It just feels so phoney," Charlotte pressed on, full steam ahead. "I mean, having your coffee morning group enter a *crafting* competition is… well, it's fine, I suppose. Bring it on, I say. But what really grinds my gears is that Amelia has to then tell the entire world about it, like everyone needs to know just how wonderful she is or something. She's all over Facebook with staged pictures of her and her gaggle, dolled up to the nines, posing seductively with knitting needles poised at the ready."

Charlotte took a deep breath to try and compose herself. "I'm sorry to go on, Moll," she said… but then immediately did just that. "I've just remembered what she said to me in the play-ground," she went on. "Amelia was taking the mickey out of my favourite jumper," she said, "when she told me knitting *wasn't even her thing*, Moll. And that was, what, two weeks ago, maybe? And now, here she is, a bloody crafting goddess, like some great Esme Young? I just don't buy it."

"Sorry, I don't know who that is," Mollie replied. "Esme Young, I mean." Mollie reached across the table and placed a hand over Charlotte's. Charlotte appeared to take this as a sign of affection and support, which of course it was. But it was also because Charlotte had been repeatedly tapping her teaspoon against the side of her ceramic coffee cup as she'd been talking, and it was getting annoying.

"The Great British Sewing Bee? No? I'll show you the next time you're around, as I've every episode recorded," Charlotte told Mollie happily. "Moll," she said, leaning forward before Mollie even had an opportunity to answer regarding the proposed crafting-themed binge-watching session, "I'm sorry for being so needy today. I promise I'll snap out of it."

"It's fine," Mollie said. "Besides, you're still in credit for the next hundred thousand years for listening to me carry on endlessly about that prat of a boyfriend, Jonathan, when I broke up with him."

Charlotte kissed the tips of her fingers, blowing gently and sending the kiss wafting over the table in Mollie's direction. "Oh, shoot!" Charlotte exclaimed, when her phone suddenly burst into life, ringing at full volume. "Sorry, I'll just pop outside and grab this," Charlotte added, not wishing to possibly disturb Mollie or anybody else who might be sitting nearby any further. She got up, pinching off a small portion of her carrot cake as she did so and popping the cake into her mouth in order to fortify herself for the long, arduous journey to the door. "Hello?" she said into her phone, weaving her way through the tables as she made her way outside.

Mollie leaned back in her seat as she waited, relaxing with her coffee in the temporary silence. Unfortunately, every time she adjusted her position, the dry leather covering of her seat gave off an embarrassing squeaking noise sounding very much like flatulence escaping from her behind. This was made all the more evident by Charlotte's present absence and the current lack of conversation to cover the noise. This happened enough times that Mollie glanced around nervously, hoping against hope that no one was in earshot of these faux bottom-burps.

Alas, such was not the case, as a rather well-dressed, respectable-looking businessman at the next table was looking straight at her. His expression was hard to read. It could have been mirth, or it could have been disgust; it was difficult for Mollie to tell.

"That noise isn't… I mean it's not…" Mollie sputtered, desperate to disassociate herself from the regrettable noises emanating from in or about her posterior region.

In response, the smartly dressed man merely extended the index finger of one hand, pointing it to his cheek.

Mollie stared at him, confused.

"Your cheek," the man whispered, when he received no reaction to his game of charades.

"Ah," Mollie said, now catching on as to his possible meaning. She then used her own finger to explore around the area of her cheek, finally locating and liberating a good-sized bit of carrot cake that had taken up temporary residence there. "I was saving it

THE CRAFTERNOON SEWCIAL CLUB

for later," she joked, shifting slightly in her chair, and loosing another fart noise in the process.

Mollie popped the remnant of carrot cake into her mouth, as there was no sense in letting any least little bit go to waste. "Thank you," she told her benefactor, holding her gaze, licking her finger clean, and then offering up a flirtatious flick of her hair once that was done. But their brief exchange was interrupted, all too soon as far as Mollie was concerned, by Charlotte's return.

"Everything okay?" Mollie asked, still half-focussed on the nearby chap.

"No," Charlotte answered with a heavy sigh, taking a seat. "No, not really."

"What's up?" Mollie asked, leaning forward and giving Charlotte her full attention once more.

"Did you just—?"

"No, it's my seat," Mollie quickly moved to clarify, and in so moving, releasing another squeak in the process. "Anyway, what's wrong?"

Charlotte took a mouthful of her coffee to compose herself. "That call," she said, wiping the cappuccino foam from her upper lip. "It was my former-sort-of-almost employer," she explained, letting out another sigh.

"Former, who's-a-whatsis? Sorry, I don't follow," Mollie answered, not following.

"I've been fired from a job I haven't actually started yet," Charlotte told her. "The company I was due to work for has been closed down while they're being investigated for something or other. Long story short, they've had to retract their job offer."

"Oh," Mollie said.

"They were full of apologies. Which was nice."

"Oh," Mollie said once more.

"Bloody hell. And I've only just told Stanley I'd book us a weekend holiday to Centre Parcs once I start my new job, as well. This is a bit of a nightmare, Moll, I won't lie to you."

"Something will turn up, yeah?" Mollie offered, trying her best to sound positive. "In fact, I could probably get you a few hours working at the farm shop if you like. You know, to tide you over?"

"I'd appreciate that, Mollie. Thank you."

"Oi. Come over here," Mollie said, standing up and moving in for a sympathetic hug. "Hey, how about I drive you up to Joan's?" Mollie suggested. "Cheer you up a little?"

"Sure, that'd be nice. Sounds lovely," Charlotte agreed, Mollie's arms draped reassuringly over her shoulders. "But... just one thing?" she added.

"Yes?"

"Are you sure you didn't, just now...?"

"It was the leather seat, Charlotte! Trust me!"

Few places on the island had the ability to make Charlotte smile just from the mere mention of its name. Joan's Wools and Crafts was one of those places. It was a location she'd frequent at least once a week, usually more, a practise started when she was a mere slip of a girl taken there by her mother. Stanley was often Charlotte's begrudging companion these days, but even he had to admit it had its particular charms. Joan's in Onchan was a staple for the island's crafters, having faithfully served those in need of a crafting fix for generations. For Charlotte, she'd have a sense of giddy anticipation on the drive there, wondering what new fabric or wool would await her. She often didn't *need* any more fabric or wool, necessarily, but that was really a moot point as she would usually buy some regardless. Being an industrious crafter, you could never really have enough, even when you *did* have enough, was her way of thinking.

"Thanks for this," Charlotte said, as she and Mollie both got out of the car, once arrived at their destination, and then made their way towards the building. "And if you see any wool you like," she advised, "I could show you how to make a square?"

Mollie wasn't a crafter by nature, but was slowly softening to the idea. At the recent CRAFTERNOON SEWCIAL CLUB, she was impressed to see, first-hand, how much joy the hobby appeared to bring to people, Charlotte included. It was a pastime that really didn't discriminate by age, ability, gender, or even physical condition, and crafting clubs — or any community enterprise, for that matter — were a lifeline for many, getting them out of the house and providing them with perhaps the only bit of social interaction they might have for the week. Mollie was proud of her friend for caring as much as she did, and if crafting was good enough for Charlotte, then Mollie was perfectly willing to dip her toes into the proverbial crafting waters as well, she reckoned.

"Hmm," Mollie said, as Charlotte opened the shop door and led her in, with Mollie following close behind. "Something pretty, perhaps? A nice pretty colour?" Mollie proposed, in answer to Charlotte's suggestion. And as far as options, there was certainly no shortage for consideration, as was now plain for Mollie to see. "Blimey," she remarked, running her eyes around the interior of the shop, "there's some right sheeps' worth in here..."

"Isn't it great?" Charlotte replied, making a beeline to one of the shelving units packed tight with row upon row of wool. She ran her fingers over the stock, caressing each item in turn with an adoring smile. "Ooh," Charlotte cooed, selecting one ball of wool in particular, dyed ballet-slipper pink, and handing it over for Mollie's immediate inspection.

"I'm actually surprised that I'm somewhat excited by this," Mollie confessed, taking a sniff of the woollen ball for some reason. "So... soft..." she added, holding the offering against her cheek.

"My treat to you," Charlotte said. "And, as it's Friday, what say you come back to ours for a takeout, and we'll get you started on your square?"

"Done and done," Mollie agreed, finding this plan of action most agreeable indeed.

As Mollie was rather more engaged at present than Stanley, her usual shopping companion, Charlotte took the opportunity before they were on their way to deliver a guided tour of her spiritual home. "This is the fabric station," she said, like she was introducing Mollie to an old friend (which essentially she was).

It was difficult not to be impressed by the vast array of vibrant fabrics to be had, many with eye-catching patterns and designs, even to the non-trained, non-crafter eye.

"Is that not…?" Mollie said, placing a finger on one brushed-cotton bale of fabric near to her, the floral print it featured looking awfully familiar.

"Yup, that's what I made *this* shirt from," Charlotte was pleased to confirm, offering up a twirl to showcase her genius creativity.

Mollie nodded her approval. "It's only when I see the bolt of raw fabric *here*…" she began. "And then I see the finished product *there*," she said, now pointing to Charlotte's lovely hand-made shirt, "that I realise just how talented you really are."

"Aww," Charlotte replied, offering a playful curtsey. "Why, thank you!"

Laura, the fine establishment's proprietor, came up behind them, measuring tape in hand. "Hi there, Lotti," she said casually, as she pulled a luminous yellow chiffon from the rack, her scissors at the ready.

"Oh, hiya," replied Charlotte, turning at the sound of the friendly, familiar voice. "Ah, this is my good friend Mollie, by the way," she added. "Mollie, this is Laura," she said by way of introductions.

"Welcome!" Laura said, always pleased to accept a new potential crafter into the fold, and with Mollie then offering salutations in return.

"I'm glad you're here, actually, Charlotte. I was hoping to speak to you," Laura added, busying herself preparing another customer's order, tape measure and scissors deployed with a brain surgeon's clinical precision, and proceeding to cut the yellow fabric in hand to the length that was required. "Charlotte, are you doing this Square If You Care thingy?" Laura asked, as she worked.

"Sure am!" Charlotte was only too happy to report. "Some of the Crafternooners are keen to get involved, as are the guys at the nursing home, too. And now, Mollie also, I think."

"Great," said Laura. "You see, I've had a handful of people dropping some squares in. They've asked if I knew of any good causes who were entering that Square If You Care competition. I expect they realise that, individually, they're not going to be topping the leaderboard by making a couple of squares apiece. They wanted to donate them to someone who might be able to make good use of them, and so naturally I thought of you."

"Well, I would be absolutely *delighted* to take them off your hands," Charlotte enthused. "We have ambitious growth plans!"

"Sweatshop," Mollie mumbled under her breath, to which she enjoyed a gentle poke in the arm from Charlotte's elbow in response.

"Excellent. It's just as well I suggested you, then," Laura told Charlotte as she moved off to attend to another customer who'd just walked in, as she was by now finished up with the yellow chiffon she'd been gathering. "The squares are bagged up behind the counter, so they'll be there when you go have your wool rung up," Laura called over her shoulder. "There's about forty or so for the taking, and I'll let you know if I receive any more."

Charlotte glanced at Mollie. *"Forty!"* she said, her eyes dancing. 'That's forty more for us!"

"Nice," Mollie answered. "With what you already have, Lotti, the Crafternooners might be soon topping that leaderboard," she offered.

Charlotte was done shopping for the day, so she stepped over to the till to pay for the wool she'd got for Mollie. Laura was still busy, however. "Laura, I'll just leave the money beside the till for you!" she called over.

Laura gave a friendly wave and nod of assent from across the room, and graciously instructed that Charlotte should feel free to help herself to the bags she'd mentioned.

With money placed down as promised, Charlotte stepped behind the counter to fetch the promised knitted squares. There were two bags, and she knelt down for a moment to survey her haul, opening up the bags and feasting her eyes on the contents of each. "Wait till you see these, Moll," Charlotte said, rising up and placing the bags on the countertop for further review. "There's *got* to be more than forty squares in here...?" Charlotte mused aloud, poking her head into each of the bags to inspect her beauteous bounty.

Charlotte extracted her head from the second bag, looking about as happy as a pig who'd just had the good fortune to stumble across the biggest, most lovely patch of mud they'd ever seen. Just then, her eyes were drawn to the large white A3 notepad one of the bags was set atop, with a good portion of the pad sticking out from underneath. She wasn't being deliberately nosey. Rather, it was more that she couldn't help but notice it, as her name (amidst other various notes scribbled onto the pad) was featured rather prominently there and jumped straight out at her.

"What are you doing?" Mollie asked, when Charlotte fell silent, deep in concentration.

"What I'm... em, that is... what I'm doing is..." Charlotte replied absently, running her finger over the scribbled notes featuring her name. "Oh, my," she said, looking up at Mollie, and then back to the notepad again.

"Are you okay?" Mollie asked, noticing the rather queer look on Charlotte's face.

"I'm fine!" Charlotte said, abruptly coming out from behind the counter, bags in hand. "Ready to go?" she asked.

"Um... Sure...?" said a slightly confused Mollie.

Charlotte bid Laura a fond adieu and the two of them, she and Mollie, were then on their way. "Want me to take one of those bags?" Mollie asked, once outside, offering up a helping hand.

"No!" Charlotte said immediately, drawing the bags closer. "Sorry. They bring me comfort," she quickly added, letting go a protracted sigh of contentment as she gave the bags a squeeze.

"Well?" Mollie asked eventually, once the pair were sat back in Mollie's car.

"Well, what?" Charlotte asked, blinking innocently.

"You know *exactly* what, young lady!" Mollie admonished. "There was obviously something written on that pad of paper that upset you."

"I wasn't upset," Charlotte assured her, "I promise. Well, I mean I *was*. But not in a *bad* way, you know?"

"Not really," Mollie answered.

"Okay, well, it wasn't anything bad," Charlotte explained. "It was just something that hit me right in the feels, you know?"

"The feels?" asked Mollie.

"Yes, the feels," confirmed Charlotte.

"Well, what *was* it?" Mollie implored.

"Hmm? What was what?" Charlotte asked, slightly losing track of the conversation.

"On the note! What did it say!" Mollie exclaimed, nearly shouting.

"Oh, that," Charlotte answered. "It was about the wool. You know, that large order that was delivered to my house?"

"You mean the order you've spoken about at least several zillion times to anybody that would listen, including me, even though I was there that day and saw it for myself anyway?" Mollie replied.

"The very one," Charlotte answered. "Well, the thing is, Moll," she said. "The thing is, I think I might have accidentally found out who sent it…"

Chapter Ten

Only me!" Sue announced, giving a quick rap on the front door and then letting herself in. "Hello!" she said, speaking a little louder this time. "Anybody home?" she asked, singing the words, and setting the bags she was carrying onto the kitchen table.

"Oh, hey," Bonnie answered, appearing from the living room. "I *thought* I heard the door," she said, moving in for a cuddle. "Thank you for coming around."

"It's in the bag," Sue advised.

Bonnie broke free of their cuddle and turned to the table, opening up one of the bags placed there. "Yum! Danish pastries?"

"No, I meant the *other* bag, silly!" Sue said, filling the kettle. "Those pastries are for the cup of tea I'm about to make us."

"Ah, okay," Bonnie replied, dipping her hand into the sadly non-Danish-filled bag. She pulled out a well-worn navy-blue t-shirt, holding it at arm's length to appreciate it in its entirety.

"I'm not so sure I could fit into it now," Sue suggested, joining Bonnie, placing her head on her shoulder. "I was a bit slimmer in my school days."

"It's how you met my mum?" Bonnie asked, eyes still fixed on the shirt, there with its embroidered patch displaying the school crest stitched into it.

"Sure was, Bonn. We both played in the school netball team. I was goal defence, and your mum was wing attack, as I recall. I'd seen your mum around the school, of course, but it was only when we both played netball that we really became friends," Sue told her. "We would have been, what, twelve...? Maybe, thirteen, at the time? Goodness, Bonn, that was nearly twenty-five *years* ago," Sue said, upon reflection. "Where's that time gone?"

Bonnie smiled in response, placing the shirt back into the bag for safekeeping. "You're sure you don't mind me using it, Sue?"

"No, not at all," Sue confirmed, moving over to the kettle. "As I said, I'll probably never be able to fit into it again. And, also, I'm really quite touched that you'd want me in there."

"You're *family*, Sue. And, after all, it's a family quilt."

"What's the difference between a blanket and a quilt?" Sue asked, opening several tins in an effort to locate the tea bags.

Bonnie's forehead creased. "I'm not entirely sure," she said, giving the question some thought. "I think a quilt is more than one layer, like a quilt sandwich, and the sort of thing you'd snuggle up to, in bed. Whereas a blanket is a single layer, I think. The sort of thing you'd sit with over your knee on a cold night. However, I might ask Joyce to clarify at the next club meeting."

"Well, you certainly sound like you know what you're talking about," Sue observed. "But whatever it's called, it's an honour to be a piece of it," she added, eventually locating what she'd been rooting around for just in time for the kettle coming to a boil and starting to whistle.

Bonnie's mum had talked for several years about making a quilt before actually starting it. It was her intention and desire to craft a family memorial using recycled clothing close to her heart. Sentimental items such as her own father's shirts, her mother's wedding dress, and even a selection of Bonnie's baby grows were in the bag of clothes that'd made the shortlist for selection. Once she'd begun, she made slow but steady progress, having completed about one-quarter of the final length before her health deteriorated to the point where she could no longer work on it. When it was still in progress, Bonnie would often help cut the pattern squares from the various garments (including her mum's old netball shirt), offering suggestions on where they should be placed in the overall pattern. It was quality time spent with her mum that she remembered fondly. It was a period in their lives when, at least for a time, the only serious concerns were related to which colour of thread and such to use in their crafting masterpiece — a creation the Newman family would surely cherish for generations to come. Sadly, her mum would never have the privilege of wrapping herself up in the finished quilt, but Bonnie hoped to do so. And when she did, it would be just as if she were in her mum's arms, enjoying a loving embrace once more.

"Ah. And here it is," Bonnie said, picking up a photograph she'd placed on the sideboard in advance of Sue's arrival. "It's what made me think that some of your shirt sewn next to my mum's would be such a lovely idea."

"Look at us! So young!" Sue commented as she took hold of the image, a team photograph of their old netball squad from secondary school. Sue's eyes lingered on the image, and she smiled fondly. "Look at your mum, Bonn," Sue remarked. "So very pretty. You really do look like her, you know. Kind eyes, just like hers. And of course the same gorgeous red hair."

"You can keep that, Sue, if you like," Bonnie offered. "I had an extra one printed, just for you."

"Thanks, kiddo. I appreciate it," Sue answered. "Right," she added, snapping herself away from her moment of nostalgia, "how's about we tuck into those pastries, then? Is your dad in? I brought along one for him as well."

"He's in the living room."

"Is he in there working on his laptop, as usual, or…?" Sue asked.

"Nope," Bonnie said, a smile emerging like she had something to spill.

"What?" Sue asked. "What's so funny?"

"He's knitting," Bonnie revealed.

"*Knitting*?" Sue replied, incredulous. "As in, actual *knitting*?"

"He's not stopped, Sue," Bonnie replied. "Since they showed him how to make a square at this Crafternoon Sewcial Club we've been going to, he's been like a man possessed!"

"That's excellent, Bonn. It's good for him to have something to focus on, something besides… *you* know," Sue told her, not wishing to say the silent part out loud.

"He was on his third square the last time I checked in," Bonnie was happy to report.

Sue flicked her eyes in the direction of the living room. "Come on," she said. "This I need to see."

Hoping to observe Benjamin in his (un)natural habitat, Sue crept like a lioness stalking a zebra, with Bonnie trailing close behind. They both took up a position in the living room doorway, taking care not to make a sound. Sue looked over to Benjamin, sat facing away from them, in his comfy chair, knitting needles clacking busily away.

Benjamin suddenly stopped what he was doing, lifting his head up and sniffing the air. "I *know* you're standing there," he said, without bothering to turn around. "I can hear the two of you breathing."

"I'm impressed," Sue answered, stepping into the room.

"Impressed with my keen, heightened senses?" Benjamin asked, flashing her a quick smile, before busying himself once more with the knitting in his lap.

"No, that you're *knitting*, silly!" said Sue, seeking to clarify. She moved over, standing behind him, leaning against the back of the chair, watching on as knitting needles clicked and clacked away. "You made these?" she asked, pointing to a small stack of knitted squares placed neatly on the chair's armrest beside him.

"Sure did," Benjamin confirmed, affectionately patting the pile of completed squares like they were a sleeping cat. "I've just started on number five, in fact."

At this point, Benjamin finally set his needles and the square he was working on down, and stood up to offer a hug. "How are you?" he asked, wrapping his arms around her.

"I'm fine," Sue responded. "And how are *you*?" she asked, once their cuddle was concluded, and with her tilting her head to one side like a puppy who'd just heard something far off in the distance. "Oh, sorry," she immediately apologised, "I must stop doing that!"

"What?"

"Tilting my bloody head when I ask how you are," she explained. "I don't mean to do it, Ben."

"It's fine," Benjamin said with a shrug, waving her concerns away. "What's wrong with tilting one's head?"

"In such an exaggerated fashion, I mean," Sue explained.

"Ah, I see," Benjamin answered, although he didn't really see.

"I always feel like I'm offering up my sympathies when I do it," Sue explained further. "Sympathy for..." she said, trailing off.

"Not to worry. Say no more," Benjamin assured her, moving in for another cuddle.

"I brought pastries," Sue offered, voice muffled from being pressed against Benjamin's shoulder.

"Well except for that. You can *definitely* say that," Benjamin joked, abruptly reversing course from his 'say no more' comment of a moment ago. "What are we doing stood here, then?" Benjamin asked, pulling away from their mutual embrace. "Let's go and get some of that tea I just smelled brewing!"

Sue had been, and remained, a rock for both Ben and Bonnie. With the two of them dealing with the grief of their loss, it was easy to overlook the fact that Sue had also, in their mum, lost her oldest and dearest friend. In the weeks and months following the funeral, Sue was the glue that held them all together, Benjamin especially. Nothing was ever too much trouble for Sue, and if ever a shoulder was needed to cry on, then hers was available at a moment's notice, day or night.

"So," said Sue, soon brushing away the remnants of the elevenses that'd escaped, landing on her jumper, "do I need to pick up some wool for you on my next trip over, Ben?"

The three of them sat around the kitchen table, with Benjamin draining the teapot's dregs into his cup. "If you'd asked me that only a week ago, I'd have laughed at the idea," Benjamin replied. "But now..." he offered with a grin and a shrug. "Well, as it stands right now, I'd be more than happy to take you up on such an offer. I was even mooching about for wool online earlier, so..."

"I think we have a crafting convert," Bonnie entered in. "Last week, Sue, I had to drag him along kicking and screaming, but—"

"Hey now, there wasn't any screaming involved, I don't think?" Benjamin countered. "A little kicking, *maybe*," he clarified. "But certainly no screaming," he added, taking a sip of his tea, pinkie finger extended.

"Anyway," Bonnie continued with a chuckle, "I think he's actually looking *forward* to the next Crafternoon session. Isn't that right, Dad?"

Benjamin nodded in agreement. "Strewth," he said, happy to confirm. "I only went along initially to stop Bonnie from nagging me," he confessed. "I'd had this picture in my head before going of a bunch of old fuddy-duddies smelling of mothballs. But it couldn't have been further from the truth, as it turns out, and everyone there was an absolute riot."

"I think Beryl had a soft spot for him," Bonnie teased, giving her dad a gentle prod in the ribs for good measure while she was at it.

"Beryl, I should think," Benjamin replied, "must be an impeccable judge of character, then, in that case," he was quick to suggest.

Benjamin then started chuckling away to himself as a train of thought shunted its way from one track to another inside his head. "Beryl was telling me," he began, shoulders wobbling like jelly, "that Joyce and the others in their gang went on a pub crawl for Joyce's ninetieth birthday."

"*Ninety?*" asked Sue, checking to see if she'd heard him correctly.

"Yep. Ninety. They all went out one Friday night in fancy dress."

"Oh, my," Sue said, laughing along at the curious image forming in her mind's eye.

"That's not the best of it," Benjamin went on, wiping away a tear from his cheek. "Beryl was tasked with ordering the costumes, but completely forgot to do so. Then, only remembering on the day of the birthday celebration, she pops along to the fancy-dress shop, but they've only got one design left in stock in sufficient quantity to cover the lot of them."

"Oh, my," Sue said again, placing her hand to her mouth. "Dare I ask? Please tell me it wasn't cheerleaders or skimpy nurse outfits?"

"No, but I'm sure they would have if they could've," Benjamin said, grinning at the very thought of it. "No, all the shop had available was Smurfette costumes for the eleven of them. So the whole bunch went out dressed head-to-foot as Smurfettes, with the blue makeup and everything. Apparently, they emptied every pub they moved through whilst on their way to the next, with many a pub-goer getting into the spirit of things and keen to join in on the revelry. From what I'm told, a photograph was taken when a huge conga line formed, which ended up on the local newspaper's front page. Eleven Smurfettes leading a load of drunks around Douglas!"

"That, I would love to have seen," Sue replied. "Also, I can't help but notice you've only been to one Crafternooners and you're already smiling like a Cheshire cat," Sue remarked warmly, giving Benjamin another one of her special looks.

"Sue, you're doing that whole head-tilting thing of yours again," Benjamin advised, though still grinning. "I do have to say, that even though I've only been a knitter for, I dunno, several days now," he went on, "I certainly can understand the appeal. It takes my mind off of things, and helps my brain, well, relax. You know what I mean?"

"Crafting is supposed to be excellent for your mental health. So, yes, I completely understand," Sue responded, adding, "And I also think it's lovely, if you don't mind me saying so, that the two of you, you and Bonnie, are doing something together."

"Ooh, in fact, let me show you how mum's quilt is coming along!" Bonnie chimed in, appearing most pleased with her current efforts. "I've attached three more squares since Joyce showed me what I should be doing," she added, pushing her chair back, and then heading off to her room, making excited, mouse-like squeaking noises as she ran up the stairs.

"Wow," Sue remarked, leaning back in her seat, and rubbing the nape of her neck.

"Wow?" Benjamin asked, uncertain as to what Sue's wowing was precisely in relation to.

"Yes, wow. I'm just really pleased to see you both happy. It's been awful, of late, so to see you smiling after… well, everything, is…"

"I know," Benjamin said, with an appreciative nod. He knew what she was getting at, so of course there was no need for her to spell it out any further. "It's baby steps," he added, lifting the teapot before remembering he'd already taken the last of it. He set the teapot back down and paused thoughtfully for a moment. "Without getting all… I don't know, William Wordsworth on you, I guess... now, when I lift my head up, I can see small patches of blue sky overhead. Only a week ago, all I saw were angry thunderclouds."

"The skies will get even bluer, eventually," Sue told him. "You just have to give it time," she added with a smile. "Seriously, though, you're both amazing, Ben."

"Ta-da!" Bonnie said, appearing in the doorway and introducing her quilt like a presenter on QVC.

"Oh, Bonn, look at that," Sue answered, getting up and walking over to her. "It's beautiful," she said, caressing the different bits of various stitched-on fabric worn over generations of the Newman family.

"I've still a long way to go," Bonnie remarked, peering over the top of the quilt as she held it up with her hands for Sue's inspection.

Sue moved her nose closer. "That's from your mum's wedding dress," she said, placing the palm of her hand flat against the piece in question.

"That's why I was so nervous," Bonnie confessed. "I even phoned Joyce before I made my first cut, just for some reassurance. Bless her, she even offered to come round, if I wanted."

"Aww," Sue said, running her eyes over the quilt. "Oh, and here's your mum's netball shirt," she said, shifting the position of her hand.

"And that's where *your* square is going," Bonnie said. "Just there, next to it. You and my mum will be right beside each other again, just like you were in the photograph."

"You've got me going," Sue replied, eyes glistening. "That's it, I'm gone," she added promptly, dabbing at her eyes with the back of her hand. "It really is lovely, Bonn. And what a beautiful thing to have in the family," she said, running her hand over the quilt once more after all necessary eye-dabbing had been completed. "I'm a little confused, though. Where do your dad's knitted squares fit into the overall design here?" she asked. "They don't seem at all the right size, as all of these other sewn-in bits look noticeably larger..."

Bonnie gently folded the blanket, tucking it carefully under her arm for now. "Dad's squares aren't for this," she noted.

"No, Sue," Benjamin said, jumping in. "At Crafternoon, they let me loose making a square as an introduction to knitting, yeah? Which I was then able to enter into the competition."

"Ah," Bonnie said, feeling the need to offer up a bit of further explanation and/or elaboration. "See, there's this whole island-wide crafting competition going on, Sue, and the aim is to make as many crafting squares as possible."

"Although I'd have to say it's certainly not *much* of a competition now that *I'm* involved," Benjamin proclaimed. "I mean, are they not aware of just how competitive I really am?" he said, raising his finger in the air for emphasis.

"This is true," Bonnie said, nodding along in full agreement. "Dad's already informed me that he'll not be sleeping for the next two weeks or so, and that we'll need to procure more wool somehow. A *shedload* more, in fact, I believe were his exact words," Bonnie informed Sue.

"Sleep just gets in the way!" Benjamin insisted, finger still held aloft.

"This competition..." Sue said, sounding like something had just occurred to her. "It's a league table, or something like that?"

"That's the one," Bonnie confirmed. "Then all of the squares all get shipped off to places where they're needed."

"Ah, yes, I remember now," Sue continued, recognition dawning. "We had an email through to school about this," she said, reaching for her phone. "Yep, here it is," she said, once the email was retrieved and opened. "Yeah. It's the same thing you're talking about. The local schools have been asked to get involved to collect squares made by students and their parents," she told them.

"Fab," Bonnie commented. "If all of the schools are promoting the initiative, then it'll hopefully be a huge success."

"Wait," Benjamin entered in, a thought occurring to him. "They've been asked by *who*? What I mean is, what are the schools doing with all of these squares once collected? Are they contributing them under their own name, entering the competition themselves, or...?"

"Oh, yes," Bonnie said. "Where did the email come from, Sue?

Was it from Oxfam directly, or was it someone looking for contributions on behalf of their group?" she asked. "It wouldn't be Charlotte from Crafternoon, would it?"

"No, it wasn't from Oxfam. And I don't believe it was from your Crafternoon group, either, as I'm sure I would've remembered that name," Sue answered. "Hmm," she said, lowering her head and scrolling through the email in question. "Yes, here we are," she said, once the particulars were located. "According to this, the person coordinating and collecting the completed squares is a woman named Amelia. One Amelia Sugden, to be precise."

"Oh, that's a shame," Bonnie said, somewhat deflated. "Because, if Crafternoon had the support of all the schools, then they'd surely be top of the league in no time. But now..."

"You should maybe tell Charlotte about this," Benjamin suggested to Bonnie. "It looks like the Crafternoon Sewcial Club is, regrettably, going to be facing some rather stiff competition for the top spot."

"Yes, good idea, Dad," Bonnie answered.

Benjamin nodded, peering into his teacup as he sat there and wishing there'd been more tea in it to be had, though sadly there was not.

"Well? What are you still doing sat there?" Bonnie asked, casting a stern glance in her father's direction.

"What? I'm drinking my tea!" Benjamin protested, lifting his cup to both illustrate the point and back up his claim, even though there wasn't a single ounce of tea left inside of it.

"There's no time for that!" Bonnie said, wagging her finger. "You need to get back to work and continue knitting, if you please, right this instant! The Crafternoon Sewcial Club is going to need all the help it can get!"

And with that, Bonnie clapped her hands abruptly, as if she were shooing the family pet from the sofa.

"Come on, Dad, those squares aren't going to knit themselves, now are they!"

CHAPTER ELEVEN

O h, hi there," Charlotte said, approaching the reception desk, a smile radiating in advance of her impending arrival. "How are you, Ken?" she asked, as she then signed her name into the visitors' book.

"Heya, Charlotte," Ken, the portly, rather well-padded receptionist replied immediately, jumping up into a standing position. He turned on a sixpence, wiggling his generously proportioned behind in her general direction. "I'm good, actually, Lotti!" he told her, running his hands over his ample derrière. "Thanks again for fixing my trousers, by the way," he offered, patting the perfectly repaired seam — so perfect, in fact, that you couldn't even tell it ever needed mending in the first place. "They're like new again," he declared, presenting an additional wiggle, and then adding, "And now, hopefully, I won't be flashing my underpants anymore when I bend over!"

"Well, I did hear the girls in the dining room saw a bit more of you than they were expecting," Charlotte answered with a laugh.

Ken turned to face her, rolling his eyes. "The girls were all wolf-whistling me," he recollected with a sigh. "Also, I'm pretty sure that when Beatrice saw that flash of white from my undies, she dropped her fork on purpose just so I'd have to bend over again in order to pick it up for her, thereby making the tear in my trousers even worse. She denies it, of course, but…"

"I wouldn't put it past her," Charlotte said, allowing the corners of her mouth to turn up.

"Here, hang on," said Ken, somewhat puzzled. "You don't usually come today, do you?"

"No, but I was just hoping to have a quick word with someone," Charlotte answered. "If that's okay?"

"Of course," Ken agreed, extending his arm as an invitation. "And if you speak to the girls, you be sure to tell them I'm not some piece of meat to be gawped at," he told her. "I'm a human being!" he said, gyrating his hips from side to side for some inexplicable reason despite the fact he'd just insisted, only seconds before, that he wasn't some cut of beef to be drooled over.

"I'll be certain to tell them that," Charlotte said, chuckling away. "But remember, Ken, they're only human. So, you know, prone to certain urges and whatnot..."

"True, true. You can hardly blame the poor dears," Ken replied. "After all, it's not every day they see something like *this*," he said, motioning to himself.

"No, I'm sure they don't," Charlotte was quick to agree, chuckling to herself, and then leaving Ken once again to his own devices as she made her way along inside the nursing home.

Charlotte first popped her head into the TV room, where Beatrice and the other girls implicated by Ken were currently occupying their time watching a Joe Wicks workout video. There wasn't too much effort being exerted by the girls in following along to any of the exercises, but they certainly appeared happy enough — especially, Charlotte noted, when a shirtless Joe commenced with a set of biceps curls. Indeed, Charlotte was briefly tempted to join them for a moment herself when she saw that. Ultimately, however, Charlotte decided to leave the girls to it and continue on with her search.

Charlotte headed towards the dining room where, if her memory served her well, a painting class would presently be underway. Each evening, once the tables were cleared away after dinner, the dining room was requisitioned as the venue hosting social activities (such as her own MAKE IT SEW club). It was a delight to see such a vast and varied social calendar that the home residents enjoyed, with one activity or another organised most evenings. The worry, of course, was that the old 'uns, having been put out to pasture, so to speak, would spend their last years leading a solitary, sedentary existence, sitting alone watching daytime TV and such, and simply marking time awaiting their eventual meeting with the Big Guy Upstairs. Not that there was anything wrong with a quiet night sat in your room, reading a book or what have you, if that is what one wished. But the knowledge that there was often a social activity happening merely a short walk down the corridor was of infinite comfort to many, at least in Charlotte's experience working with the residents.

Sure enough, Charlotte's memory had not failed her. Opening the dining-room door, she was greeted by the inspiring sight of fifteen or more residents forming a large circle, each with an easel positioned directly before them. Charlotte moved closer to see what sort of subject matter the aspiring artists had chosen to depict this day. She wondered briefly if it were a live-model figure drawing class in progress, as she'd overheard that very possibility being discussed earlier in the week. She was slightly relieved — and yet also mildly disappointed — to see, however, that there were no nude bodies to be had on display. No, it was merely a bowl of fruit and such set up on a small table. So, only still-life drawing today, it would seem.

Charlotte tiptoed around the periphery, for fear of disturbing the class (even though, considering the intense concentration levels on view, a bomb going off could well have passed unnoticed). Seeing Emma, the home manager, in the circle, Charlotte came up behind her and gently tapped her on the left shoulder so as not to startle her.

"Ah. Evening, Lotti," Emma responded, lowering her brush from her own work in progress, as she'd joined in with the others while leading the class. "Lovely to see you," she said. "I'm sure we've a spare easel about, if you wanted to have a go…?"

"No, I'm fine, but thanks," Charlotte whispered, taking a peek at Emma's artwork. "Looks good," she offered encouragingly, though one might have called this a rather friendly extension of the truth on Charlotte's part. "Anyway, I was hoping to have a quick word with someone, and I thought they might be here," she said, getting closer to the point. "Oh, wait, I've just spotted the very person I'm looking for," Charlotte added quickly, extending her index finger to point in said person's general vicinity. "Do you mind if I—?"

"Go right ahead," Emma replied graciously, brush poised, nose pressed up against her canvas and ready to add further strokes to one particular object in her painting that might have been an apple. Or, a large grape, perhaps. Or maybe... well, actually, truth be told, it was difficult for Charlotte to tell.

Charlotte continued her circumnavigation, slightly picking up her pace now that her intended target was in view. Her intended target, Charlotte couldn't help but notice, had jumped headfirst into the spirit of the evening, wearing a striped Breton-style shirt, paired with a black beret sat slightly askew atop his head, and looking very much like one Pablo Picasso. And, to be fair, once stood behind and clearly able to view the person's canvas, Charlotte was pleasantly surprised by the lovely splashes of colour to be found there.

"*Pssst*," said Charlotte, again, not wishing to startle. "*Pssst*," she repeated, when no reaction was forthcoming. She took a step closer, choosing to adopt her previously employed tapping-on-the-shoulder strategy. "Larry," Charlotte whispered. "Larry, it's only me."

Larry looked over his shoulder, with his brush still engaged on the canvas. "Charlotte!" he boomed, rendering her stealth-like approach redundant in an instant, breaking the concentration of those who stood on either side. "Lovely to see you!" he said, even louder this time, and disturbing those fortunate few who hadn't been disturbed the first time around. "What do you think?" he asked, taking a step back to show off his handiwork. "You like the kiwi fruit I just added?"

Charlotte looked at the painting. Then to the bowl of fruit sat on the table. And then back to the painting. There were no kiwi fruits in or around the bowl on the table, but Larry had included one in his painting anyway. The confusion on her face must have been evident.

"I like kiwi fruit!" Larry proclaimed merrily, with this serving as explanation.

Larry was a full-grown adult, so Charlotte reckoned he could add whatever fruits he liked into his bowl-of-fruit still life painting. She placed her finger to her lips, giving the painting a good once-over, as Larry had, after all, asked for her opinion.

"It's actually pretty good," she said after a moment, nodding her head in approval. "Really it is, Larry. From the clothes you're wearing, I was expecting something rather more Picasso-like. But, with your use of colour and bold brushstrokes, I'd say this has more of a Vincent van Gogh feel to it, yeah?"

"I was going for Paul Cézanne!" Larry answered happily. "But I'll take the compliment!"

Juggling. Lion-taming (possibly?). And now Impressionist-style painting. Larry was certainly full of surprises, thought Charlotte.

"Larry, might I have a quick word?" she asked. "Maybe..." she suggested, pointing to the door, not wishing to cause any further disruption to the class than her current interruption already had.

"Ehm... Yeah. Sure!" Larry said brightly, giving his canvas one last glance, before taking his paintbrush and placing it behind his ear, the same way a builder might store their pencil.

"Larry..." Charlotte said, walking towards the door. "Larry, you've got a dollop of paint about to drip right down onto your shoulder," she cautioned.

"Ha! It'll make me look like a serious artist!" Larry declared, just as a splotch of paint, as predicted, hit his shoulder. He rubbed the kiwi-green pigment into the fabric with enthusiasm, appearing not the slightest bit concerned at ruining his special shirt.

"Here, you've not come to shout at me about my blanket, have you? For not finishing it yet?" he asked, once outside the dining room, lowering his head like a hungry dog caught snaffling the Sunday roast.

"No, of course not," Charlotte assured him, unable to take her eyes off his paint-stained shoulder. "Besides," she continued, "I suspect your true creative talents lie more with painting than with fabric, so no worries on the blanket front," she told him.

Larry removed his hat, placing it over his heart. "What is it, then? Is everything okay?" he asked, just as another dollop of kiwi-green paint was readying itself to make the descent from brush to shoulder. "Charlotte...?" he added, deep furrows appearing across his forehead.

"Sorry. Yes. All is fine," she answered, taking note of his obvious concern. "No, I was in Joan's Wools the other day..." she began.

"Oh," he said, fidgeting, and shifting his weight from one foot to the other. "Was it, ehm, fun?" he asked, in a manner which suggested he didn't really know what to say.

"And while I was there..." Charlotte went on.

Larry didn't say anything at all now, merely closing over his left eye, as if he were possibly bracing for something.

"While I was there, I found something out..." Charlotte continued.

This time, Larry scrunched both eyes shut. He held that pose for several seconds, then opened his eyes again, appearing disappointed that Charlotte was still standing there as opposed to, say, him merely experiencing a bad dream.

"Larry," Charlotte said. "Larry, did you buy that ginormous batch of wool for the Crafternoon Sewcial Club? The one that was delivered to my house?" she asked, deciding to come straight out with it instead of beating around the bush.

Larry's jaw swung open as if he were unable to speak, which, temporarily, he was. "Yes," he said eventually. "Yes, that was me," he admitted.

Charlotte stepped forward, wrapping her arms around the portion of him unsullied by paint, and taking care not to disturb the precariously balanced brush over his ear. "Thank you, Larry," she said. "Larry, that's one of the loveliest things anybody's *ever* done for me."

"You're squeezing me too hard!" Larry joked, but, judging by his broad smile, was appreciative of the sentiment expressed. "Anyway, you're most welcome," he said softly, checking his palms were free of paint before patting Charlotte on the back.

"Just so you know, Larry..." Charlotte began, releasing the artist extraordinaire from her clutches. "Just so you know, the shop didn't reveal to me who paid for the wool, okay? I found out on my own, completely by accident. Well, alright, maybe not *completely* by accident. It *was* an accident at *first*, but then I got a touch nosey as well," she said. "But, anyway, why the big secret? Why didn't you tell me?"

"Well, I..." Larry answered, appearing somewhat reluctant to say out loud whatever it was he was thinking. "I didn't... well, I suppose I didn't want you to think of me as some sort of weirdo," he explained, looking down to his feet.

Charlotte stared blankly, uncertain as to Larry's possible meaning. "Weirdo...?" she asked, hoping for some kind of elaboration.

"You know," Larry replied. "A weirdo. A pervert. Or what have you."

But, actually, Charlotte *didn't* know. Because a weirdo was in fact one thing, and a pervert something else again. And in either case, Larry was neither of those things. Charlotte wasn't at all following his line of reasoning, leaving her more confused than ever. "Larry, my love, what the heck are you on about?" she asked, hands now planted on hips. "How on earth could you possibly think that?"

"Old man giving lovely young lady gifts?" Larry offered up by way of clarification. "You can see how that might look, right?" Larry said sheepishly, eyes still fixed southward. "I wanted to help you with your new project, and figured that keeping quiet about it was the easiest way. I didn't want you, or anyone else for that matter, getting the wrong impression. You know how people can get the wrong idea and jump to the wrong conclusion about such things..."

"Oh, Larry," Charlotte said, placing her hand on his shoulder (the clean one, that is). "Larry, I would *never* think you were anything but the charming, polite, perfect gentleman I know you to be," she said, giving his shoulder a gentle squeeze.

Larry lifted his head slowly until his eyes met Charlotte's. "So you don't think I'm a weirdo?"

"Of course I think you're a weirdo, Larry!" Charlotte replied. "Just not *that* sort of weirdo. Only a *nice* kind of weirdo such as yourself could possibly have at his disposal such a vast array of naff jokes as you do, for instance," she suggested, laughing playfully.

"Well, you do have a point there," Larry was happy to accept, placing his hat back on his head, patting it down into position.

"Thank you, Larry. It's a lovely thing to do," Charlotte continued. "I'm just a little surprised that somebody who isn't especially keen on crafting would make a donation to a crafting club. No offence meant about your crafting skills, of course."

"None taken," Larry confirmed, waving away the offence that was neither meant nor taken. "Charlotte, do you know just how much we think of you up here?" Larry asked. "Do you know what you've done for us?"

"I... well, that is... I suppose, ehm..." replied Charlotte, somewhat flustered.

"I'll *tell* you," Larry gently cut in, saving Charlotte the trouble of trying to come up with a response. "We all adore you, Charlotte," Larry told her. "And as for what you've done for us, you've brought us all together like one big happy family. I mean, sure, we've always had activities to do together. But it's different with you. With you, it was so much fun. You challenged many of us to learn a new skill, and that, along with your sparkling personality—"

"Oh, stop, you're going to make me blush," Charlotte interjected. Even though it was too late, as she was already blushing.

Larry pointed in the general direction of the painting class in the dining room. "It's because of you that people are now even more receptive to trying out new things, which is why the art class is in full swing tonight," he said.

"It does look like fun," Charlotte replied. "Although not everyone's in there," she remarked. "There's a group of girls in the TV room watching a video of some muscly, shirtless chap in tight shorts performing a workout routine. I saw them as I passed by the room earlier," she said.

"Yeah, I heard about that. I wasn't sure I fancied being in on that one, to be honest," Larry answered. "I mean, what would be the point, right?" he asked, flexing the biceps of his right arm to illustrate what he meant. "Why work on perfection? There's just no need," he said, kissing his muscle affectionately.

"Quite," Charlotte agreed with a smirk.

"Anyway," Larry added, turning serious again, "we all

appreciate what you've done for us. And seeing how much everyone *here* has enjoyed the crafting experience, I reckoned there were more people out *there* who might enjoy it as well. And so that's why I made that wool donation to you. I figured it was the least I could do."

"Well thank you again, Larry," Charlotte replied. "It was a lovely thing you've done."

"You're very welcome," Larry answered. "But just, if you wouldn't mind seeing your way clear to keeping it our little secret? Because of, you know, what people might think...?"

"Mum's the word," Charlotte assured him. "And don't worry, we'll make sure to put your wool to good use, Larry," she told him. "So. Will we be seeing you at Crafternoon this week?" she enquired, by way of conversation, and speaking of putting said wool to good use.

"Of course!" Larry replied immediately, as if the answer should never have been in doubt. "I've also been busy signing up some more of the troops," he informed her. "So we might need to hire a double-decker bus to fit us all in!"

"Excellent!" Charlotte said. "Well, I won't take up any more of your time, Larry. I'd best leave you to it, to get back to your painting," she told him. "I just wanted to come round, in person, to say thank you. So, mission accomplished."

Larry offered a cheery wink, turning to head back to the dining room. "Oh," he said, raising his finger in the air and pivoting back around. "Tell young Stanley that in our next juggling lesson, I'll add one more item into the mix! We'll go from juggling three objects to four!"

Charlotte nodded. "He'll look forward to that!" she called out, and then, once Larry had gone, made her way back to the reception desk in order to sign herself out.

"That you heading off?" Ken asked, emerging from the TV room, clutching the small of his back with a grimace. "There might be a further requirement for your needle and thread," he advised, releasing a pained groan.

"Oh?" Charlotte answered, tilting her head, and scanning Ken's trousers for any key areas in sudden need of further repair.

"No, not for me this time," Ken said, noting her current visual inspection. "It's that bunch of keep-fit loons in there," he indicated, tipping his head in the direction of the TV room. "Anabelle decided that attempting the splits, like that Joe Wicks fellow in the video was doing, would be a wonderful idea," he went on to explain, shaking his head. "And muggins, here," he said, jabbing the tip of his thumb into his chest, "was the one who had to help her up when she found herself stuck and couldn't right herself."

"Is she okay?" Charlotte asked, stifling a laugh, as she was unsure of the gravity of the situation at this point (though one could say gravity had certainly been the culprit here).

"Oh, she's fine," Ken assured Charlotte. "Although my lower back isn't," he added, kneading the lumbar region of his spine with his knuckles. "Lift with the knees, they tell you! Well I always forget to lift with my knees, don't I?" he moaned.

"And Anabelle?" Charlotte asked.

"Oh, yeah," Ken answered, nearly forgetting the point of his story. "Well, see, the fabric on her Lycra leggings is going to need some serious attention judging by the sound of the tear I heard. Can those be mended? Anyway, I didn't hang about to see how much of either her unmentionables or bare flesh might be left on display. You may want to poke your head in before you leave and have a look…"

CHAPTER TWELVE

L ife was ticking along quite nicely right at the present moment, Charlotte was pleased to report, to anybody who might be inclined to listen. In the last two days alone, she'd received a commission to make three memory bears for a doting new mother and her family. Also, a booking for a series of private, one-to-one sewing classes had recently presented itself. What all of this meant was that the wolf would thankfully be kept away from her door, financially speaking. Bolstering her mood even further was the encouraging number of attendees at her Crafternoon sessions. She was thrilled she'd entered into the double-digit range on only the second time of asking. So, for Charlotte, things were currently tickety-boo.

And as if all this good fortune hadn't been enough already, Charlotte had now also been invited along to the local radio station to talk about the SQUARE IF YOU CARE initiative. As such, Charlotte made her way along the steep coastal road towards her destination, and then parked up on Douglas Head once arrived.

Douglas Head was a popular area offering a sweeping view of the entire bay below and, looking back towards land, a view which included the hilly island's only true mountain, Snaefell, imposing as it was, up there in the distance. It was an impressive vantage point that'd been enjoyed by generations, from the Victorian tourists, arriving in their droves at the start of the previous century, to present-day families parking up to enjoy their fish 'n' chips, with an enviable vista looking out past Douglas Head Lighthouse and on to the Irish Sea. It was also a firm favourite with Stanley, who loved to sit on the grassy hillside, ice cream in hand, taking full advantage of the eagle's-eye view as he watched the island's ferries coming and going to the nearby port. However, it wasn't for the aesthetic beauty that Charlotte had come this morning, sat with butterflies swirling around in her stomach ...

"Doh-Re-Mi-Fa-So-La-Ti-Dohhh!" she sang to herself in her car, practising her solfège scale for the first time since primary school choir some years earlier. "You can do this," she said, twisting the rear-view mirror until she could see her face. She held her gaze, staring at her reflection with a determined *you've-so-totally-got-this* type of expression, motivating herself on.

With her vocal cords adequately warmed up and sufficiently radio-ready, Charlotte grabbed her handbag from the passenger seat, took a final glance at her watch, and then stepped out into the fresh morning air. It was only a short walk up a winding drive-way to the offices of Manx Radio, but her heart was already racing, her hands clammy. She'd never been particularly comfortable being the centre of attention. Indeed, it had taken three large vodkas to get her down the aisle at her own wedding due to nerves. Still, it had done the trick (though it wasn't so much a walk down the aisle as it was a gentle stagger). She'd considered a nip of something to settle her nerves today, but as she was due on air at ten-thirty in the morning, she thought it a little too early to partake in such liquid-based courage.

Without the shelter offered by her car, what had been a gentle breeze back at her house was now a bloody *firm* breeze here by the shore. Charlotte observed a fishing boat, down below, being tossed about like a cork as it left the harbour wall's protective embrace. "Shoot," she said, running her hand over her hair. She'd spent a good deal of time that morning getting it just right, and it now felt like it was quickly becoming a mess. She quickened her pace, which was a challenge in itself against a brisk sea wind doing its best to impede her progress, not to mention further ruffling her hair.

Through wind-induced, watering, blurry eyes, Charlotte managed to make her way to the entrance door, which was helpfully identified by the subtle "WELCOME" sign on it. Once inside the building proper, she shook herself down, very much feeling like she'd just fallen out of a tumble dryer. She wiped the excess moisture away from both eyes, helping to restore her vision in the process.

"Morning!" a cheerful voice called out from behind the oak-veneer reception desk, a raised hand being offered in case Charlotte should be in need of assistance.

Charlotte approached with a smile, vigorously rubbing her chilled cheeks in order to restore blood flow. Just to the left of where she now stood was a glass window with a clear view of the broadcasting studio behind. Her stomach fluttered, watching the presenter, Sandy Branson, talking into his large, rather imposing-looking professional microphone. Charlotte often listened to Sandy over the airwaves, so to be here watching the man himself in action, live, in-person, added to her already heightened stress levels.

"Morning," Charlotte eventually replied, turning her attention to the friendly young woman sat behind the desk. "It's a bit fresh out there," she offered, throwing a thumb over her shoulder to point outside, indicating where "out there" was just in case there might be any doubt.

"It's good weather for kites, as my dear old dad would say," Holly (as identified by the name badge pinned to the breast of her jacket) suggested. "You're here for the ten-thirty interview?" Holly ventured, twirling her hair around the blue biro in her hand.

"Yes. Yes, I am. Charlotte Newman, at your service," Charlotte replied, extending her hand across the desk, and then laughing nervously as she wondered to herself if it was even proper protocol to shake hands with the receptionist like that. "Ehm... do you have somewhere I could freshen up?" Charlotte asked, glancing about anxiously. "I must look like I've arrived on a motorbike," she went on, motioning to her wayward hair. "It's very windy out there," she was keen to point out for the second time.

Holly stood up out of her chair, pointing to the area of the office Charlotte had just walked through. "Sure, if you—" she began, but then cutting herself short as a sudden rattling of fingertips on glass took her attention. Holly and Charlotte both turned in response, finding Sandy, earphones dangling around his neck, looking at Holly but pointing in Charlotte's direction. He held up a note that appeared to be hastily scribbled, pressing it against the glass. It said: *"If that's our ten-thirty, can we start now?"*

Sandy lowered his message, followed by a smile for Charlotte's benefit, and Holly nodded her head in confirmation.

"Sorry, looks like Sandy is going to start the interview early now that both of his guests are here," Holly said, looking back to Charlotte. "We've something of a hectic schedule at present, what with it being election season and every would-be politician and their dog looking for airtime," she explained.

Holly indicated to a door directly behind her. "The waiting room is right through here. You can take a seat inside," she instructed. "You'll see a red lightbulb inside, above the door to the studio. That means the presenter is live on air. You'll be able to see Sandy through another window in there, so don't worry. And then, when the lightbulb changes to green, Sandy will wave you both in. Is that all right?"

"Ehm, I just…" Charlotte said, grimacing. "I just wanted to, uh, freshen up a little…?"

"You're fine," Holly assured her. "Honestly, it doesn't look that bad at all, this wind-swept thing you've got going on!" she said breezily, adding, "And besides, the beauty of radio is that no one can see what you look like anyway!"

Charlotte turned, reaching towards the waiting room door. "Wait, hang on," she said, looking back over her shoulder. *"Both* guests, you said?" she asked Holly, Holly's previous words finally registering.

"Yes, your colleague is already in there ahead of you. She arrived earlier!" Holly reported happily, before then shifting her attention to the phone ringing on her desk.

"Wait, *what* colleague?" Charlotte asked, but it was too late, as Holly was now otherwise engaged.

Call it a sixth sense, a funny feeling of impending doom, but the tingling down the back of her neck was telling her she wasn't going to like what she'd find once she pushed open that door. And she had a sneaking suspicion she knew exactly *who* she was going to find behind it.

Charlotte eased the door open with immense trepidation. "Oh, bloody marvellous," she said under her breath as the door edged open and revealed her so-called "colleague" seated inside. It was Amelia, just as Charlotte had suspected and feared. Amelia looked up at her, smiling, then looked briefly shocked, and then smiled once more.

"It's me," Charlotte confirmed.

"Yes, I know it's you," Amelia answered. "I just didn't expect… all of this," she said, drawing a big circle around her face in indication of what *"this"* was. "My goodness, Charlotte, you look like you've stuck a knife into an electrical socket!"

Charlotte proceeded inside, resisting her initial urge to turn tail and run. She looked for someplace to sit that was as far away from Amelia as possible, wishing to distance herself both figuratively and literally. This was made difficult, however, on account of the small waiting room being little more than a converted broom cupboard, and therefore somewhat uncomfortably intimate given the present company.

"Would you like to…?" Amelia asked, patting the empty seat next to her.

"Thanks, but I think I'll stand," Charlotte answered, noting the red lightbulb above the studio door and willing it to turn green.

"I imagine you must feel right at home in here," Amelia offered, waving her hand through the air to indicate their present enclosed location (an action that didn't take that long to perform, as the room was very small), after which Amelia chuckled madly to herself as if she'd just made the cleverest of jokes.

"What? I don't…" Charlotte replied, not understanding what was so funny.

"You know, what with the red lightbulb above your door and a viewing window?" Amelia was happy to elaborate, appearing quite tickled with herself as she did so.

Charlotte glared at Amelia, as she now took Amelia's meaning, though of course not liking that meaning very much at all.

"Oh, relax, Charlotte," Amelia began, "I'm only—"

"At least people would *pay* me for it," Charlotte quipped, cutting Amelia short, and happy at the razor-sharp quality of her instant retort (and with *"unlike you"* being the unspoken but implied addendum to that retort).

"I'm sure they would?" Amelia replied with a casual shrug, with Charlotte's witty comeback appearing not to have produced quite the response Charlotte had been hoping for.

"No, that is…" Charlotte stammered. "I mean I wouldn't actually… I mean I'd never actually sell…"

"Charlotte, relax," Amelia said again. "I'm only kidding. Honestly. There's no need to take offence, and no need to be so serious, yes?"

"What are you doing here, Amelia?" Charlotte asked, folding her arms against her chest, and steering the conversation well away from the subject of bodily commerce.

"To talk about Square If You Care, Charlotte," Amelia responded. "Which, I presume, is the reason you're also here?"

At this point, Amelia casually pulled a compact mirror from out of her purse, opened it up, looked into it, and then decided there was nothing to be done as her makeup was perfect already. "Here," she said, handing the mirror over to Charlotte. "Would you like to fix yourself?"

Charlotte eyed her with suspicion, but Amelia's voice had been soft and gentle, and she seemed absolutely genuine in her desire to help. "Thank you," Charlotte said, accepting the mirror, and then having a look.

She hadn't brought a hairbrush along with her so there wasn't much she could accomplish, but she did straighten herself out as best she could, after which she passed the mirror back to Amelia. "Thank you," she said again. "I'll have to live with the skydiving hair for the most part, I suppose, as there was only so much I could accomplish," she commented.

"It looks fine, don't worry!" Amelia assured her, smiling warmly.

This sudden kinder, gentler, more sincere version of Amelia was going to take some getting used to, and it was leaving Charlotte a little disoriented.

"Oh! Looks like that's us!" Amelia announced, looking up to the green lightbulb. This was further confirmed by Sandy, who'd risen up in his seat, offering an inviting wave through the window. "You coming?" asked Amelia, already at the door, and holding it open for Charlotte.

"What? Oh. Oh, yes," Charlotte answered, still trying to get her bearings. Perhaps Amelia wasn't quite so intolerable when she was by herself and not surrounded by her sycophants, Charlotte considered. Maybe she could actually be a decent person when she wanted to be?

"Ladies. Welcome," Sandy greeted them, gesturing to the empty chairs where they were meant to sit. "We'll be on air right after Duran Duran has finished. So, please, get comfortable, be yourselves, and above all, have fun."

"Lovely. Just lovely," Charlotte answered, parking herself down and making herself cosy.

"Right. I've been looking forward to this!" Amelia said, looking over at Charlotte, eyes sparkling, and a big dumb smile on her face.

"Me too," said Charlotte, sharing a rare moment of solidarity and comradery with Amelia. "And I reckon I've got just the right hairstyle for a Duran Duran concert," she joked, receiving a sympathetic nod from Sandy.

"And that was *Hungry Like the Wolf*," Sandy announced into his microphone, pressing down on several buttons in quick succession. "And coming up after the ad break, I've two crafty guests joining me to talk about all things knitting. So, don't go away..."

"She's a devious, conniving, wretched little two-faced so-and-so!" Charlotte declared, with no effort made to hide her contempt, pacing around the free-range egg display of Mollie's farm shop with a face like a slapped arse. "Pretending to be all nicey-nicey and then making me look stupid on live radio!"

Mollie had been offering up the occasional grunt of encouragement, just to demonstrate she was still listening from her kneeling position on the floor. "Hmm? Oh, you were fine," she entered in, right as she was readying another crateful of produce to be stocked on the shelf.

"It's what she does," Charlotte continued, seething, and clenching and unclenching her fingers, balling her hands into fists over and over again as she spoke. "She often plays off like she's being nice, but she says things which could be taken two ways, her *real* meaning hidden just below the surface. I've always said that about her."

"Oh?" Mollie said, clapping the dirt loose that'd gathered on her hands, and looking up at Charlotte. "Such as...?" she asked.

"Well, for starters," Charlotte began, in a tone that suggested there might well be several such examples and the conversation might go on for quite some time. "For starters, making out that I copied her idea for having a social club. And then suggesting that I only entered the Square If You Care competition because *she* was doing the same."

"Did she say that?" Mollie asked with sincerity, shuffling over on her knees to attend to the tray of carrots sat there patiently waiting their turn to be stocked.

"Exactly!" Charlotte replied. "She didn't *say* that, word for word, but that's precisely what she *meant*."

"It is?"

"Sure. When Sandy asked us about our inspiration in forming our respective clubs, Amelia immediately chimed in, saying she was flattered that I'd set one up shortly after hers. In Amelia-speak, this translates as saying that I'd *copied* her. Which I bloody *didn't*."

"Right, right," Mollie replied, nodding along, and figuring it was the duty of a good friend to be agreeing at this point.

"And what about the situation with the hall booking?" Charlotte asked, in exasperated disbelief. "She made out, on-air, like she was the hero of the hour, stepping in to remedy my error in booking the wrong timing slot. As if it were *my* error! Amelia then implied I'd only moved Crafternoon to Union Mills because I'd thrown my toys out of the pram, at the considerable inconvenience of my members. Only it was *her* deliberate attempt at sabotage that made me do that! Then she even made fun of my hair, live on the radio, Mollie. My *hair*!"

"It does look a little, I dunno, maybe... nineteen-eighties-era Dolly Parton? As in, all poofed out, and going every which way,"

Mollie offered. "Did it look like that earlier as well?"

"It was windy outside!" Charlotte protested. "Anyway, that's not the point," she said, taking a seat on top of the large burlap bags of potatoes stacked nearby. "Aww, why do I let her get to me so?"

Mollie pushed herself upright, appearing satisfied that her vegetable displays were pleasing to the eye and looked sufficiently inviting to the next group of customers who might venture in. "Stop it," Mollie said, looking her friend directly in the eye. "Stop worrying about Amelia, and just do what you're doing, Lotti. You're doing an amazing job, and Amelia is just grinding you down."

"I know, I know," a frustrated Charlotte replied, slapping her hand down on the topmost potato sack, and sending a cloud of fine dust into the air in the process. "From this moment forward, I swear I'm going to ignore anything Amelia says, because it's mostly rubbish," she vowed.

"Apart from the hair," Mollie said. "She was right about that."

"It was windy outside!"

"Come on," Mollie said, extending her hand, and gently pulling Charlotte up from her seated position. "We've just had some local Manx honey dropped off," she advised, licking her lips at the mention of said honey. "Honestly, it's like... like... liquid gold," she added reflectively. "You need to meet the adorable couple that bring the honey in, Norrie and Esther. What they don't know about bees isn't worth knowing, and they've got a veggie patch that makes Monty Don's look like a window box. Esther likes crafting, so I'm sure you could sign the pair of them up! Anyway, you can start unpacking the honey and help stock the shelves, if you like. Take your mind off Amelia, yeah?"

The radio interview hadn't been a *complete* car crash, necessarily. Amelia had put in something of a polished performance, taking the occasional swipe at her fellow guest. Even so, Charlotte managed to make a positive account of herself and the members of her two clubs. She spoke passionately about the gang at the nursing home and their willingness to get involved in new projects. For a moment, she'd even been concerned she might tear up at the recollection of Larry's kind words of appreciation to her earlier in the week. However, she'd laughed to herself as she re-called Ken nearly putting his back out while bravely rescuing Ana-belle from her attempt at the splits.

Sandy, the presenter, had enquired about the SQUARE IF YOU CARE competition and, specifically, what each of his guests in-tended to do with the cash prize if they topped the leaderboard. In truth, Charlotte hadn't given the prospect much consideration, but the answer still came quickly to her. After seeing the positive, transformative impact crafting had on Larry and the rest of her MAKE IT SEW group, Charlotte declared her intention to ensure that every nursing home on the island would have a healthy stock of crafting supplies. Any prize money received would go some way to helping that become a reality, she had decided.

However, Charlotte's confidence in actually winning was dealt something of a blow, listening to her fellow guest. Amelia spoke enthusiastically about how she'd secured the support of most of the island's schools in contributing squares to her cause. She hap-pily went on to announce that she'd already received over two hundred squares at the last count, looking rather smug as she de-livered this revelation. It was for this reason that Charlotte couldn't help but feel somewhat defeated at the start, knowing there were thirty-seven schools on the island, by Charlotte's count, the majority of which had fallen neatly in Amelia's crafting camp.

"It's a lovely place to work," Charlotte suggested, pottering around the farm shop, taking her mind off the interview, and ad-miring the wide variety of fruits and vegetables on display, all products straight from the earth. "You always have it looking so appealing," she added, taking the opportunity to fill her own shopping basket. "Tops still on the carrots from when they were pulled up from the ground. Can't get fresher than that," Charlotte remarked to herself, marvelling at the bunch in her hand.

"Don't forget to use those greens!" Mollie called over, spotting Charlotte's selection. "Full of nutrients, and exceptionally good for you!"

"Duly noted," Charlotte answered, moving on now to inspect a plump cabbage, and then placing that in her basket as well.

The farm shop was situated within a renovated cattle shed on a working farm. It was full of rustic charm and old-timey features, as Mollie had opted for fixtures and fittings that you'd typically have found in a Victorian corner shop, adding to the overall nostalgic character. She'd even sourced a wonderfully vintage, antique cash register, resplendent with brass trim and a cheery bell each time she rang through an order.

The items on offer were a little more expensive than, say, your local supermarket. But folk were willing to travel a little further and happy to pay a bit more for the tasty, excellent, organic stuff. It was worth taking a little extra time to look around, too, as you never knew what goodies you just might find (such as fine local honey). And for Charlotte, of course, there was also the added advantage of having a natter with your best friend while shopping for your weekly veg.

"Here we go," Charlotte said, returning from the storeroom with a cup of tea for the pair of them, joining Mollie by the till. "I even found your stash of Jammie Dodgers in the cutlery drawer," she added, with the packet of biscuits safely tucked up under her arm.

"Thanks, Lotti," Mollie replied, accepting the cup gratefully. "This is the first one I've had today, as it's been rammed in here all morning right up until recently. And thanks for stocking that honey earlier, by the way."

"My pleasure," Charlotte answered, setting her own cup down on her side of the counter, and then popping open the packet of Jammie Dodgers and taking the liberty of helping herself to one.

"You know, I was just thinking..." Mollie began, leaning over with cup in hand and elbows on the counter.

"Oh?" Charlotte said, partially submerging her biscuit in her tea.

"I don't think Amelia's going to be too much competition for you," Mollie put forth. "Not so much that you have to worry about it. I wouldn't assume, just yet, that she's got the contest all sewn up..."

"She's got every school, or nearly every school, on the island on board," Charlotte was quick to point out. But Mollie appeared unconvinced, or at least, was busy giving Charlotte a very peculiar look. It took Charlotte a moment to work out why. "Wait… Did you just say, *sewn up?*"

"I did," Mollie was happy to confirm. They shared a laugh, and then Mollie continued. "No, but think about it," she said, back on subject. "How many children do you know that come running home from school to jump headfirst into a crafting project? Most of them can't even be arsed to brush their own teeth."

"Hmm, fair point," Charlotte conceded.

"As for the parents," Mollie went on, "most have full-time jobs and just want to collapse on the sofa with a glass of wine at the end of the day, right? Of course, you'll get *some* jumping on board, but I doubt Amelia's going to be inundated with submissions. You, dear Lotti, have a particularly impressive ace up your sleeve, however."

"I do…?" Charlotte asked, curious to know what this ace of hers was, as this was certainly the first time she'd heard about it.

"Sure you do. Whereas Amelia is targeting the island's *youth*, you, Charlotte, can go after the folk that are *actually* more inclined to get on board."

"The elderly?" Charlotte said, now figuring out what Mollie was getting at.

"The elderly!" Mollie happily affirmed. "You've seen, first-hand, how motivated they are. So, throw in a little healthy competition and you'll have a veritable *army* of crafters, all ready and willing to smash the island's kids to pieces!"

"Not so sure about the *pieces* part, Moll. But, yeah, I take your point."

"*And…*" Mollie continued, finger raised and apparently not yet finished with that same point. "And, any cash you win is going to directly benefit the island's nursing homes, right? So why *wouldn't* they want to help?"

"Ah, bugger," Charlotte said, suddenly noticing that her biscuit, unattended as they'd been speaking, had disintegrated amidst her tea, leaving only half of it left held in her hand and the other half dissolved into oblivion. "You're right," Charlotte said with a shrug, quickly gobbling up the portion of Jammie Dodger that was left. "You're right, they're insatiable. In fact, I'd put my money on *one* single, motivated pensioner crafting more than an *entire school*."

"So you know what you need to do, then?" Mollie said, like a battle-hardened general readying their troops for combat.

Charlotte set her teacup down, a steely-eyed, resolute expression taking over her face. "I need to strike hard and strike fast!" she said with a snarl.

"Yes...?" Mollie said, encouraging her on.

"I need to form a crack squad of crafters!" Charlotte continued, eagerly entering into the spirit of things. "An army so deadly with the knitting needle or lethal with the crochet hook that no enemy will be able to stand against us!" she declared, like Mel in *Braveheart*.

"To the Wrinkly Warriors!" Mollie shouted, lifting her cup.

"To the Wrinkly Warriors!" Charlotte concurred, repeating the toast, and then taking a dainty sip from her cup. "Ooh, this tea tastes like Jammie Dodger..."

CHAPTER THIRTEEN

L arry, by his own admission, wasn't overly proficient at crafting. For this reason, he'd put forward to Charlotte that his services at her new club might be best utilised on the catering front, with him volunteering on that side of things. With over twenty members expected at the day's proceedings, Charlotte was grateful for the offer. It meant she could now spend her time on the shop floor, so to speak, rather than continuously heading in and out of the kitchen. Mollie also hoped to pop along at some point, work permitting, as she genuinely enjoyed the atmosphere at the previous session.

Larry hadn't quite settled on the official job title for his new role just yet. As the club was operated from inside a place of worship, he mulled over the possibility of calling himself, say, the *Reverend of Refreshments*, or perhaps the *Archbishop of the Brew*. Although, he wondered if this might be sacrilege, and thought it best to first consult with the appropriate authorities before adopting any such title for fear of being struck down by lightning if he did.

Regardless of whatever title Larry would eventually settle upon, Charlotte knew his current handling of the tea urn and such would allow her to focus on the operational aspect of things, which was a relief. Also close at hand was her young assistant, Stanley, who had promised to help in any way he could. Right now, in fact, he was presently helping himself his third helping of cake. It was a delectable little affair, a small, delightful sponge cake with a delicious vanilla topping, drenched in soft fondant icing.

"Are you eating *another* French Fancy?" Charlotte asked, but the presence of pink icing on his cheek told her all that she needed to know. "Save some for the crafters, you!" she admonished, wagging her finger. But her gentle reprimand was interrupted by the alarm on her mobile phone suddenly sounding. "Right, Stanley," she said, quieting the alarm, "you know what that noise means. That means it's three forty-two p.m. And *that* means that the bus is due to arrive momentarily, so off you go!" she told him, giving him a playful slap on the bum as he sprinted past on his pre-appointed task.

Charlotte knew that Joyce and Beryl would be arriving on this bus. With Joyce now knowing precisely where she was going, she had insisted that she and Beryl would make their own way to the meeting this time around, rather than impose upon Charlotte. Joyce had informed Charlotte, with great excitement, that the two of them had in fact planned on making a full afternoon of it. A trip to the hairdressers was first on the agenda, followed by some light shopping, and topped off with a gin & tonic by the quayside, enjoying the fresh air and watching the boats bobbing on the tide. Indeed, Joyce apologised in advance just in case they both rocked up a little squiffy, as she so eloquently put it, as they arrived after the last leg of their journey to Union Mills Methodist Church. There was a bus stop less than fifty yards from the church hall, so at least they wouldn't have too far to navigate. Plus, they'd have each other to lean on, Charlotte reasoned. However, it didn't prevent Charlotte from pre-emptively assigning a chaperone in advance, in the form of Stanley, to help escort them inside, just in case.

"The bus is in!" Stanley shouted, upon his return, peering around the door and into the church hall. "And they smell like you do when you've had your Mummy's Special Happy Juice!" he added, turning up his nose.

Charlotte stopped what she was doing, looking over to Stanley, who'd ventured back inside, unaccompanied. "Well where are they?" Charlotte said, placing the knitting patterns down on the table.

"I asked, but they said they didn't need any help, Mum," Stanley answered, shrugging his shoulders. "I even offered to carry their bags, but they said they'd sort themselves out. Also, I thought it was just going to be the two of them on this bus, but there must have been about fifteen of them, so..."

"Fifteen?" Charlotte asked, incredulous. "As in... *fifteen* of them, in Joyce and Beryl's group?"

Stanley nodded. "Yeah, so quite a lot of bags," he said, with one eye on the cake table. "Joyce said that I'd need a pack horse if I wanted to bring all of their bags in on my own. I didn't know if we had one of those, so I said I'd come and check."

"You're going to need to fire up the other tea urn, Larry!" Charlotte happily shouted through to the kitchen.

"Roger that!" Larry called back, without question or hesitation.

Knowing that Stanley was prone to the occasional bout of exaggeration, Charlotte headed for the door to see for herself. But, sure enough, once outside, Charlotte observed a steady stream of people coming up the path, like a column of ducks, one following the other, with Joyce taking the lead as the mama duck.

"Here," Charlotte said, scampering down the steps to meet them. "Welcome!" she said, extending a hand to Joyce, and admiring the row of people trailing behind her. "They're all with you?" she asked, unable to contain the grin on her face.

"This lot?" Joyce said, pointing behind her. "Sure," she added, with a playful wink, "a social club with cake to us old folk is the same as soaking a Gremlin. We multiply!"

"I'll take your word for that, Joyce," Charlotte said with a laugh, waving at the group. "Let's get you all inside for a nice cuppa!" she offered invitingly.

Joyce leaned in close as she passed Charlotte, having something of a confidential nature to share, it would seem. "Keep an eye on Eileen at the back," she advised, tapping her nose in a knowing fashion. "She smuggled a hipflask on the bus, and she's a liability when she's had a few."

"Thanks for the warning," Charlotte whispered, laughing again, and then ushering everybody in.

Once everyone had settled in and the other attendees arrived as well, Larry, unsurprisingly, played the perfect host in his catering duties, effortlessly replenishing cups while serving up a healthy dose of charm to go along with it. Also, the copious amount of cake on display was dispatched without delay, so Charlotte's fears of perhaps baking too much were quickly dispelled (and with additional cake remaining in reserve, which was fortunate, as it looked like it would definitely be needed). Larry was in his element, it seemed, happy to be at the beck and call of such a lively and entertaining bunch. The fact that most of those present were of the female persuasion was also, no doubt, an added bonus as far as Larry was concerned. On his most recent trip from the kitchen, he'd taken the opportunity to unveil his new apron, specially designed, as it was, for his new role as the official Reverend of Refreshments — the title he'd settled upon after much deliberation (and after clearing it, as well, with a quick call to the church's minister).

"What do you think?" Larry asked, offering a twirl, delighted at the effort he'd gone to in jumping into his new role, and quite pleased with the results — that effort being the image of two large balls of wool printed on the front of his apron, and with those balls of wool being accompanied by an extended measuring tape standing tall and proud emerging from between them.

"Wonderful!" came the collective cry from Joyce and the rest, along with an assortment of hoots and hollers. Larry placed his hands on his hips in response to this encouragement, strutting his stuff like a catwalk model. It's fair to say he wasn't exactly a spring chicken, but in the company of those presently wolf-whistling, Larry could be considered something of a youngster by comparison.

Charlotte did a double-take upon noting the custom, crafting-inspired illustration on Larry's apron. She moved in for a closer inspection, wondering if what she was seeing was actually what she was seeing, as on first impression it rather looked like something else. "Oh my," she said, offering a smirk, but not wishing to make further comment in case it was just her dirty mind playing tricks on her.

Stanley noticed it too, apparently. He stood there giggling, head cocked this way and that, as he looked in alternating views at what he obviously considered to be a very comical image. "Mum..." Stanley remarked, tugging on Charlotte's shirtsleeve, "Mum, there on Larry's apron. Is that not a—?"

"Stanley!" Charlotte said, cutting him short before the words she knew he was about to say could escape his lips, but struggling not to laugh at the same time. "It's two balls of wool and a measuring tape, nothing more!" she explained for his benefit, even though neither of them, she knew, could ever quite unsee what they'd already seen.

Poor Larry, for his part, appeared genuinely puzzled by Charlotte and Stanley's reaction, and seemed as if he assumed the various hoots and hollers from the women a moment or two ago were made merely in appreciation of his keen fashion sense.

Just then, Joyce raised her hand. "Lotti!" Joyce called out, waving Charlotte over to their station. Charlotte was most grateful for the interruption, as it prevented the need for any further discussion with Stanley in regard to what the image depicted on Larry's apron may or may not have looked like.

"I'll be right there, ladies!" Charlotte replied, then skipping over as requested. "Oh, Bonnie," she cooed, once arrived, "that quilt is a thing of beauty." She ran her hand gently over the fabric squares. "A true thing of beauty," she said, reiterating her point as she marvelled over Bonnie's work-in-progress. Bonnie was flanked by Beryl and Joyce, like two mother hens sitting either side of her, with the quilt laid out on the tabletop before her.

"I know," Bonnie replied, fit to burst. "I actually can't believe how it's coming along, and it's thanks in very large part to these two terrific ladies right here. I should be finished stitching on all of the squares next week, I reckon."

"And then it's just a matter of the binding to bring it all together," Beryl entered in, looking up from her own knitting project, smiling.

Charlotte looked around their table, seeing no sign of Benjamin. "Here, Bonnie, we didn't scare your dad off last week, did we?" she asked.

"Not at all," Bonnie replied. "I was only just telling the girls about that..." she said, grinning as she began to explain the situation to Charlotte. "No, no, my dad is hooked, make no mistake. In fact, I've rarely seen him without his knitting needles lately! It's actually quite sweet, watching him work. But he'd gone a bit overboard, apparently, because his hand started to cramp up. The doctor suggested it was tendon strain, and then strapped it up for him. Told him to lay off the crafting for a few days, which my dad is finding difficult. I even caught him trying, unsuccessfully, to knit with one hand last night!"

"Oh, no!" Charlotte answered. "Although, as a crafter, if you're going to get any sort of injury," she offered, "then that's a pretty cool one to lay claim to, I suppose."

"I know! But he can still drive, at least. He's picking me up later, so might pop in and say hello."

"It'd be good to see him," Charlotte responded. "Oh! Sorry, Joyce," Charlotte then added, remembering why she'd headed over in the first place. "You called?" she asked Joyce. "What can I help you with?"

"Rather, it's what I can help *you* with," Joyce answered, reaching for her handbag.

"Sorry?" Charlotte asked, not sure how Joyce could help any more than she already was.

Joyce placed her handbag onto her lap, plunged her hand in, and then, after a brief rummage around inside, produced a large manilla envelope. "Here we go," she said. "Take this."

Charlotte did as she'd been instructed. "Ooh," she said, giving the plump, well-stuffed envelope a gentle little squeeze. "This is like something from a gangster film," she suggested. "It's not a bribe, is it?" Charlotte teased open the flap of the envelope, peered inside, and then looked back to Joyce. "Oh, Joyce!" she exclaimed, "I was a bit worried there for a moment, but this is even *better* than money!"

Charlotte encouraged the contents of the envelope out onto the surface of the table with a gentle shake, watching with love as square after square fell out, like woollen snowflakes wafting down from the heavens.

"There's roughly two dozen there," Joyce was pleased to report. "A bunch of us made at least one, and there's more to come!"

"Joyce, that's wonderful, thank you!" Charlotte replied. "And this will go some way to trouncing those pesky school kids," she added, in her finest cartoon villain voice, thinking of her arch-enemy Amelia's face as she said it.

"Sorry? I don't follow," Joyce said.

"It's nothing," Charlotte answered, leaning in to plant a kiss on Joyce's cheek. "Anyway, I'll just go and thank the others responsible for this," she said, collecting her bounty back into its envelope carrier, and then being off on her way.

The hall where the Crafternooners were presently beavering away was separated from the chapel by way of a sliding partition wall. It was often left open, with the chapel on full view; it was a delight to see the daylight casting through the delicate stained-glass windows, bathing the individual congregational chairs in soft, warm colours. It was normally a calming place of quiet reflection for its loyal flock who were honoured to call this place their spiritual home. Today, it was providing a sanctuary for Larry, allowing his ears a brief respite from the incessant clicking of needles and constant chatter. Still, Larry wouldn't have had it any other way, enjoying those noises just the same as he sat there taking a moment for himself. He'd counted thirty-one crafters in attendance — including seven of his fellow residents from the nursing home — so that was a considerable volume of tea he'd served up. Larry took a load off his weary feet, sat on the raised platform at the front of the chapel, right beside the pulpit, affording him a complete view of the crafting class there in full swing. He nursed a well-deserved brew himself, watching on intently should someone's empty cup be raised aloft, requiring his attention. He hoped it wasn't too disrespectful to be sat there so close to the pulpit, but he was, after all, a Reverend of sorts for the day, he reckoned.

"Ah, there you are," Charlotte said, coming to the head of the chapel to join him. "I just popped into the kitchen to see how you were getting on, but you weren't there. Everything okay?"

"Wonderful," Larry replied, raising his cup of tea to toast the amount of wonderfulness he was currently feeling. "Look at that," he suggested, using his teaspoon to point the way. "*You* did that," he offered, now that Charlotte had turned to see where he was pointing. "Thirty-one people here today, Lotti," he told her. "I've just counted them all."

Charlotte allowed that fact to sink in for a moment. She moved her eyes slowly along from one table to the next, appreciating the smiling faces, laughter, and all of the new friendships likely being forged.

"That lady there?" Charlotte said, discreetly pointing out a dark-haired woman who was trying her darndest at present to thread her needle. "That's Carol, and—"

"Lovely lady," Larry entered in. "She was very impressed with my apron when I introduced myself."

"She's got a definite eye for fashion," Charlotte remarked, shaking her head with a chuckle. "Anyway," she continued, "Carol's husband is a doctor who's just taken up a position here on the island. Sadly, she's finding it difficult to make new friends, both because she's new here, and also because she has a bit of social anxiety and so doesn't often leave the house. Fortunately, she found us on Facebook, and even came along last week, but then couldn't pluck up the courage to actually come inside. She dropped me a message about her anxiety, though, so I suggested I'd meet her outside this time around in order to escort her in, which I was of course only too happy to do," Charlotte explained.

"We've made her feel very welcome," Larry observed.

"Ab-so-lute-ly, Larry. Welcomed her with open arms," Charlotte answered, in full agreement. "Just look at her now. The lady she's talking to has just had twins and is largely in the same boat, stuck at home and finding it a challenge to get out and socialise. They've just told me they're meeting up for a coffee tomorrow. Larry, they look so happy."

Larry nodded, smiling fondly. "That's the power of these community hubs, Lotti, and why they're so important," he said. "People think it's just us old duffers who are sometimes sat at home lonely. But it's not. It can happen to anyone at all, and for a variety of different reasons. Those two lovely ladies over there are the perfect example of that, and why these sorts of clubs are so beneficial."

Larry looked into his cup, which was now empty, and realised he'd soon have to get himself up and re-enter the fray. "Right. I'll need to get back over there and attend to this lot," he said. "Can I get you anything while I'm at it, young lady?"

"Oh, I don't know, Larry. How about a handsome, eligible bachelor to sweep me off my feet, for starters?" Charlotte proposed.

Larry looked straight past Charlotte and into the main hall behind her. "There you go," he said casually, as if his work here were done. "Mission accomplished."

"What, now?" Charlotte replied, uncertain if there was actually someone there of interest, or if this was just the set-up for another one of Larry's jokes.

"Turn around," Larry suggested.

Charlotte did as he asked. "What the...?" she said, shooting a quick glance back at Larry, and then looking to the main hall once more. There, in the hall, appearing slightly out of place surrounded by the crafters, stood an immaculately dressed gentleman in a handsome, fitted, charcoal-grey herringbone suit. She couldn't see his face yet, as he was turned the other way, but it was almost as if he'd been made to order, not to mention conjured out of thin air.

"How on earth did you manage that so quickly, Larry?" Charlotte asked, mystified and not a little shocked by the apparent miracle she'd just witnessed, thinking Larry must have suddenly gained some kind of divine powers or something.

To this, Larry pointed heavenward. "Maybe the big fellow upstairs was listening?" Larry offered as possible explanation, along with a grin.

"If that were the case, then I'd have wished for bigger boobs at the same time," Charlotte whispered under her breath. "So, you're all good, Larry?" she asked, loudly enough for Larry to hear her this time.

"Yes, just wonderful, I promise. Now go and see who the mystery man is," Larry answered, waving her away.

Charlotte moseyed back into the hall, offering a friendly wave to everyone in advance of her arrival. "Yes, hello," she said, zeroing in on the one unsuspecting chap in particular, who at present had his attention directed towards the stuffed-bear table. "Hi there," she reiterated, once she was beside him. "Welcome," she added, smiling at him as he turned to face her. "We've got sewing, knitting, crochet, needlework, quilting…" she offered, running through the laundry list of various options to be had, although the new arrival's piercing blue eyes were proving something of a distraction for her. "Oh, and stuffed bears, of course!" she added with a laugh. "I knew there was something obvious I'd forgot," she said, picking up a completed teddy and taking its paw so it could offer a little ursine wave of its own. "I'm Charlotte," she said, placing the bear back down, and introducing herself with an extended hand. "Charlotte Newman. Welcome to the Crafternoon Sewcial Club."

"That's an impressive list of choices," the suited chap said in response, shaking Charlotte's hand. "I'm Calum," said Calum. "Calum Whitlock," he elaborated, as if this might well elicit some form of recognition on Charlotte's part (though clearly it didn't). "And I've brought along custard cream biscuits, as instructed?" he added, in hopes of clarification.

Calum stared at Charlotte, and Charlotte, in turn, stared back at Calum. Neither of them spoke. It was like a showdown, with each gunslinger sizing the other up and neither wishing to be the first one to draw their pistol. Sensing this awkward standoff could potentially continue on indefinitely if no action were taken, Charlotte took the lead in breaking the impasse. "Sorry, are you perhaps picking someone up, or dropping them off…?" she asked, with nothing else of use coming to mind.

"I suspect you're not expecting me?" Calum put forth, stroking his stylish, well-manicured beard, and putting his powers of deduction to fair use.

"Should I be?" Charlotte asked, laughing off the awkwardness of the situation.

"How about I start again?" Calum suggested with a playful sigh. "I'm the owner of Microcoding," he announced.

Charlotte raised her eyebrows, smiling like she had trapped wind. "Oh, yes. Right. Microcoding. Exactly. Of course. Ehm…"

"You've no idea who I am, do you?" Calum asked, shaking his

head sadly, though smiling.

"No. No I don't," Charlotte admitted. "But you're most welcome here, I promise!"

"My company, Microcoding," Calum explained, "are the ones sponsoring the Square If You Care initiative through Oxfam."

"Ah!" Charlotte said, slapping her forehead. "I *thought* I recognised the name," she added, lying, and doing a pretty bang-up job of it she hoped.

"So, I'm guessing you didn't get the phone message I left you yesterday?" Calum enquired.

"Phone message?" Charlotte asked, staring blankly again.

"Ah, okay, so that would explain your confusion, at least," Calum answered. "Your phone number was on your competition application form," he told Charlotte. "I was calling to organise a time to pop along to introduce myself and understand a little more about your club. But when I rang, you were indisposed, apparently. The young gentleman I spoke with assured me he would absolutely pass along the message that I'd be coming along today, and also suggested — very *strongly* suggested, I might add — that I bring along custard creams, and so..."

"Stanley Newman!" Charlotte turned and called, realising precisely who'd received the very important message but had nevertheless somehow neglected to share the information with her.

"Yes, Mum?" Stanley asked, trotting over. "Ooohh, custard creams!" he said, suddenly taking note of his favourite biscuits being in this new fellow's hand. "Oh, crap," he added quickly, realisation dawning as to who this new fellow might be. "Mum, you know yesterday, when you were in the bath...?" he began.

"Button it, shrimpy!" Charlotte said, cutting him short. "Some answer machine *you* are," she added, casting him a look, though not without some degree of affection.

Stanley stood there a moment, not knowing what he was meant to do at this point. "Do we... do we get to keep the custard creams?" he asked, this being his area of primary interest at present.

"We'll talk about it later," Charlotte advised, eyes narrowed.

"But—"

"*Later*," Charlotte reiterated, and then shooed him off.

Charlotte then turned her attention back to her previously unexpected guest. "My apologies, Calum. It appears that our lines of communication at home need something of a fine-tune," she told him.

"At least we got there in the end," Calum said with a grin, wiping a bead of imaginary sweat from his forehead.

"Sorry about that," Charlotte offered with a grimace, giving her apologies once again. "Honestly, if I'd known you were coming, I'd have—"

"Baked a cake?" Calum asked, finishing her sentence for her.

"Ah. Well. About that, actually..." Charlotte replied, pointing over to and introducing the refreshments table, where a small handful of untouched cakes yet remained.

"Ah, splendid!" Calum remarked with a laugh.

"So, now that you're here, Calum, how about I take you for the guided tour, tell you what we're all about, and introduce you to a few of the troops?" Charlotte proposed, getting down to business now that introductions and such had finally been sorted.

"That would be perfect," Calum answered. "Lead the way."

Charlotte nodded, first bringing their guest to meet with Bonnie and the quilting team, eager to showcase some of the fantastic work the ladies had accomplished. "Oh. And Calum," Charlotte said, before any further introductions were made. "You should be aware that all guests absolutely *must* join in with at least one of the crafts, yes?"

"Is that so? That's the rule?" Calum replied.

"The rule I made up just now, yes," Charlotte answered.

"Very well, then," Calum agreed, taking off his suit jacket and rolling up his sleeves. "I'm rather looking forward to this..." he said with a grin.

CHAPTER FOURTEEN

In the days following her radio debut, it became apparent that Charlotte's efforts had struck something of a chord with the tremendous Manx public. Her stated goal of supplying every nursing home on the isle with crafting supplies was something that seemed to touch a lot of hearts, and when Sandy, the presenter, rang her up in response to all the calls he was receiving, asking Charlotte where people wanting to donate squares for her campaign should deliver them, Charlotte, on the spur of the moment, suggested Joan's Wools as a drop-off point. This plan of action was advanced without clearing it with the shop ahead of time, so she very much hoped Joan's would be okay with it and wouldn't mind terribly. The last thing she wanted was to be an imposition, of course. But she remembered they had been kind enough to provide this service for her once before (though it had been a complete surprise to her), and hoped it wouldn't be too presumptuous on her part to expect them to do so again. Also, Charlotte really wasn't expecting too many squares to flow in their direction because of this anyway.

Charlotte was tickled pink, then, when Laura from over at Joan's phoned to say they'd been inundated with donations, with over forty squares having been dropped off over the previous two days alone. Charlotte was also relieved to hear that she hadn't made a nuisance of herself, with Laura assuring her that collecting the squares on Charlotte's behalf was no trouble at all. Not only that, but Laura expressed her delight at the unexpected influx of charitable-minded crafters to her store. It was a well-known fact among the crafting community, a sort of unwritten rule, as it were, that it was very nearly illegal for a crafter to visit a crafting shop without actually purchasing something crafting-related! So Joan's, as one might well expect, were nothing but grateful for the increased footfall and the subsequent boost in sales.

With this welcome contribution of squares to her crafting coffers, Charlotte could easily be forgiven for developing an air of confidence and being guardedly optimistic about her chances of quite possibly being in the mix at the top of the league table. Her two crafting clubs, both MAKE IT SEW at the nursing home and her more open-to-the-general-public CRAFTERNOON SEWCIAL CLUB, were chugging along quite nicely. Now, add the radio-related windfall into the mix and things weren't looking half bad.

As for the SQUARE IF YOU CARE initiative, each participating group in the competition was asked to have their current week's worth of squares at the charity's office each Monday. The organisers would then compile all of the totals and would update the leaderboard online at ten a.m. on Tuesday. It was for this reason, come Tuesday, that Charlotte had been anxious all morning, flittering around the kitchen and trying to occupy her time. Although presently, at least, she'd managed to lose herself in a particular project...

"Ah, fudge knuckles," Charlotte remarked, noting her cup of tea on the table in front of her, and how it had remained untouched and was, by now, probably cold. "This is all *your* fault, Peter," she said. "If I wasn't so wrapped up in *you*..."

Charlotte laughed, as she'd just made a joke without even realising she'd been making it. In her hands was a stuffed rabbit, and one of her hands literally *was* wrapped up in it, inserted as it was deep within the rabbit's guts.

The rabbit was named Peter, with great originality and thought, and was the third in a recent trio she'd been commissioned to create by a series of different customers. With a bit more padding added and the application of a pair of eyes, she'd soon be done with Peter #3. Once he was complete, this current creation would be ready to deliver to his new owner, just as his other two rabbity brothers had been. The process of converting a bag of old surplus school uniform into an adorably cute keepsake was something Charlotte thoroughly enjoyed. Also, the money such projects brought in was not at all unwelcome at the current time (and nor were the one-to-one sewing lessons she'd been booked in, either).

As she busied herself putting the finishing touches on Peter, she couldn't help checking the kitchen clock periodically. It was quickly approaching ten by now, and the closer it got the more nervous she became as she awaited the results of her SQUARE IF YOU CARE weekly tally. Charlotte was determined not to allow her competitive nature to get the better of her in what was, after all, a charitable endeavour. Still, drifting off to sleep the previous evening, half-dreaming, she imagined herself walking into the nursing home, with all of the residents anxiously awaiting her arrival. Initially, she'd tease them by sporting a glum expression, making it seem as if she were the bearer of bad tidings. Then, she'd erupt with a furious roar of delight, jumping in the air, shouting out the news of their unassailable lead at the top of the league table, and dancing a happy jig. She may have fallen straight into dreamland at that point in her imaginings, as things got rather more fanciful. She recalled firework-wielding acrobats soon appearing on scene, for instance, astride a pair of African elephants, no less. But things got murky after that.

It was two minutes past ten when Charlotte placed Peter #3 on the table, completed and able to remain upright all by himself for the first time. Charlotte waited for a moment to see if he'd fall over, but he didn't. Satisfied, she reached for her phone, loading up the charity's website. It was the first week the current league standings were initially being published, and at this early stage in the game Charlotte had no clear idea of how she might be doing, or even for that matter, how many groups may have actually entered the competition — for all she knew, it could be just her and Amelia's Laxey coffee morning group. She ran her eyes over the phone's screen, using her index finger to scroll through the information displayed until she found the league standings. "What the heck...?" she said, scrolling further.

A line formed across her forehead, which quickly turned into a full-on crease. "Oh, come on!" she yelled, turning to Peter for support, although with Peter saying not much of anything at all. Charlotte placed her phone on the kitchen table, followed a moment later by her forehead down there on the tabletop as well.

According to the updated league table, *eleven* teams were competing. Which was great news for the charity, of course. However, what wasn't so great was that the CRAFTERNOON SEWCIAL CLUB was languishing in a woeful eighth place. Further compounding Charlotte's unhappiness was the fact that Amelia's coffee morning group were perched securely in the top spot.

"How's that even possible?" Charlotte moaned to herself, followed by a series of pained groans. Her despondency might well have continued for some time had the doorbell not rang, rousing her from her current lamentations. She peeled her head up from the wooden surface where she'd been sulking, offering an apologetic smile to Peter, as her gloomy despair hadn't been his fault, after all.

Postman Harry's cheery face at the front door was just the pick-me-up that Charlotte needed. "Hiya, Harry," she said, opening the door and greeting him. She wasn't just pleased to see him because he brought her crafting supplies on a regular basis. No, he was also just a thoroughly pleasant chap to have around, with a personality to brighten even the darkest of mornings.

"Ms Lotti," Harry said, offering an exaggerated bow, and swirling his hand in the air in an *at-your-service* sort of gesture. "I bring you happiness in a brown jiffy bag, if I'm not mistaken," he added, straightening himself up.

"Oh, is that so?" Charlotte replied.

"Indeed," Harry continued, giving the jiffy bag a gentle shake. "Is that the sound of cotton spools I hear?" he asked, as if his expert ear, honed over many years of delivering parcels, could determine the package's contents (whereas the shape and feel of the spools within the packet were more of a dead giveaway, as was the return address, clearly identifying the sender as being one *Spools of Thread R Us*).

"Ooh, it could well be," Charlotte said, taking possession of the delivery with the hint of a smile emerging, all thoughts of the league table forgotten for the time being. "It's a good job I'm not a drug smuggler Harry, as you'd be on to me in a flash!" she joked, in reference to his apparent X-ray vision, to which Harry gave her a quizzical look. "What? I'm *not* a drug smuggler, Harry, I promise," she assured him.

"No, I believe you," Harry replied. "It's not that. It's just... have you got an eye stuck on your forehead?" he said. "Do I need to start calling you Cyclops?"

"I think Cyclops only had the one eye, didn't he?" Charlotte asked, running her fingertips along the upper portion of her face until she worked out what Harry was referring to, offending article located. "Ah, here we are," she said, plucking it off and examining it. "Yes, it's a rabbit's eye," she explained casually, polishing it with her thumb and forefinger.

"A description like that would ordinarily concern me, Lotti. But, strangely enough, not where you're concerned," Harry answered with a laugh. "Anyway, is everything okay?" he asked. "You don't appear your usual lively self today."

"Self-pity," Charlotte replied. "Not to worry, as this cotton spools delivery should cheer me up in no time," she told him. "Here, I'm just about to pop the kettle on, Harry, if you've time?" she offered.

Harry snapped his arm smartly forward, taking a peek at his watch. "Alas, I'll need to take a raincheck, Lotti," he answered. "I've got a whole van full of election manifestos that need delivering. You should see the delight in people's eyes when they come to the door to meet me, hoping I'm bringing them a delivery they've ordered, and all I hand them is a bunch of electioneering pamphlets!"

"I can well imagine," Charlotte replied, grateful that *she*, at least, had been fortunate enough to indeed receive a package instead of said unwanted pamphlets. "Try and get here for about the same time tomorrow, Harry. I'm baking fruit loaf. And, if you're able to linger for a few, I'll have the tea made for your arrival!" she suggested.

"It's a date," Harry confirmed, taking an appreciative glance at Charlotte's glorious roses as he started to make his way back down the path, out towards the road. "Hang on, what am I like?" he asked rhetorically, suddenly spinning round and shaking his head. "Here," he said, reaching into the canvas bag slung over his shoulder and handing over a pile of the very same pamphlets he'd only just mentioned. It was a whole large stack of them, secured with an elastic band causing the edges of the pile to curl up.

"Do you have to?" Charlotte joked, holding up her hands in protest so that she wouldn't have to take possession. "You could just pop them in the wheelie bin on your way out of the garden?"

"Tempting, but I'm not allowed. Not worth losing my job over, I'm afraid."

"Well, in that case," Charlotte conceded, taking the collection from Harry's hand. She rolled off the elastic band, bending the shiny paper to straighten out the lot. "Just think how many trees have been sacrificed to make..." Charlotte began as she sorted through the pile, noticing the portrait shots of all the campaigners dressed in their Sunday best and offering up their most endearing smiles. "Oh, you've *got* to be bloody kidding me!" she said, suddenly pausing.

Harry took a step back, for he was well aware of the old adage about shooting the messenger, and he of course was the messenger. "I'll just, em... shall I...?" he said, reaching out in the general direction of the garden gate.

Charlotte took hold of the one particular pamphlet that'd caught her eye, featuring as it did the mugshot, so to speak, of a certain someone, and hence drawing her ire. She pulled it from the pile and held it up for Harry's inspection. "This has to be some kind of joke...?"

"I take it you're not a fan?" Harry gamely ventured. "Though I suppose she *is* something of an acquired taste, isn't she?" he added, as his considered opinion.

Charlotte shook her head in disbelief. "Amelia *Sugden*," she said, grumbling half to herself and half to Harry. "Amelia Sugden as our elected *representative*? Can you just *imagine* it? I don't *think* so..."

"I should probably leave you alone with your pamphlets," Harry gently suggested, figuring he'd best be on his way.

"Yes, of course, Harry. Sorry, it's just the effect that woman has on me!" Charlotte answered. "See you at ten tomorrow?"

"See you then!" Harry agreed, waving enthusiastically. "And here's hoping I'll bring you only nice things tomorrow, yeah? Like wool, for instance?" he added, hoping to brighten her day.

After seeing Postman Harry off, Charlotte returned to the kitchen, at which point she found Peter #3 sprawled prostrate across the table. Either the stuffing he'd received could keep him upright for only so long, or he too was expressing his displeasure over this whole sordid Amelia affair in the only way he knew how — by lying face-down on the tabletop and having none of it. "I couldn't agree more," Charlotte told him, to which he didn't reply, as no reply was really necessary.

Charlotte sat down, thumbing through the manifesto outlining Amelia's intention to stand as an MHK, a Member of the House of Keys, part of the island's local parliamentary government. Charlotte wasn't particularly hot on politics in general, but, as the election concerned the village she lived in, she certainly had a vested interest in this one. "*Pfft,*" she said, reading the opening gambit where Amelia outlined her credentials as an upstanding, respected pillar of the community. "*Pfft,*" she said again, at regular intervals, with the turn of each page. What frustrated her more than anything was how the content made Amelia sound so good, like a cross between Florence Nightingale, Greta Thunberg, and Mother Theresa, all rolled into one. Indeed, such was her persuasive rhetoric that Charlotte, if she hadn't in fact known any better, might well have sprinted down to the local polling station, that very instant, in order to mark a massive cross over Amelia's name.

Amelia's main pledges, as described, *did* resonate with Charlotte. As a Laxey resident herself — where Amelia was seeking election — and with a young son, the subjects broached were close to Charlotte's heart. Amelia spoke passionately (if she was to be taken at her word) about the scourge of cars speeding through the village, the lack of afterschool activities for the local youth, and the need for additional funding for elderly care initiatives. It was difficult for Charlotte to conceive that this person, dripping with compassion on the printed page, was in fact the same spiteful person she knew and loathed so well. But it did make her wonder.

Was it possible she may have got Amelia all wrong? Had she perhaps misjudged her? It did cause her to question herself for a moment.

Fearing she was bordering on becoming a fully paid-up member of the Amelia Sugden fan club if she wasn't careful, Charlotte dropped the pamphlet on the table to return her attention to the currently poleaxed Peter. Charlotte's eyes, however, were then drawn to the rear cover of the manifesto where Amelia stood, proud as Punch, holding a pair of knitting needles aloft — as if Amelia was, and had *always* been, a devoted crafter. Charlotte took particular umbrage at this, as she knew Amelia had never indicated even the slightest bit of interest in crafting previously. Indeed, it had always been quite the opposite, and in fact with Amelia often enjoying a jibe at Charlotte's expense at Charlotte's own dedication and devotion to the hobby.

"Oh, come *on!*" Charlotte shouted, as she read the text around the photo. There, Amelia waxed eloquently about her supposed passion in founding her official LAXEY COFFEE MORNING CREW. She went on to say how proud she was to be partaking in the SQUARE IF YOU CARE initiative. That wasn't so bad in itself, but Charlotte's eye started to twitch as she read the bit where Amelia outlined her motives for getting involved in the exciting enterprise, all of which sounded *identical* to Charlotte's own explanation on the radio interview. As if that weren't bad enough, Charlotte was aghast to read that Amelia's ultimate goal, as laid out, was to get crafting supplies into all care homes across the island — blatantly appropriating Charlotte's *own* plan that she'd, again, *explicitly* stated on live radio. Amelia even closed off her rhetoric with an impassioned plea for the tremendous Manx public to send her their crafted squares. As if badgering all the schools on the island wasn't enough for her!

Of course, Charlotte wasn't precious about who arranged for the care homes to be furnished with crafting supplies, just that it would actually happen. What infuriated her was that Amelia had clearly jumped on Charlotte's bandwagon, plagiarizing *her* ideas with the likely motive of winning voter support ahead of the next election. With this in mind, it immediately made her question

Amelia's other election pledges. Were they actually genuine, or were they merely political waffle designed to hoodwink what Amelia no doubt saw as gullible voters? Charlotte certainly hoped that wasn't the case, but had real concerns Amelia was doing precisely that.

"A wolf in sheep's clothing, Peter," Charlotte observed. "A bloody wolf in sheep's clothing."

To which she could only take Peter #3's continued silence as agreement.

CHAPTER FIFTEEN

"Oi, you little maggot!" barked the irate young lady. "Watch where you're going!" she said, in response to having been barged unceremoniously out of the way by the younger lad. She dusted herself down, conscious of the giggling in the corridor emanating from her fellow pupils at her expense. It was a jungle in the school corridor, this she knew. And if the situation had been reversed, she could well have found herself among the throng sniggering at someone *else's* expense. She shrugged her shoulders and carried on, conscious this delay, minimal as it was, would mean a position anywhere near the front of the lunch queue would be seriously compromised.

"What's with that tie, Melanie?" Miss Stead, her math teacher, appearing suddenly in the hallway, asked with a stern expression, further impeding Melanie's immediate progress.

"Sorry, Miss, I'll straighten it up right away," Melanie responded, raising her hand to her throat in such a practised motion that it was clear this was the exact type of question she was asked at least several times each day. She continued on her way, clutching at her neck for Miss Stead's sustained benefit, until she'd safely progressed further away from any potential scrutiny about the errant nature of her attire, and at which point, feeling safe, she dropped her hand again.

"Hey!" Melanie called out, picking up her pace, just then, as she spotted her friend Bonnie some distance ahead. "Hey, Bonnie!" she said, attempting to cut through the rabble of ravenous pupils heading to the dining room, but her progress was impeded by the sheer numbers trying to squeeze through the main doors' bottleneck, like sand through an hourglass.

Thirty seconds or so later and finally in the lunchroom, Melanie partially jumped the lengthy queue, pushing her way back into it ahead of several lads. They were much younger and smaller than she was, so they didn't offer up much resistance. But it was clear they were none too pleased at having their place in line usurped. Melanie ignored them and turned her attention to Bonnie, her flame-haired friend, and the reason Melanie had chosen that particular place in line to cut in.

"Oh, heya, Mel," Bonnie said, turning round in response to the hand placed on her shoulder.

"This queue is savage, Bonnie. How's about we go somewhere else for a nice sausage bap?" Melanie suggested.

"Have you been making friends?" Bonnie asked with a laugh, upon noticing the scowling, glaring faces of the lads stood just behind her friend.

"Who, them?" Melanie replied, casting the boys a look, prompting the lads to fall into order, finding something fascinating on the floor with which to suddenly focus their attention. "What do you say, Bonn?" Melanie asked, now that any potential youth uprising had been brought under control.

"Yeah," Bonnie agreed, looking up the line of pupils moving at less than a snail's pace. "Yeah, let's do it. We'll be here all day, otherwise."

"See ya!" one of the braver lads said to them from behind, although focusing once again on his shoes when Melanie turned in response.

Bonnie forged a path through the influx still spilling into the dining hall, which showed no signs of abating. "It's never this busy for the early lunch sitting," she remarked, looking to Melanie for any possible answers.

"Mr Gilhooly's lunchtime crafting club starts in twenty minutes, so they're probably trying to get fed before then," Melanie suggested.

Bonnie walked several paces further before what Melanie had just told her suddenly registered. "Hang on, did you just say *Mr Gilhooly's crafting club*?" she asked with a laugh, fully expecting some kind of punchline that hadn't yet arrived.

"Yup," Melanie said, nodding her head in confirmation.

"The lunch club I went to last year and was on my own on each and every occasion? *That* one?" Bonnie asked, at a bit of a loss as to how such a club might become popular all of a sudden.

"That's the one," Melanie replied, spotting an incoming teacher and instinctively fumbling with her tie. "It's the hottest ticket in town right at the moment. Especially for the lads."

"Oh...kay," Bonnie answered, still a mite confused. "You sound like you've got your finger on the school pulse, Mel, so could you fill me in as to what's going on?"

Melanie smiled politely as the teacher walked on by. "There's a knitting competition or something," Melanie explained to Bonnie. "You've got to make squares, I think. But I don't know much more than that."

"Ah! The competition!" Bonnie answered. "Mel, that's what I tried to sign you up to, remember? The Crafternoon club I go to is involved in that, as I said."

"Oh," Mel said, easing her tie loose again. She sucked in air through her teeth, trying to recall that conversation, the one Bonnie was referring to, but failing miserably. "You're sure?" she asked.

"Yes, I'm sure. But anyway, why would all the lads in school want to give up their lunch hour for Mr Gilhooly's crafting club?"

"Well, duh. He's teaching them how to knit, I suppose," Melanie said, picking up the pace now they'd made it safely to the corridor.

"And this doesn't strike you as at all strange?" Bonnie asked, scurrying behind to catch her up. "The lads in our school having a sudden interest in learning to knit so they can enter a charity knitting competition? Nothing about this sounds in the least bit peculiar to you?"

"Oh, that. Well, the new PlayStation might have something to do with it, I expect," Melanie elaborated. "Bonn, do you not read the flyers displayed around the school?" she asked, taking a step over to her left to a nearby corkboard, plucking off one of the particular flyers in question, and then handing it over to Bonnie as the two of them walked along.

Bonnie slowed to a dawdle, running her eyes over the details in her hand. She slowed further, eventually coming to a complete stop and lifting her head. "Is this not bribery?" she asked, and then added further, "Can you even bribe people to enter a charity competition? Is that even legal?"

"Wow, three questions on the bounce," Melanie replied, taking a gentle grip of Bonnie's arm, pulling her along in the direction of the exit, eager, as she was, to attend to her hungry tum. "Anyway, I think it's just a way of encouraging participation," she offered. "Young people will do anything for the new Xbox or PlayStation, I reckon. Especially boys. Dunno why they didn't offer a different prize for the girls, though. Maybe that would be considered sexist? I mean, it's not like girls don't play video games as well, but still, I would've—"

"But this..." Bonnie protested, cutting her now slightly rambling friend off. "*This*," she said again, jabbing her finger down, poking an index-finger-sized hole in the middle of the paper. "This Laxey Coffee Morning Crew is in direct competition with *our* club. And now they're bribing kids in order to gain an advantage? That can't be fair, can it?"

"Cheese and crackers, you make it sound like it's some sort of life-or-death struggle or something," Melanie replied, gently rolling her eyes. "Like gang warfare!"

"Very funny," Bonnie answered. "They're offering one entry into the raffle for each completed square," Bonnie went on, reciting what she'd just read, and apparently not finished on the subject. "You know, that's actually rather clever," she grudgingly allowed. "All the kids are going to get everyone they know making squares for them, getting family members in on the act, I'll bet, in order to increase their chances of winning the prize. Quite genius now that I think about it. Insidious. But genius."

The two girls walked in the direction of the nearby petrol station, which was also a convenience shop offering a considerable array of snacks as well as hot food items served up. It was a popular lunchtime destination for the local school kids as the queue was generally processed quicker than the school dining room. The food was often quite good, too, if not especially healthy.

"Guess what, Bonn!" Melanie said, once inside the shop and stood before the hot food counter. "Sausage bap, please," she quickly added, directed to the hard-working woman behind the counter, whose white apron, plastered in dried egg yolk, looked as if it had originally been white at some point in the distant past.

"Me too, please!" Bonnie chimed in, receiving a nod from the server in acknowledgement.

"Bonn," Melanie said, picking up from what she'd started to say before, as their sausage baps were being assembled. "Bonn, guess what!"

"What?" Bonnie replied flatly, eyeing her friend with suspicion. "I can always tell when you're up to mischief."

"*Moi*? But how?"

"You open your mouth," Bonnie replied, her lips curling into a grin.

Melanie pressed on, undaunted. "*Anyway*, there's a certain lad in school who, only this morning, asked me about your availability for the school prom," Melanie revealed, flapping her eyebrows up and down in quick succession.

"Melanie," Bonnie groaned (although, to be fair, the groaning noise could just as easily have been her stomach gurgling in anticipation of her lunch), "I'm still not decided if I'm going to the prom. I've told you."

"Oh but you've *got* to," Melanie insisted. "Daryl Stenson is having an after-party, see, and we're both on the invite list, Bonn. He's got a swimming pool and a tennis court."

"Tennis? After the prom?"

"Well, no..." Melanie answered, exchanging cash over the glass counter for her lunch. "No, I was just saying about the tennis court so you'd be able to imagine how big his house was," she explained. "So, are you not interested in who was asking after you?"

"What? I thought you just said it was Daryl Stenson?"

"No, no," Melanie clarified, "that's unrelated."

"Then what does...?" Bonnie began to say, taking hold of her own lunch. "Actually, it doesn't matter," she said. "As I say, I just don't think I'm up for going."

With lunch now in hand, the girls headed back in the direction of school, where they'd soon locate a wall to perch on and enjoy their respective culinary delights.

"Go on, then," Bonnie asked eventually, kicking a pebble along the pavement. "I s'pose it wouldn't hurt to know."

"No. No, you said you weren't interested," Melanie teased, turning her head away.

"Mel! Spill it!"

"It's Todd Ramsay," Melanie answered, snapping her head back, unable to keep the information to herself for even one more second.

"Oh," Bonnie said, playing it cool, but with the gentle flushing of her cheeks betraying her true feelings on the matter.

"You're *blushing*," Melanie said, noticing this and jumping straight on it. "I *knew* you liked him!"

Bonnie liberated her sausage bap from its bag as they walked, taking a gerbil-sized nibble, her thoughts appearing to be elsewhere. "I suppose he's okay," Bonnie replied with a shrug, nonchalantly, not really committing herself one way or the other.

"That's why I told him you were certain to say yes if he asked you," Melanie responded, taking Bonnie's rather noncommittal response as a ringing endorsement.

"You didn't! Tell me you're joking!" Bonnie replied.

But any further reprovals, rebukes, or protestations on Bonnie's part would have to wait for a moment as she was abruptly distracted, her attention being taken away as she noticed a familiar car driving towards them.

"Is that not your dad, pretending he didn't see us?" Melanie asked, noticing the same car, now passing by, that had evidently drawn her friend's attention.

"Eh, yeah. I think so…"

"Who's the woman in the passenger seat?" Melanie asked, turning to follow the car with her eyes as it made its way past. "Has he got a hot date?" she joked. "He must have a hot date, and that's why he was covering his face with his hand?" she speculated, still joking and laughing, not really thinking too hard about what she was saying, and then immediately regretting it as she saw her friend's shoulders sag and demeanour change. "Oh my goodness,

I'm so sorry," she added quickly. "I didn't mean—"

"It's fine," Bonnie replied. "I mean, no, of course he's not on a date. It must be just a friend…" she said, although not appearing entirely convinced of her own words.

"Yes, it's probably just a friend," Melanie agreed, trying to sound positive for Bonnie's benefit. "Anyway, so Todd…" she said breezily, attempting to steer the conversation back into previously charted waters. But it didn't seem to work, as she saw her friend's eyes start to well up.

Bonnie took a slight detour, just inside a narrow lane intersecting the road, and leaned back against the side of a building. Melanie followed, and once safely away from prying eyes, used her napkin to wipe her friend's cheek. "Aww, Bonn. Is this about seeing your dad?" she asked sympathetically.

"I guess I always knew he'd meet someone else, Mel," Bonnie told her, sobbing gently. "I just… I just don't think I'm ready for that quite yet…"

"What you're feeling is perfectly natural, Bonn. Nobody can ever replace your mum," Melanie assured her. "Anyway, as you said, it was probably just a friend, yeah?"

Bonnie returned her lunch into its grease-stained bag, not feeling very hungry anymore. "No," she said, shaking her head. "No, there's something going on, Mel. Dad's been a bit cagey all week. He's never off his phone, and when I ask what he's up to, he goes all weird on me. I did wonder already if he weren't perhaps messaging a woman."

"Here," Melanie said, handing the napkin over to her friend. "You know, when I saw the tears I panicked, thinking you were upset about the whole Todd situation. Or possibly that your sausage bap was of substandard quality!" she joked, trying to lighten the mood.

"No, you're fine," Bonnie said, dabbing at her eyes. "Although the bap wasn't nearly as good as I expected."

"Come on," Melanie said, "I've *just* the thing to cheer you up."

"Oh?" said Bonnie.

"That's right. Just the thing," Melanie confirmed, sinister devilment dancing in her eyes. "Let's get rid of your competition and sabotage Mr Gilhooly's crafting club, Bonn!" she offered gamely.

"How exactly do we go about sabotaging a school crafting club?" Bonnie enquired, not exactly sure she liked the sound of whatever it was that Melanie was proposing, but not discounting out of hand the possibility of going along with it either.

"Well…" Melanie replied, linking Bonnie's arm and leading the march, back in the direction of the school. "Well, we could start by bending all of their knitting needles, for one!" she suggested, glancing over to gauge the initial reaction to the plan she was only just now devising on the fly.

Bonnie nodded, one corner of her mouth turning upward. "If that doesn't work, then I suppose we could just steal their wool?" she said, the other corner of her mouth now joining the first.

"Or kidnap Mr Gilhooly?" Melanie ventured, getting a little carried away in exploring the endless possibilities of this plan.

"Too far, Mel. Too far."

CHAPTER SIXTEEN

"Nope, it's no use," Mollie declared, having no luck in her present internet search. "It's hopeless, Lotti. I just can't find him anywhere," she advised, lowering the mobile phone in her hand. "You're sure that was his name?"

"Yes, that's what he told me it was. I'm certain of it," Charlotte answered, keeping her eyes on the road ahead. "Keep looking, Moll. I mean, it's not like he would have given me a false name or something," she said with a nervous laugh. "Would he?"

"Well, actually…" Mollie began. "Actually, my dear, need I remind you about that chap who worked in the pizza shop, Lotti? As I recall, he gave you a wrong name, *and* a wrong phone number to boot, after your one and only date with him at that very same pizza shop."

"Yeah, I did wonder why everyone always called him Bob at the shop when he told me his name was Steve," Charlotte admitted with a shrug.

"Wasn't it an Indian restaurant's number he gave you? Just to get rid of you?"

"Yes it was. And it was a very *good* Indian restaurant, as it turned out, so he actually ended up doing me a favour!" Charlotte informed Mollie. "So good, in fact, that I never went back to that rubbish pizza shop," she was happy to report.

"Ah, so that's how you found that Indian shop. They do make some lovely curry," Mollie remarked.

"They do indeed. And you wouldn't believe it, but I actually saw that cheeky blighter about two weeks ago."

"Steve-Bob?" Mollie asked.

"Yeah. And he's still working at that same pizza shop, and even had the nerve to ask me why I'd never been back around!" Charlotte told her.

"What did you tell him? And why *haven't* you been back around?" Mollie said with a snigger.

"I told him that pizza of his left a bad taste in my mouth," Charlotte replied, flicking her eyes over to the passenger seat for a moment. "But I told him I've got a *friend* of mine who might like to try it," she added with a chuckle, putting her eyes back on the road.

Mollie laughed, knowing Charlotte was most likely joking about that last bit, and put her head down in order to resume her thus far fruitless search instead. "Sorry, Lotti," she said, after some further investigation. "There's nobody with that name on either Facebook or Twitter that fits his description, at least that I can find."

"Hmm, what about LinkedIn, Moll?" Charlotte suggested. "Try on there, as that's for the business type, right?"

Mollie did as instructed, loading up the website in question, and then pressing her nose closer to the screen as she performed a search. "Ah, yes, here we go. Calum Whitlock," she said, after soon getting successful results. "Yep. Got him, Lotti," Mollie was happy to confirm. "Calum Whitlock, CEO of Microcoding, Ltd. This is the one."

"That would be him. Brilliant," Charlotte answered. "Does he have a picture there?" she asked. "Oh, but don't click on his profile, Moll!" she quickly warned.

"What? I don't understand," Mollie said, not understanding. "You told me to look for a picture, so that's what I'm doing."

"Yes, but don't go all the way into his profile," Charlotte explained, "as LinkedIn tells you who's been looking at your profile if you look at their profile! I only know that because I set up an account of my own to promote my crafting items."

"Ah. Too late. Sorry," Mollie replied with a shrug, not seeing what the big deal was.

"Mollie! Now he's going to know you've been stalking him on social media!" Charlotte scolded her, pressing down on the indicator and driving into the carpark. "And as you've got an account of your own for your business, he'll be able to see that *you* know *me*, and… and…" Charlotte went on, almost hyperventilating.

"Relax, Lotti, just looking someone up on social media isn't *stalking* them, for goodness' sake," Mollie answered. "And besides, there's no chance he's going to know that I've been stalking him anyway," she offered, allowing Charlotte a moment to regulate her breathing.

Charlotte eased the car into the first available parking space with a sigh of relief. "You're absolutely sure?" she asked, shutting the vehicle off, and then applying the handbrake. "Is your own profile set to private or something?"

"No, it's not that," Mollie replied. "Don't forget my phone battery's dead, so I've been using *your* phone just now, not mine," she told her friend. "So, he's going to see that *you've* been stalking him, not me."

"Ah, bugger!"

"Ooh, Lotti, he *is* rather dashing," Mollie commented, using her thumb and forefinger to spread out the image before her onscreen, achieving a magnified view. "Hmm, he's something of a silver fox," she remarked. "And looks fantastic in a suit, I might add," she added.

"Yes, he did have that George Clooney thing going on," Charlotte agreed. "That is, in the early, ER stage of George's career, when he first started going grey, and not how he looks now," she clarified, having given this some considerable thought previously, it would appear. "Right. I'll be ten minutes, I promise," Charlotte said, climbing out of the car. "And then we can head to our spin class. Coming in?"

"Nah, I'll wait here," Mollie answered. "Leave your phone, so I can do a bit more research on the new hunk in your life, yeah?"

"Not a bloody chance," Charlotte said, snatching her phone from Mollie's clutches. "Knowing you, I'll end up with a restraining order!"

"Fine. Be a party pooper, then," Mollie said, giving Charlotte an exaggerated sad-faced frown. "I'll just have to sit and listen to the radio, then, won't I?" she pouted. "That's right, don't worry about me, I'll be fine. I'll just..." she said, trailing off and not finishing, as by this point Charlotte had already gone.

Charlotte had a black folder tucked under her arm, with several crocheted squares secured in plastic display sleeves inside. She was like a travelling saleswoman intent on hawking carpet samples to bored housewives. However, it was a very different audience she was hoping to appeal to today. Still reeling from the poor showing on the league table — despite the Herculean effort by her club members — Charlotte was determined to get their numbers back on track, and if that meant taking their recruitment drive on the road, then so be it.

First up on the campaign trail today was the Appledene nursing home — first up by virtue of it being at the top of the alphabetical list of the island's nursing homes. She'd phoned earlier and had managed to secure a meeting with the duty manager, Samuel. He sounded broadly enthusiastic about the idea of the residents crafting squares on behalf of Crafternoon and was happy to meet to discuss further.

"Charlotte!" boomed a deep male voice, from a figure heading directly her way, before she had even made it completely across the gravel driveway.

Slightly startled, Charlotte smiled awkwardly as a blond-haired chap bounded down the steps with his hand extended. If this was Samuel, his outward appearance didn't match his serious phone voice, Charlotte thought. With his unkempt, wind-strewn hair and his kaleidoscopic, colourful attire, he could easily have been mistaken for someone belonging more at the Woodstock music festival than as the manager of a nursing home.

"Samuel?" Charlotte hazarded, reasoning that nobody else would have known she was coming and so it must have been him.

"That's me! But you can call me Sam! Or Sammy!" Sam replied, smiling broadly. "I *thought* that was you," he said, and then, adding cryptically, "You look exactly like your photograph!" Sam extended an arm to her. "Welcome, welcome," he said, escorting her up the driveway and towards the front door he'd just appeared through.

It certainly was a rather grand establishment, Charlotte couldn't help but notice, marvelling at the handsome exterior. She'd driven past it a thousand times, but the dense covering of trees restricted the available view from the road. She stopped for a moment, staring up at the imposing stone turret towering above the corner of the property. "It's like something from a fairytale," she remarked, imagining herself peering hopefully through the window, lowering her hair to the prince who'd arrived to rescue her. She blushed for a moment when realising the face of Prince Charming in her fantasy was none other than Calum.

"It's something special," Sam agreed, following her eyeline. "The estate was once owned by a Victorian shipping magnate, by all accounts," Sam told her. "The extensive grounds are just one of the reasons our residents are so happy here."

"You're fortunate to call this your office," Charlotte said, breaking away from her daydream. "Wait," Charlotte added, finally catching up with something Sam said a moment earlier. "*What* photograph?" she asked, looking at him.

"What's that?" Sam asked, cocking his head.

"I just wondered how it was that you had a photograph of me?" Charlotte asked jovially, not wishing to sound like she was accusing him of something at this early stage of their relationship.

"Oh. Oh, that," Sam said, shaking his head. "What am I like?" he joked, chastising himself. "You'll be thinking I've been outside your house with a telephoto lens!"

"Well… no. No, that hadn't even really entered my head, actually," Charlotte replied, wondering if there *was* something she ought to perhaps be worrying about, suddenly very aware that there wasn't another person within view should assistance be required.

Motivated, most likely, by the concern on Charlotte's face, Sam elaborated further before his guest should decide to turn around and leg it. "Ah. I was speaking with Emma earlier," Sam explained. "As in Emma the manager from where you have your Make It Sew club?" he added. "We have a weekly call to share best practices and the like."

"Oh, yes. Emma's lovely, isn't she?" Charlotte said, perking up, and more confident now that she wasn't about to be bundled into the boot of Sam's car, and thus deciding it safe to resume her journey towards the building's entrance.

"Anyway," Sam continued, "I mentioned that you'd been in touch, and she kindly sent me some photographs through of your crafting class in full swing, you see. They're wonderful pictures, and you all look like you're having the jolliest of times."

"Oh, we do. We always do," Charlotte said, walking through the front door that Sam was, like a gentleman, holding open for her. "Which is what brought me along today," she said, holding up her ring binder. "I was hoping to show you an example of some of the squares we've been working on, as I mentioned on the phone earlier. I thought that some of your residents might be interested in getting involved?"

Sam led the way, guiding Charlotte up the corridor. "Interested? Yes, you *could* say that," he replied with a laugh, soon coming to a halt outside an imposing set of wooden double doors. "I may have let it slip that you were coming along," he added, in response to Charlotte's questioning look, at which point he pushed open one of the doors and held it open, inviting Charlotte to enter.

Charlotte walked inside, with Sam following close behind. "Oh my," she said.

"With you being something of a crafting legend in the nursing home community, some of the residents were very eager to meet you," Sam explained.

Charlotte ran her eyes around what looked very much like a grand ballroom from a costume drama. Staring back at her were about thirty or so faces sat on either side of the most enormous dining room table Charlotte had ever seen. Instead of platters of food laid out before them, however, there were a number of wicker baskets stuffed with balls of wool.

"They were all hoping to help you with your crafting square campaign," Sam whispered through the corner of his mouth.

"Do they know how to knit or crochet?" Charlotte asked, offering a warm smile and a friendly wave to the group.

"A few of them do," Sam replied. "But those that don't are very willing to learn if you had the time to set them on their way?"

"Of course!" Charlotte answered, only too happy to oblige.

"Wait, hang on, you mean right now?" she said, glancing down at her watch. "Well, I was supposed to be going to a spin class very soon," she said, chewing her lip while weighing her options, and also thinking about Mollie sat twiddling her thumbs in the car waiting for her.

"Oh. Would you like to perhaps schedule another—?" Sam began to suggest.

"No, it's fine," Charlotte assured him. "Trust me, if there's a choice between crafting or dripping in sweat on a static bike, then there's only ever going to be one winner when making that decision."

Charlotte took her phone from the rear pocket of her jeans.

"I just need to make a quick call, as I've got a friend waiting for me in the car," she advised. "Maybe I can bring her in, as I think I could do with some reinforcements to help with this lot anyway," she added, indicating the array of seated volunteers. "Oh, wait," she said, "the battery on her phone is flat. Give me two minutes, and I'll be right back in so we can get this crafting party started!"

"On the way home, Chinese takeaway, on me," Charlotte said, placing her arm around Mollie's shoulders, impromptu crafting party now in full swing. "You're certain you don't mind missing the spin class?" she asked.

Mollie pursed her lips, playing off like she was really struggling at coming up with an answer. "Chinese takeaway or a spin class, Lotti? Hmm, I don't know, that's a toughie," she said with a chuckle. "Only I don't think changing into my gym attire in advance was the best idea, under the revised circumstances," she offered confidentially, leaning in.

"You're fine," Charlotte said, waving away her concerns. "Besides, I think the two chaps at the end of the table appear to appreciate your Lycra leggings."

"Them two?" Mollie said with a sniff. "Yeah, that's precisely my point. They've already dropped their knitting needles twice, calling me over to pick them up, cheeky old devils."

"I'm sure it's purely a coincidence. Maybe they're just clumsy?" Charlotte suggested wryly. "You know, Moll, I really do appreciate you agreeing to help," she added, turning serious. "I like doing things like this with you."

"It's fine, Lotti," Mollie answered her. "And you know what?" she whispered, face grave as if she were about to deliver some type of deathly worrying news, "I think I'm turning into a crafting convert." Mollie lowered her head, as if what she'd just said was something to be deeply ashamed of. "I was even browsing crafting websites last night! Do you think I have a problem? Do I need to talk to someone?"

"It's too late, Moll. You're one of us now. *One of us*," Charlotte told her, patting her friend's shoulder, welcoming her into the fold with a sinister laugh. "You only need to be genuinely concerned if you're having a difficult time making the choice between buying new fabric or paying the electricity bill," she advised sagely, as if she had a little too much experience in matters precisely such as this.

Charlotte's simple ten-minute visit that was planned initially to showcase her squares had turned into a quite-a-bit-longer, full-on crafting class. Stanley was sleeping over at his dad's, so that wasn't a worry, at least. So long as their new friends were eager to participate, then, Charlotte was delighted to lead, assisted admirably by Mollie.

The group's skillset was similar to the folks at MAKE IT SEW. Some of them had some previous crafting experience, while others were complete newcomers, with the group being happy to either learn from scratch or hone their skills. There were a few scattered grumblings and the assorted salty language bandied about as the evening progressed, due in the main to some of their fingers not being quite as nimble as they once were. But progress was made, and before too terribly long the gang were knitting away like seasoned professionals. Also, Charlotte made it a point not to neglect the knitters with previous experience, as they were a valuable resource. If she could upskill them or refresh their prior knowledge, they would be able to assist the broader group moving forward. It was a strategy that'd worked wonders with her other

groups, meaning there was always help on hand in between classes when Charlotte wasn't there. It was also a great way to promote collaboration between them, as well as greater socialisation
and interaction.

"When I'm older, I'm staying here," Mollie confided to Rita, the
woman she was assisting at the present moment. "Honestly, this
building is like something from Downton Abbey," she remarked,
admiring the delicate gilding on the moulded ceiling.

"It's alright, I suppose," Rita answered. "Not much eye candy to
speak of, if you know what I mean," she said, throwing a disap-
proving glance over at the scant selection of men to be found
around the table. "I think I'm going to invest in a pair of leggings
like yours, though," Rita suggested.

"Oh?" said Mollie.

"Yeah, I've seen the effect they had on those two frisky buggers
over there," Rita answered, using one of her needles to furtively
point in the direction of the two particular buggers in question.
"I'm confident those leggings would ramp up my social life a fair
bit, if you take my meaning," she suggested, offering a cheeky
wink.

"Oh. But I thought you just said you didn't fancy any of
them...?" Mollie asked, a mite confused.

"One takes what one can find, my dear, and makes do with
what's at hand," Rita offered, speaking from many years' worth of
gathered wisdom. "Anyway, we should go out shopping together.
You can show me where to pick up a pair of those lovely leggings!"
she added brightly.

"Now that sounds like a date, Rita," Mollie confirmed, holding
her hand out to seal the deal.

"Right ho!" Sam eventually announced, after two hours or so
had gone by, clapping his hands together smartly, with the noise
echoing about the spacious room. "Are you going to release these
poor ladies so they can go home, or do I need to call the police on
their behalf?" he asked, good-naturedly, placing his hands on his
hips. Then, he walked over to Charlotte. "It appears that you
might just have a few more volunteers for your crafting square
campaign, yes?" Sam asked somewhat rhetorically, as the answer

was already obvious.

"And what a fantastic bunch they are, the lot of them," Charlotte answered. "Thank you ever so much for gathering them together. Me and my friend Mollie both had so much fun getting to know them all!"

"Although you might want to throw a bucket of cold water over those two over there," Mollie entered in, though stated not entirely seriously.

"Let me guess. Henry and Sid, is it?" Sam replied, without even having to see where Mollie was looking. "Yes, they fancy themselves as quite the ladies' men, a right pair of charmers."

"Yeah. But smashing blokes, to be fair, once you do get to know them," Mollie allowed.

"So, you were saying you're doing the grand tour of the island's nursing homes to drum up a band of volunteers?" Sam asked, turning to Charlotte again. *"That'll* be fun," he said, although quite sincerely, and without a trace of sarcasm.

"Well, yes, that was the intent," Charlotte replied, standing now, and enjoying a nice little stretch after being seated for so long.

"Oh?" Sam answered. "Change of plans? Our friends here haven't frightened you off, have they?"

Charlotte shook her head in the negative. "No, no. Not even a little bit. Quite the opposite, as it turns out," she informed him happily. "The problem is that I'll..." she began, until, that is, Mollie happened to throw her a glance which indicated they were both in this together in regard to whatever it was that Charlotte might be about to say. "What I mean to say is, *we'll* end up spending probably several hours in each home doing the same thing there as what we've done here tonight. And, while that's my idea of heaven, there just aren't enough hours in the day, I don't think, to get around to them all and give them each the attention they deserve."

"Tell you what," Sam said, raising his finger in a eureka moment. "I'm in a WhatsApp group with most of the other nursing home managers on the island. Why don't I send them a little note and tell them how enthusiastic our residents were to get involved with your crafting initiative? I'm sure they'll be happy to get their residents onboard also. Plus, it'd give you a foot in the door to all the homes without, say, having to necessarily set foot past each door, or spend hours at each location."

"That'd be amazing if you would," Charlotte said, looking to Mollie with a grin. "If we do get a chance to go along and visit them, though, we absolutely will," Charlotte added, still entirely happy to entertain the prospect. "Oh, and Sam, you'd be most welcome to come check out our Crafternoon club," she offered. "Some of the folks here have suggested they might be interested in popping along, in fact."

"Sounds good," Sam replied. "And seriously, thank you, both of you, for tonight. You can see how much it meant to them all."

Henry (of Henry & Sid fame), stood at the far end of the table, holding his hand out, his knitted square's humble beginnings on display. "You're coming back next week, aren't you?" he called over, with hope-filled eyes. "You must!" he insisted. "We've loved having you here!"

"Uhm..." Charlotte answered, uncertain as to how she ought to respond. She wasn't really sure she could make such a commitment, but then neither did she wish to cause offence.

But any possible reply she might have been considering was promptly cut short by those sitting around the table.

"Yes, please come back!" another of the residents pleaded, with this quickly turning into a collective chorus of thirty or so voices conveying the same sentiment, with everyone doing their very best to persuade the two girls to return the following week.

Charlotte turned to Mollie, receiving a raised eyebrow in response, which was all the approval she needed. "We'd love to," Charlotte said to the crowd, resulting in a generous round of applause in response.

"See you next week!" Henry called over, blowing a kiss in Mollie's direction.

Once outside in the late evening air, Charlotte pointed out the Disneyesque turret, although choosing to leave out the details of her earlier Calum-related fantasy associated with the tower. "What a place, right?" Charlotte remarked, taking the whole thing in. "You can imagine yourself stepping down from a horse-drawn carriage in your finest gown," she suggested, her mind starting to wander off once more.

"You know," Mollie said, her mind wandering to her own set of thoughts, "there's something quite attractive about him…"

"*What?*" Charlotte replied. She only wished she'd been drinking coffee or tea as she said this, so that she could have spit it out right then. "Mollie, he's a bit old for you, don't you think?"

"He's not *that* much older than us, is he?" Mollie answered, puzzled by Charlotte's reaction.

"Wait… Who're we talking about?" Charlotte asked, puzzled that Mollie was puzzled.

"Sam, of course," Mollie clarified, as if there should have been any doubt. "Who are *you* talking about?"

"I thought you were talking about Henry!" Charlotte replied.

"Henry? Don't be bloody daft!" Mollie told her. "Although…"

"Although?"

"Ha-ha! Just kidding!" Mollie responded. "You should've seen the look on your face just now!"

"Blimey, you had me worried there for a tick," Charlotte said, breathing a sigh of relief. "I suppose there *is* something about Sam, though," Charlotte offered, taking into consideration Mollie's actual suggestion. "It's the quirkiness, I suppose?" she mused aloud. "Maybe the caring nature of his career choice?"

"A sort of scruffy sophistication?" Mollie suggested. "If that's even possible? A kind of paradox-type thingy? A pleasing juxtaposition?"

"Oh, I wouldn't know anything about that," Charlotte answered, as they made their way back to her car. "It's a bit early in the game, I should think, to be speculating as to what sort of positions he may or may not—" she began, but then cutting herself short as she felt a sudden vibration in her pocket. "Hello, who's this?" she asked, pulling her phone from her pocket and taking a gander. "Holy crap," she mumbled to herself, a few moments later, after viewing her onscreen messages.

"What is it?" Mollie asked. "Is everything okay?"

Charlotte opened the car door, her eyes remaining fixed on her phone as she fell into the driver's seat. "It's a LinkedIn notification," she told Mollie, as Mollie joined her inside the car. "Calum's sent me a connection request."

"Ah. You're *welcome*," Mollie replied, a self-satisfied grin across her chops as she fastened her seatbelt.

"What do I do?" Charlotte asked, appearing absolutely pathetic in her abject indecision, and in danger of throwing her phone straight out the window.

"Accept it, of course," came Mollie's wise counsel.

"But I can't, can I," Charlotte stated, her voice verging on panic. "It might make me overly keen, and that would be—"

"*Charlotte!*" Mollie interjected.

"Okay, okay. There. I've accepted it. You happy now?" Charlotte answered. "Jayzus, I just hope Calum doesn't think I'm a stalker who likes him…?"

Mollie sighed a loud sigh. "Charlotte, you *are*, and you *do*."

"Fair point," Charlotte conceded. "But *he* doesn't know that, now does he?" she added. "Wait… Oh my god," she said, looking down at her phone.

"What now?" Mollie asked, wondering if she should be concerned.

"He's just messaged me," Charlotte revealed.

"And?"

"He's asked me for a coffee," Charlotte said. "Mollie, he's asked me for a coffee!" she repeated, even though her friend had no doubt heard her perfectly the first time around.

"I say again, Charlotte. You're welcome!"

"But what do I do now?" Charlotte asked, staring at her phone as if it were some kind of alien device she'd never seen before.

"Well," Mollie answered, "What you do is—"

"Yes…?" Charlotte said, leaning in close, anxious to hear what advice Mollie had to offer.

"What you do is, you put your keys in the ignition. You then start the engine. And *then* you drive me to the Chinese takeaway place for some Szechuan chicken, because I'm bloody famished! *That's* what you do now!"

CHAPTER SEVENTEEN

Amelia Sugden stalked the school playground yet again, picking unsuspecting parents off with what appeared to be relative ease. A cursory glance down at her fancy, leather-bound, monogrammed clipboard seemed to tell her all she needed to know about whether the mark before her was one she'd targeted previously, or was in fact new, fresh meat ripe to fall victim to her polished sales patter.

Watching on from the relative safety of the carpark, Charlotte marvelled at the sheer brass neck of the woman, pestering these good folk first thing in the morning when they were likely at their most vulnerable. Amelia was very much like a peregrine falcon, thought Charlotte, menacing a murmuration of starlings and waiting for just the right moment to periodically make her move, dive in, and strike.

For the past week, Charlotte had mastered the art of the covert school drop-off and pick-up. Amelia was hard work to deal with at the best of times, but with her coffee morning crew currently topping the crafting square leaderboard she was apt to be even more of a nightmare than usual. Best to simply avoid her entirely, Charlotte reckoned. Also, the thought of possibly being canvassed to vote for this woman as well was another reason for Charlotte to give Amelia a very wide berth right at present.

"Are... are you avoiding Amelia also?" came a voice from behind, enquiring tentatively, and breaking Charlotte's attention away from the unfolding tableaux on the playground below.

Charlotte turned to locate from whence the voice was originating, finding another school mum she didn't know crouched down behind a nearby white VW Beetle. The poor woman appeared shellshocked, her sunken, weary eyes offering a glimpse of the many horrors she'd perhaps been witness to. Charlotte, sympathetic to her plight, waved the lady over, inviting the woman to join her in her car.

"Avoiding, yes. And also carefully observing," Charlotte said, in reference to the question being offered, once the woman was safely ensconced on the passenger seat beside her. "Best to keep her in plain sight so evasive action can be taken if and when required," Charlotte explained. "You never know when she might change course and head this way, for instance."

"I'm Fenella," the woman said, extending her hand. She appeared grateful for the refuge and the present company, but still seemed rattled. "She keeps asking me to make squares," she said, voice brittle. "I told her I didn't knit, but that didn't deter her one bit, not one least little bit. The next time she saw me, she came prepared with printed instructions. *Printed instructions!* This way, I had no excuse, you see. She's relentless!"

"Oh, terrible, terrible," Charlotte commiserated, though secretly wondering if this weren't perhaps an approach she might try for her own crafting square recruitment drive efforts. "Did it, ehm... did it work?" she asked, not wishing to pick the scabs from poor Fenella's wounds, but still curious nonetheless.

"Yes," Fenella replied, darting fearful eyes to the playground for just a moment. "Yes, but I've hardly seen my own kids lately because I spend all of my time knitting!" she confessed. "I made Amelia five squares last week," she told Charlotte. "*Five* squares. And you know what she said to me when I handed them over to her?"

"Erm... no?" Charlotte said, concerned by the size of the vein currently pulsing in Fenella's temple.

"It's a good start!" Fenella replied. "That's what she told me. That my efforts were *a good start*. A bloody *good start* is all she could offer me in return for hours and hours of work. Yesterday, I even had to miss an appointment at the dentist in order to finish the square I was working on. I've got an infection in my wisdom tooth, but I skipped it for her!" She caressed her tender jawbone, wincing from the pain. "I'm in bloody agony," she declared. "And now, not only do I have to wait another two weeks for an appointment but I also have to pay out of pocket for the one I've just missed because of the cancellation fee."

"Oh, dear," Charlotte said, unsure what else she could say to ease this unfortunate woman's obvious distress. "So..." Charlotte said, searching around for something positive to say. "So, em, I take it you won't be voting for her in the upcoming elections, then?" she asked gaily.

This question, of course, was meant to lighten the mood. And yet, curiously, it seemed to have precisely the opposite effect, with the vein on Fenella's temple now appearing as if it were about to rupture at any given moment.

"I'm now also on her campaign trail," Fenella answered, in a voice that was barely audible.

"You're what, now?" Charlotte asked, uncertain she'd correctly heard what was being said to her.

"I'm... on... her... campaign... trail..." Fenella answered, very slowly, as if merely saying the words was causing her considerable physical pain, more physical pain, that is, than she was already in. "She's got me *canvassing* for her. I went to tell her I couldn't make any more squares. But not only am I *still* making squares, but she's somehow roped me into working on her *campaign trail* as well."

Charlotte sat open-mouthed, as she was currently gobsmacked.

"Look at this monstrosity," Fenella said, unfastening her jacket, with obvious contempt at what she was about to reveal.

"Is that...?" Charlotte asked, screwing her eyes up, and moving in for a closer look to confirm what her eyes were trying to tell her but that she was still not believing.

"Yes. Yes, it is," Fenella said, with a sigh of defeat. "Amelia's given each of her canvassing team a t-shirt with her face printed on the front. She wants us to be instantly identifiable as being a proud member of the winning team. *Go, Team Sugden.* Her words, not mine."

Charlotte placed a hand over her mouth, stifling a laugh. Not that Fenella's obvious distress was in any way amusing to her. It's just that Fenella was a rather large-chested woman, and the image of Amelia plastered across her bountiful breast was therefore stretched out as if printed on an overinflated balloon. As a result, Amelia's mug was thus comically distorted. "Well, erm... Go, Team Sugden?" Charlotte offered, in the absence of anything more intelligent coming to mind.

Charlotte turned her eyes back to the playground, but Amelia was now nowhere to be seen. Sensing this to be her best opportunity to collect her son, Charlotte exited her vehicle, bidding adieu to her new acquaintance. As she walked down the steps to the playground, she glanced back, spotting poor Fenella crouching beside her Volkswagen once again, unwilling or unable to brave the battlefield ahead.

It was only a few minutes to school chucking-out time at this point, so Charlotte's intention was to just find a quiet spot to wait in peace. Now that Amelia was gone, it shouldn't have been too difficult, except...

"Oh, bollocks," Charlotte said, upon realising it was not an Amelia-free zone after all, as she had believed.

"Count on your vote for a better and safer Laxey?" Amelia said, as if she were reciting a line from a script, which essentially she was, and presenting herself before Charlotte.

"Amelia, how do you *do* that?" Charlotte asked, disgusted, and yet with a grudging sort of respect for Amelia's ability to do the very thing she'd just done. "I swear, you were nowhere to be seen not ten seconds ago, and yet here you are, like a shark after someone's just chummed the waters."

"That's because you *are* my chum, chum!" Amelia answered, her voice cloyingly sweet. "Plus, I'm just passionate about what I do!" she added cheerfully.

"Well, now that you're here, I may as well speak to you. There's something I *have* been meaning to have a word with you about," Charlotte told her, narrowing her eyes to indicate her displeasure.

"Oh?" Amelia replied, though not really interested now, casting her eyes about in search of a victim perhaps more pliable.

"I looked through your manifesto," Charlotte informed her.

"Oh. You did?" Amelia answered, returning her attention to

what might now be a potential vote stood before her.

"Yes, very interesting. I couldn't help but notice that one of your major commitments was to get crafting materials into the various nursing homes on the island," Charlotte remarked dryly.

Amelia wavered for only just a moment, like she knew what was to follow, before jumping straight in to deflect the incoming strike. "Yes, it's a splendid idea, isn't it!" she suggested cheerfully, grinning inanely.

"And this splendid idea of yours. It doesn't sound at all *familiar* to you in any way?" Charlotte asked, folding her arms across her chest.

"Why, I'm sure I have no idea what you—" Amelia began.

"This wonderful idea of yours sounds exactly like *my* idea, don't you think, Amelia?" Charlotte put forth, cutting her off, and then waiting for a response that didn't arrive. "You do remember when we were both on the radio?" she continued, laying it all out for her. "On the radio, where I said *precisely* the same thing? And that *you*, Amelia, later printed in your manifesto passing it off as your *own* idea? And as if that weren't bad enough in itself, I've come to learn that you're now bribing kids with the promise of a new gaming console, just so you can win the crafting competition. Is all of this so you can pretend to the voters what a charitable and compassionate person you are, Amelia?"

Amelia placed her hands to her face, shocked, and visibly upset, if one could believe one's eyes, at such a hurtful, untoward accusation. "Oh, Charlotte!" she said, crocodile tears arriving just in time to keep her trembling lower lip company.

At this point, as if right on cue, two compatriots of Amelia suddenly appeared, rushing in on either side to provide comfort, each throwing a scowl in Charlotte's direction for being so shamefully insensitive. It was getting a little awkward for Charlotte at present, as several other parents standing nearby were now turning to see what the kerfuffle was all about as well.

Sensing that an even larger audience would be the likely outcome, Amelia added a bit of sobbing to her performance, ramping up the volume to produce the desired effect. "Oh, but I wasn't *copying* you, Charlotte!" she wailed. "I was *inspired* by you!" she insisted, with such apparent conviction that Charlotte was beginning to squirm.

"Yes, I plead guilty, Charlotte!" Amelia went on, getting altogether into her stride and attracting even more attention thanks to her bravura performance. "I plead guilty of caring too much for the elderly in our community! And if that's a crime, well then you'll just have to lock me up and throw away the key!"

Amelia held out her hands, head bowed, inviting the shackles to be placed onto her wrists, ready, it would appear, to surrender her liberty, martyr that she was for such a worthwhile cause.

Charlotte wasn't quite sure what the hell had just occurred, how the situation had somehow come to this. It hadn't played out at all like she expected it would only a few short moments before. Right now, she felt as if she'd been trying to attack someone as innocent as Bambi, for god's sake. Or at least that's certainly the way Amelia made it appear, such was the force of her Oscar-worthy acting on display. A large number of waiting parents were now looking over, wondering who would dare upset such a kind-hearted, selfless soul as Amelia was portraying herself to be.

"Ha... ha...?" Charlotte offered, shifting her weight from one foot to the other uncomfortably. "You can put your hands down, Amelia," she said, fidgeting with her hair, and very much wishing a sinkhole might have the courtesy to make an appearance and swallow her up just then.

To Charlotte's immense relief, Amelia didn't attempt to milk the situation any further, at least for the most part. Instead, amidst a few lingering sniffles, Amelia lowered her hands, wiping away a tear that Charlotte could clearly see was never there in the first place. With any excitement to be had now having passed and no more of it imminent, the crowd around them began to disperse, and Amelia's two sidekicks also buggered off as well, all, again, much to Charlotte's relief.

"I can't believe... that is... what you thought... just then..." Amelia stammered, like a boxer on the ropes after suffering one too many blows to the head. Amelia only had an audience of one at this point in Charlotte, but she wasn't ready to give up entirely on her performance quite yet, it would appear, as she did so enjoy the spotlight.

But her punch-drunk boxer impression notwithstanding, Amelia had clearly won this bout, and the only bell Charlotte heard was the one belonging to the school, indicating the end of another day of lessons. Hundreds of kids swarmed rapidly from the building, and Charlotte stood there waiting for Stanley to catch up with her, Amelia still present, unfortunately, and looking to Charlotte as if Charlotte owed her some kind of apology or something.

"Look, I'm sorry, Amelia," Charlotte said, even though she'd done nothing wrong. "I didn't plan on—"

"No, no. No need to apologise," Amelia assured her, patting her shoulder. "If anything, I should be thanking *you*."

"What? You should?" Charlotte asked, not understanding this new direction Amelia was suddenly taking, the conversational winds having abruptly and inexplicably changed course.

"Yes," Amelia whispered, leaning in close, and glancing about to make sure there were no other ears nearby to hear. "You see, that tour-de-force exhibition I just pulled off has probably won me at *least* a dozen more votes. I have to thank you for that, Charlotte, as I simply couldn't have done that without you."

CHAPTER EIGHTEEN

For those green-fingered folk appreciative of a fine bloom, late April was a particularly glorious time of the year. The dreary, bone-chilling days of winter's frosty embrace had moved steadily aside, reluctantly making way for Mother Nature's miraculous rebirth. And as much as Charlotte appreciated the dark nights, cosying up with Stanley to watch a cheesy film next to the roaring log burner, she was always thrilled to see springtime emerge, erupting majestically into life.

As such, the only other retail outlets that could compete for her affections, the same way the crafting shops could, were the garden centres. Charlotte simply adored them. In fact, no weekend from April through September was quite complete without dragging Stanley around one of many such fine establishments on the island. Still, Stanley didn't seem to mind too much, safe in the knowledge as he was that most of them also had an onsite coffee shop and hence delicious cake to tempt the two of them after their often-prolonged traipse.

And so, with her love of such locations already firmly in place, when Calum suggested meeting up for a coffee, with Riley's Garden Centre as their destination, well, Charlotte didn't really need asking twice. However, it absolutely *wasn't* a date, though, as Charlotte had sought to remind herself multiple times since Calum's first message arrived. No, it was just an innocent coffee with a man she'd just met. The fact there was no alternative agenda suggested by him — other than grabbing a coffee — meant that this was most certainly *not* a date. No way, as why would someone suggest a first date held at ten in the morning in a busy coffee shop? Muddying the waters, though, was Mollie, implying that if there was no other agenda proposed, then what else *could* it be if not a date?

Oh, the turmoil running through her mind was all-consuming!

As she didn't in fact know what Calum's motives were — romantic or otherwise — at this particular point in time, Charlotte opted for the smart-casual approach rather than the smart-glamorous option (the latter being her default had it been confirmed as an actual date). Her woollen tweed blazer over a cream-coloured shirt was, she thought, entirely appropriate for a breakfast appointment at a garden centre; that is, demonstrating she'd made an effort, but not *too* much effort. She didn't want to appear overly eager, of course.

However, one aspect of the day that might well indeed have been considered overly eager was her arrival at the garden centre some forty-five minutes earlier than the scheduled, agreed-upon meeting time. For Charlotte, it meant she wasn't running around at the last minute, fighting the heavy traffic and such, and eventually arriving in a stressed, sweating heap. This way, with time on her side, it meant she could spend some quality alone time inspecting the floral arrangements on display, wondering how much of the money she didn't actually have could be spent enhancing her own garden.

Charlotte ambled through the indoor plants and pots section, a contented smile on her face, sniffing liberally as she went along.

"Can I help you, madam?" a chirpy fellow in green overalls asked, wiping his soil-covered hands on the sides of his thighs.

"No, but thanks," Charlotte replied. "Although I'm sure I want to buy nearly everything!"

"I'd be happy to oblige," the fellow said optimistically, hopeful of a sale. "Shout if you need any assistance!"

Charlotte offered a friendly wave as she saw the man off, and then continued on. She was now approaching Stanley's absolute favourite spot in the store (apart from the café, of course), which always introduced itself to them through the smart, uniform row of proud, impressive-looking garden machinery sat there just waiting to be chosen for their moment to shine.

Charlotte felt a tinge of guilt for being there on her own without her normal garden centre companion at her side. By now,
Stanley would ordinarily be sat astride the largest of the racing-
green ride-on lawnmowers, similar in stature and proportion to
that of a prize bull. The shop assistant would usually suspect there
was no intention or likelihood of an imminent sale but would often oblige Stanley by handing him a product brochure anyway,
once, the year before, even playfully going as far as discussing fi-
nance options with him, much to Stanley's delight. This sales patter must have struck a chord with Stanley, as the previous Christmas he was fairly determined that the lawnmower should be the
only item on his list for Santa. Sadly, as Charlotte was at pains to
point out, they had no grass to speak of in their garden to cut. And
even if they had, the mower was unlikely to even fit through their
garden gate in any case. For this reason, amongst others, Charlotte
suggested Stanley may wish to consider revisiting his list, but the
boy was not for turning. Of his own volition, Stanley later wandered down to the local cricket club to offer his future grass-cut-
ting services (once his Christmas present had arrived, as it surely
would) in return for the modest fee of a Coke and a packet of crisps
from behind the bar. The plucky would-be gardener even appeared in the local paper after the cricket groundsman regaled a
journalist friend with the tale of young Stanley's generous offer.
As for Stanley, the new bicycle that eventually *did* arrive via Saint
Nick's reindeer-powered sleigh proved, much to Charlotte's relief,
to be a perfectly acceptable alternative gift.

Once past the mowers and such, Charlotte stepped outside into
the warm spring air, gazing longingly at the selection of green-
houses on display. She could totally see herself in one, tending to
her homegrown produce, like Barbara from *The Good Life*. But
again, sadly, the modest size of her garden wouldn't accommodate such an addition, incredible as it might have been, and so a
dream it would need to remain.

"Ooh," Charlotte said, directed to the roses by her twitching
nostrils, the roses tantalising her with both their vibrant colours
and magnificent scent. Located just behind the floral display was
an old potting shed that she'd watched the resident gardener

working his magic in on previous occasions. Directly outside the shed was an old wooden door lying across four barrels and currently repurposed as a makeshift worktop. The surface was jam-packed with rose bushes and clippings. Judging by the earthen mess surrounding them, they'd just been re-potted, perhaps in preparation for their appearance in front of the paying public.

Charlotte looked the bushes over, wondering which one she might buy if she in fact had the money to buy one. It was silly, she knew, but she always worried about those plants and flowers left behind, as if their feelings could be hurt at having not been chosen by anyone.

Just then, interrupting her ruminations about the possible worry and distress felt by neglected plants and any lasting psychological harm they might suffer as a result, Charlotte felt a small splash of water land on her shoulder. She glanced skyward, wondering if a passing shower could be the culprit, but with not a cloud in sight this scenario seemed unlikely. "What's all this, then?" she said, wiping the water droplets from her blazer, looking about in order to locate their potential source. "Hello?" she said, in the direction of the potting shed, wondering if someone there were perhaps playing silly beggars at her expense. Then, without warning, a full stream of water arched through the air before Charlotte had any chance to move, or even react. The full force hit her squarely in the face, knocking her back a pace in surprise. "Blllawwa!" she spluttered, mouth full of cold water.

Instinctively, she raised her hands to protect herself, but all this succeeded in doing was to disperse the flow in all directions, drenching both her jacket and her jeans in the process. Charlotte jumped to her left, so the water hitting the ground now splashed at her feet, beside her. "Stop it!" she yelled to persons unknown, and wondering, for a moment, if it was an automated watering system she'd perhaps inadvertently triggered somehow. However, this was not the case, as the water flow immediately ceased in response to her command.

"Hello...?" came the tentative, squeaky, worried-sounding voice of what seemed to be an adolescent male youth. "Hello?" the voice could be heard again, with the person in question appearing into view from behind the potting shed, hosepipe in hand, and with the hose still dribbling water from the nozzle. The lad, maybe sixteen if he was a day, gawped in Charlotte's direction with a *what-on-earth-are-you-doing-stood-there* type of expression painted over his confused and surprised face. "Uhm..." he said, scratching the inside of his ear. "Are you okay...? I mean..."

"I'm bloody soaked, is what I am!" Charlotte barked at him, shaking herself down like a Jack Russell terrier fresh out of the bath. "What on earth do you mean by turning the hose on me?" Charlotte demanded, stamping her foot to show this young rotter she was none too pleased with the current situation.

The lad, for his part, stood rooted to the spot, looking anxious, perhaps realising his safety was in imminent jeopardy. "Erm..." he said in response, finger still wedged firmly in his ear, "I was watering the roses I've just re-potted...?"

"Do the roses *look* like they've been watered?" Charlotte asked, extending her hand to introduce the wooden door, pointing at the bone-dry blooms sat atop the makeshift table with not a drop of water to be seen anywhere on or about them or even in the same general vicinity.

"No. No, I suppose they don't," the lad was forced to admit. "I'm sorry, I didn't mean to soak you," he explained. "It's just that if I stand exactly where I was, behind the potting shed, then I can water all the plants from that position without having to move each time."

"Only you *didn't*," Charlotte was quick to remind him. "Your roses are still dying of thirst, and I look like a drowned rat."

"I'm sorry, miss," the lad said, apologising again, head bowed and duly chastised. He went quiet for a moment, then slowly lifting his bumfluff-covered chin, staring vacantly off into the distance, and quite possibly questioning his career choices. "Wait, hang on," he said, suddenly slightly more assured now, while raising up the limp hosepipe in his left hand to take a peek at his watch. "Yes, I thought so. You shouldn't even be *in* here," he advised, polite yet firm. "This part of the store doesn't open until ten. Which is why I was watering the plants just now, safe in the knowledge that there shouldn't be anybody walking around to accidentally soak, see?"

"And how am I meant to bloody know that?" Charlotte answered, unfastening the buttons on her blazer to further survey the water-borne damage. "Look at the state of my shirt!" she said, looking down to the sodden V-shaped area on her chest where the shirt hadn't been protected by her blazer.

The lad stood up onto his tiptoes, looking over to the entrance Charlotte had arrived through. "A-*ha*," he said, using the yellow nozzle on his hose to point the way. "Look," he said, tipping his head in the direction of the entranceway. "Two traffic cones connected by a rope were blocking the way. I put them there myself. And there's even a sign dangling from the rope between them saying we're not open until *ten*," he told her. "Oh, and wouldn't you know it. Somebody appears to have *moved the cones*," he added, affording himself the merest hint of a smile, and allowing his remark to be delivered with just the slightest suggestion of sarcasm.

Charlotte pursed her lips, choosing not to glance in the direction he was pointing as she knew exactly what she was going to see there. "Yes, well, I may have shifted them just a little, just a *teensy bit*," she confessed. "I was captivated by the petunias, so I moved the cones to get through," she explained, and then adding, although not terribly convincingly, "I reckoned someone must have simply left them there by mistake or something."

"It's fine," the lad offered. "I should probably have still looked before I started anyway," he graciously allowed. "Can I do anything to help?"

"Well, unless you have a hairdryer, then I don't suppose there is," Charlotte answered, removing her jacket and shaking off the excess moisture from it as best she could. She then draped her blazer over her arm, looking down at the damp patch on her chest with a sigh.

"Ah!" said the lad, dropping his hosepipe. "I might be able to go one better than a hairdryer!" he proposed, and at which point he scurried away, disappearing into the confines of the potting shed.

Moments later, Charlotte was startled by what sounded much like an old motorbike engine bursting into life. "What the devil...?" she said, taking a few cautionary steps backward.

Like one of the Ghostbusters readying themselves for action, the lad burst back onto the scene, appearing from the potting shed with an industrial leaf blower strapped on over his shoulders. "THIS WILL DRY YOU OFF IN NO TIME!" he hollered over the hellacious racket of the spluttering two-stroke engine, pleased as Punch, and eager, it would appear, to remedy the drenching disaster of his own making.

"Oh, *hell* no," Charlotte said, immediately raising her hands in a defensive posture.

"Wait until you feel the power of this thing!" the lad said. "Ah! Let me just show you!" he suggested, noticing Charlotte's rather obvious reticence. "And then you can decide if I should continue, okay?"

He raised the blower, taking care to direct the tip of the device away from a somewhat panic-stricken Charlotte. He gave the trigger a gentle squeeze, releasing a stream of air similar to that of a Boeing 747's jet engine roaring to life. "Eh…?! Eh…?!" he shouted excitedly, waggling his eyebrows. He swivelled his hips slightly, directing the flow of the air so it just caressed Charlotte's right arm (if by "caressed" one means being buffeted by hurricane-force winds). "What do you reckon?!" he asked, hoping to receive the green light to crank things up a notch, increasing the airflow even more (although Charlotte didn't know how this might even be possible, as after all, what could possibly be stronger than a hurricane or a typhoon?).

"I'm fine!" Charlotte shouted, vigorously flailing her hands to indicate she wasn't entirely on board with this idea and wished to proceed no further. "I'm just going to go!" she called out, over the roar of the machine.

He'd done his best, the lad. So, with Charlotte clearly not too enthused about his plan, he decided they could only go their separate ways at this point and, he hoped, part on good terms. He slung the blower around, from off of his back, releasing his finger from the trigger as he did so.

But as he repositioned the blower, attempting to set it down on the ground, the engine winding down still produced a firm burst of air. Even faced with only a quickly decelerating engine, in fact, the bone-dry overflow compost on his makeshift potting table was blown clear off the door in less than a second from the remainder of the suddenly redirected airflow. "Shit," he said, immediately realising the error of his ways, as Charlotte was stood right in the line of fire. He dropped the blower, letting it fall the final foot or so and clatter to the ground. "Shit," he said again, afraid to look up and survey what sort of damage he might possibly have wrought. When he eventually did, he was greeted by the sight of a startled Charlotte, still stood there with her hands raised in protest. Fortunately, most of the propelled compost had scattered harmlessly, landing on the concrete path, but alas, not all. Indeed, a smattering had landed on her chest, hitting the soaking-wet fabric of her shirt, and, in the process, leaving it a dirty shade of chocolate brown.

"Absolutely marvellous. I didn't think it could get any better, but now it has," Charlotte said with a sigh, looking down at the muddy mess on her chest. "This is just wonderful."

Charlotte's efforts to dry herself off in the ladies' lav had failed miserably. The hand dryer there didn't have as much drying power as she'd hoped, and besides that, there was still the matter of her soiled shirt (and bra, too, as it turned out). With no time to head home and change, she briefly considered going commando underneath her blazer, but the wool of her blazer was itchier than expected and was also, with no shirt underneath, a little too revealing — so that idea was quickly chucked in the bin. Her only other option that she could see was to purchase something to wear from the garden centre shop. Unfortunately, the selection of clothing on offer in-store was limited, to say the least, what with it being a garden centre and all. She could have her pick of Wellington boots in a variety of colours, for instance, or even gardening trousers with a padded knee if she so desired. But anything else was likely to be in short supply, as one might expect. There were t-shirts, however, and after requesting assistance she was directed to a small selection located next to the garden tools. But the issue with these, as she soon discovered, was that they were all novelty shirts printed with a variety of gardening-themed images and slogans on them. Oh, and the fact that the smallest size they had in stock was a Men's Large didn't help matters any, either. Still, with no other option available and her meeting time rapidly approaching, she bought the least offensive one she could find, figuring most of it would be covered by her blazer anyway.

So, after a quick change into her new t-shirt — which sported the following catchy phrase: *SOMETIMES I WET MY PLANTS* — Charlotte headed to the café where she was pleased to see Calum seated and awaiting her arrival. Her blazer was still damp to the touch, but she was looking reasonably presentable overall, she felt confident, all things considered.

"Fancy meeting you here," Charlotte said with a chuckle, acting casual, and trying her best to act as if nothing at all was out of the ordinary.

"It's good to see you," Calum said, standing like a true gentleman to welcome his guest. He moved around the table, easing her chair out from under the table.

"Why, thank you, kind sir," Charlotte said, appreciative of the old-fashioned chivalry on offer.

Calum smiled, taking a small step forward, readying himself to push her chair in once she'd sat down. Charlotte, however, misread his sudden movement, offering up her right cheek at the same time as Calum extended a hand, inviting her to sit down.

"Oh. Sorry," she said, flustered and embarrassed. "I thought you were going to, erm..." she explained, motioning to her cheek.

"Not a bad idea, necessarily," Calum suggested with a grin. "But, moment's probably gone now?" he advised, lowering his hand as she took her seat. "Coffee?" he asked, with one eye on the waitress who was floating past.

"Please!" Charlotte answered, eager to move past the awkward moment just experienced.

"Two coffees, please," Calum asked of the waitress, who slowed by their table in response. "So..." he said to Charlotte, once the waitress had headed back to the kitchen to gather their order. "How's the craft squares coming along?"

Charlotte nodded her head enthusiastically. "Terrific," she said. "Sadly, I don't think we're going to be topping the league table. But the folks involved are having a lot of fun, and that's what it's really all about, I suppose."

"Ah," Calum said. "That kind of ties in with me suggesting a coffee today."

"It does?" Charlotte asked, a little confused, not too sure what he meant. Also, she wasn't exactly listening to him at this point. She wasn't trying to be rude; rather, she'd simply found herself lost in his face. She ran her eyes over him, trying to work out his age. Ordinarily, she was usually fairly good at placing someone's age, but with Calum, it was a bit of a struggle. It was the grey that was throwing her off, she reckoned. While he looked relatively young, his brown hair had bits of grey here and there, as did his closely cropped, well-trimmed salt-and-pepper beard. She guessed he was in his early forties, though she wasn't overly confident in this estimate. As for his broader appearance in general, once again, he was impeccably dressed in a charcoal-grey herringbone suit with crisp white shirt. Also, as an important bit of information, she did happen to notice the absence of any ring on his finger.

"Yes. This is my gran," Calum announced, opening his wallet and removing a passport-sized photograph from inside.

"Oh? Oh, yes," Charlotte replied politely, sensing that she must have missed a portion of dialogue while daydreaming, as this would otherwise have been a somewhat odd way for Calum to start off a conversation. "She's, ehm… pretty?" Charlotte offered, thinking this to be a safe enough answer no matter what Calum may have been speaking about.

"You're very kind," Calum answered, returning the picture and closing his wallet over. "Just so you understand, I'm not in the habit of showing pictures of my gran to every woman I'm only just getting to know," he added, laughing gently. "Only, as I was saying, she's the reason I'm involved in sponsoring the competition."

Charlotte smiled, nodding at him to continue.

"She's gone now," Calum revealed. "Sadly, she had dementia," he told her, the strain of what was obviously a painful memory showing across his otherwise handsome face.

"I'm sorry," Charlotte replied sympathetically. "That must have been difficult."

"It was," he said. "But she was a fighter, was Gran. Anyway, a long story short, Charlotte, do you know what kept a smile on her face right until the day she died?"

Charlotte wanted to offer him an answer but didn't wish to get it wrong, put her foot in it, and possibly cause offence. For this reason, she merely nodded again, encouraging him to continue once more.

"Crafting," said Calum, answering his own question. "Knitting, in particular. Even in her most challenging days, it was the one thing that always made her happy and kept her going. And that's why I was pleased to get involved in sponsoring the Square If You Care initiative, you see. Knowing what a boon it was to Gran, I hoped it would bring passion and joy to others as well, and groups of all ages, mind you, not just old folk, as they all got into the competition."

"It's working," Charlotte was entirely happy to report. "I think there are eleven or so groups taking part in total, if I recall, with plenty of different people within those groups, and with help being solicited from the broader community as well. So lots and lots of people have taken the plunge, and are up to their elbows in squares."

"Thank you," Calum said, looking up to the waitress unloading their coffee from her tray just then.

"I did wonder," Charlotte said, taking possession of her cup. "And this explains much, as your company didn't quite sound like the type that would ordinarily concern itself with such matters as the local crafting movement. Not that I actually know what your company does, if I'm frank."

"We're in technology," Calum explained (though this didn't tell Charlotte an awful lot, actually). "Anyway, my sister, knowing me as well as she does, told me about the league competition and suggested it would be a nice idea if I sponsored it. And she was absolutely right."

"Well, my gang at the Crafternoon Sewcial Club were delighted to see you," Charlotte said, blowing the steam from her coffee.

"I've been around and visited every group," Calum confided. "And I've loved every minute of it."

"Every group?" Charlotte asked, impressed, but also wondering if he had indeed visited quite *every* group, as she couldn't imagine him loving "every minute" of being in *Amelia's* presence.

"Every one!" Calum was pleased to confirm. "There was a mother-and-toddlers' group in Peel, a retired nurses group in Castletown, you guys in Union Mills, and of course the coffee morning group in Laxey. That's just to name a few."

"Wow," Charlotte said, duly impressed. "It's nice to see you're actually getting involved as well as providing a good portion of the prize money."

"Do you know what I've noticed, and is so good to see?" Calum asked, before pressing ahead, answering his own question again. "Amongst all these groups, I've observed a wonderful mix of people involved. We've got folks of all different ages involved, both male and female, and all with varying levels of ability and experience, novices working side by side with seasoned pros. And what they've all got in common, each and every one, is the sheer enjoyment of crafting bringing them all together. It's exactly what I hoped for when I got involved, and to see it happening around our island is certainly inspiring and encouraging. If my gran were still alive, no doubt she would have enjoyed getting stuck in."

Charlotte wanted so much to reach over the table and take Calum's hand right then, but wasn't sure it would be appropriate. "It's a good thing you're doing," she told him, smiling fondly.

"Thanks for that," Calum said, smiling back.

There was something Charlotte was very anxious to find out about, and she hoped she wasn't being too terribly insensitive for bringing it up just then, but she was simply dying to know. "So..." she said, easing into her enquiry as gracefully as she could, which, as it turned out, wasn't really all that graceful, actually. "So, if you were with the Laxey coffee morning group, did you happen to see Cruella de Vil, by chance?"

"Cruella de Vil? I'm... not sure...?" Calum answered with a

laugh, appearing not to mind the slight conversational redirect Charlotte had employed, but also appearing not to get her joke.

Charlotte waved away her slightly unsuccessful attempt at humour, explaining, "Sorry. Just teasing. The lady in Laxey, the head of their group, is something of a battle-axe, as I guess you might call her. They're top of the leaderboard, but that's probably only because she's running a sweatshop over there."

"A sweatshop...?" Calum said, once again appearing not to be in on the joke. "Are you talking about Amelia?"

"Yes, that's right," Charlotte replied. "Although I'm not entirely serious about that whole sweatshop thing, of course," she added, feeling the need to backpedal a bit. "But I think it's fair to say she *is* something of an 'acquired taste,' as my postman has so aptly put it."

"Ah," Calum offered, lowering his head for a moment. "This is a bit awkward."

"What? Oh, sugar, I've not put my foot in it, have I?" Charlotte asked, panicked, sensing she'd said something awful though not sure precisely what it might be. "Wait, she's not your girlfriend, is she?" Charlotte asked, casting about for possible explanations as to why Calum had suddenly reacted the way he just did. "Oh my god, she's your girlfriend, isn't she?" she said, now convinced this must be so. "She's your girlfriend, and here's me just now going and accusing her of running a sweatshop, and—"

"She's *not* my girlfriend," Calum jumped in, promptly reassuring the flailing Charlotte, and saving her from prattling on further.

"She's not?"

"No," Calum answered. "But you know when I mentioned earlier about my sister talking me into sponsoring the event...?"

"Amelia's your *sister*?" Charlotte replied, quickly putting two and two together.

"Yes," Calum confirmed with a smile. "And for what it's worth, she *can* be a bit... difficult, on occasion," he offered.

Charlotte buried her face in her hands. "I'm so sorry," she said, peeking out from her fingers, cheeks red. "I'm sorry. Honestly, if I'd have known—"

"You're fine," Calum entered in, reassuring her once again, and graciously putting her out of her misery. "So, anyway," he went on, moving things along. "The reason for dragging you out here today..."

"Yes?" Charlotte answered, fanning her burning cheeks with her napkin.

"Would you be willing to model for me?" Calum asked, coming fairly straight to the point.

"Oh! Not like... that is, I don't mean..." he quickly added, realising what he must've sounded like just then, and attempting to explain. "I don't mean in an unsavoury sort of way or anything."

"That's a shame," Charlotte joked, thrusting her chest out, and accompanying this with a sultry pout.

It was now Calum's turn to blush. "I should probably clarify," he said. "What I mean to say is, would you and your fellow *club members* consider being models?" he asked.

Seeing a blank look facing back at him from across the table, Calum explained further. "I'm hopeful of funding a website and then a promotional video for the charity," he said. "When people see how it's really pulling all areas of the community together, my hope is that it will encourage others to get involved. And, as you and your group were having so much fun, I thought you would make ideal subjects, and your enthusiasm would really come across on camera."

"Will I need to get used to signing autographs?" Charlotte asked, swirling her hand, writing her name in the air.

"Yes. I would expect so."

"Well, in that case, I'm in," she said. "Of course, I'll need to check in with the others to ensure they're okay with the idea as well. But they're not exactly shy, so I don't imagine it being a problem."

"That's wonderful, and I'm really looking forward to this," Calum replied. "Can I take a note of your mobile number?" he asked. "It'll be easier to get in touch if I have your number, I reckon, as opposed to communicating through LinkedIn messages or trying to get through to your answer machine at home."

"Yes, of course. In fact, I've had some Crafternoon business cards printed, so I'll give you one of those," Charlotte answered, reaching down for her handbag. "The shop in town just did them for me, so you'll have the honour of being the first person to receive one."

"Splendid," said Calum.

Charlotte set her bag on the tabletop, delving into its dark recesses, and humming along to herself as she performed her search. "Just a tick," she said, rummaging around in what was essentially her mobile office, beauty station, A&E department, and small sewing item haberdashery. It was impressive how much stuff Charlotte was able to cram in her bag, but it did sometimes make finding things a bit of a challenge.

"Ah! Here we go," she said, finally locating what she was looking for. She grabbed hold of the clear plastic case protecting her new business cards, excited to take the box out on its maiden voyage. "I even had the lettering on them embossed," she explained. "It cost a little extra, but not all that much, really, and I think it makes them look so..."

But as Charlotte started to remove her arm from the bag, box in hand, her watchstrap caught on the clasp of the muddied bra she'd stuffed into her bag when changing in the women's loo earlier.

"... nice," she said, finishing her sentence at the same time as her bra, now dangling from her wrist, was drawn free from her bag. She flapped her hand furiously, hoping to shake the thing off, but the intimate article in question was nothing if not tenacious. Mortified, and having no luck to speak of, she plunged her hand back into her bag — unyielding undergarment still attached — where it would at least be concealed from the prying eyes of any patrons of the coffee shop possibly sat nearby.

"It's... it's brown because of compost!" she told Calum desperately, certain he wouldn't believe her (and unsure how to explain it even if he did).

"I'm not even going to ask," a bemused-looking Calum replied.

"It's probably best you don't," Charlotte agreed, continuing her struggle inside the bag, unable to make any headway.

Calum watched from a distance, from over on his side of the

table, thinking it best not to try and interfere. "I'd offer to help, but you know how bloody useless us men are at removing bras," he said with a grin.

"It's... it's still caught on my watch," Charlotte told Calum, updating him on the situation. "I... I might need to just take this watch off and untangle the rest when I get home," she said, troubleshooting out loud. "Ehm, do help yourself to a business card while I try and sort this out...?" she suggested.

"Thank you, I will," Calum said, removing the plastic lid from the box that had fallen to the table during the earlier hand-flapping stage of Charlotte's struggle, and then helping himself to one of the cards held therein. "Ah. The embossing *does* look quite nice, doesn't it?" he offered, admiring the card by running his thumb over the surface.

"Yes, yes..." Charlotte replied, distracted by the task at hand.

"Right. Em... there was just one other thing I wanted to ask you, Charlotte?" Calum put forth.

"Hmm? What's that?" she replied, still wrestling with her bra, which was by now hopelessly entangled about her wrist, her struggle with it only having made it worse.

"I wondered if you'd like to go out with me one evening? Say, on a date?" Calum ventured bravely. "As in a proper date?"

Charlotte stopped what she was doing, looking over to Calum, certain he was having her on. "You do know I'm presently wearing a men's t-shirt that says, *Sometimes I wet my plants,* yes? And that the shirt I *was* wearing is crammed inside my bag, covered in muck, just like my bra that's currently stuck to my wrist?"

"Well, I suppose things can only improve, right?" Calum replied.

"Yes, it's a date, then. That sounds lovely," she happily agreed. "But... for now... You, erm, couldn't possibly ask the waitress if she might have a pair of scissors, could you?"

CHAPTER NINETEEN

L axey really was a most splendid place to call home at any time of year and under any possible conditions, but throw in a generous helping of golden sunshine and it became an absolute utopia. Living a stone's throw away from the beach was a godsend for both Charlotte and Stanley. With the longer evenings returning, they'd think nothing of taking advantage of the extended hours of sunlight by packing a flask of tea, along with a few snacks, and heading through the narrow cottage-lined streets to spend an hour or two or more exploring the rocky tide pools at the coast or ascending the bordering cliff walks up to the headland to enjoy a panoramic view over the village. These simple pleasures had been enjoyed by Charlotte when she was a child, and to witness Stanley splashing about now, using his pond-dipping net to see what marvels had been left behind from the previous tide, both warmed her heart and brought her own fond childhood memories flooding back.

Of course, it wasn't just Charlotte and Stanley out enjoying the great outdoors, whenever they could, during the warmer weather. Peppered intermittently across the gilded sands were other families making use of this pearl on their doorstep as well. Some of them enjoyed a BBQ, with the delicious mix of aromas wafting gloriously on the sea breeze, tantalising the senses. Others were content to merely sit and relax, listening to the gentle waves of the Irish Sea lapping rhythmically against the shore. And still others might dare to take a paddle in the cold, briny ocean waters whenever the mood should strike. What was apparent, though, in all cases, and was wonderful to see, was the distinct absence of iPads, or any other form of electronic types of distraction for that matter. It was a throwback to a much simpler time overall, where the casting of a fishing line into the water brought a special kind of pleasure, for instance, or the nimble plucking from the air of a moving frisbee brought forth squeals of delight from any of the children who might be involved. And Charlotte wouldn't swop this seaside paradise for anything.

Presently, on one such evening's happy outing to the coastline, Stanley and Charlotte spotted Mrs Ringwald, Stanley's teacher, sat on the seawall, running her tongue over a generous serving of Whippy ice cream. She looked as if she were in a contented world of her own just then, so Charlotte thought it best to leave good Mrs Ringwald undisturbed as she and Stanley continued their current journey of exploration along the beach. This, however, did not appear to be a mindset shared by Stanley…

"Hiya, Mrs Ringwald!" Stanley shouted, apparently deciding his teacher hadn't seen quite enough of him for the day.

Charlotte instituted a slight course correction, so that Stanley and herself were now walking up the beach's gentle slope towards where Harriet — or "Mrs Ringwald," to the children in her care — could be currently found.

"That looks lovely," Charlotte offered, admiring Mrs Ringwald's frozen treat once stood before her. "Anyway, sorry. You looked like you were in a trance, so I wasn't about to bother you, but m'laddo here clearly had other ideas," she said with a smile.

"I've been doing my homework!" Stanley announced proudly, holding up his sketchbook to his teacher for her inspection. "I drew a picture of a shore crab! But then I dropped my book in the water and it got kinda ruined, I guess, so I suppose I'll need to draw it again once I get home!"

"I very much look forward to seeing the final result, Stanley," Mrs Ringwald told him, before quickly attending again to her ice cream for a moment, catching up any possible drips to prevent them from making a mess over her clothing.

As far as schoolteachers went, Mrs Ringwald was, in Stanley's own words, pretty cool. Charlotte was also fond of her, impressed by how Stanley had really come out of his shell, so to speak, under her expert stewardship this school year. She was also a keen crafter, Charlotte knew, which of course only endeared her even further to Charlotte. Unfortunately, Charlotte had not been quite quick enough out of the starting gate to secure Harriet's membership in the Crafternooners, Amelia being one step ahead in that respect and recruiting several teachers to join her LAXEY COFFEE MORNING CREW. Fortunately, at least, where the relationship between Charlotte and the teaching faculty was concerned, the squares competition was viewed purely through the lens of a very friendly rivalry (although the same, of course, may not have been said about Amelia, who seemed to consider the squares competition a much more cutthroat affair).

"Oh, and congratulations on winding Amelia up so much," Harriet joked, turning to Charlotte from Stanley. "I don't think I've ever seen her so animated as she was after school today."

"Oh?" Charlotte replied. "I'm not sure how I did *that*, exactly. But I'd be delighted to learn more," she said with a grin.

"I take it you didn't bump into her today?" Harriet asked, stepping down from the seawall, and joining Charlotte to stand on the beach's pebbly portion.

"Mum, can I explore a bit?" Stanley asked, the conversation having apparently turned to slightly more grown-up topics of discussion, and thus becoming suddenly too boring for him.

"Go ahead. Just stay close!" Charlotte answered.

And then, turning her attention back to Harriet, Charlotte said, "And no. No, I didn't bump into Amelia earlier today, to answer your question. Although I definitely would have enjoyed witnessing the poor dear getting herself all worked up into a lather, I have to admit."

Charlotte, as it transpired, had done a fairly admirable job of avoiding Amelia after suffering through the unpleasantness of the previous week's histrionics session at the school playground. And so she wondered what she could conceivably have done to set Amelia off, as Charlotte had been making it a point to steer well clear of her.

"It wasn't anything to do with... with a man, was it?" Charlotte proposed tentatively, in the absence of any other possible issue she imagined might provoke Amelia. She was wondering if perhaps word had somehow filtered back about her planning to go on a date with Amelia's brother, and if this was in fact what had kicked up the proverbial hornet's nest.

"A *man*?" Harriet asked, looking surprised but intrigued. "Not that I know of, Charlotte. Is there something you're not telling us...?"

"Oh, I wish!" Charlotte replied, laughing the suggestion off, and pretending as if there were no reason — absolutely none at all! — that she'd brought such a thing up. "So, did she, you know, give any clue as to why she might be annoyed with me?" Charlotte asked, fishing around for answers.

Harriet looked as if she was unsure if she was being teased at this point. And that was because she was, in fact, unsure if she was being teased at this point. "About the *league table*, of course," she offered after a moment, when Charlotte continued to stare at her blankly.

"Oh! Right!" Charlotte replied, in a way that suggested she totally understood, even though she totally *didn't* understand. "The league table has annoyed Amelia...?" she asked, hoping for some manner of clarification. Because, as far as Charlotte was aware, Amelia's group maintained quite a considerable lead, and there was no real reason to believe this could have changed.

"Well, yes. Of course," Harriet said with a laugh. "In particular, the fact that your crafting group is now above her group? Well, above *our* crafting group, I should say, as I'm a member of Amelia's group also."

"Wait, hang on," Charlotte answered, raising a finger in the air as she tried to catch up. "Are you saying the Laxey Coffee Morning Crew have dropped down the league table?"

"I'll take it from the surprised expression on your face that you've not looked at the current scores?"

"We were eighth place last week," Charlotte recalled, painfully. "So I didn't think there was really very much point in checking the present status," she explained. "But... I don't understand. Amelia's group *cannot* have dropped so far down the leaderboard, could they? And that quickly, in only one week? How is that even possible?"

Harriet dispatched the small remaining portion of her ice cream cone, appearing quite excited on Charlotte's behalf at what she was about to reveal to her. "Charlotte," Harriet told her, "Charlotte, your Crafternoon Sewcial Club are not only ahead of Amelia, you're top of the league! You've overtaken everyone, *including* Amelia!"

"Shut the front door!" Charlotte replied, a broad grin emerging as she realised Harriet was being completely serious here and not at all having her on. "How on earth are we top of the league??"

Harriet raised her palms to the heavens. "You've got me, Charlotte. But you are."

Charlotte could barely contain her excitement. She ran her fingers through her fringe, looking around for Stanley so she could share the fantastic news. Stanley, however, was down by the water's edge, just outside of easy reach, shoes and socks off, busy being chased by the incoming waves and getting his feet wet. Charlotte thus returned her attention to Harriet. "Hmm. There's only one full week or thereabouts left of the competition," she said, thinking aloud. "I wonder if we could actually win this?"

"You could," Harriet offered.

Even though Harriet was technically amongst the opposition, it was obvious to Charlotte that Harriet was genuinely pleased for her.

"Although, I should probably warn you that Amelia's already on the offensive," Harriet added.

"Oh?"

"Yeah. She's been cajoling more of the parents in the playground, and she's already sent two emails through to the members' email list, ramping up the pressure for the final week. Just keep doing whatever it is you're doing, Charlotte. It appears to be working!"

"Oh, I will," Charlotte said, punching her closed fist into the palm of her other hand in a show of steely determination. "I just wish I knew what I've done, exactly, so that I can keep on doing it!"

"Well, good luck," Harriet told her. "Ah. I should go," she added, glancing at her watch. "Amelia has scheduled an emergency crafting Zoom call in half an hour. I'm only joining in to see just how worked up she gets! Anyway, please tell Stanley that I'll see him tomorrow."

"Of course," Charlotte said, her head still reeling from the most excellent — if slightly inexplicable — news she'd just received. "Enjoy your Zoom call, and you'll have to let me know how it went."

Harriet went quiet for a moment, looking down towards Stanley at the water's edge, reflectively. "You know, you should be very proud of yourself, Charlotte," she said after a bit.

"Oh? How do you mean?" Charlotte asked, certainly happy enough to receive such a compliment, but in the dark as far as what it was in reference to.

"No, honestly. Stanley tells us all about your volunteering work at the nursing home, and now also with the Crafternooners," Harriet explained. "It's quite inspiring, I have to say, and it's actually one of the main reasons I originally agreed to get involved in the crafting square competition in the first place. I only wish now that I hadn't agreed to be in Amelia's group in particular, as I don't think I was prepared for Amelia being..."

Harriet seemed to be searching for the right words, and perhaps struggling to refrain from having those words include any profanity. Charlotte jumped in, finishing Harriet's sentence for her and saving the day. "For Amelia being the way she is," Charlotte offered.

"That's a good way to put it!" Harriet replied with a laugh, settling on that description. "Anyway, keep up the amazing work!"

"Thank you, Harriet," Charlotte said. "That really does mean a lot."

"Right. I better start walking home," Harriet advised. "I don't want to get shouted at for being late to the Zoom session..."

An hour later, and the entire stretch of Laxey beach had been scoured for anything at all Stanley felt was deserving of his attention. He'd also spotted two intrepid fellows armed with metal detectors during his investigations, which had rather captured his imagination, and because of this, the short walk home was filled with less-than-subtle hints from Stanley. He felt confident that it was his duty — as a proud Manxman! — to uncover the countless priceless cultural treasures buried underfoot, something he would absolutely be pleased to do if only he had his very own metal detector.

With Stanley's birthday rapidly approaching — as he well knew, and thus the hints — Charlotte told him she'd have to see how things went, as she was currently fairly skint (though she didn't use those exact words), but that she would absolutely keep it in mind. For now, at least, the Manx Indiana Jones would need to settle for his current pond-dipping net and plastic shovel setup in pursuit of his treasure hunting goals, he was told.

Once home, and with the taste of salty sea air still fresh in their lungs, Charlotte felt that a mug of hot chocolate would be just the ticket to round off a thoroughly splendid evening. Stanley was totally on board with this plan, of course. But first, he scurried away to his room to find another sketchpad so he could start in on redrawing his currently water-damaged portrait of Mr Crabby from earlier.

Charlotte's laptop was fired up in the kitchen while the milk for the hot chocolate was heating on the stove. She had no reason to doubt Harriet Ringwald, but she couldn't shake the feeling that there must have been some sort of mistake, and so she had to check for herself. Of course, whatever she was to find, she knew that her two crafting clubs had put in an admirable shift either way, and that was all Charlotte could ever ask of them. Victory in the competition would have been sweet, obviously, but the underlying goal had always been to bring people together for a collective purpose and to have fun, something they'd achieved and then some.

So, at this point, even if the CRAFTERNOON SEWCIAL CLUB were bringing up the rear, trailing in very last place, well, it *still* would have been mission accomplished as far as Charlotte was concerned. However, that didn't stop Charlotte from wincing in anticipation — bracing herself for the worst, yet daring to believe — as she waited for her ancient, lagging computer to respond.

"Holy guacamole," Charlotte said, shaking her head in disbelief, once the charity website was finally onscreen. She started to laugh, as sure enough, the CRAFTERNOON SEWCIAL CLUB was sat firmly at the top of the league with a big, bold number one right next to their name. Amelia's group was in second place, Charlotte saw, nipping at her heels. Charlotte couldn't tell just how close the margin was, however, as the charity appeared to have removed the precise tally of completed squares for each group. Charlotte didn't know why this might be, but thought perhaps it was to help build tension and stop any one group from taking their foot off the gas.

Unfortunately, it was too late in the evening to phone the charity about how or why they were at the top, if in fact the charity could provide any details anyway. Charlotte wondered if it might be some sort of accounting error, or simply the result of a member of staff with fat fingers hitting the wrong digit on their keyboard. Or, could their lead really, actually be genuine? Had Joan's Wools, for instance, received a generous windfall and sent them directly to the charity, maybe? Whatever the case, Charlotte couldn't help but savour the moment, deriving a bit of guilty pleasure as well by imagining Amelia squirming in her seat as she pleaded for a final, desperate push in the Zoom call to her members. All that was left for Charlotte to do now was to call around to her own members and apprise them of their current status, if they weren't already aware, so they could all enjoy it too.

Charlotte had no real cause to venture into the school playground the following day. Lately, after her last encounter with Amelia, she'd simply walk only as far as the entrance gate and then wave Stanley on his way, where his friends would be waiting further on. This particular morning, however, Charlotte was determined to escort Stanley well onto the tarmac of the school playground.

"I'm okay, Mum," Stanley declared, when he could still feel her shadowing him. He looked back, unsure why his mum was still there. "Mum," he said, coming to a stop. "What's going on?"

"Oh, nothing," Charlotte said nonchalantly, looking over Stanley's head towards the climbing frame in the far corner.

Stanley followed his mum's eyeline, wondering what could possibly be so interesting over in that direction. "Oh," he said, once he'd clapped eyes on his mum's arch-nemesis. "Go on, then," he told his mum.

"Hmm? What's that?" Charlotte replied, acting as if she didn't know what he could possibly mean.

Stanley placed his hand on his hip, adopting the stance of the sensible parent. "You can gloat once, and then on your way, Mum. All right?"

"Agreed," Charlotte said, agreeing. She blew Stanley a discreet kiss, as physical lips on cheeks would surely be frowned upon by Stanley's mates nearby. They were much too old for that sort of thing at the ripe old age of nine. "Love you, handsome," she added.

Charlotte flicked back her hair, heading across the playground with a confident spring in her step. With Stanley dropped off, she could of course have simply headed back the way she'd arrived, but where would the fun be in that? This way, she'd have the opportunity of seeing Amelia's face.

"Morning, Amelia!" Charlotte said, once she was near, and saying it loud enough so there wasn't any chance Amelia couldn't hear her. "Lovely morning for it!" she added cheerily, slowing as she passed by on her way towards the other exit.

Amelia, for her part, merely raised one eyebrow in response. Perhaps it was partially because the rest of her cheerleaders weren't stood beside her egging her on, and also the fact that she was currently with her children. But mostly, Charlotte suspected, it was because there wasn't an awful lot that Amelia *could* respond with. This particular time, Amelia had, for once, precisely *nothing* to say, and this was something that Charlotte found most agreeable indeed.

Charlotte certainly enjoyed her moment in the sun, rubbing her league standing in Amelia's face and leaving Amelia at a distinct loss for words. "That felt good," she said to herself as she headed off, her spirits buoyed, and ready for the day ahead.

With that bit of business sorted, next up for Charlotte was a stop at Oxfam. She had another matter to attend to (picking up four balls of eagerly awaited wool that had arrived at the craft shop) and Oxfam was right along the way, so Charlotte figured she'd swing by the charity's office en route to Joan's Wools, for two reasons: firstly, to attend to the mystery of the surge up the league table, and secondly, to drop a bag of her completed squares off and swell her group's numbers even further.

It was a jolly pleasant morning for a drive, and Charlotte certainly did enjoy the coastal views on the journey from Laxey. Still, Charlotte couldn't help but feel just slightly anxious, worried that there'd been some possible cock-up somewhere along the line which resulted in her (erroneous) first-place position on the leaderboard. Was she about to be told her group were, in actual fact, sat in the last place, and then offered an apology for the mix-up? The Crafternooners and the folks at the nursing home had indeed been industrious over the previous week, but not nearly enough, she felt, that it would have propelled them into first place. She'd even messaged Sam as well, the previous evening, wondering if the other nursing homes he was in regular contact with might have been responsible. He was pleased to report that he'd garnered some positive support, but it wasn't more than a couple of dozen completed squares. He knew this, he said, because he'd kindly collected them himself, dropping them off at the charity only the day before. This was brilliant news to Charlotte, but, again, unlikely to have had a huge impact on the league table.

Charlotte pulled up outside the charity's office in an estate on the outskirts of Douglas. The building was painted the colours of the rainbow, bringing a burst of welcome cheer to an otherwise drab stretch of industrial units. Besides the building serving as their HQ, there was also a popular onsite retail area selling donated second-hand household furniture and other items, further raising funds for the charity.

"Hello," Charlotte said, once inside, and approaching the reception desk with an *I'm-about-to-ask-you-a-very-daft-question* look written all over her chops. "I wonder if you can help?" she asked, resting her elbows on the countertop.

"Fire away," the perky lass behind the counter answered.

"I'm Charlotte. Charlotte Newman from the Crafternoon Sewcial Club?"

"Ah, yes. I'm Trudy. And I know *exactly* who you are, Charlotte," the girl replied, flashing a toothy smile.

"You do?" Charlotte asked.

"Yes, indeed," Trudy answered brightly. "We spoke on the phone when you first registered," she explained. "And also, there's *this*, of course," she added, reaching for a clipboard, and then turning it round so Charlotte could see it. "Top of the league!" she said, tapping her finger on the page. "How good is that?"

"It's amazing!" Charlotte said. "So... it's not some sort of mistake or other...?"

"No, ma'am! I counted them all myself," came the reply.

"Do you mind if I ask where they came from, Trudy? All those squares?" Charlotte asked, delighted that it wasn't all a huge mistake, yet thoroughly perplexed.

Trudy gave a little laugh, thinking Charlotte must be joking. Then, when it became clear she wasn't, she said, "Wait, do you mean the big batch we just got in recently? If so, I just assumed one of your team had dropped them off?"

"No," Charlotte answered. "Or at least, if they did, they've not told me," she said, raising her shoulders with a shrug. "I've honestly not a clue. Last I knew, we were languishing near the bottom of the league table, and yet, somehow, here we are now..."

"Oh, my. How curious," Trudy said. "Well, all I can tell you is that I turned up for work the other day and there was a good-sized bag sitting by the front door. At first, I thought it was just a donation from someone, something for us to sell in the shop. But when I stuck my nose in, I saw the bag was full of squares!"

"How many were there?" Charlotte asked her.

"Three hundred and five!" Trudy happily announced. "I counted them twice, just to be sure, as I always do."

"And that's why the Crafternooners are now at the top?" Charlotte asked. "Wait, how did you know they were for us if they were stuffed in a bag and left at the door?"

"There was a note inside the bag," Trudy explained. "But the only thing written on it was that it was care of Crafternooners. No other details, names, or anything else, I'm afraid."

"So we've no idea where they came from?" Charlotte asked, though already knowing the answer. "That's a shame," she said, shoulders drooping. "I'd really like to have thanked whoever was responsible."

"You should know..." Trudy said, lowering her voice and speaking as if she were about to reveal something that perhaps she shouldn't. "You should know that there's not too much in it between first and second place. So, the next week is going to be absolutely crucial."

"Ah," Charlotte answered, offering a nod of appreciation, "I hear what you're saying, Trudy."

Charlotte's attention moved slightly away from Trudy, towards the monitor sat on a set of filing cabinets behind her. "Is, ehm... that CCTV?" Charlotte asked, even though she obviously knew it was, as she could see her own car parked up outside right there on the screen.

"Sorry, I can't," Trudy replied, appearing to know precisely where Charlotte was heading with this.

"But it would've captured who dropped the bag off, wouldn't it?" Charlotte responded. "Come on, you must be just as intrigued...?"

"Sure, yeah, I guess so," Trudy allowed. "Still, it's a matter of client confidentiality and all that, you know?"

"Come *on*," Charlotte wheedled, using her most persuasive tone. "I mean, it's not like we're talking about someone's *medical records*, now are we?"

"I suppose not," Trudy said, mulling it over. "It's just a bag of wool, really," she said, mulling it over even further.

"Exactly," said Charlotte, sensing Trudy was softening to the idea. "Also, with several nursing homes currently volunteering for us, you can see how it's possible if one of them had simply forgotten to attach their details?"

"Oh, can you imagine how upset they'd be if you didn't even thank them for their efforts? They'd feel awful!" Trudy agreed, softening to the idea even more.

"Precisely," Charlotte said. "Can you just imagine?"

"Help yourself to the coffee machine," Trudy suggested with a wink, after which she spun around on her chair. "I'll have white with one, if you're making one?" she said over her shoulder.

Charlotte busied herself with preparing the coffee, casting the occasional glance across the reception area. "This is like something from a movie," Charlotte said, filling the silence even though there was no requirement to do so. "You know," she went on, "how you'd see them in the old American cop programmes having to fast forward through hours of videotape, trawling through the evidence until they identify the perp. Is it perp? Is that what they say, *perp*? I think it is, isn't it? That's a funny word, perp. Perp..."

Trudy didn't respond, as she was presently distracted, carefully examining the motion-activated footage for the previous evening. "Yes! The eagle has landed!" Trudy announced, after several minutes of diligence. "Come around and have a look," she said, tapping her finger on the display.

Charlotte wandered around to the other side of the reception desk as instructed, handing Trudy her coffee, and then setting her own down as she focussed her attention on the monitor. "Is that them?" she asked, saying it in a hushed whisper, as if the onscreen person could possibly hear her.

"I think so, yes," Trudy answered. "It definitely looks like the same bag, and it's left in the same position I found it in the next morning." Trudy rewound the footage for Charlotte's benefit. "According to the time stamp on the footage, this fellow carrying the bag arrived just before eight in the evening," she advised. "Do you recognise him?"

Charlotte screwed up her eyes, focussing as the scene replayed, on what appeared to be a youngish lad, climbing out of a blue car, and walking to the front of the building carrying the bag in question. "No..." Charlotte said, moving her head this way and that, to and fro, as if this desperate side-to-side motion head-wagging action would somehow improve her view of what was appearing there on the flat, two-dimensional screen. "No, I don't think I do."

"He only looks to be about, maybe, twenty or so?" Trudy offered. "Interesting. Not exactly someone you'd think to be a prolific knitter, is he?"

"No," Charlotte answered. "No, definitely not. Well, in any case, I guess it'll have to remain a mystery for now, as I can't say I recognise him."

"Hopefully, somebody might phone in to see if we've received the squares?" Trudy suggested. "And if they do, then I'll be sure and—"

"Ooh, wait," Charlotte said, shifting her attention away from the lad, and towards the car he'd just climbed out of. "In that car..." she said, pointing to the monitor, and then moving in for a closer look, her nose positioned millimetres from the screen.

Both of their focus had, until now, been on the deliveryman, and not the car he'd arrived in. In the corner of the screen, just within view, fortunately, was somebody sat in the passenger seat with their head hanging out the opened window, giving what seemed to be a series of instructions to the lad.

"Do you know them?" Trudy asked.

"Yes, I know *exactly* who that is," Charlotte declared, pulling away from the screen, and clapping her hands in delight. "I also know who the person sat behind her in the rear is, also."

"Well?" Trudy said. "Who is it?"

"The pair of elderly passengers in that car are two of my sewing ladies," Charlotte revealed. "In the front is Beryl," she said, "and in the rear, with her face pressed up against the window, is her partner in crime, Joyce. I'm guessing the lad is Beryl's grandson."

"So what are they doing skulking about after-hours like they don't want to be seen?" Trudy wondered aloud.

"Well, Trudy," Charlotte answered, tapping the crease on her upper lip with her index finger, "that remains an excellent question, and one I honestly have no answer to. But, you can be sure that I'll find out what those two wily old birds are up to!"

CHAPTER TWENTY

From about lunchtime on Thursdays, Charlotte started to feel a giddy excitement building up inside. It began in the tips of her toes, and ran all the way up to the top of her head. Her phone was often pinging away from first thing, with first-time Crafternoon attendees checking in for things like directions or to find out what they should be bringing along with them. And while she was busy with her own memory bears and whatnot, fielding such phone calls was anything but a chore. In fact, she loved welcoming new members into the fold, and she enjoyed seeing new friendships being forged as they joined the group. Many of her older members were relatively isolated at home, Charlotte knew, often having very limited social interaction. So, to see them bonding at her Crafternoon sessions and getting on so well, and to learn that some of them were even getting together outside of the crafting sessions as well, really warmed the cockles of her heart.

There was no doubt that crafting was a passion for Charlotte. But she took just as much enjoyment from seeing the progress others were making each week. It was a delight for her to witness and to be a part of their crafting evolution. Someone who first arrived not knowing which end of the crochet hook to hold could be crafting like an old pro in no time at all. As their confidence grew, so did the glimmer of light in their eye, Charlotte observed. And once that faint glimmer reached a bright spark, Charlotte was confident this meant they'd caught the crafting bug for good — because, as Charlotte knew from experience, once it'd got hold of you, there was no shaking it loose!

As for what the various club members got up to during the

Crafternoon meetings, a fair number of them would bring along their own crafting projects, happy enough to crack on with their current work in progress over a cuppa and a friendly chat. For the rest, Charlotte got her creative on, preparing a range of projects that they could pick and choose from depending upon their level of experience. You could simply work on crochet or knitted squares if you wished, or, if you fancied something a little more adventurous, then Charlotte had you covered there as well. She'd diligently prepared a prospectus of projects to keep even the most adventurous occupied for at least the next eleven years. You could set about making a handbag, for instance, knit a cardigan, sew yourself a purse, or even crochet a unicorn if the mood took hold. Whatever you wanted to do, Charlotte couldn't wait to guide you along and be a part of that journey.

Stanley also enjoyed the club's increasing popularity, eager and willing to attend without requiring too much persuasion by Mum. Charlotte suspected this was due in large part to the steady supply of cake always on offer, in addition to the scintillating company. She was pleased to see Stanley mixing with people of all ages, feeling it was a good thing for him. It wasn't that he was shy, necessarily. But she could see his social skills coming on leaps and bounds by spending time with such a diverse group of people.

And so, expecting a bumper crowd from the number of calls she'd received earlier in the day, Charlotte headed to the church hall later in the afternoon, straight from the school pick-up, in order to get the tables set up and supplies laid out. Stanley may have still been knee-high to a grasshopper, but he could fair old shift when required and was proving to be a rather splendid and indispensable assistant.

"Am I too early?" Bonnie asked, sometime later, peering around the door leading in from the foyer.

"Of course not, come and grab yourself a seat," Charlotte said, offering a warm welcome. "Is that your quilt?" Charlotte asked, looking to the generously stuffed bag tucked under Bonnie's arm.

Bonnie nodded her head. "It is, Charlotte," she said, a beaming smile emerging. "I actually can't believe that I've nearly finished it."

"Way to go, kiddo," Charlotte replied. "I knew you could do it."

"A few weeks ago, I could barely thread a needle, and now..." Bonnie said, setting her bag onto the table and patting it affectionately. "It's all because of you, Joyce, and Beryl," she told Charlotte.

"May I?" Charlotte asked, rubbing her hands together in gleeful anticipation.

Bonnie didn't need asking twice to show off her material masterpiece, gripping the bag firmly, and liberating her folded quilt from inside. "Grab a corner?" she suggested to Charlotte.

"Oh, my word," Charlotte remarked, as they unfurled Bonnie's handiwork, laying it out flat so they could both appreciate its magnificence. Charlotte took a step back, one hand placed over her mouth. She'd seen the quilt before, of course, but it was nearly complete now, with loads of new sections added on since she'd viewed it last. "It's beautiful," Charlotte added, moving in close again, and running her hands over the neatly stitched squares. "You must be so proud of yourself, Bonnie, and what an amazing heirloom for your family to enjoy."

"I just need to finish a little bit of the binding," Bonnie advised, pointing to the area she wanted to work on today. "Oh, and this," she said, reaching into her trouser pocket, and then holding up a well-worn leather patch for Charlotte's inspection. "I was hoping to find a home on the blanket for this," she said with a chuckle.

"Is that not...?" Charlotte asked.

"Yep! Mr Bean!" Bonnie confirmed. "Apparently, when Mum and Dad first met, he made out like he was some sort of serious biker dude. When Mum eventually agreed to go out with him, he did turn up on a motorbike, but it was one of those pasty-warmer types."

"More like a moped?" Charlotte joked.

"*Exactly* like a moped," Bonnie said with a laugh. "In fact it *was* a moped. Mum always used to tease him by saying it wasn't a proper bike, but more like something Mr Bean would likely ride. His moped must have done the trick, though, as they were married a year later. Anyway, Mum made this badge initially as a joke, but my dad loved it so much that she ended up stitching it on her denim jacket and wearing it with pride whenever they went out for a ride. That's both of their initials above Mr Bean's face."

"That's lovely, Bonn," Charlotte said, taking the patch in her hand and admiring it. "Hmm, it's a bit thick, though, isn't it?" she asked, turning it over to inspect the leather.

"Right, and sadly that's exactly the problem I've run into at home," Bonnie replied. "My poor little sewing machine tried valiantly but couldn't quite cut the mustard."

"Unfortunately, I doubt I'd have anything here that would pass muster either," Charlotte said, continuing her inspection. "You could always sew it on by hand, I suppose, same way as your mum did on her jacket. But I expect you're looking for something that looks a little nicer, and is also longer-lasting? Although, as I said, we really don't have anything here that might—"

"Maybe glue?" Bonnie entered in, unsure of what available options there might be, and appearing dejected for a moment.

"No, you just need a sewing machine with a little more *oomph!*" Charlotte told her. "Something a little more industrial. I'm pretty sure the guys at Joan's would have something that could tackle this. Or, wait a minute, what about at school...?"

"Oh, yes!" Bonnie said, perking up again. "Mr Gilhooly has some proper medieval-looking beasts in his classroom! I'm sure he'll have something that would make light work of this. As for the rest, I guess I'll just need to focus on tidying up the binding this afternoon."

"Sounds like a plan," Charlotte said. "And it does look brilliant, Bonn. You've done an excellent job, and just shout if you need me."

Charlotte had so much time for Bonnie. It was heartbreaking that Bonnie had lost her mum at such a young age. And yet, amazingly, considering the emotional turmoil she'd been through this last year, she was rarely seen without a smile on her face, maintaining such a positive, can-do attitude. Charlotte was pleased to have her, and pleased to see the other ladies in the group such as Joyce and Beryl taking her under their wing. Charlotte knew crafting offered Bonnie something to focus on, and hoped that it was a hobby she'd continue even once her quilt was completed. Charlotte certainly enjoyed her company, as did the rest of the group.

"Mum!" Stanley shouted from his position stood there out in

the foyer, keeping watch on the road outside. It was, at this point, getting close to starting time. "Mum!" he repeated, popping his head in. "The bus just pulled up outside. I'll see if anyone needs any help with their bags!"

The numbers in the church hall soon swelled as the four o'clock start time drew ever nearer, and the quiet solitude was now replaced with conversation and sporadic bursts of raucous laughter. It was a joy to see, but Charlotte was worried that if the numbers continued to grow, they'd soon run out of tables to accommodate them all. However, it was an excellent problem to have and one that Charlotte, even in her wildest dreams, couldn't have imagined.

It was nice to see a good handful of new faces in attendance, many of whom appeared to have accompanied Joyce & company, arriving on the bus from the far-flung north of the island. Two of the new gentlemen in their group were acting somewhat dazed and confused, appearing as though they weren't entirely sure how they'd managed to end up in their current surroundings. Indeed, Stanley even joked to his mum that they might well have been kidnapped by the girls. Charlotte suggested that Stanley should keep an eye on the two fellows and raise the alarm if assistance was requested.

Larry, meanwhile, as per usual, was proving himself to be quite indispensable. Once again, as things got started, he effortlessly moved between the kitchen and the hall, replenishing cups, sharing a joke, and just being the attentive host. Overall, it really was a contagious atmosphere, and anyone walking by outside must have wondered what in heaven's name was going on inside that was causing such a din in a place of worship.

After twenty minutes or so had elapsed from the start of the session, Charlotte sidled over to the table where Joyce and Beryl were sat next to Bonnie, each of them engrossed in their latest projects. Charlotte stood over them, watching what they were up to for a moment. "Ladies," she said, in greeting.

"Hello, Lotti!" Joyce and Beryl both answered in unison, and with Bonnie giving a friendly wave and a smile.

"We've brought a couple of new handsome, strapping young

fellows along this week," Joyce said, with a mischievous sort of cackle.

"We found them by the bus station," Beryl entered in. "They didn't put up too much of a struggle once we had them pinned down on the ground," she added, setting the two of them off into a fit of the giggles.

"I don't even think they're joking," Bonnie suggested, looking both ways.

"I've got Private Investigator Stanley keeping a careful eye on them, just in case they're in need of help," Charlotte answered with a laugh. "Oh, by the way, I tried to call you yesterday, Joyce," Charlotte said, turning back to Joyce. "I even left a message for you on your answer machine."

"Oh?" Joyce replied. "Hrmm. Some of us went ten-pin bowling yesterday, so I must have been out."

Charlotte walked around to the opposite side of the table so she could stand directly in front of them, leaning over and placing her hands flat against the tabletop. "So. The two of you been up to anything *else* of interest this week, besides bowling?" she asked, in a manner suggesting she might well already know the answer, which of course she did.

Joyce looked up to Charlotte, then across to Beryl (who was remaining silent), and then back up to Charlotte. "Such as...?" Joyce asked, blinking innocently.

"Oh, I don't know, ladies. That *certain something* you pair did the other evening, perhaps?" Charlotte answered, casting them both a look.

"It was all *her* idea!" Joyce offered, perfectly willing to throw her mate under the bus. "*She* made me do it!" Joyce added, edging her chair away from Beryl, increasing the distance between them.

Charlotte couldn't really understand why Joyce was acting so guilty, as if she'd done something naughty, or bad, when surely what they'd done was a *good* thing?

Bonnie, for her part, appeared completely in the dark as well, same as Charlotte, and watched on in confusion as Beryl dropped her partially-knitted jumper on the table and gave her partner in crime a stern glance.

"Oh, so it's *my* fault, is it?" Beryl shot back at Joyce indignantly. "And yet I don't recall you putting up *any* kind of fight at *all* when that fellow was covered in oil and gyrating his hips inches from your face! In fact I rather thought you were going to have a stroke, and I don't mean of the medical variety either, you wicked thing!"

Charlotte let this exchange go on a little bit longer, allowing the girls to bicker, as they seemed to enjoy it. Finally, when there was a pause in the conversation between them, Charlotte took the opportunity to very gently interrupt. "Ladies. I've no idea what you're both talking about. I was referring to the *big bag of squares* that was dropped off at Oxfam."

"Oh, that," said Beryl.

"Oh, that," said Joyce.

"Yes, but the two things are related, actually," Beryl informed Charlotte.

"Right, they're really the same thing," Joyce agreed.

Charlotte pulled up a chair, as she was more confused now than ever, and it looked like this might take a fair bit of explaining on their part. "Go on," she said, raising an eyebrow.

It was a jolly good thing that Joyce and Beryl weren't spies, tasked with securing state secrets, because the two of them cracked quicker than a glass trampoline. Charlotte listened intently, as did Bonnie, as did those earwigging close by, while Joyce began with the confession.

"We just wanted to help you win that league competition," Joyce explained. "So, we came up with the idea of organising a dinner dance for the girls who live up our way."

"Only without the dinner part," Beryl entered in.

"Okay?" Charlotte replied, no closer to understanding how any of this could possibly have any connection to a large batch of knitted squares for the charity competition, but intrigued, nonetheless, to find out. "And...?"

"Elsie, who we know from bingo, lives next door to a dancer," Joyce said.

"He's in a group with some of his friends. They're all dancers," Beryl said.

"That's right," Joyce continued, picking up where Beryl had left off. "And so we arranged a dinner dance. Well, there wasn't food, as I said. Just alcohol. So, a drinking dance would be a better description, I suppose."

"Lots of alcohol," Beryl entered in.

"Lots of alcohol," Joyce confirmed. "Anyway, so we suggested, as the modest cost of admission to this most magnificent of spectacles, you see, at least one crafted square, made as per competition specifications."

"Two squares if you wanted alcohol along with the dancing," Beryl added.

"And three squares if you wanted alcohol along with the dancing, *and* a Polaroid with the boys afterwards," Joyce added, the two girls bouncing off each other quite happily now.

Charlotte looked at Bonnie, and Bonnie looked to Charlotte, neither of them knowing quite what to make of all this. "So you're saying you collected over three hundred squares as an admission fee for a dance you organised?" Charlotte asked, turning once again to Beryl and Joyce.

"Yes," Joyce said, appearing immensely pleased with the results of her efforts, and also pleased at the recollection of that particular evening's events.

"Well, not exactly. Not at first," Beryl pointed out, chiming in. "I mean, there was the matinee performance the next day as well," she said. "You see, when the first one sold out, we had to put another one on the following afternoon to satisfy demand. That's when the police turned up."

"The police?" Charlotte asked. "Why would the *police* have turned up?"

"Ah. And this is exactly why we didn't want to tell you," Joyce said.

"We knew you'd disapprove," Beryl said.

"And why we discreetly dropped the squares off at the charity," Joyce added. "We didn't think you'd find out."

"Wait, something's missing here. I still don't understand why the police would raid a dinner dance," Charlotte replied, perplexed. "Ladies...?" she said, inviting further explanation.

"A drinking dance," Joyce replied, gently correcting her. "And we didn't exactly have permission to use the community centre as we did. And the police, you see, weren't very impressed that we were technically selling homemade spirits also."

"Technically," Beryl said with a shrug. "Always hung up on details, the police."

"Bloody rocket fuel is what it was," Joyce admitted. "They were worried people might have ended up going blind from drinking it, or some such rubbish," she added.

"Utter tosh. They worry about the silliest of things, don't they?" Beryl added further.

"Also, you apparently need some sort of special licence for that particular type of dancing," Joyce explained to Charlotte.

"That particular type of dancing?" Charlotte answered. "And what *particular* type of dancing would that be, exactly, that it could possibly require a licence?" Charlotte asked, afraid she already knew the answer, but still choosing to hope for the best.

"You know..." Joyce replied, shaking her torso around in her seat as if she were having a mild seizure. "The type involving baby oil and Velcro trousers."

"Tear-away Velcro trousers," Beryl added helpfully.

"Tear-away Velcro trousers," Joyce confirmed happily, smiling at the thought of seeing them employed in action. "Anyway, to answer your question, Lotti, exotic dancing, I suppose you could call it? To put it politely."

"But what she really means by that is—" Beryl began.

"A strip show? You lot put on a bloody strip show??" Charlotte said, loud enough to bring a collective hush to the hall. "You broke into a *community* centre, selling *moonshine*, at a *strip* show, *twice*?"

"Well, when you put it like *that*..." Joyce replied.

"*Pfft*. You make it sound so *tawdry*," Beryl scoffed.

"I know, right?" added Joyce, in perfect alignment with Beryl, and not understanding why anyone would get their knickers in a twist over the whole affair.

"Also, Elsie is the cleaner there, so we technically didn't need to *break into* the community centre, necessarily," Beryl pointed out.

"Mmm-hmm, mmm-hmm," Joyce added, and nodding along as Beryl spoke.

Charlotte had to take a moment to process all this. She didn't know whether to be cross with the girls, or to see the humour in the whole situation. Finally, the humour won out, and Charlotte started to laugh to the extent that snot bubbles were in danger of forming in her nose. "Oh my stars and garters. You two..." she said, shaking her head and gasping for breath. "What are you two like?"

"Her hands have never been so moisturised," Joyce suggested, looking over at Beryl. "She was especially liberal with the baby oil, you see. Applied it to the lads herself," she explained to Charlotte.

"You're one to talk, Joyce," Beryl countered. "You went up for a photograph three times!"

"Four times, actually. And I was worried the first three had come out looking a bit fuzzy, wasn't I?" Joyce shot back.

"Anyway," Beryl said. "With the police turning up and all, we didn't want to associate Crafternoon with our innovative type of fundraising endeavours."

"*Pioneering*, I'd say, even," Joyce added in. "Anyhow, you're not too annoyed, are you?"

"Annoyed...?" Charlotte replied, standing with her hands on her hips, and pausing for dramatic effect before she provided her answer. "Yes, of course I'm annoyed!" she said. "I'm annoyed because you didn't invite me!"

CHAPTER TWENTY-ONE

"Wait, hang on," said Sue, turning down the car radio in order to verify that what she thought she just heard was in fact what she had just heard. "Did you just say a leopardskin thong? Seriously?"

"Yep," Bonnie replied, confirming her previous statement. "Beryl was telling us that one of the male strippers threw it into the crowd during his performance. But when he went to recover it later on, it had mysteriously disappeared. He's been phoning around a few of the ladies in attendance to try and locate it, but so far, no luck."

"Eurgh!" Sue offered, making a gagging noise. "Who on earth would want to take a stripper's filthy thong home as a souvenir, and why would he even bother phoning around trying to recover it?"

"Apparently it held some form of sentimental value to him, from what I understand," Bonnie explained. "Although nobody, I'm told, was quite sure what could possibly add sentimental value to a leopardskin thong, and I don't think anybody cared to ask."

"It sounds like the Crafternooners are leading you astray, young lady," Sue joked, slowing the car on the approach to the staff carpark. "Do you want to jump out here, away from prying eyes?" Sue asked, finger poised over the indicator.

"You're fine," Bonnie answered. "Being dropped off in the staff carpark is only an issue when you're a daft fourteen-year-old who thinks she's cool when she really isn't. So, I'm well past that stage now, I reckon."

"So I can honk the horn and wind the window down and sing at the top of my voice while you're in the car? You don't mind?"

"Go for it," Bonnie replied with a laugh, daring her, and calling Sue's bluff. "By the way, though, I truly do appreciate the lift, Sue. I really didn't fancy bringing this quilt on a bus stuffed with filthy, grubby lads who'd probably end up throwing and kicking it around like a bloody football or something," she told her. "Boys will turn absolutely *anything* into a football given the slightest opportunity," Bonnie remarked, letting loose an exasperated sigh.

"My pleasure," said Sue, pulling into her allocated parking spot. She looked over at the heavy canvas bag across Bonnie's lap. "And as for that quilt," she said, "you learned how to sew, and finished what your mum started, Bonn. I think that's wonderful. I really do."

"Hopefully Mr Gilhooly will be able to help me with the final touch," Bonnie said, holding up the Mr Bean patch. "And then it's all finished, and ready to snuggle under."

Sue reached over. "May I?" she asked, taking possession of the patch, admiring it, and smiling fondly. "I remember your mum talking about this new bloke she'd met, Bonn. She told me in great detail about how wonderful he was, and also how athletic. Quite the rugby player, apparently. And she was *especially* excited to find out he rode a motorbike."

"That made him something of a catch, did it? The bike?"

"Oh, yes!" Sue answered. "You see, when you're seventeen or eighteen, most of the lads are driving about in rust buckets, and that's if they're lucky! More often than not, they'd just be borrowing their mum or dad's car on a Friday night. So, having a motorbike was absolutely brilliant. Very sexy. Like Tom Cruise in Top Gun."

Sue drifted off for a moment, in seeming recollection of Tom Cruise's character riding his motorbike in *Top Gun*.

"It's funny because after that first date, your mum didn't really mention the motorbike again," Sue continued. "And then, a few days later, your dad rode up the high street with your mum on the back, and your mum dying of embarrassment when she caught sight of me and a few of the other girls standing outside the video rental shop. She was *especially* thrilled when your dad tooted that ridiculous little horn on the bike, waving furiously over at us. But from then on, Bonn, they were never apart, girly little moped not-withstanding!"

"He's still got the thing, believe it or not," Bonnie informed her. "It's in the back of the garage, at the house. Do you want me to ask him if it still starts? I'm sure he'd be delighted to take you for a spin over to the video shop! If they still have video shops, that is?"

"Don't you dare!" Sue said with a laugh, handing back the Rowan Atkinson Mr Bean patch. "Tell you what," she went on, "do you want me to give you a lift home at lunchtime? Save your quilt hanging around in school all day with those dirty, filthy boys?"

"Yes!" Bonnie immediately replied, grateful for the suggestion. "It shouldn't take me too long to sew the patch on, assuming I'm successful in that, and I'm really not too keen on carrying the whole thing around with me all afternoon, as I'm sure it's too big to stuff into my locker. And I don't know *what* I'm going to do with it when I have to go out onto the field for PE this afternoon!"

"Meet you here, then?"

"Yes, please. And thanks so much."

"My pleasure," Sue answered, as they both climbed out of her car.

Bonnie waved goodbye, walking away to catch up with two friends she spotted walking through the carpark, the both of them chomping down on a thick piece of toast apiece.

"Oh!" Sue added, causing Bonnie to turn and look back over her shoulder. "And don't forget to let me know if that male stripper's thong turns up!" Sue called out, much to the bemusement and amusement of Bonnie's two toast-eating pals.

Bonnie's nerves were on edge all morning. She cradled her quilt-stuffed canvas bag with the tender devotion of a mother leaving the maternity ward for the first time. She did try placing it in her locker but as suspected it was too big to fit, and navigating through the corridors between each class was a minefield for someone carrying something so precious. At every turn, she was met with grabby, inquisitive, racoon-like hands, with everyone reaching for it and wanting to paw at it and have a look. In the classroom, as well, her closest friends were all eager to have a butcher's at her handiwork and get a view of the thing that'd been taking up so much of her free time. This was nice of them, of course, and completely understandable. However, removing the quilt from its canvas covering was like liberating a carefully-rolled-up sleeping bag from its carrying case whilst on a camping trip — easy enough to pull out, yet all-but-impossible to get back in without considerable effort. For that reason alone, Bonnie had to politely decline their enquiring advances.

Bonnie was relieved when the lunch bell eventually sounded and she was thus able to escort her cherished package to Mr Gilhooly's crafting room, forgoing any actual lunch and heading straight there instead. It was still surprising to see the crafting room so well attended during non-mandated crafting classes, the allure of a new PlayStation system appearing to draw quite a crowd judging by the number of bums on seats. Fortunately for her, everyone in attendance was much more focused at present on the fine art of knitting, towards that very end (increasing their chances of winning a new gaming console), than to be bothered with anything sewing-related. As such, Bonnie was pleased to see the line of sewing machines on a heavy wooden workbench over by the window near the fire escape unattended. Like pretty maids all in a row they were, and yet sadly, currently untouched and un-loved.

"Let me guess," Mr Gilhooly said in Bonnie's direction, hearing her come in, but without looking up from the young lad he was assisting. "You want to learn how to make knitted squares?" he asked wearily, already certain he knew the answer.

If ever there was a teacher you suspected was counting down the days to retirement, Bonnie thought, it was Mr Gilhooly. He always looked glum and exhausted these days, like all the wind had been taken from his sails.

"No, sir," Bonnie said, holding up her Mr Bean patch. "I was hoping you'd have a sewing machine capable of stitching this onto a quilt?"

Mr Gilhooly stood upright, leaving the young lad he was working with to crack on without him. "A quilt, eh?" he asked, walking
over and taking hold of the patch, running his fingers over the
surface. "And this quilt is in there?" Mr Gilhooly surmised, looking
to the large canvas bag held in Bonnie's other hand. "May I?" he
asked, reaching out.

"Please do," Bonnie said, handing the bag over. There was a fair
bit of weight to the quilt, and so she was happy now to be able to
shake out her fingers and restore the flow of blood to her digits.

Mr Gilhooly made his way through the crew of assembled knitters, heading towards the sewing station, Bonnie following close
behind. Once in front of the workbench, he ran his hand over the
wooden surface, ensuring that it was clean, and clear of any possible debris. Cautiously, he eased the quilt from the bag, carefully
tugging it out the final few inches. "You made this?" he asked,
without turning around.

"Mostly, sir. Yes."

Mr Gilhooly partially unrolled the quilt, moving his head closer
for an improved view. "This is really rather excellent," he said,
with an enthusiasm rarely seen in recent days. "Why have you not
been in my class if you can produce work like this?"

"I have, sir," Bonnie replied. "I was in your class all last year.
You called me Bunny rather than Bonnie, although, to be fair, that
may have just been your Irish accent."

"Ah, yes. I remember you now," he said, looking over his shoulder. "How could I forget that rather remarkable red hair of yours?"
he added. "Sorry, I haven't been myself lately. Anyway, here, try
this one," he said, introducing one particular sewing machine
with a wave of his hand, and inviting her to have a look. "This one
should do the trick, I would think. I couldn't imagine you having
any trouble getting through the leather of that patch with it."

"Thank you, sir."

"And just shout if you need any assistance."

Tentatively, Bonnie took charge of the formidable-looking be-
hemoth. Previously, she'd only used her mum's machine on the
quilt for the most part, which was about half the size of this brute

before her. Not knowing what to expect, she'd even brought extra fabric so she could have a trial run before committing to the job proper. "Right, girl, you can do it," she whispered to herself.

When she applied pressure to the foot pedal, the machine burst into life, and startlingly so. It caused something of an almighty din, in point of fact, vibrating loudly enough to loosen one's fillings, and attracting the attention of the assorted knitters in the room.

"Everything okay?" Mr Gilhooly called over, once she'd released the pressure on the foot pedal.

"Perfect, sir. I feel like one of those workmen digging up the road with a pneumatic drill!"

"Just take it steady, and you'll be fine, Bunny."

After a few trial runs with the scrap fabric she'd brought along, Bonnie took several calming breaths, placing the Mr Bean patch over the desired location on her quilt. "Steady on, girl, here we go," she whispered, before pressing down her shaking foot. Her apprehension had however been fortunately unfounded, because in hardly any time at all, Bonnie was finished, sitting upright and admiring her stitchwork. And just like that, Mr Bean was a permanent fixture on her family quilt.

"Ah. Excellent," Mr Gilhooly said, looking across her shoulder and having come over to check on her work. "You should consider coming along to crafting club more frequently," he suggested. "It'd be nice for the rest of the group to realise what you can actually achieve when you put your mind to it."

"I might just do that, sir," Bonnie said, rolling up her finished quilt and carefully fitting it back into its canvas bag, which was no small feat. "Thank you again," she said, with one eye on the clock hanging by the door.

Her fellow pupils must have thought her quite mad, gambolling about the corridor as she was, with an overly jubilant grin on her face, and cradling the canvas bag lovingly in her arms as she went along. Little did most of them know, Bonnie held something she would treasure for years to come and future generations in her family would no doubt treasure as well.

"Sorry I'm late, Sue," Bonnie said once outside in the carpark, still grinning like a Cheshire cat.

"You're fine, Bonn. I did stick my nose into Mr Gilhooly's class, but I could see you were engrossed in the task at hand, so I didn't want to disturb you. You ready to go?"

"Sure am," Bonnie said, climbing into the car with her canvas bag placed lovingly on her lap.

"It'll just be a flying visit, Bonn, if that's okay?" Sue said, strapping herself in. "I've an appointment with the headmaster to talk about the riveting subject of budgets as soon as I get back in the office. And plus it's your lunch period, of course, so we'll need to get you back as quick as possible."

"No problem, Sue, I'll only be two minutes. I'm just so happy to be taking it home so I don't have to worry about lugging it around and it possibly getting ruined somehow," Bonnie answered. "You know, because of this quilt," she added, "I've started to understand why Dad used to get stressed out about keeping certain things protected, like the time we had a new carpet put in the house when I was younger. He was so worried about keeping that thing clean!"

"You're getting old and wise, Bonn," Sue remarked, giving Bonnie a wink as she pulled out of the school and onto the road. "So, have you decided what you're going to do with the quilt?" she asked. "Are you going to put it on your bed, or...?"

"Well, the *first* thing I have to do is to show it to the girls at Crafternoon!" Bonnie replied. "After that, I'm not sure. But, yeah, I think I'll keep it on my bed for the time being, though ultimately I may hang it up on the wall?"

"Sounds good, Bonn," Sue answered.

It was only a short drive home from school for Bonnie, not more than five minutes or so, but of course a little too far to walk home in your lunch hour and be back in time for your first lesson of the afternoon afterwards. Sue's offer of a ride was thus very much appreciated and just what the doctor ordered, and soon they were approaching Bonnie's house.

"Oh, good. Dad's home," Bonnie remarked, noting his car in the driveway and hoping she would see it there. "Do you mind if I very quickly show him what I've done?" she asked, looking over to the driver's seat. "He doesn't know about Mr Bean, and I wanted to see his face."

"Go right ahead," Sue answered. "I won't come in, but tell your dad I'm not being rude, okay? It's just that we're pressed for time."

"Okay. I won't be long," Bonnie replied, patting her canvas bag affectionately as the car came to a halt.

Conscious of the time constraints, Bonnie ran up the drive, hoping the kitchen door was unlocked so she wouldn't have to fumble with the key. It was, fortunately, and so she was able to walk straight in. "Dad, it's only me!" she shouted, placing the bag on the kitchen table. "Come and have a look, Dad!" she called out. "I've got a little surprise I want you to see!"

"Bonnie?" Benjamin replied from the other room, surprise evident in his voice. He appeared from the living room, filling the kitchen doorframe. "You're... home," he said, stating the obvious. "You don't normally come home for lunch," he added, stretching his arms above his head and, in the process, filling even more of the doorframe.

"Well, I didn't fancy the quilt's chances of safely lasting the day in school," she explained, "and Sue was kind enough to drop me home for a moment. In fact she's waiting in the car, and said to say hello, and that she's not being rude for not coming in, but that..."

Bonnie had been rolling out the quilt as she'd been talking, but something about the way her father was behaving struck her as odd. She turned to face him directly. "Dad... you're acting peculiar," she said, running her eyes up and down him.

"Me? What, peculiar? Ah-ha-ha, heh, ha-hah," he said, sounding like a madman from a low-budget horror film. "Love the quilt, by the way," he added quickly, without moving from his somewhat awkward and uncomfortable-looking position filling the doorway. "That you... all finished, then...?" he asked, sounding like he was reaching and struggling for something to say.

Bonnie trained her eyes on her dad, walking closer to him without breaking her gaze. "Have you been smoking something you shouldn't have, Dad?" she asked, taking a deep sniff of the air. "Because you *are* behaving a little bit strangely."

"Oh, just a busy morning," her father replied, shifting his position to somehow fill up even *more* of the doorframe.

"So why are you stood like that, Dad?"

"Like *what*?" her father asked with a nervous laugh.

"Like you're trying to *hide* something," Bonnie shot back, looking through the gaps that his torso and arms were unable to conceal.

Bonnie poked him in the ribs a few times, causing her father to lurch backwards, and now rendering the doorway unobstructed in the process.

"Quit it!" Benjamin said, giggling like a schoolgirl in reaction to the digit-based assault on his ribs.

"I need to leave in a moment," Bonnie said, flicking her eyes up and down the hallway. "But before I do, come and have a quick look at..." she said, trailing off, suddenly distracted by what she'd just spotted at the foot of the stairs. "Whose are *those*?" she asked, looking back to her dad.

"W–w–what? Th–those?" Benjamin answered, sounding as if he knew precisely what Bonnie had clapped eyes on.

"The shoes. The women's shoes," Bonnie said, walking over and kneeling down to pick one of them up. "They're not mine, Dad. So either you've taken to cross-dressing, or—"

"Ben!" a distinctly feminine voice called out from one of the rooms upstairs. "Ben!" it said again, increasing in volume slightly as it drew a bit closer to the top of the stairs. "Ben, can you hear me? I think I've dislocated my shoulder with this zip! Can you come up and help me out?"

Bonnie placed the shoe back down, just where she'd found it. She looked over to her dad, startled.

"It's not what you think," Benjamin said quickly, attempting to explain.

"Can you help me out of this dress?" the mystery woman upstairs called down, from somewhere around the top of the stairs, effectively placing a spanner in the works as far as any possible explanations from Benjamin went.

"Not what I think?" Bonnie said. "Not what I *think*?" she said again. Bonnie raised her index finger, using it to point in the direction of the upper floor. "It would appear to be *exactly* what I think it is. And what makes matters even worse is that I know exactly *who* it is that wants help out of their dress, as I now recognise that voice."

"Bonnie," Benjamin said, moving closer. "Bonnie, I swear, it's not what—"

"Hello, Charlotte," Bonnie said, getting a glimpse of Charlotte, who was now just visible on the first-floor landing. "I'm sorry to interrupt you both," she said, emotion taking over her voice.

"Bonnie," Benjamin said, reaching out, placing his hand on her shoulder.

"No, it's fine," Bonnie said, though her trembling lower lip suggested differently. She pushed her father's hand away, eyes welling up. "It's my fault for coming home during the day when you're not expecting me. I should just... I should go."

"Bonnie. Stop," Benjamin said, grabbing at her arm, preventing her exit.

"I always knew you'd find someone else eventually, Dad. I suppose I just didn't think it would be quite so soon," Bonnie answered, tears falling down her cheeks. "I'm sorry, I'm just a bit emotional because there's the shock of it as well. And by that I mean the shock that you're with somebody *pretending* to be my friend, just so that certain somebody can jump into bed with you, apparently, while I'm out of the house at school."

Benjamin opened his mouth to speak, but didn't get the chance to respond. Bonnie snapped her arm forward, breaking free from her father's grip.

"I'll let you know, next time I'm coming home early," Bonnie told him, pushing past and walking into the kitchen. "Oh, and Dad," she added, snatching the quilt from the table. "*Do* be sure to show this to Charlotte, and pass along my gratitude for her help in finishing it," she said sarcastically, tossing the quilt to the floor.

Bonnie didn't look back, throwing open the kitchen door and heading outside, wiping her face with her sleeve. On the way down the drive, their neighbour, Irene, looked up from mowing her lawn. At first, she smiled, but then, upon seeing Bonnie's face, her expression changed to one of deep concern.

"I'm fine!" Bonnie assured her, offering up a half-hearted wave in response.

Sue, sitting there in her car listening to the radio as she waited, had a reaction similar to that of the neighbour. At first, she was singing merrily along to an Oasis song she liked, and then, upon seeing Bonnie sprinting towards the car, face wet with tears, Sue's expression changed to one of alarm. "Are you okay? What's wrong?" she said, as Bonnie reached for the car door.

"Can we head back?" Bonnie asked, talking through her tears as she climbed inside the car.

"What's going on?" Sue pressed, looking first to Bonnie, and then up the driveway to where Benjamin was now stood, calling after his daughter. "Bonnie? What's going on?"

"I'm fine. Honest," Bonnie said. "It looks like my dad has managed to move on with his life, that's all. Found himself a new girlfriend," she added, between sobs. "Which is fine, of course. Please, can we just go?"

Sue reached for the keys in the ignition, appearing unsure about what exactly she should do in this situation. "Wait, is that not the woman who runs your crafting club?" she asked, just as Charlotte appeared, joining Benjamin at the top of the drive.

"Yes, it is," Bonnie confirmed, without looking up, face buried in her hands. "That's my friend Charlotte. And I'm sure they'll make a lovely couple."

"Right, ehm..." Sue responded, seeming confused by Bonnie's assessment of the current situation. "So why... why exactly is Charlotte wearing a red ballgown at one in the afternoon?"

"What?" Bonnie asked, lowering her hands so she could see for herself. "That looks like my dress," Bonnie remarked, confused, as she observed Charlotte, stood there barefoot beside her father, looking decidedly sheepish. "She's wearing the dress that *Mum* was making me! What the hell!" she shouted, climbing back out of the car she'd just climbed into.

"Bonnie!" Benjamin said, running down the driveway, arms extended, and ready to scoop her up. "Bonnie, you need to shut up for a moment and listen to me!"

"*Why's she wearing my dress?*" Bonnie demanded, the tears now replaced with anger.

"Bonnie," Benjamin pleaded, "Bonnie, you need to listen to me, yeah? Look, Charlotte and I haven't, well, you know, been doing what you *think* we've been doing, honestly. Bonnie, Charlotte's been teaching me to *sew*."

Bonnie heard her father's words well enough, but they didn't really register; they were making no sense to her. "What on earth are you on about, Dad?"

Benjamin smiled as Sue joined them from the car. "Hiya, Sue," he said, before returning his attention to the matter at hand. "Bonnie," he said, holding both of her shoulders, "Bonnie, the reason I started knitting was that I thought it would make you happy. But the truth is, it's made *me* happy. Crafting has taken my mind off all the rubbish that's happened this year and made me refocus on what's important. And that's me and *you*, Bonn. I then asked Charlotte if she'd mind giving me sewing lessons as I wanted to challenge myself. I kept it quiet as I had a special project I wanted to work on. Bonnie, nothing is going on between Charlotte and me. She's teaching me to sew, that's all."

"Oh," Bonnie said, lowering her head. "I just thought that…"

"I know what you thought, Bonn," Benjamin answered. "And it's okay. I can completely understand why you'd react as you did. You thought I'd forgotten Mum and moved on already, but I haven't." Benjamin cradled Bonnie's face in his hands. "I'll always love your mum," he told her. "And right now, the only other lady I want in my life is *you*, Bonnie."

"Is that what you've been sewing?" Bonnie asked, pointing over at the ballgown Charlotte was wearing and looking quite splendid in, actually.

Benjamin nodded. "It tore me up every time I went into the spare room, Bonnie, to see the prom dress your mum started for you but didn't get to—"

"I'm sorry for behaving like a brat," Bonnie interrupted, wrapping her arms around her father and squeezing him tight. "And, Charlotte, please forgive me for being such a—"

"It's nothing," Charlotte said, waving Bonnie's concerns away. "I was just trying it on so that we could make some final adjustments, but seeing as *you're* here now, maybe you could try it on yourself...?"

Sue took a few steps back for a moment, reaching for the phone inside her trouser pocket. "I think I'd better phone the headmaster and reschedule our budget meeting," she said to nobody in particular, perhaps sensing this emotional exchange might take a few minutes longer to resolve between them. She didn't appear to mind, however, smiling warmly, watching on as Bonnie and her dad shared a cuddle.

"Well, I suppose I should go and change out of this," Charlotte suggested, looking up and down the street. "As lovely as it is, I'm not sure what your neighbours are going to think," she said, smiling over to Irene, who'd given up any pretence of mowing her grass, having a bloody good nosey instead. "Bonnie, you couldn't help me with the zip, could you?"

CHAPTER TWENTY-TWO

C harlotte's inability or, to be more accurate, reluctance to say no to anything crafting related was proving to be something of a challenge for her. Spare time was already a commodity in short supply, she found, and that was without even the further commitment of gainful employment. So when her crafting square recruitment drive ramped up significantly in the closing week of the competition, she barely had time to lift her head out of the water and take a breath. Not that she'd change it for anything, however, as she was having an absolute whale of a time.

She hadn't made a formal list of names to cross off, but there couldn't have been many nursing homes on the island she hadn't yet had the pleasure of visiting over the course of the previous few weeks. It was a genuine delight to meet the lovely residents, and at each and every location Charlotte recruited folk for the crafting competition and promoted the various benefits of crafting with a class while she was there. She was usually accompanied by young Stanley on these outings, and that just made things even more lovely as far as Charlotte was concerned.

The difficulty — and it was an excellent problem to have — was that the residents often enjoyed themselves so much that they were keen to turn the one crafting class into a regular event. This was not an unforeseen circumstance, as Charlotte suspected it may well happen. But it was a request she wasn't sure she could accommodate, as much as she would certainly love to — especially once she was able to secure paid employment, which would of course severely limit her available time even further.

Now, with only a few days remaining in the crafting square

J C WILLIAMS

competition, Charlotte was feeling some mixed emotions. Yes, the Crafternooners were top of the league. But Charlotte wasn't daft, and she knew their current standing was due in the main to Joyce and Beryl's stripper soirée and the impressive influx of squares that particular affair had generated for the cause. However, that rather formidable affair had been merely a one-time occurrence (albeit spread over two days), so Charlotte knew she wouldn't benefit from those remarkable numbers again during the competition's closing stages. And as for where they stood now, with the charity not releasing any figures, they were all pretty much knitting in the dark, so to speak. For all Charlotte knew, the Crafternooners could have dropped league positions like a stone, languishing at the foot of the table, rendering their final push fruitless. On the other hand, they could also be sat at the top with an unassailable lead. The truth was, Charlotte simply didn't know either way. One thing she was sure of, though, was that those involved were still having a great time regardless.

From speaking with her mole inside of Amelia's inner circle (namely, Stanley's teacher, Harriet), Charlotte knew they were also giving it their all in the closing days, with the proverbial whip being well and truly cracked. Still, Charlotte could always take comfort in knowing that if Amelia & co romped to victory, the prize money was at least committed to the same cause as her own. Of course, Charlotte didn't wish to see Amelia's smug face parading around with the trophy. But if the unthinkable happened and she did, then there would be some consolation in the knowledge that the prize money won't have gone to waste.

Not that Charlotte would be leaving things in any way to chance. On the contrary, she would do everything she could to win. A few days of the competition remained — time enough to increase their final tally by a good amount, she reckoned.

So, with Stanley dispatched for another day in front of the school blackboard on this particular morning, Charlotte was planning to collect knitted squares from two of the nursing homes she'd visited the previous week. And, of course, such visits were deserving of the generous-in-size Victoria sponges she'd baked the previous evening. As such, Charlotte headed for the door of her Laxey cottage, car keys secured in her mouth and a sponge cake balanced in each of her hands.

"Mmm," she murmured to herself through pressed lips, having not really thought through the issue of the closed door and her occupied hands. She raised her left elbow with impressive dexterity, using it to lift the door's metal latch without dropping her cakes. After a couple of failed attempts, the door opened enough to stick her foot in the gap and ease fully open.

"Mmm!" she said, louder this time, mouth still full, and startled by the figure standing on her doorstep.

"Morning, Charlotte," Postman Harry offered, in his customary cheery fashion. "How very kind of you, Charlotte!" he said, chuckling away to himself as he feasted his eyes on the Victoria sponges before him. "Just the one cake will do for me, thanks," he suggested gamely. "Though they *are* a magnificent pair. And very tempting indeed," he said, running his tongue over his lips. "Oh, wait!" Harry added abruptly, suddenly realising what he'd just uttered and what it must have sounded like. "I didn't mean... that is, I meant the *cakes* were a magnificent pair... of course I would never—"

"Mmm!" Charlotte said in response, eyes pointing southward towards the keys, where a trickle of saliva was now running down her chin. "Mmm!" she added, a little louder this time, nodding her head like she was trying to communicate in mumbles, which in fact she was.

"Ah!" Harry offered with a hearty salute, eventually catching on and understanding this modified form of communication. He reached for the dangling keys, liberating them from Charlotte's mouth, and shaking the excess saliva free.

"You scared the bejesus out of me," Charlotte playfully scolded him once her mouth was unobstructed. "And I nearly dropped my magnificent pair!" she teased, with a wry smile. "You couldn't take one of these, could you?" she asked, thrusting one of the cakes in his direction.

"Of course!" Harry replied. "I was only joking a moment ago, but if you're offering, then certainly I'll be happy to... Wait, hang on. We're taking these to your car, is that what you're saying?"

"Please," Charlotte said. "I'll come back and lock up in a tick."

"So, where are these culinary delights destined for?" Harry asked, walking through the gate Charlotte held open for him as she passed through.

"This one," Charlotte said, raising the cake in her hand an inch or two further aloft, "is going to the Cherry Woods nursing home. And the one in your hand is going to Cedar Grange. Some might call the cakes bribery, but I like to think of it as motivation!"

"Cedar Grange, is it?" Harry replied, handing over Charlotte's keys as they approached her car. "Oh, how nice. Cedar Grange is where my mum stays."

Charlotte's face lit up. "Oh, Harry, what a beautiful place it is," she said, placing the cake she was holding onto the passenger seat once she'd unlocked the door. "They all appear to be so happy up there. And talented, too! They were practising their rendition of a Gilbert and Sullivan opera when I visited last week."

"The Pirates of Penzance!" Harry was pleased to report. "I've been up there most nights helping them decorate their set, as you can see," he added, holding up the paint-stained palm of his free hand. "Wait," he said, a thought presenting itself to him. "Mum and her friends were busy knitting squares the other night before rehearsal. I've only just twigged, but I'm guessing they're for the competition you were talking about the other day?"

"Guilty as charged," Charlotte said, taking the other cake from Harry's possession. "Fingers crossed, your lovely mum and her friends will have a few more to add to the final tally. We need all the help we can get, as the competition is hot on our heels," she told him. "And help from any quarter is appreciated, in fact. So, if you're at a loose end...?" she suggested playfully.

"Ordinarily, I'd say yes in an instant, Charlotte," Harry answered. "But once the curtain comes down on The Pirates of Penzance, you see, then it's straight onto the H.M.S. Pinafore. So, no rest for the wicked, as they say."

"No worries. And that's really lovely of you to get involved like that, Harry," Charlotte remarked. "It's selfless acts like those that really make a difference in people's lives. So, well done, you."

"Well..." he said with a shrug of his shoulders. "Well, it was either work backstage, or get dressed up as a pirate and perform," he admitted. "And I was never blessed with much of a singing voice, I'm afraid."

"Right, then," Charlotte said, now the cakes were safely stowed in the car. "I must lock up and be on my way," she advised politely, as otherwise she knew she could easily stand about chatting for most of the day with Harry. "Should I take my post?" she asked. "Save you a walk back up my path?"

"Oh, none today," Harry replied, patting his mailbag.

Charlotte looked at Harry, appearing slightly confused. And this is because she was slightly confused. "Oh? But you were just at my front door, Harry," she pointed out, quite reasonably.

"Sorry to disappoint, Lotti. To be honest, I'd not seen you all week, and was just checking in to make sure everything was okay while I was on my rounds," he explained.

"Aww, Harry, that's sweet of you," Charlotte answered. "I've just been swamped this week, out and about, drumming up support from the crafting army. Thank you, though. I mean it."

"Here..." Harry said, lowering his voice, and offering a furtive glance over his shoulder. "Your mate down the road..." he said cryptically.

"Who, Mollie?" Charlotte asked, interest immediately piqued.

"No," Harry clarified. "When I say *friend*, I don't actually mean *friend*."

Charlotte ran her eyes over his face, trying to figure out who he could possibly be referring to, and where this might be leading. "Who do you mean?" she asked, when no clue was forthcoming.

"The other crafting woman," Harry said matter-of-factly, as if she should have known exactly who he meant. "The one with the silicone you-know-whats?" he added. "Looks to be a rather high-maintenance affair?" he went on, in furtherance of his description. "Wants to be a politician?"

"Amelia?" Charlotte said, venturing a guess.

"That's the one," Harry confirmed.

"Okay...?" Charlotte said, swirling her hand in the air, hoping to move the conversation forward. "Wait, you don't really think they're fake, do you? Her you-know-whats?" she asked, suddenly giving the idea some serious weight.

Harry raised one eyebrow, effectively indicating his position on the matter leaning decidedly towards the affirmative. "Anyway," Harry continued, shifting the convo away from what may or may not have been natural or unnatural, and back over to what he'd wanted to convey. "Anyway, she's in the same competition as you, right? The crafting square thing?"

"Yes. Along with her group, the Laxey Coffee Morning Crew, yes."

"I thought so. And that'll explain it, then," Harry offered, folding his arms across his chest and nodding his head, like a detective who'd just successfully put several clues together and unlocked the key portion of a perplexing mystery.

"Explain what, exactly?" Charlotte asked.

"Well..." he said, taking another furtive glance over his shoulder, just in case somebody might have snuck up behind him during the course of the last minute or two. "Well, I didn't tell you this," Harry cautioned, while proceeding to do just that, "but *someone's* just had two large boxes of woollen products delivered to their house." He then tapped his nose, in a *you-heard-it-here-first* sort of manner.

"Fancy that," Charlotte replied, giving her keys a less-than-subtle jingle while glancing sharply over towards the door of the house, indicating she was anxious to get going. "The organiser of a group in a crafting competition getting balls of wool delivered to her house? I mean, heavens to Betsy, who would ever imagine such a thing," she said teasingly.

But Harry wasn't quite finished making his point. "No, silly," he told her, giving his nose a final tap. "No, according to the delivery note she had to sign, it wasn't balls of wool, but *crafting squares*. As in, *completed* crafting squares. There were even pictures of them printed on the box," he explained. "I wouldn't usually have noticed, but they looked just like that breakfast cereal. What are they called...? Oh, yes, that's right. Shreddies, that's them!"

"It couldn't be, could it?" Charlotte asked.

"Yes, definitely. Shreddies is the cereal I'm thinking of, I'm sure of it!" Harry replied.

"No, I mean, crafting squares? You're certain?"

"Ah," Harry answered, leaving the topic of breakfast cereal to fall to the wayside for the time being. "Well, the delivery note contained a description of the contents, and it clearly said crafting squares. So make of that what you will," he told her. "Honestly, Amelia has been bending my ear for days, demanding to know where her delivery was, as if it were *my* fault they've been taking longer to arrive than expected. I mean, talk about shooting the messenger, am I right?"

Charlotte walked over to her garden, placing her hands on the perimeter wall, mulling this new information over. "So, Amelia receives a delivery of two large boxes of knitted squares from..."

"China," Harry entered in, joining her by the wall.

"*China?*" Charlotte answered, taken aback.

"Oh. Did I not say that part?" Harry asked.

"Good lord. So Amelia receives a large order of finished knitted squares, from China of all places, a few days before the competition comes to a conclusion," Charlotte replied, the significance of what Harry was telling her sinking in.

"That'll be why she's been jumping up and down for the delivery," Harry noted. "She needs them for the competition," he added, stating what Charlotte was already keenly aware of at this point.

"Something stinks here," Charlotte observed, turning her head, and looking off into the distance.

"Oh, sorry. Is it me?" Harry said, taking a wide step to his right, away from Charlotte. "Walking up some of these hills, carrying this heavy bag..." he explained worriedly. "Well, it doesn't half make you sweat."

"No, not *you*, Harry!" Charlotte said with a laugh. "I meant about Amelia, silly."

"You'd tell me if I did, though? Stink, I mean?"

"Yes, of course," Charlotte assured him. "Tactfully. Somehow. But seriously, though, Harry, Amelia's up to something."

"Told you!" Harry said, raising his finger to his nose again, but resisting just one more tap.

Charlotte sighed, looking off to the sea in the distance. "Amelia must be buying extra squares to win the competition, to win a *charity* competition," she said, stating the obvious, and yet shaking her head at the absurdity of it. "It's the only thing that makes sense. Amelia must be that concerned about her league position that she's resorted to shipping additional squares in to cheat her way to victory. And that's if she wasn't doing it from the *beginning*, which, knowing her, I wouldn't put past her."

Harry glanced at his watch, unsure now of his decision to bring the matter to Charlotte's attention, as there was still loads of mail left for him to deliver. "Why would she spend her own money like that?" he asked. "Is there a big cash prize or something? Is that the reason?"

"Well, there is, yes, but it wouldn't go directly into her pocket," Charlotte revealed. "You see, the cash prize is to be used for charitable purposes," she told him, "not to reimburse her or directly benefit her financially."

"So she wouldn't even recoup what she's spent on those squares?" Harry asked. "But that's even more confusing to me, then, because why would—?"

"Because she's Amelia," Charlotte gently cut in. "And to Amelia, winning is everything."

"But, still," Harry said, frowning.

"There's more," Charlotte explained. "She's doing this because of the upcoming election. By winning this competition, she knows she'll end up with her photograph plastered all over the front page of the local newspaper, thus making her look like a hero to the electorate. There's not a genuine bone in her body, I don't think, so I suspect it's all about the votes for her."

"It's rotten. It's rotten, I agree," Harry agreed. "Still, in the end, it doesn't sound like the crime of the century, I suppose," he supposed. "I mean, her selfishness and ulterior motives aside, any squares she's paying for out of her own pocket are still going towards the charity. All for a good cause, in that regard, at least, right? So things could be worse, is what I'm saying."

Harry had a valid point, and Charlotte knew he was trying to make her look on the positive side of things. She mulled his comments over, giving them due consideration, but then something occurred to her. "Oh my god, Harry!" she said, jumping at least an inch off the ground as it suddenly came to her. "Harry, even if we park the cheating aspect of all this for just a moment and also ignore the bit about her doing this purely for votes, I know for a fact she's been handing out sponsorship forms for *weeks*."

"Okay?" Harry said, unclear as to what point Charlotte might be making.

"She's duped her sponsors by artificially boosting her numbers with imported squares from China," Charlotte elaborated. "I'm fairly certain many of her sponsors are paying her for *each and every square completed*, with the natural assumption that they're all being knitted locally. And then here comes Amelia, on the sly, having huge shipments flown in from overseas! How many do you reckon were in those two boxes she's just had delivered, Harry?"

"Quite a lot," Harry answered. "Hundreds, at least. Possibly even a thousand."

"Exactly," said Charlotte. "So take a typical sponsorship rate of, say, fifty pence per square, and that's hundreds and hundreds of extra pounds that one sponsor alone might potentially be paying! Now, granted, the sponsorship money is still ultimately going to a good cause. But, still, it's just not cricket, is it? She's capitalising on and taking advantage of people trying to do a good thing for the community, Harry. Also, think of all the other groups in the competition! They're all hoping for a fair shot at winning, when here's Amelia scuppering their prospects with underhanded tactics. It stinks to high heaven!"

"Right, I see what you mean there," Harry offered, seeing what Charlotte meant. "Yeah, that's not good, now you mention it," he said, now in perfect agreement.

"I know, right?"

Just then, Harry's face turned pale. "Bloody hell, thinking about it now, she collared me a few weeks ago for sponsorship myself," he revealed, suddenly recalling the conversation. "She wouldn't take no for an answer. Stood in her doorway, she did, until I said yes and signed her blasted form! Blimey, this could cost me a bloody fortune," he moaned.

"I'm sorry to hear that. But thank you for mentioning this to me," Charlotte told him, exhausted from all the thinking she'd just been doing, and deciding she was now in desperate need of a large dose of caffeine.

"So what are you going to do?" Harry asked.

"Well..." Charlotte began, perking up at the thought of what she was going to do about it. "Well, I'll tell you just what I'm going to do! What I'm going to do is... That is, what I'm thinking is... Erhm, what I had in mind was... I mean..."

"You don't really know, do you?" Harry suggested.

"Haven't a bloody clue."

"Well, just one thing, Lotti," Harry advised, doing that looking-over-the shoulder thing again. Once he was certain the coast was clear, he continued, "If you let on about the squares from China being delivered, then Amelia's probably going to know where the information came from, see? If you catch my drift?"

"Don't worry, I catch your drift, Harry," Charlotte assured him. "Mum's the word. And, again, thank you!"

"Right. Well I'll let you get that cake to the nursing home, then," Harry replied, setting off to resume his delivery route. "You would tell me, wouldn't you?" he called out, turning round and walking backwards as he spoke.

"When I've delivered the cake?" Charlotte asked, on her way to locking the door of her house.

"No, about the, *you* know..." he said, lifting one wing and making a proper show of giving his underarm a good sniff.

"Of course, Harry!" Charlotte confirmed, with a cheery wave and a laugh. "We both look out for each other, don't we?"

"That we do!" Harry said, returning the wave. "Have a nice day, Lotti, and say hello to my dear old mum!"

CHAPTER TWENTY-THREE

"Hello?" Charlotte said weakly, eyes closed, voice croaking as a result of her vocal cords not yet being lubricated with coffee and warmed up. She allowed her head to sink back into her fluffy pillow with her phone pressed to her ear. "Larry," she said, struggling to focus on the bedside alarm clock due to the sleepy bugs in her eyes, "Larry, it's like..." she said, squinting, "six a.m."

It took a few seconds before the significance of the time hit her, and when it did, she sat bolt upright in bed. "Larry, what's wrong?" she asked, realising that even Larry wouldn't be phoning at this time of the morning simply to chat. "Right. Okay," she said in response to his answer, jumping out of bed in a shot, phone still in hand and pressed to her ear. "Larry, give me a moment. I'm going to put you on speakerphone so I can get dressed while I'm talking, all right?"

Charlotte pulled the phone away from her face and stared at it like it was a foreign object and the first time she'd ever clapped eyes on such a device, searching hopelessly for a speaker symbol or similar. "Where the hell are you...?" she asked. "Oh, there we go," she said, locating the function. "Larry, can you hear me?"

"Contact made, Lotti. I hear you loud and clear."

"Great. I'm putting my jeans on as we speak," she said, setting her phone down now, and reaching for her jeans. "Tell me again what you were saying?" she asked him, now liberating a pair of socks from her allocated sock drawer.

"Noreen hasn't responded to Larry's Lookout," Larry explained, concern evident in his voice.

J C WILLIAMS

"Right," Charlotte said, mouthing the words *Larry's lookout* back to herself, and wondering why Larry had all of a sudden started referring to himself in the third person. Between her abrupt, unexpected awakening and the distinct absence of any available caffeine immediately at hand, her brain was not performing at peak processing power just yet. "Ah!" she said, catching up, eventually, and understanding his meaning.

As the Crafternooners family expanded, Charlotte was acutely aware of their members' varying age ranges, and that a good number were of a rather more mature vintage. What concerned Charlotte was that many of the older folks in the group lived alone, without a support network like Larry and the others in the various nursing homes enjoyed. Crafternoon helped, of course, but Charlotte knew, through speaking to them, that some of them rarely left their homes outside of the crafting sessions, spending hours with only the TV for company. And this was a concern she had happened to share with Larry.

Larry was deeply sympathetic, having experienced a similar living situation before moving into the nursing home where he currently resided. As such, he'd suggested to Charlotte, and then the broader group, that he hoped to form a WhatsApp group called *Larry's Lookout*, which in fact he did, the primary purpose being that they could all keep in touch with each other. Besides the usual back-and-forth banter you'd expect in a chat group, Larry, every evening at ten, sent his daily *Larry's Laugh* message. These would consist of one of Larry's usual trademark cringeworthy jokes, or perhaps a whimsical musing relating a humorous anecdote about one of the day's events. The group members were requested to respond with a smiley face emoji in acknowledgement following that final message of the day. This wasn't just to tickle Larry's inflated ego, but also so that Larry could, more importantly, confirm that all members were present and correct before he went to bed. Of course, he wasn't overly bothered if one of the group's younger members like Bonnie didn't come back, or others he knew lived with their respective family members. Yes, he'd be slightly disappointed if they didn't immediately appreciate his comedic genius with a smiling emoji, but their lack of response wasn't something which should elicit much cause for concern, he reckoned. This was not the case with Noreen, however, who was one of the elderly members he knew lived alone, and who had not responded the previous evening.

"Are you still there?" Larry asked Charlotte.

"Yes, Larry. I'm just putting my shoes on now."

"Right," Larry continued. "Well, I did my evening roll call, as usual, receiving a high-yield, bumper crop harvest of crying-with-laugher emojis, again, as usual and per expectations," he said, voice perking up for a moment. "So, I went to bed. But, still, I tossed and turned all night, Lotti."

"Okay, Larry. Jump to the end, if you'd be so kind?"

"Ah, yes. Well, when I woke up, I just had a feeling in the pit of my stomach that I'd forgotten somebody. You know, like the mum in that Home Alone movie when she realises. So, I looked through my responses and saw I'd had nothing back from Noreen. She's often a little slow to respond, and I've pulled her up and taken her to task for this in the past, telling her—"

"Larry!"

"Sorry! In short, she didn't respond to me last night. I've tried phoning her this morning, but she's not picking up, Lotti. I'm worried, and I don't know what to do. I don't even know her address, and I'm ashamed to admit that I'd never asked for her surname."

"Okay, all right," Charlotte said, softening her tone. "I should have the addresses for all our members, including Noreen," she told him. Charlotte could sense the real strain in his voice. "Larry," she said, "I don't want you upset by this, do you hear me? If it wasn't for your brilliant idea to set up Larry's Lookout, then we wouldn't even be having this conversation at all, would we?"

"No," Larry said. "I'm just a little bit worried, Lotti."

"I know, Larry, I know. Look, I'll disappear right now so I can check through my paperwork. I'll make some calls and come back to you as soon as I can, yeah? Thank you for the call, Larry. You're truly one in a million."

After ending her phone call with Larry, Charlotte threw on an old jumper (hand-crocheted, naturally) before shaking a fast-asleep Stanley awake from slumberland and apprising him of the situation. Then, she bolted down the stairs, making a beeline to her Crafternoon filing cabinet — which was, in actual fact, a little plastic bucket used for dishwasher tablets in its former existence, now repurposed, having received something of a promotion.

"Right," Charlotte said, grabbing a handful of papers, and making a mental note that she was absolutely going to sort this into some semblance of order at some point in the near future. Fortunately, she quickly laid hands on the application form she was searching for, and mercifully, all sections appeared to have been completed.

"We need to go!" Charlotte shouted out, proper information now obtained, and in the circumstance, Stanley didn't dillydally.

She grabbed her phone, sending a quick message out to Larry's WhatsApp group, of which Noreen was a member:

> Guys – We need to check on Noreen. Noreen, if you're reading this and you're okay, sorry to wake you up 😊
>
> I'm heading there now, and I'll ask Stanley to send out the address for anyone living closer than us.

With Stanley present and correct, Charlotte grabbed her car keys and was out the door, Stanley in tow. Noreen's house was a little bit of a drive, but not too terribly far. Charlotte reckoned it would ordinarily take about twenty minutes or so to get there, but with minimal traffic at this time of the morning, she was hopeful of fifteen.

"Mum?" Stanley said in response to Charlotte sitting in the driver's seat, staring dead ahead without moving. "Mum, we need to go."

"I know," she replied, tapping her fingers on the steering wheel. "Pass me my phone before you text them the address, will you?" she asked.

"Mum?"

"Just one minute, honey. I think maybe we should also phone the police," Charlotte explained, while at the same time trying to figure out if this was in fact the proper thing to do and warranted under the circumstance.

Charlotte was in a genuine quandary about what to do. On the one hand, Noreen not checking in was concerning. Noreen was in her late eighties, and given her advanced age something dreadful could easily have happened to her. On the other hand, with Noreen being in her late eighties, it might well be the case that she merely went to bed early. Or, it could also have been that she was simply fed up with Larry's lame comedy stylings, which was also a distinct possibility. Either way, Charlotte felt reasonably confident that the police would rather receive a call, as responding to what might turn out to be a false alarm was still preferable to only hearing about something when it was too late.

In the end, Charlotte went ahead and made the call, and then handed the phone back over to Stanley, at which point she pulled out of the drive and put the pedal to the metal.

Stanley, as previously instructed, furnished everyone in the group with Noreen's address. Then, he pressed himself back into his seat, knuckles turning white due to his firm grip on the passenger-side grab handle.

"You okay there?" Charlotte asked, what with Stanley being a little quieter than usual.

"Just not used to you driving quite this fast," the boy replied, through gritted teeth.

Charlotte did indeed have her right foot planted down a little heavier than usual. But the roads were clear, with only the most minimal of traffic to contend with, and so she pressed on, making good time. Soon, however, she was distracted by the flash of a blue light rapidly approaching from behind, visible there in her rearview mirror. "Oh, fudge," she said, fearing she was about to be pulled over for speeding.

Stanley twisted around in his seat, watching as a police car hurtled towards them, travelling along at a fairly good clip, but then sailed straight on by. "Maybe they're responding to your phone call?" he suggested. "Catch them, Mum!" he said, perhaps overestimating his mum's driving abilities, as well as the limited horsepower available from her car's already-overtaxed motor.

Charlotte didn't chase the police vehicle, of course, though a short time later they did turn into the cul-de-sac where Noreen lived, and sure enough, just as Stanley had suspected, the same police car they'd seen a few miles back was parked outside her bungalow, lights now turned off.

Charlotte didn't pull into the modest drive, parking up a short distance away on the street instead, leaving plenty of room should any additional police vehicles be on their way and require access. "Wait there a moment, pumpkin," Charlotte advised, looking over to her passenger as she unfastened her seatbelt. "I'll just have a quick word with the police officer, okay?" she said, patting Stanley on the leg. "I won't be too long."

Charlotte walked up towards the property gingerly, having a quick look to see if the police car was empty once she was in the drive, which it was. "Hello?" she called out tentatively, easing open the metal gate leading to the garden path. "Oh, no," she said, breaking into a canter as she noticed the open front door. Once arrived at the door, Charlotte saw the back of a police constable, with the PC leant over and attending somebody lying on the floor a short distance inside.

"Are you family?" the officer asked, without stopping what she was doing or turning round, as she heard the sound of Charlotte's footsteps behind her.

"What...? No," Charlotte said, hands now shaking. "I–I'm the one who called you."

"What's the lady's name?"

"What...? Oh. Noreen," Charlotte replied, clearly rattled. "Sorry, it's Noreen," she said. "Is she... is she okay?"

"Noreen," the officer said, her attention focussed once again, and quite understandably, on Noreen for the moment. "Noreen, my love. My name is Susan, and I'm a police officer."

Officer Susan looked up for a moment. "Can you find a blanket or something?" she asked, over her shoulder, to Charlotte.

Charlotte had a quick glance about, in order to pinpoint the location of the bedroom. "Yes, of course," Charlotte said, spotting now what looked to her like the correct door. "Should I get a pillow also?" she asked, although not receiving a response, as the officer was busy again.

"Noreen, my love," Susan said, a little louder this time than before. "Noreen, there's an ambulance on its way, and we're going to get you a nice warm blanket, okay?"

"Is there anything else I can do?" Charlotte asked, returning with Noreen's familiar-looking, patterned crochet blanket, as well as a pillow, from Noreen's bedroom.

Susan took the blanket, laying it gently over Noreen, and then placed the pillow beneath Noreen's head as well. "No, but thank you," she told Charlotte. "The ambulance should be here in a few moments, so we're just going to sit with this lovely lady and keep her comfortable until it does. How does that sound, Noreen?"

Charlotte didn't want to ask what had occurred, but due to Noreen's position on the floor, she could only assume Noreen had fallen at some point. Choking Charlotte up was seeing Noreen's phone no more than two or three feet away from where she lay. The thought of her having help so close at hand, but just out of reach, was heart-rending.

"Noreen's one of our star crocheters," Charlotte offered affectionately as she watched on, taking a step back to give the two of them some room.

"Is that right?" Susan asked, running her hand over the blanket. "And I'll bet you made this beautiful blanket, Noreen?"

From where Charlotte stood, she could see Noreen was conscious but appeared to be in some degree of obvious discomfort. Charlotte was certainly grateful she'd made the decision to phone the police, because she knew she'd never have managed to be as calm and composed as Susan had she been the one to arrive first by herself.

Charlotte glanced over to the living room, and there, folded neatly on the sofa, was the cardigan Noreen had been working on. It was her current project, and one that Noreen had brought in the previous week at Crafternoon. "Oh!" Charlotte said, as a wave of anxiety washed over her. She put her hand to her face, certain she was going to start weeping.

"Why don't you look out for the ambulance?" Susan suggested gently, likely hearing the emotion from behind.

Charlotte nodded, heading outdoors, where Stanley was now

waiting for her outside of the car, stood at the foot of the drive.

"Mum?" Stanley asked, once Charlotte had walked over to him.

"It's fine," Charlotte said, wiping her cheek. "I don't know exactly what's happened, but Noreen is conscious, and the police are with her. We need to keep an eye out and direct the ambulance when it arrives. That's our job now," she told him.

"Should I go to the top of the street in case they drive past, Mum?"

"Brilliant idea, Stanley," Charlotte said, and with that, he was off quick as a flash to act as a lookout.

Charlotte couldn't help but notice a few of the curtains starting to twitch in the windows of the nearby houses. This was perfectly understandable, however, what with the sound of voices early in the morning and the police car parked in their street, as they were most likely concerned for their neighbour.

"Come on, come on," Charlotte said, pacing up and down the garden path, willing the ambulance to arrive. Abruptly, she stopped, certain she'd heard the sound of an approaching vehicle engine carried on the gentle morning breeze. This was confirmed by the sight of Stanley suddenly coming to attention at the entrance to the cul-de-sac. However, it didn't appear to be the ambulance just yet, a fact confirmed a moment later when a silver car drew up in front of the house. "Emma?" Charlotte said, peering over the gate as the car's window wound down. "Emma, what are you doing here?" she asked, but her question was answered in large part by the appearance of Larry climbing out of the passenger seat. "I'd only just arrived at work," Emma explained, "and Larry here asked me if I could drive him straight over."

"How is she?" Larry asked, approaching the garden wall.

But before Charlotte had a chance to respond, the sound of another vehicle approaching took her attention, followed by another. It was turning into something of a convoy. Fortunately, one of the vehicles turning into the street was the ambulance, prompting Stanley into his most passable impersonation of an airport ground controller, flailing his arms in the direction of the bungalow.

Considering the early hour, it still hadn't stopped half a dozen cars from arriving, with a concerned group of friends responding to the WhatsApp message sent from Charlotte's phone. As such, those curtains in the neighbourhood that hadn't previously been twitching were most certainly doing so presently, as their sleepy little street now resembled something of an airport runway with a squadron of aeroplanes having all just come in for a landing. As for the assorted Crafternoon members in attendance, the group watched on quietly as one of their own was soon wheeled away to the waiting ambulance. Bonnie, standing alongside her father, blew a kiss in Noreen's direction, whereas Larry raised a clenched fist, offering Noreen a spirited *show-them-what-you're-made-of!* type of gesture.

It still wasn't clear at that particular stage what precisely had transpired. Though Noreen was conscious, she was exhausted and in a lot of pain, and so wasn't able to communicate very well. The attending medics, based on the available evidence, suspected a broken hip due to a fall at some point during the previous evening. Whilst obviously in a great deal of distress, however, Noreen *had* still managed to muster up a wave to her crafting friends as she'd passed by them, trooper that she was.

Poor Larry was in pieces as the ambulance pulled away. His shoulders heaved as the emotion poured out of him.

"Hey now," Charlotte said, by this time standing with the others, and moving closer and placing her arms around him. "What's all this?"

"It's all my fault," Larry answered, a pronouncement which only resulted in the sobbing intensifying. "If only I'd checked my bloody phone later on last night, I might have…" he said, trailing off, unable to finish his sentence.

Charlotte was joined by Emma, with the two of them now giving him a cuddle. "Larry," Charlotte told him, "this is absolutely *not* your fault. If it wasn't for you, then poor Noreen could likely have been lying there all day on her own, and then who knows how things might have turned out, yeah?"

Susan, the police officer, walked over to take some details so she could reach out and contact Noreen's family, if possible. "I didn't mean to eavesdrop," she said. "But I couldn't help overhearing what you were all talking about, and I have to tell you, I've responded to many calls such as this where, sadly, nobody shows up or comes to the person's aid. All I have to do is look around and see the concern on your faces to know how fond you are of that lovely lady, so well done. I'm sure it means the world to her to have you here, and to know that all of you care."

Larry appeared to take some comfort from this, settling down and calming his breathing. "Thank you, lass. Thank you for saying that," Larry told the officer, smiling warmly. "And thank you for all you do," he added, a sentiment that was echoed by the others in the group as well.

Once the officer got the information she needed and moved away, Bonnie entered in with something to try and lighten the mood. "You know, Larry…" she said with a smirk, and pausing for dramatic effect. "You know, maybe Noreen was so distracted by the sheer awfulness of that terrible joke you sent around last night, that the poor dear fell arse-over-teakettle after reading it," she suggested, flicking her eyes around the group in expectation of their reaction.

However, her quip was met with abject silence, with nobody appearing to know if this was quite the appropriate time to break into laughter.

"I'll have you know, Bonnie…" Larry said, after a rather long, painful moment, and wagging his finger as if he were about to admonish her. "I'll have you know that joke was comedy gold, young lady," he said, with a cheeky grin emerging, at which point the others felt it safe to laugh.

"Right, then," Benjamin said, enjoying a little stretch now that the atmosphere was a little less tense. Judging by his wayward hair, it looked as if he'd been dragged out of bed at short notice, which of course he had, just like the rest of them. "Come on, you lot. There's a little café up the road that does a lovely bacon sarnie and a smashing coffee," he proposed. "What say we reconvene there, and Larry can tell us some more of those dangerously awful jokes of his? We'll just have to make sure we're all sitting down first before he starts! And, Bonnie, don't worry, if you end up late for school I'll give you a note."

Everyone was in agreement in regard to Benjamin's plan, and before they left, Charlotte just wanted to quickly check in again with the police in order to see if there was anything else they might need. Once that was sorted, she took a moment to look back over to the group. It had been a terrible morning, of course, but it could also easily have been much worse, and she was grateful that it hadn't.

She watched her people there, all stood round giving Larry appreciative claps on the back, offering words of support, and just generally being there for each other. She hadn't known most of those in attendance until a few short weeks ago, but now they were all like friends she'd known for years, a big happy family. It really struck Charlotte then as to just how vital social clubs like her Crafternoon were to the community. If you were fortunate enough to be surrounded by friends and loved ones, it made all the difference in the world. And if ever she needed reminding of that fact, she'd just need to recall the convoy of compatriots willing to look in on a friend at a moment's notice with no concern for the time of day.

At this point, Stanley, who'd followed his mum, didn't really know what to do with himself. Watching the others, he decided to suddenly jump back into the fray. "Larry!" he said, bounding over excitedly. "Larry, what do you call a pig that does karate?" Stanley asked, drawing alongside.

Larry stopped for a moment, giving this question from Stanley serious consideration. He may well have heard the joke before — many times, in fact — but if he did, he didn't let on. "I don't know," Larry answered. "What *do* you call a pig that does karate?" he said as the quick follow-up response, giving the sort of appropriate and expected kind of reaction to a line that Stanley had obviously been rehearsing in preparation for its delivery.

"A pork chop!" Stanley said, jumping in front of Larry, jazz hands in full effect.

"Brilliant," Larry said. "Well done. A pork chop! I love it!"

CHAPTER TWENTY-FOUR

C harlotte approached the charity headquarters, a relieved expression on her face, and letting loose a contented sigh. She'd just completed a whistle-stop tour of the final three nursing homes on her rounds that morning, gathering up those last-minute squares that could very well be all-important to her group's final league standings.

With this final roundup of knitted squares she'd collected from her MAKE IT SEW group, the Crafternooners, Joan's Wools and Crafts, the various nursing homes, and now these final few nursing homes, there were a fair few squares to add to her final tally. She'd not bothered counting them all up individually, but the large plastic carrier bag in her hand was plump, to say the least, and had some nice weight to it.

It had been a busy few weeks, of that there was no doubt. But it'd been bloody good fun, as well. Still, a teensy-weensy ickle part of her didn't want to see another bloomin' crafting square for at least... well, not until the same time the following year, assuming they chose to repeat the campaign, at which point she'd be knee-deep in squares once again, glutton for punishment that she was.

Charlotte was genuinely interested in finding out their final, ultimate total, just so that she could feed the number back to the assorted participants who'd provided so much of their time. There was no doubting that Charlotte had her eyes firmly set on first place, but in all honesty she didn't realistically hold out too much hope. However, she wouldn't be overly concerned if they didn't top the leaderboard, because either way, it was the charity (and, by extension, the broader community in general) that would ultimately benefit from their collective endeavours. Plus, if they didn't happen to win it this year, there was always the next. The CRAFTERNOON SEWCIAL CLUB was going from strength to strength, so their chances could only improve, she felt confident.

Charlotte stopped suddenly just outside of the charity's main entrance, turning on a sixpence, certain she'd caught her name floating on the wind. She raised her right hand to her forehead in a sort of salute, shielding her eyes from the midday sun in defence against the harsh light, and was able to just make out, against the glare, a figure advancing at pace.

"Charlotte!" came the voice again, louder and more distinct this time as the figure to which it belonged approached. "Charlotte, wait up!"

The person didn't need to get too much closer for Charlotte to know precisely who it was that was calling her name. "Oh, great," she said under her breath in response, reaching for her phone so she could keep it poised and at the ready in order to pretend an urgent call was coming in if the need should arise.

"Wait up!" Amelia called out, in an unnervingly friendly voice. "You're making me run in my expensive shoes!" she joked, before finally coming to a halt in front of Charlotte. "So..." she said.

"So," Charlotte replied, offering up a forced smile.

Amelia ran her hand through her perfect hair, ensuring every single strand was in its proper place. "Are you dropping off the last of your squares?" Amelia asked, looking down to the bag held in Charlotte's hand.

Charlotte instinctively pulled her hand back, like a schoolkid protecting a treasured possession from the class bully. "What can I do for you, Amelia?" Charlotte asked, eager to move this conversation along to a swift conclusion.

Amelia exposed her veneers, and to anyone who may have been passing by, the pair of them would have appeared like two old pals having a friendly little catch-up and chin wag. "I just wanted to..." Amelia said, appearing unsure of what exactly she wanted to say next, despite having run all the way over like she desperately wanted to say something.

"Yes...?" Charlotte pressed, moving her bag-laden hand back a bit further in response to Amelia's prying eyes.

"That bag looks jolly full," Amelia noted, following this with a weird little snort of a laugh thingy that made Charlotte sick to her stomach.

"Two, maybe three hundred in there…?" Amelia suggested, sizing up the bag with an expert eye, like a jeweller spotting a large, valuable gemstone.

"Amelia, are you following me?" Charlotte said bluntly.

"What? No, of course not!" Amelia replied, laughing nervously as she did so. "No, I've just been in to drop my final squares off, and who should I see as I walk away and turn to get in my car but yours truly," she said.

"Oh…kay…?" Charlotte answered. "Right, well I suppose I should probably…" she said, pointing over her shoulder, and then pivoting towards the entrance of the charity once again in order to resume her journey inside. "Good luck and all," she added, without spinning back around.

"Your ex-husband George!" Amelia then blurted out, rather strangely, and apropos of absolutely nothing at all.

Charlotte half-turned in response, wondering where on earth this could possibly be going. "Yes…?"

"He's a wonderful worker, your George," Amelia added cryptically. "Just wonderful. Efficient, also."

"Well, sure, that's generally what happens when you *pay* him, Amelia," Charlotte replied. "But ask him to change a lightbulb when you're *married* to him, and it's an entirely different story, however," she remarked.

"I've enjoyed having him around the church hall these last few weeks," Amelia went on. "Terrific worker."

"Amelia," Charlotte said, turning fully now, and eyes narrowing. "Amelia, what are you on about? I thought you were married?"

"Me? Yes, of course I am," Amelia responded, placing her hand across her chest to protect her virtue. "No, no, I'm not interested in George like that," she said. "Good heavens, no," she added, grimacing like she'd sucked a lemon dry.

"So why have you chased after me after having almost made it back to your car, and then pounced on me to prattle on about my ex-husband, who you don't at all fancy, and his impressive work ethic?"

"Well," Amelia said, in a tone indicating she had some grade-A gossip to spill. "It turns out that we're going to have at least another six months of work available on the church hall. And, if that turns out well, which I'm sure it will, then there should be another contract in the community centre also available."

"Great," Charlotte said, raising her eyebrows, feigning interest.

"Your husband — sorry, *ex*-husband — mentioned how difficult building work has been to come by lately," Amelia continued, blathering on. "A terrible state of affairs for a hard-working man, I'd say. So, it must be nice for him to have some regular money coming in, and to, you know, be able to treat young Seamus now and then."

"It's Stanley!" Charlotte shot back, seething, and with no attempt to conceal the daggers flying out of her eyes. "Get to the point, Amelia, and save us from having this bloody little dance with each other," she said, until a moment of realisation hit her hard as to what Amelia might possibly be getting at. "Wait, are you trying to bribe or extort me or something...?" she asked.

"What?" Amelia said, appearing mortally wounded by the very suggestion. "No, of course I'm not," she insisted, offering her most pleasant of smiles to a woman suddenly walking out of the building. Amelia turned her head, following the woman with her eyes until she felt the woman was well out of earshot. "It would be so nice to win this competition, is all that I'm saying," Amelia continued, her attention now back to Charlotte. "All the time we've invested, it'd be so disappointing if we were to fall at the final hurdle," she suggested. Amelia sucked in air through her expensive teeth, shaking her head sadly. "A real shame," she added, sighing ruefully, for full effect.

Charlotte glanced down to the bag in her hand, and then back up to Amelia. "You're something else, Amelia," she remarked, rolling her eyes. "So let me see if I understand you correctly here, she went on, cocking her head. "Let's say, in a purely hypothetical scenario, of course, that I was to donate the considerable number of squares in my hand to bolster your effort. That would mean that not only does my group's tally *not* increase as it should, but that *your* total does, stretching any potential lead you may have even further. And, in *return* for this becoming a reality, again, purely *hypothetically*, of course, might my ex-husband, say, miraculously find himself as the frontrunner for a generous new contract?"

"Perish the thought!" Amelia said, appearing most offended by what Charlotte was implying. "I'm sure I could speak to someone, however…?" she quickly added, as if this were an afterthought, something she'd never before considered but an idea she was quickly warming to nonetheless. "That is, if you'd like me to, of course?" she offered magnanimously.

Charlotte didn't often struggle for words, but this little exchange had temporarily taken her tongue. "So…" she said, after a long few moments' pause. "So, not only are you cheating by importing knitted squares from China, but you're here, now, trying to bribe me into handing over the squares my team has worked so hard on? Amelia, need I remind you that this is a knitting competition for *charity*, and not an episode of the bloody Sopranos?"

Amelia stared at Charlotte's plastic bag with the fiery intensity of Gollum after having clapped eyes onto The One Ring and never wanting to let it go. "Hang on!" Amelia snapped, once Charlotte's words had sunk in. "How the hell do you know about the China thing? Very few people know about that!"

"I don't know, perhaps a spy has infiltrated your organisation?" Charlotte suggested casually, of course not wishing to throw good Postman Harry under the bus. The subterfuge appeared to have worked, thank goodness, as Amelia, unhappy though she was, didn't seem to suspect the truth.

"Anyway, so not only have you artificially inflated your group's numbers by importing squares from overseas, but now you're trying to bribe me into handing over additional squares as well?" Charlotte continued. "For a *charity* competition? Seriously, Amelia, the press would have a field day if they knew what despicable lengths you'll go to in order to impress the local voters!"

"Fine!" Amelia said, holding her hands up in submission. "I was only trying to help out your ex, and *this* is the thanks I receive in return," she whinged. "As for the ridiculous accusations of bribery and cheating, Charlotte, *tut-tut,* my dear. After all, who's going to believe such a load of old flannel? Especially, to use your words, when it's only a knitting competition for charity? So, even if it *were* true, who's going to believe the ramblings of little old you? Certainly not the slack-jawed bunch of idiots that live in Laxey, that's for sure."

Charlotte unwrapped her fingers, revealing the phone in her hand, holding it up for Amelia's benefit. "Well, it's just as well that I recorded our pleasant conversation, then, isn't it?" Charlotte said, allowing herself a broad grin. "I'm sure the local press and your potential electorate could draw their own conclusions as to what you did, or did not, mean to say. And what did you call them, Amelia? Slack-jawed idiots, was it? I'm sure they'll appreciate that come election day."

Charlotte held her steely gaze for several seconds, enjoying each and every one of them, hoping for some form of reaction that didn't arrive. "Right," Charlotte said eventually, breaking the silence. "I'm going in there, and when I come back out, I really don't want to see you, Amelia."

Charlotte offered her leave with an impressive flick of her head, bag swinging gently in her hand as she set off. "Oh, and Amelia?" she said, turning just slightly as the building's automatic doors slid open for her, and speaking just loud enough that only Amelia could hear her. "I've got a funny feeling that when George next pops round to my house, he'll be telling me all about his new contract," she suggested. "Or else…" she added, wiggling her phone in the air as she went inside, not waiting around to hear Amelia's response but confident that Amelia would come to the correct conclusion.

Ordinarily, Charlotte wasn't somebody who relished conflict, and in fact was eager to avoid it at all costs whenever possible. Indeed, Mollie often joked that if you stole Charlotte's seat at the cinema, she'd likely give you her popcorn and tell you to enjoy the film. It was one of those things that Charlotte told herself she really ought to work on. Not that there was any desire on her part to start dragging people from their car if they cut her up at a junction or anything. Nothing like that. But she did wish to have a little more bite if such a need were to present itself. As such, she was delighted with the calm yet assertive manner in which she handled the situation earlier, and was keen to regale Mollie with every detail of her bravery. After leaving Oxfam, then, Charlotte headed to the farm shop after a bit. Mollie's farm shop also sold a gorgeous selection of fresh-cut flowers, which was an added bonus and worked out well, as Charlotte was planning to pop by the hospital to see Noreen on the way home…

"And *then*…" Charlotte said, with Mollie hanging on her every word. "*Then,* I turned away from her, like *this*," Charlotte said, reenacting the moment without sparing any detail. "Flicking my hair in her *face*," Charlotte added, curling her top lip into a snarl, and putting in a performance worthy of an Oscar.

"Yeah? And then what?" Mollie asked, waving the price gun she was currently holding, anxious to hear more about her best friend's heroic exploits.

"Well…" Charlotte said, perfectly happy to continue. "*Then,* I walked over towards the door without looking back, all tough and whatnot, like *this*," she explained, inflating her chest, and illustrating further by introducing a swagger into her walk that looked to Mollie as if Charlotte either had a very bad limp, or she was maybe experiencing a type of leakage of some sort or another, or possibly both things at once.

"What the hell was *that*?" Mollie said, bursting into a fit of giggles. "Please tell me you didn't walk like that?"

"Like what?" Charlotte asked, coming to a sudden halt next to the beetroot stand.

"Like *what*?" Mollie replied. "Like John Wayne staggering out of a saloon with a stone caught in his boot, that's what!"

"I'm probably just not doing it justice," Charlotte suggested. "It was a lot more… well, more angry and convincing if you were to see it in person, if you know what I mean. I could probably ask the receptionist for the CCTV footage if you like? She's done it for me once before, and I could probably convince her to do it again."

"You're fine, Lotti. But well done, babes," Mollie said, offering her best mate some much needed praise. "So, did you send her away with a flea in her ear, then?" Mollie asked. "After you showed her who's boss?"

"Well, yes and no," Charlotte said. "I mean, away, yes. But not *away*, away. I could see her through the window, actually, waiting for me in the carpark," Charlotte revealed, with her level of bravado waning somewhat as she recalled this. "However, I wasn't for intimidating," she declared, now perking up again, and rolling her fingers into a tight fist. "Charlotte Newman can hold her own when the need arises!"

"You went out the back door, didn't you?" Mollie surmised.

"That's one way to put it, I suppose," Charlotte confirmed, before adding, "There's a lovely coffee shop just down the road where I sat in the window, watching her. I ended up having two coffees while I waited, so my head was spinning by the time she eventually left. I won't sleep tonight after all that caffeine in the afternoon. Anyway, thirty-five bloody minutes she waited, pacing back and forth like a caged bear before she finally got bored and left. I honestly thought I was going to have to abandon my car and phone for a taxi home."

Charlotte proceeded to fill Mollie in on all the finer details of the attempted bribery and fraud, as well as the electoral deception. The picture Charlotte so eloquently painted was that this heinous, hideous crafting square scandal was at least on the same scale as Watergate, with Amelia's tentacles also likely reaching the highest echelons of the Manx establishment.

"So..." Mollie said. "Now what?"

"I told you, I'm going to see Noreen. It's a fractured hip, but they're confident that—"

"No, I meant what about Amelia?" Mollie said, gently cutting across. "Though I'm pleased Noreen is being well looked after."

"Ah," Charlotte said, removing a carrot from the wooden crate next to her, and dusting off a bit of remaining dirt. "Well... what I was going to do was..." she began, but then drifting off, fidgeting with the carrot in her hand.

"You don't have a plan, do you?"

"Not in the slightest, Moll. Why? Do you?" Charlotte said, moving closer to her, eager to hear what pearls of wisdom Mollie might be able to impart on the current situation.

"You need to dust yourself down," Mollie replied.

"Excellent idea," Charlotte replied, taking a mental note. "Yes? And then what?"

"No, I mean, literally, dust yourself down, Lotti. You've got a little bit of soil on you, just there," Mollie remarked, motioning towards Charlotte's shirt. "But as for Amelia, well, I can't really say. Has the competition now closed?"

"Yes, today. That's how we both met at HQ."

"Ooh," Mollie said, a devious thought appearing to present itself to her. "What you could do..."

"Yeah?" Charlotte said, edging closer.

"Is there a prize presentation?"

"Yeah. The participating groups are invited to charity HQ tomorrow for tea and sandwiches for the grand unveiling of the winner," Charlotte replied. "Why?"

"Great," Mollie answered. "So, if Amelia and her gang were to win, what you do is let her saunter up on stage..."

"I'm not sure if there's a stage, but go on."

"Okay, you let Amelia saunter up to collect her prize, and then BOOM!"

"Boom?" Charlotte asked, eager to understand the next stage of the cunning plan.

"You offer up a cough, loud enough to attract everybody's attention," Mollie explained. "And when everybody turns to look at you, that's when you press play on your phone and wipe the smug, satisfied expression straight from Amelia's chops. You could even bring along a Bluetooth speaker to make it that much louder."

"Brilliant!" Charlotte declared. "But why do I press play on my phone, exactly?" she asked, diligently taking mental notes so she could visualise every detail in her mind's eye.

Mollie went silent for a moment, running her eyes over her friend's face. "Why do you think?" she said. "So everybody can hear the conversation you recorded, obviously?"

"Ah. Well I do love the plan, Moll," Charlotte answered. "But there's just one teensy-weensy flaw."

"Which is?"

"Well, I didn't actually record Amelia. Apologies, I thought you'd picked up on that point."

"Wait, what? You said you did!" an exasperated Mollie shot back. "Just earlier. You told me."

"Ah. Sadly, no. Not really. Not for real. The fact of the matter is, I wouldn't have the slightest clue about how to do that even if you gave me all day to figure it out. And as for attempting it under pressure, in the heat of battle, well, there was never a chance."

Mollie returned to her station behind the counter, shaking her head in exasperation. "Well," she said, "if you didn't actually really record Amelia, then I'm afraid to say I don't think there's anything you can do. At least nothing that comes to mind."

However, in response to this sombre conclusion, Charlotte offered up a confident smile. A smile that belied the fact that their plan had just been blown up, destroyed before it'd even had a chance to hatch. "No!" Charlotte said, approaching the counter, repeating her palsied John Wayne too-long-in-the-saddle swagger from earlier. "Whilst it may be true that I'd not recorded Amelia's confession, *Amelia* doesn't know how useless I am at working my phone."

"Ah, I see," Mollie said, nodding. "So, to be clear, as far as Amelia is concerned, you recorded the conversation in full?"

"Every last word. Or so she *thinks*," Charlotte was happy to report. "Her face was a picture," she recalled fondly.

"Excellent!" Mollie said, reaching for the pen tucked safely behind her ear. "In that case, young Lotti. Let's get back to the drawing board on Operation Amelia."

CHAPTER TWENTY-FIVE

S top telling me you're on your way, you little monkey, when you're quite clearly not!" Charlotte said, calling upstairs as she placed a neat pile of clothes into Stanley's backpack, though how long they'd remain neat was anybody's guess. "Stanley, your father is going to be here for you in…" she began. "Scrap that, he's already here!" she added abruptly, looking through the kitchen window with a wave. "Stanley!" she shouted once more, for good measure, as she headed over to the door to greet their visitor.

"Heya," said Charlotte, opening the front door before George had a chance to ring the bell.

"Hi," George answered, head slightly down, staring intently at the bedside table placed strangely, just there, where it was. "Is this some kind of new design feature?" he asked, apparently wondering why it was exactly that a piece of *indoor* furniture would be placed *outdoors*, on the steps. "Most people usually put a potted plant or something here. But whatever works, I s'pose?"

"Oh, that?" Charlotte said casually, as if the item's sudden appearance on the doorstep had inexplicably slipped her mind. "I completely forgot I'd left it there," she said, though not being terribly convincing.

"What?" George said with a laugh. "I just saw you put it there when I was driving up the street towards the house!"

"Oh," Charlotte replied, her minor subterfuge quickly unravelling. "Ehm… well, the bottom has dropped out of one of the drawers, you see, and I was going to—"

"Bring it out just before I arrived?" George suggested playfully.

"Want me to take it and have a look? See if I can fix it for you?"

"Oh, would you?" Charlotte asked, acting surprised but delighted, as if this thought had never occurred to her, and as if this in fact had in no way been her plan all along. "My unmentionables keep getting mixed up with my mentionables, and…" she started to explain. "In fact, you know what, never mind about that. If you'd take a look, yes, I'd be grateful."

"Come on, Stan-the-Man!" George shouted through the opened door. "We've got a boys' weekend to get started!" he said, bursting with enthusiasm at the prospect of said weekend.

"Sounds fun," Charlotte offered, handing over Stanley's backpack. "In that bag, George, I've packed a change of clothes, as usual," she said. "Now, you may have noticed that I tend to include a spare pair of underpants, also. And the reason for this is so that Stanley doesn't wear the *exact same* underpants for several days on the bounce," she advised pointedly, though not without some degree of humour.

"He told me he was trying to set a new world record!" George protested, apparently quite pleased at his son's endeavours. "I was just encouraging his get-up-and-go!" George added, appearing well chuffed at the little lad's attempt at holding a place in the record books.

"Hmm, are you quite certain that's something you haven't made up just now?" Charlotte commented, sceptical but amused. "And besides, his undies nearly get up and go all by themselves by the time he finally gets round to changing them! So that I'll not need to remove them eventually with a pair of kitchen tongs and a hazmat suit, can you kindly make sure he puts on a clean pair tomorrow morning? I'd be eternally grateful if you did."

"Ah, the good folks over at Guinness will be sorely disappointed, then," George answered, shoulders slumped in defeat.

"Plenty of time for Guinness when he's older," Charlotte replied with a wink.

"True, true," George agreed with a laugh.

"Anyway…" Charlotte said, taking a detour away from the topic of Guinness, be it record books or otherwise. "How's work?" she asked.

"How's work?" George said, a little taken aback at this sudden and unexpected change of subject. "Work's... work," he said, succinctly summarising his present employment situation. "Why?" he asked, scratching the top of his head.

"Oh, no reason," Charlotte said, looking over her shoulder for a moment to see where Stanley was. "How is it working with Amelia?" she enquired. "She *is* your current boss, isn't she?"

"I dunno," George replied, offering a shrug. "I mean, she signs the cheques, so I suppose she is," he said. "Again, why do you ask? You rarely talk to me about work, Lotti."

"No real reason," Charlotte said nonchalantly, though again, not awfully convincingly. "Only you mentioned previously that it was a short-term contract. So I was just interested, that's all."

"Ahh," said George, nodding, certain now that he knew what was going on with this peculiar line of enquiry. "You're worried about my ability to earn money, aren't you?" he suggested. "And, in turn, my ability to give *you* money."

"George, that's not fair, I was just interested in—"

"It's fine," George said cheerily. "I'm just teasing, as you've actually been very understanding when I've experienced the occasional lean spell in that regard. It's actually a bit spooky, though, that you should mention Amelia. Because I had a missed call from her only just this morning, as it should happen."

"Oh?" Charlotte said.

"Yeah, I'll speak to her on Monday, as we've got our boys' weekend." George took a step forward, offering up a high-five for Stanley, now present and stood in the doorway next to Mum. "Let's get going, buddy."

Charlotte gripped Stanley in a bear hug, kissing the top of his head. "You have a wonderful weekend, Stanley," she said. "And not too much sugar or fast food, yeah?" she added, although she knew there was about as much point to telling Stanley this as there was to advising Popeye not to eat spinach.

"Good luck in the crafting competition," Stanley offered up in between the kiss-based assault upon his person.

"Oh, yeah. The prize ceremony is later today?" George asked. "Do you want us to drop by?" he proposed, looking to Stanley for concurrence, which was duly given.

"Oh, would you?" Charlotte said, genuinely appreciative of the offer. "If you could, it would be wonderful, George. I'll text you over the address."

"Right, let's go, short stuff," George said, making sure to take hold of Charlotte's strategically placed bedside table, as well, as he and Stanley turned to leave. "Next stop, McDonald's!"

"Yay!" Stanley replied, adjusting the straps on his backpack.

"But I just said…" Charlotte began to protest, but it was no use. Charlotte well knew that once the idea of McDonald's was planted inside a child's head, there was no getting it out.

"Have fun!" she called after them. "And I'll hopefully see you very soon!"

As Amelia had apparently already phoned George — probably to discuss a shiny new contract, no doubt — Charlotte felt safe in assuming she had Amelia dangling on the end of her fishing line like a prize trout. Indeed, Charlotte kept one eye on her phone for most of the morning, half-expecting a call from her beleaguered nemesis.

The difficulty, as of right now, was that Charlotte still didn't know quite what to do with the recorded conversation situation that'd presented itself, or what she hoped to achieve by it — and made more challenging, also, by the fact that there *was* no actual recorded conversation. Sure, Mollie had offered some innovative ideas during their subsequent Operation Amelia battleplan discussions, but Charlotte simply didn't know which possible course of action might be best in pursuing.

Also, while Amelia may have been guilty of many things, it transpired that sponsorship fraud didn't appear to be one of them, as Charlotte had located and reviewed a copy of the form in question on Amelia's social media. Detailed on it, those sponsoring the Laxey Coffee Morning Crew agreed to pay a fixed amount regardless of the total amount of squares created. So, Amelia artificially inflating their final tally with foreign imports didn't fraudulently increase the amount of sponsorship due after all, and on this one point, at least, Charlotte had been mistaken.

However, buying in the additional squares from overseas still afforded Amelia an unfair overall advantage, and this was the issue that really grated with Charlotte (that, and of course the unsavoury matter of attempted bribery to help further achieve her nefarious ends). Playing devil's advocate, Mollie had pointed out previously that Charlotte herself had accepted many squares from what might easily be considered a questionable source — namely, the strippers-and-moonshine event. Charlotte was able to reconcile this in her mind, however, as the squares had at least still been crafted on the island by the local crafting community. The friskier ones, granted. But still the local crafting community.

She'd still to settle on a final decision as to what she'd do, but all things considered and reviewed, Charlotte (along with Mollie) felt it would be unfair and unsporting for Amelia to win the competition by buying in the items they were supposed to craft. As far as Charlotte could see, the only proper and equitable solution would be for the Laxey Coffee Morning Crew to withdraw from the competition before the awards ceremony later in the day — a suggestion it was hoped Amelia would agree to, even if the threat of the (supposed) phone recording was required to give her a gentle nudge in the right direction. Following this course of action wouldn't come easy to Charlotte. She felt awful for Amelia's members, who were only guilty by association. But, on the same token, what Amelia had done was unfair to hundreds of other crafters who'd entered into the proper spirit of the competition.

The issue now, though, was that Amelia hadn't yet made contact, and so Charlotte would need to do just that, a prospect that she really didn't relish. But the clock was ticking, with the awards ceremony only a few short hours away, so Charlotte would need to get her skates on, so to speak.

Charlotte returned to the kitchen, after having seen George and Stanley off. She had a seat, and then scrolled through the contacts saved on her mobile phone, uncertain if she still had Amelia's phone number there. At one point she did, from when they were both on the school disco organising committee a while back. But she had a feeling she'd since deleted it, likely when Amelia had become a complete pain in the—

"Bollocks!" Charlotte said, startled, dropping her phone onto the tabletop. She looked like she'd seen a ghost as, just then, a text had suddenly arrived in her inbox from Amelia at the very same moment she was looking for Amelia's number.

Panicked, Charlotte swept her eyes around the interior of the kitchen, wondering if she were somehow being observed or, perhaps, bugged. This was a notion she quickly dismissed as absurd, although it didn't stop her from having one last lingering look about the room, before then bravely picking the phone back up in order to read her incoming message:

> Charlotte. I wondered if we might have a quick talk? If you're available, I'm at the Laxey coffee morning from 11 till 1.
>
> Tnx - Amelia

"Oh," Charlotte said, somewhat unnerved. "Oh," she said again, slightly perturbed by the unexpected cordial nature of the text, and also wondering as to what she ought to do next in light of it. Whatever she decided to do, however, Charlotte would need to do it sooner rather than later, as a glance at the clock confirmed it was now a little after ten a.m.

Rather than procrastinate for the next hour or so, as she knew she otherwise might, Charlotte instead settled on phoning her most trusted advisor, hopeful of some wise counsel. Mollie didn't know what advice she could offer, but she did volunteer to accompany her bestie to Charlotte's meet-up with Amelia.

Shortly thereafter, Charlotte spotted Mollie through the kitchen window, with Mollie stood there peering over Charlotte's garden wall admiring her roses, before then making her way up to the house. "I didn't mean for you to come over immediately!" Charlotte said, as she opened the door and let her in.

"It's fine," Mollie said. "Reporting for duty, as requested. I've got someone minding the till, and I was going to pop around in a bit anyway, ahead of the awards ceremony. Will there be food there?"

"At the awards ceremony? I imagine so. Sandwiches and such, from what I understand," Charlotte said. "But I've bought a couple of steaks and a lovely bottle of red for later. Are you staying over?"

"Pyjamas are in the car," Mollie replied, giving a little salute.

Whilst Charlotte hadn't specifically asked for it, she was grateful to have Mollie by her side on her trip to see Amelia. She didn't suspect Amelia to be capable of physical violence, but knowing how devious she'd been of late, it certainly didn't hurt to bring along a witness, at the very least.

It was only a brief stroll over to the Laxey church hall, and Charlotte's mind was working overdrive. She genuinely didn't know what to expect from Amelia once she would arrive there, and the butterflies were out in force, having a party in Charlotte's stomach.

"Here we are," Charlotte said, a short time later, looking at the wooden notice board welcoming visitors at the foot of the concrete path. The first thing she noticed was Amelia's eye-catching COFFEE MORNING CREW poster displayed behind a Perspex sheet. It was considerably better than her own graphic design efforts, and something she would certainly take inspiration from on her next attempt.

"Right. This is the sweatshop where they've been churning out crafting squares for weeks," Charlotte joked to Mollie, attempting to lighten the mood, and at the same time hoping to relieve the knot in her tum. "I'll bet the poor members are chained to wooden benches, with Amelia walking around whipping them into submission when their productivity levels drop."

In truth, Charlotte didn't know what she'd find behind those heavy oaken doors up ahead, but there was only one way to find out. Lifting the large, ornate iron latch to ease the door open, Charlotte glanced behind to Mollie, confused about the sound she could hear emanating from within the church. "Does that sound like a guitar?" she asked.

"Ukulele, maybe?" Mollie answered, venturing a guess, though appearing uncertain herself.

Charlotte opened the door fully now, enough to walk through, which she then did, and with Mollie following closely behind.

There in the corner sat on a stool was a smartly dressed chap plucking the strings of what turned out upon closer inspection to be a mandolin, as near as the girls could tell. He warbled out a rather catchy ditty, and whilst Charlotte didn't recognise the lyrics, the tune itself seemed very familiar to her. "He's quite good," Charlotte said, patting her thigh along in time to the music.

On first impressions, Amelia's coffee morning wasn't anywhere near as expected. No wardens were patrolling, beating those who dared to break ranks, and no chains were visible, or at least none that Charlotte could see. Indeed, as far as Charlotte could observe, those folk inside appeared to be there very much of their own free will. Several tables were spaced out inside the modest hall, each filled with people singing along to the music while they crafted. And rather than feeling intimidated, Charlotte felt perfectly at ease. In fact, the general atmosphere felt just like her own Crafternoon club, if not perhaps even a little bit more lively.

"Room for two over here!" a friendly lady said, pointing to the pair of empty seats near to her. "Not to worry, we don't bite!" she added amiably, accompanied by a friendly wave of laughter from the others presently sharing the table.

"Oh, thanks," Charlotte said, keeping her voice fairly low so as not to possibly disrupt anyone's enjoyment of the current musical serenade. Charlotte's overriding reaction was to sit down, pick up the wool and needles sat there on the tabletop, and get stuck in. But she remained resolute and focused on the task at hand. "I was hoping to find Amelia?" Charlotte said, having a cursory glance around the room.

The woman Charlotte was speaking with repeated the same process, glancing about the room herself. "Hmm," she said. "She might be in the kitchen helping with the refreshments," she suggested, in the absence of anything else immediately apparent. "It's at the back of the hall through the door on the left."

"Terrific, thanks," Charlotte said, just as the music came to its natural conclusion. "Oh, and by the way, I absolutely adore your cardigan. Such beautiful colours!" she added, taking advantage of the short lull between now and when the next song might start.

The two girls wended their way through the maze of tables,

offering and receiving courteous smiles as they progressed.

"Charlotte...?" an enquiring voice called out, bringing Charlotte to an abrupt halt.

"Yvonne?" Charlotte said, upon locating the voice's owner, who was huddled over one of the tables, needles in hand. "Yvonne is one of our Crafternooners," Charlotte said by way of introduction, turning to Mollie for a moment. "I didn't know you came here...?" Charlotte asked Yvonne, in a tone she hoped didn't come across as accusatory in any way.

"Crafternoon, Laxey, Peel, and Ramsey," Yvonne replied, receiving several nods around the table from her crafting compatriots. "We'd turn up to the opening of an envelope if there was crafting, tea, and conversation to be had," Yvonne joked.

"Gets us out of the house," Yvonne's friend sat to the left of her suggested.

"Yvonne's told us all about Crafternoon, so we'll be seeing you on Thursday," her mate to the right then chipped in.

"Excellent," Charlotte responded. "Well, we'll make you all very welcome, and I look forward to seeing what you're working on. Anyway, I'll leave you to it, and lovely to see you all."

Charlotte continued making her way towards the kitchen, taking an appreciative glance at the various crafting projects in progress as she went along. It was apparent there were some fine, seasoned crafters amongst the group, and also those perhaps newer to the hobby. Either way, they were all having a blast, and the friendly conversation and gentle laughter filling the room was a delight for Charlotte to hear.

"*Ahem*," Charlotte said, clearing her throat to announce her presence, as she was soon stood in the kitchen doorway.

The figure Charlotte believed to be Amelia remained crouched down, with her head positioned close to the opened door of an oven. "Jimmy, if that's you again, then the scones are going to be ten minutes, at least," the person said firmly, although following this with a friendly laugh.

"It's not Jimmy," Charlotte said softly, recognising Amelia's voice, but not wishing to startle her, what with Amelia's head positioned so near to the oven and all.

"Oh," Amelia said, looking over her shoulder, and then returning to a standing position with a tray of freshly baked scones held fast in one oven-gloved hand. "One moment," she added, placing the scones on a baking rack to cool.

Seeing Amelia like this took Charlotte a bit by surprise. Rather than the perfect, flawless face — with makeup precisely applied — that Charlotte had always come to expect, Amelia now had a generous smear of flour running across the width of her cheek. She was also wearing flat shoes (no heels), which was unusual, and the absence of any visible designer clothing was also striking as well. To be fair, she looked great either way, but this was just a side of Amelia that Charlotte had never seen.

"This is Mollie," Charlotte said, introducing her friend. "Mollie, this is Amelia."

"Would you like a scone?" Amelia asked with a smile, noticing Mollie staring intently at them. "When I thought it was Jimmy come begging for more, I said ten minutes, but really I've got an earlier batch that should be right at optimum temperature just now."

"Ehm..." Mollie replied, looking over to Charlotte for approval and appearing uncertain if she should be taking gifts from the perceived enemy. "Yes, that would be lovely, thank you," Mollie told Amelia, after receiving a shrug and a nod from her friend.

"I've seen you before," Amelia said, narrowing her left eye, and cocking her head for a moment. "Ah!" she said, butter knife poised and readied for action. "Do you work at that marvellous farm shop?" she asked, liberating a generous portion of clotted cream from the tub on the table in front of her.

"Yes, that's me," Mollie answered. "I'm the manager," Mollie was happy to report.

"You run a tight ship," Amelia remarked. "The veg up there is to die for."

Amelia then stood with her head bowed, preparing the scone. "Thank you for coming, Charlotte," she said, without looking up. "I'm not really sure what to say to you. So, I'll just begin by saying how sorry I am."

"You are?" Charlotte replied, unnerved, as she half-expected

Amelia to go on the offensive.

"I am," Amelia confirmed. "Actually, Charlotte, I'm ashamed of myself," she added, applying a delightful dollop of strawberry jam to Mollie's scone. "I'm too competitive," she went on, popping the scone onto a side plate, and then handing it over to the now-salivating Mollie. "I won't lie, Charlotte. I've not really slept, with everything running through my head thinking about how I've behaved. And I don't just mean the other day, either. I've been absolutely horrid to you when I've seen you at school recently, and I'm ashamed."

"Oh," Charlotte said, in the absence of anything else coming to mind.

"This may come as a surprise to you, Charlotte, but you make me feel inadequate," Amelia offered. "Not that it's deliberate on your part, of course."

"What?" Charlotte said, looking over to Mollie, wondering where this was possibly going. "I do?"

"Indeed you do," Amelia answered. "Again, not that it's your fault," Amelia was quick to add. "What I mean to say is that I find you quite inspiring, if I'm honest."

"I... you– you think I'm...?" Charlotte stammered, with nothing else more sensible presenting itself. "What?" Charlotte said again, uncertain if this weren't perhaps some sort of mind game Amelia was playing.

"I'm not teasing in any way," Amelia said, reading the scepticism that must have been written across Charlotte's face. "You come into school wearing adorable clothes you've made yourself, all while juggling being a single mother, and you *still* make the time to set up social clubs and volunteer at the nursing homes, which I think is amazing. It's inspiring, as I've said, and if I'm honest, it's the reason I set up my own coffee morning."

"Why didn't you tell me all of this before?" Charlotte asked. "I thought you were just being a witch to me recently because, well, you're a witch."

Amelia considered her response for a moment, using the back of her hand to wipe the flour from her cheek. Her bottom lip began to tremble like a bowl of jelly. "I didn't tell you, because I *am* a witch," she said, eyes welling up. "Or at least I can be. But I don't *want* to be, Charlotte. I don't *mean* to be, honestly, I don't. And I have to say I deserve anything that might be coming to me, Charlotte, when you make that recording of yours public. I've been doing a lot of soul-searching, and who knows, perhaps it'll even help make me a better person in the end."

At this point, Charlotte remained silent, suspecting these might well be crocodile tears on display. After all, Amelia had form for putting in an astonishing, award-winning performance when the situation demanded it.

"I'm going to withdraw from the crafting competition," Amelia revealed. "As you know, I bought in a large number of squares to artificially inflate our figures, five hundred to be exact, which I absolutely shouldn't have done. And, as for the shameful act of attempted bribery, well, I've genuinely no excuse for that other than I was so focussed on winning I became blind to my actions. Stood here, right now, I realise how completely bonkers I must have come across."

"Oh, come on now, Amelia," Charlotte said, placing hand on hip. "You wanted to win the competition so much because you thought it would impress the voters of Laxey," she pointed out. "You acted like a madwoman with me in service of reaching your goal, to win, and thus sway the election in your favour, just admit it."

"What…? No!" Amelia said, appearing upset by the insinuation. "Charlotte, if you only believe one thing I tell you today, you need to know that it wasn't for that reason. I genuinely adore Laxey and the people living here, despite the derogatory remarks I stupidly made about them. If anything, I'm now unsure about running in the election, as I'm no longer confident I'm doing it for the right reasons. It all comes back to that whole feeling-of-inadequacy thing again. I wanted to feel good about myself, which is why I threw my name in the hat in the first place."

"Okay…" Charlotte replied. "But…"

Amelia lay her hands flat on the table, head bowed. As if precisely on cue, a tear fell down her cheek, landing on the dusting of flour on the table's surface. If this was a performance, then it was a bloody masterclass, Charlotte thought.

"Charlotte," Amelia went on, sounding very much like a broken woman, "I wanted to win because I was so afraid to embarrass myself for being an abject failure. After I managed to convince the lovely people sat out there in the hall to get involved, along with the school kids," she confided, "I just didn't want to let any of them down after all of the hard work they'd put in. I was convinced we'd done enough to win it, and then you pulled the rabbit out of the hat at the last minute. That's why I ended up buying in the extra squares, hoping that might put me back in first place. Stupid, I know. Anyway, I didn't ask to speak to you hoping for forgiveness, Charlotte."

"Okay?" Charlotte said, still not convinced that Amelia was being entirely sincere, but still willing to let her continue and to hear what she had to say.

"Your forgiveness would be a wonderful thing, but I'm certainly not expecting it," Amelia continued. "No, the reason I asked you here was that I wanted to tell you in person that I'm withdrawing from the competition. And as for the conversation you recorded, well, you'd be well within your rights to play it on social media or to give it to the press, and I couldn't blame you at all if you did."

Charlotte looked over to Mollie, who remained silent due to her face presently being full, still happily chomping away, having finished her first scone and then secretly stealing another while the others were busy talking. "Amelia..." Charlotte said, feeling the need to finally come clean, herself, after Amelia's own surprising revelation. "Amelia, there is no recorded conversation. I didn't actually do that."

"But I saw you," Amelia responded. "You showed me the phone."

"Yeah, about that. I lied," Charlotte replied, looking down to her feet. "I can barely send a text message, and I'm not entirely sure my phone even *has* a record function. I just thought it was a good way to stop you from being a..."

"A witch?" Amelia suggested, along with a somewhat relieved laugh.

"Yeah, a witch," Charlotte said, laughing as well. "So. Now that you know there's no recording, is this where you show your true colours and throw us out on the street?" Charlotte asked, raising one eyebrow, and bracing herself for the possibility of being thrown out on the street actually happening.

Amelia laughed again. "No, you're fine, I promise," she assured Charlotte. "Besides, I've seen Mollie here carry a large burlap sack of potatoes across each of her shoulders, so I wouldn't be so brave as to even *try* to kick you out," she joked.

Charlotte and Mollie's strategy planning, what there'd been of it at least, had now fallen by the wayside. None of the strikes or counterstrikes they'd envisaged had played out as they'd imagined, as there was ultimately no battle at all to be had. "Look," Charlotte said, feeling slightly guilty now, "Amelia, please don't withdraw from the competition, okay? As you say, all of your people out there have given their all for this."

"Oh. Okay," Amelia agreed, surprised, but definitely grateful. "Thank you. That's very kind."

"However," Charlotte continued, "there are nine other groups in the competition. They've all put in just as much effort and devoted just as much time. So I'm not sure it would be fair on them if you were to win under what really are deceptive practices, even if you have seen the error of your ways."

"Oh. Okay? So I *should* withdraw?" Amelia asked, willing to agree, but not quite clear on what she was meant to agree on.

"Why don't you wait until the award ceremony this afternoon and see if your team actually win," Charlotte proposed. "If you don't, well, then I suppose it really doesn't matter. If you *should* happen to win, though, I'm not going to tell you what you need to do. You'll just need to do the right thing, Amelia. Do what your heart tells you."

Amelia wiped her hand on her pinny and then walked over, extending her hand. "Thank you, Charlotte," she said, sounding contrite. "And I genuinely mean it."

"Amelia," Charlotte replied, sincerely, "if ever you're feeling inadequate again, just look out into that hall and remember how many people you're helping, and how many of them might be sat at home, on their own, with nobody to speak to. Look out there now, and you'll see a room full of people talking to their friends and doing something they enjoy. *You* did that!"

"Thank you, Charlotte," Amelia said again, escorting her guests from the kitchen, whereupon Amelia did precisely as Charlotte had suggested, running her eyes around the bustling church hall. "Ah, on you go, Jimmy," Amelia said, as Jimmy approached.

Jimmy, it turned out, was the most excellent mandolin player whom Charlotte had seen earlier strumming away. Jimmy had also, it would appear, agreed to delectable scones in lieu of any payment for his services, from the looks of things, and was eager to sample more of them judging by the way he was anxiously sniffing the air.

"They *were* cracking scones!" Mollie offered passionately, wiping her top lip free of a bit of jam that'd stuck itself there.

"Oh, and Charlotte, before you go..." Amelia said, raising her hand like she'd just remembered something she wanted to say.

"What's that?" Charlotte asked.

"What I said to you about George," Amelia began. "I tried to phone him earlier to offer him the contract extension. I wanted you to know that I did that purely because he's an excellent worker, and not because I thought you'd recorded our conversation. It's important to me that you know that. He secured the work entirely on his own merit. You do believe me when I say that?"

"I do," Charlotte said. "And thank you. I'm sure he'll be delighted."

"Great! So, I expect I'll see you later this afternoon?" Amelia said, seeing them off. "And it was nice to formally meet you, Mollie."

"You should get back to your scones," Charlotte advised. "Jimmy there has got one in each hand, and lord only knows how many he's already stuffed in his gob," she said with a laugh.

"On it," Amelia answered. "Oh, and if you wanted to stay for a bit, I'm sure there's plenty of wool for you. They'd all make you most welcome."

Charlotte glanced straight over to Mollie, like a child asking their mum if they could go on the bouncy castle.

"Go on, then," Mollie replied. "And I can get a nice cuppa to wash that delicious scone down."

"Excellent," said Charlotte, reaching into her handbag. "This is why I always carry an emergency project for impromptu crafting sessions just such as this!"

CHAPTER TWENTY-SIX

With the benefit of hindsight, it became clear that the charity had been rather conservative in its forecast of the numbers attending their inaugural crafting square competition prize presentation. The original plan was for the awards ceremony to take place indoors, and with refreshments to be served in the modest-in-size boardroom afterwards, all nice and cosy and civilised. At least that had been the idea.

Unfortunately, the organisers had failed to appreciate the sheer amount of crafters involved, along with their friends, supporters, and assorted eager well-wishers, who all desired to be on hand for the day's events. And as the starting time of the event drew ever nearer, the number of attendees kept on rising. It was like a festival for crafters — a sort of Woollen Woodstock, if you will. But certainly nothing that an adaptable organisation like the charity couldn't handle. And the man tasked with ensuring the smooth and orderly schedule for today's proceedings was Justin, the charity's calm, experienced, unflappable, imperturbable PR manager...

"Shit, shit, shit, shit!" Justin shouted, each time his foot hit the tarmac. He came to a sudden halt, placing his hands to his face, like the figure in Edvard Munch's most famous of paintings, *The Scream*. He covered his eyes, and then gradually splayed his fingers, daring to peek through at what lay before him. "They just keep on coming!" he shouted to nobody in particular, watching as yet another busload appeared into view.

Fortunately, being on the outskirts of town on a large industrial estate, the parking facilities were ample, and the neighbouring units happy to accommodate any overspill. However, Justin's meticulously organised event — weeks in the planning — was unravelling like a ball of wool being pawed at by a cat. "Who's stolen my walkie-talkie!" Justin screamed, raising a hand above his head to try and attract the attention of those ambling by, as if the screaming wouldn't have been enough in itself. With the vein in his forehead in real danger of erupting, he bent over, palms against his thighs, taking several deep lungful's of air to compose himself, but failing miserably.

A nearby Charlotte, spotting the wayward walkie-talkie in question, reached down into a sea of feet, snatching up the misplaced piece of equipment before it could be either crushed or possibly kicked into oblivion. "Were you shouting about this?" she asked, returning the missing device to a relieved-looking Justin.

"Yes," he said, examining the casing for damage. "Thank you," he added, wide-eyed like a madman. "They just keep on coming," he whispered, left eye twitching uncontrollably.

"Oi, slick! I've got just the answer!" said Joyce, trundling close behind Charlotte and stepping forward to save the day. "Take a nip of this, and you'll be right as rain in no time!" she offered, extending her hand and prodding Justin with her hipflask.

Justin, it would appear, was too far gone at this point, waving away the offer of liquid medicine, and walking away like a man who wasn't exactly sure whether he was coming or going.

"Suit yourself," Joyce said, re-holstering the life-saving elixir into her handbag (for a short while, at least).

"Are you expecting this afternoon to be particularly thirsty work?" Charlotte asked, raising her arm like a bird's wing so Joyce could link back in as she had been previously.

"It's *her* fault," Joyce suggested, looking across Charlotte's chest to the person now swooping in and linking Charlotte's other arm, the trio back together again as they'd been not long before.

"It's bloody well not!" Beryl shot back, offended by the insinuation.

"You're the one who bought a bottle of Johnnie Walker!" Joyce said, deflecting any blame. "And you *know* I can't resist a drop of Johnnie."

"I didn't make you fill up your flask with the stuff and drink it, though, you old lush," Beryl countered. "You can pass it here if you don't want it, then."

Joyce shook her head. "No, it's fine," she said. "I'm happy to help you out," she added, selfless hero that she was, of course. "Besides, we'll hopefully be celebrating soon."

"Come on, you two," Charlotte said, chuckling to herself. "Let's go and find the rest of the club before you two end up too tiddly to see."

Justin, or perhaps someone from the charity who was a little more composed, had started the transition process of the day's proceedings from inside the building to outside. Fortunately, the often-unpredictable Isle of Man weather appeared receptive to this last-minute change of plans, offering up a blanket of blue sky and a generous application of warm sunshine for good measure. Also, rather than the minor change in venue being something of an inconvenience, it was the perfect recipe for a party atmosphere, as it turned out. Word of the gathering crowd must have quickly spread, as several industrious catering vans descended en masse, appearing to sniff out the prospect of a quick buck the same way sharks smelled blood in the water. And before you could say the words "crafting square," there was a queue ten deep over at the ice cream truck, and the aromas wafting from the burger vans were divine.

The growing numbers included a healthy contingent present from Charlotte's own CRAFTERNOON SEWCIAL CLUB and MAKE IT SEW gangs, swelled even further by at least twenty residents from the other nursing homes, accompanied by family members eager to see for themselves what the competition was all about. It was a similar story all around, as Charlotte could see from glancing about the carpark. Overall, there were eleven groups involved, and it appeared that each of them was represented in force, all contributing to the lively mood.

Charlotte escorted Beryl and Joyce through the friendly throng, keeping one eye out for Mollie, who'd gone on ahead to find the others. Charlotte stood up on tiptoes as she walked in order to see over the ocean of heads, searching all around until her calf muscles started to ache under the strain. "Mollie texted me and said to look out for Larry's hat, but I don't see how…" she began. "Oh, there it is," she said, finally spotting the hat in question.

Charlotte adjusted their trajectory slightly to the left, keeping the top of Larry's hat in view so they didn't veer off course. Larry probably didn't realise it when he'd dressed earlier, but his J. R. Ewing-inspired ten-gallon hat was the perfect beacon to guide them through the mob, and it was clear now why Mollie had recommended to Charlotte that she use it for this purpose.

"Howdy, partners," Larry said to Charlotte & co as they arrived, tipping his hat, cackling happily away.

"Looking sharp, Larry," Charlotte said, looking him up and down. "And there was me thinking the cowboy guise extended only to the hat. So, why a cowboy outfit, exactly?"

"Because Stanley double-dared me to?" Larry said in response. Larry then adopted his very best squinty-eyed Clint Eastwood impersonation, finger-pistols extended and hanging loose next to his leather chaps. "Do ya feel lucky, punk? Well, do ya?" he asked, continuing to keep his eyes scrunched up.

"Ehm, Larry, I think you're mixing up your Dirty Harry with your High Plains Drifter…?" Mollie, beside him, offered gently. But Larry wasn't listening, as he was currently enjoying himself too much.

"I bought the outfit from one of those TV shopping channels!" he explained. "With today being a special occasion, I thought this was the ideal opportunity to offer the get-up its first outing. Plus, it's all a bit of fun!"

"He can show me his pistol anytime he likes," Beryl remarked, a little louder than she'd perhaps meant to, her lips loosened courtesy of the Johnnie Walker she and Joyce had shared earlier.

There was some sudden movement in the area directly in front of the charity building just then, with Justin and an assistant dragging out and placing several office folding tables in a semi-circle, creating a dividing line between the crowd and this newly designated presentation area. In only a short space of time, he'd also secured himself a high-viz yellow jacket and, once the tables were in place, was now in the process of wheeling out an oversized speaker that he'd somehow managed to procure. He may have been highly strung but was, evidently, resourceful enough when the situation required it. He plugged in a microphone, connecting it to the speaker, and then it looked like he was ready to go.

"Yes, hello," Justin announced into the microphone — which was connected without success, it would appear, judging by the muted volume of his voice. "Hello," he said once more, adjusting a couple of dials on the speaker casing. Justin recoiled when the speaker burst into life, releasing in the process an ear-splitting screech. "Sorry!" he apologised, playing with the dials so that optimum settings could be achieved.

"Ah," Justin said, standing upright now, chest out, shoulders pressed back. "There we go," he announced happily, tapping the microphone with the tip of his finger, using it as one might ping a crystal glass with a knife around the dinner table to attract attention. "Can you hear me all right at the back?" he asked, cupping his ear and slipping into the role of MC with relative ease. "Excellent," he declared, upon receiving a handful of grunts in response from those waiting by the doughnut van that'd just turned up. "Right," Justin went on, as a collective shush rippled through the crowd and those who weren't already doing so turned to see who was speaking and hear what was being said. "Just a quick announcement to let you know that we'll be getting things underway in around ten minutes or thereabouts," he said, slowly and deliberately, over-enunciating each word. "So, please. Eat, drink, and be merry."

"You heard the man, Beryl," Joyce responded, immediately rummaging in her handbag.

Several official-looking persons emerged from inside the building a few moments later, stepping outside to convene and converse with Justin.

"Oh, *hello*," said Mollie, moving closer to Charlotte, and giving her friend a gentle tap in the ribs with her elbow. "*Someone's* certainly made an effort," she remarked, giving a sly glance over at Calum, who was amongst those making their way out, before looking back again at Charlotte.

"That's the way he *always* looks," Charlotte replied. "And he does wear that suit well, doesn't he?" she observed, offering a mildly flirtatious wave in Calum's general direction.

"You're not wrong there," Mollie confirmed, sneaking another quick peek over towards Calum. "So when's he taking you out?" she asked.

"Monday," Charlotte answered, a statement which brought a most serene smile to her face. "He's taking me to the theatre," she added, causing her smile to falter just a bit, becoming slightly less serene.

"The movie theatre?" asked Mollie, a mite confused, as she'd never known Charlotte to frequent the other type.

"No, the *theatre* theatre," Charlotte clarified.

"Oh?"

"Yeah... I think I might have suggested I was a regular there. You know, to make myself sound more cultured than I actually am."

"Well," Mollie said, "that's what you get for trying to act more sophisticated than you really are."

"But I *am* sophisticated!" Charlotte countered. "And very in tune with the local arts movement! At least that's what I might have let on. Several times, in fact."

"*Pfft*," Mollie scoffed. "You wouldn't even watch the movie Frozen with me because you said it had too much bloody singing in it."

"Well..." Charlotte said, turning up her nose. "Maybe I'll just have to add it to my Netflix queue tonight, won't I?"

The delicious smell of doughnuts arrived a split second before Charlotte felt someone tugging on her sleeve. "Stanley!" she said, bending down and moving straight in for a cuddle. "Your mouth's covered in sugar!" she said, an observation that didn't prevent her from planting a sloppy kiss right on his lips.

"Muuummm," Stanley protested, wiping his mum's yucky, public kiss away, and sadly, in the process, most of the surplus sugar as well.

"Yoink," Mollie said, dipping her hand inside the grease-stained white bag in Stanley's mitts, and liberating one of the delectable, tasty treats from within. "Thanks," she offered, giving Stanley a cheerful wink for good measure, as if he'd had any choice in the matter anyway.

"I've just seen that Amelia," George announced, appearing a few paces behind Stanley.

"Good afternoon to you also," Charlotte joked.

"You'll not believe what she said," George continued, undaunted. "She's offered me a new contract."

"She hasn't...?" Charlotte said, acting surprised, her reaction giving nothing away about her prior knowledge in regard to that very subject.

"Not only that," George said, caressing his bushy beard, "but she's offered me a pay rise as well!"

"Way to go," Charlotte replied, punching George playfully on the arm. "That's great news."

"Here..." George went on, something apparently puzzling him, judging by the confusion on his face. "You don't think she's buttering me up, do you?" he asked. "You know, for a bit of..." he said, winking several times, followed by a click of his tongue, and all topped off with a whistle. "I'm spoken for, after all."

Charlotte looked blankly at him for a moment, processing that whole tongue-clicking, etc thing he'd just done. "George, you're a fine specimen of a man, of that there's no doubt. But, on this one, I think I'm confident in saying you're safe. She was complimenting your work ethic only just earlier today, so I reckon it's likely down to your ability rather than your rugged animal magnetism. Plus, she's happily married."

Shortly after, a collective, pained groan broke out as the familiar squealing, squawking noise emanating from the speaker indicated the award ceremony was about to begin. "Sorry about that," Justin said into the microphone, plugging his ear for comic effect. "There, that should fix it," he suggested, twiddling more knobs in quick succession. "Okay," he continued, sweeping his hand over the tables in front of him. "This is what we're all here for," he said, introducing the three trophies sat there, all alluring and on display for all to see. "Can I first take the opportunity to thank each and every one of you here today, and especially to those who kindly participated in the charity competition. You just need to look around and about at the impressive crowds, and you'll know just how popular this initiative has been. So, again, thank you. And, without further ado, I'd like to introduce our lead sponsor, Calum Whitlock, CEO of Microcoding."

Calum stepped forward, taking the microphone from Justin and acknowledging the warm applause. "Thank you," he said. "Wow," he added, running his eyes around the area of the carpark. "When I pulled up in my car earlier, I wasn't sure if I'd come to the right place. To see you all here, the vast numbers present, is simply staggering, and I'm pretty sure poor Justin here was on the verge of a nervous breakdown a little while ago!"

Justin rebuffed the suggestion with a wave of his hand. "All under control!" he shouted, receiving a laugh in return.

"So," Calum said, returning to the script, "when I first heard about this competition, the organisers were mildly optimistic about the amount of participation. But I don't think that even in their wildest dreams they'd have envisioned the roaring success it has become, and neither did I. Now don't shoot me, but my ill-informed perception had been that crafting was the preserve of the mature lady knitting a blanket by the fire."

"We do!" one old dear quipped from the audience.

"Quite so," Calum said, raising a smile. "I suppose what I'm trying, quite badly, to say, is that I didn't fully understand or appreciate the true extent of this wonderful hobby. Over the previous few weeks, I've enjoyed visiting schools, nursing homes, hospitals, and even a firm of motor mechanics, to see your craft squares in progress. What struck me the most is how all-inclusive your hobby is. I witnessed all sorts of different people making all sorts of different things, all having a fine old time, and all involved in a worthwhile cause. When my sister suggested I get involved in sponsoring this competition early on, I'm a little embarrassed to say I initially turned my nose up at the suggestion."

"Boooo!" a raucous heckler entered in, but it sounded like it was delivered in fairly good humour, at least.

"*Exactly*," Calum replied, agreeing with the heckler's sentiments. "Yes, to think that I nearly missed the opportunity to get involved in this project! It would have been a huge mistake on my part, and I genuinely mean that."

"Hurrah!" the fickle heckler said, chiming in once again.

"Thank you," Calum said, looking into the crowd, but failing to locate the owner of the voice. "I'm humbled by the caring, generous, and talented people that I've had the pleasure to meet on my brief journey with you all," he went on. "And I've also learned how to crochet in the process, though I think I may need a few more lessons," he suggested, picking Charlotte out from the masses and looking directly over to her. "So. Let's get to it, then, shall we?" he said, looking to Justin for the first stage of the presentation. "And here we go," Calum said, taking possession of the trophy Justin kindly provided to him, along with a sheet of paper.

"And, first up..." Calum began, glancing at the typed page. "We've got the award for the most squares produced by an individual. And having attempted to make one myself, I can appreciate just what a herculean effort this must have involved. With *one hundred and forty-three* completed squares to her name, I'm thrilled to announce, the winner is... Phyllis Lyon! Come on over here, Phyllis."

"Bloody hell, that's going some!" Charlotte whispered to Mollie. "We need to get Phyllis onto the Crafternoon Sewcial Club team," she suggested, taking a mental note to track the woman down after the award ceremony. "We'd be unbeatable next year with her on board!"

"What about that," Calum said, joining the applause as Phyllis, having received her trophy, wandered off with it clutched to her chest, a beaming smile on show for all to see. "What a truly talented lady," Calum added, along with a contented sigh.

"Right. Moving on to the next award," Calum said, moving on, and glancing down to his trusty sheet of paper. "This is an award we've called the *Spirit of the Stitch*, and one that's been nominated by you, the crafters. We wanted to recognise those who selflessly give their time and devotion to the hobby, those who are the backbone, organising community events island-wide, promoting crafting to a wider audience. Now, I've had the pleasure to see this person in action myself, first-hand. And to say she's a crafting superstar is probably the biggest understatement you'll hear today.

Ladies and gentlemen, I give you Charlotte Newman, founder of the Crafternoon Sewcial Club, Make It Sew, and serial crafting teacher around the Isle of Man."

"Oh, bugger," Charlotte said, not expecting this, and not really one for the limelight, her cheeks turning crimson in an instant.

"Way to go, Mum!" Stanley squealed, jumping up and down in excitement. "That's my mum!" he shouted, pointing at her in case anyone should be unsure as to who Charlotte Newman was.

"You deserve this, you wonderful person," Larry said, smiling proudly as Charlotte was nudged forward by Mollie.

"Where are you?" Calum said, looking in the general direction of where he'd last clapped eyes on her.

"She's here!" Stanley was pleased to announce, waving his arms wildly. As Stanley was quite a bit shorter than most in attendance, George took the liberty of picking his son up so that all could see him, with Stanley pointing vigorously at his mum from this somewhat higher, advantageous elevation, leaving Charlotte with absolutely no hiding place.

"You go, girl!" Beryl shouted, followed by Joyce also chipping in with, "One in a million, that one!"

Reluctantly, Charlotte trudged to the front, smiling politely to those offering their congratulations. It was clear from the rapturous applause what Charlotte meant to those gathered. Charlotte smiled, accepting a kiss on both cheeks from Calum. She took hold of the trophy, looking out, happy on the outside, blushing on the inside. Well, actually, she was blushing on the outside as well. "Thank you," she said timidly, into the microphone. "But really, I should be giving all of *you* an award, for letting me do what I love doing most in life. And that would be crafting, eating cake, and meeting wonderful people."

With her short, impromptu acceptance speech duly delivered, she began to move away. Calum, however, had other plans, preventing her departure with a gentle hand on her arm.

"Along with the votes," Calum said, resuming his place at the microphone, "the organisers, as many of you know, also asked for any comments supporting the nominations. There were, as you would imagine, a good number we could choose to read out. But

I've been asked to relate to you just one, this one, from Elouise Sibbald, aged eleven. Elouise writes:

"My grandad recently passed away, and my wonderful Nan was so very sad. They did everything together and were best friends. She stopped going out, and hardly ever left the house. I tried to get her to come to the park with me, but she kept on making excuses not to because I think she was just too sad. Her normally bubbly, happy spirit I was so used to was gone, and I was worried all she wanted to do was to go and join my grandad. Then my mum saw the advert for the Crafternoon Sewcial Club and thought it might help. It wasn't easy to convince Nan to go, but once she finally agreed we all went along and it was the three of us. The moment we walked in, it felt like home. Everyone was lovely. Nan recognised many of the people there and spent quite a lot of time in particular catching up with one lady she used to work with. Nan has put her crocheting skills to good use and especially enjoys the cake. There's always lots and lots of cake. She still gets sad but smiles more than she cries now. I like having my nan back in my life, and Nan now has more friends than she knows what to do with. It makes me so happy to see her with a sparkle back in her eyes, so thank you, Charlotte, and thank you to the special group of people who are now our friends.

"Ladies and gentlemen," Calum said, "I couldn't have put it any better than Elouise Sibbald, eleven years of age. And there you have it. Charlotte Newman, everybody."

Calum waited a few moments, allowing Charlotte to return to her group now that she was very thoroughly embarrassed by all the fuss made over her. He watched on as Larry, Joyce, Beryl, Bonnie, Stanley, Mollie, and the rest of her great extended crafting family welcomed her back into their arms, smiles all around, and giving her plenty of assorted pats on the back and the like.

"Well, then," Calum said, after the applause for Charlotte had come to its natural conclusion. But then he noticed some folks were distracted over at the rear. "The ice cream van's not going anywhere just yet!" he joked, tapping the microphone politely, encouraging everyone's attention to be directed towards the front once more. "Well, then," he resumed. "This brings us on swiftly to the main event, the award for the group who produced the most crafting squares during the course of the competition. It's genuinely mindboggling to think about how many collective hours have been invested in reaching the final tally. It's also humbling to think about how your combined efforts will be used by those who need them the most. For that, and on behalf of the charity, we're genuinely grateful. Now, I should tell you, the grand total of the squares made on the Isle of Man, as a whole, is a whopping forty-three thousand, seven hundred and sixty-two! Just let that register for a moment, folks. It's completely staggering."

Calum lubricated his vocal cords, taking a drink from the glass sat on the table before him, allowing people the opportunity to let that huge number sink in, as he'd suggested.

"So, in third place..." Calum continued, a few moments later, and pausing dramatically to build up the suspense, drawing out the reveal for slightly longer than was really necessary. "In third place, the team from Stitch N Bitch!" he announced, clapping one hand against the microphone. "I had the pleasure of spending some time down at the Stitch N Bitch HQ with Trudy and the gang," Calum remarked. "And let me tell you, my sides are still hurting from laughing along with them all. What a great bunch."

Watching on anxiously, Mollie leaned in close to Charlotte's ear. "You could be in with a shot here," she suggested, whispering to Charlotte as she clapped along politely for the fine third-place winner.

"Moving on to second place..." Calum announced, taking a gander at the sheet in his hand, and repeating the process of implementing a very long pause for dramatic effect. The crowd of hundreds stood in silence, willing Calum to get the words out from his mouth. "The runners-up are..." Calum said. "The Crafternoon Sewcial Club and friends!"

"Ah, bollocks," Joyce said, evidently not somebody who was too magnanimous in defeat it would appear, though fortunately the noise from the rest of the appreciative crowd managed to drown out her frustration.

Those standing in front of Charlotte parted like the Red Sea, allowing her safe passage to the makeshift stage area once more.

She was disappointed her group had not won first place, yes. But more so for the rest of the team than herself, as they'd worked so hard and she really wanted them to bask in the glow of victory. (If they'd won first place, she'd even planned to bring each and every one of them up with her in order to share their collective moment in the sun.) But, alas, that was not to be, at least not for the current year. Still, second place was certainly nothing to sneeze at. And also, Charlotte received a further two pecks on the cheek from Calum, so there was that as well.

She held the handsome trophy aloft, giving it a little wiggle for the benefit of the other Crafternooners watching on. And it was just then Charlotte caught a glimpse of Amelia clapping, stood there with her own group of able crafters. It would be fair to say, noted Charlotte, that Amelia gave the appearance of someone very much wishing the ground would open up to devour them. Amelia wouldn't necessarily have had any insight as to who the group in first place might be, but her grave expression suggested that she was hoping it *wouldn't* be hers. Naturally, this was a sentiment, as one might expect, not shared by her colleagues, who were of course not privy to Charlotte and Amelia's earlier conversation. Many in Amelia's group, in fact, were clinging to each other in excited anticipation as they waited upon Calum's all-important next words.

"This is it!" Calum said, whipping the crowd into a cheering frenzy by holding up the shimmering winner's trophy in his hand. "In first place, and winning the inaugural crafting square competition, is…" he said, pausing as Justin handed him a cream-coloured envelope with a red ribbon tied neatly around it. "Sorry. One moment," Calum advised with a chuckle, placing the trophy on the table so he could free up his hands. He unfastened the ribbon, eased open the flap on the envelope, and removed the card from within. "The winner is…" he said, unfolding the card to reveal the answer. "The winner is, the Laxey Coffee Morning Crew!" Calum announced happily, looking straight over to where his sister was standing.

They were a popular winner, judging by the deafening cheer that erupted, but Amelia stood like a rabbit in the headlights, looking very much like she didn't know what to do next. "Come on up here!" Calum said, encouraging her to come forward.

For a brief moment, it appeared as if Amelia was getting ready to turn and run, though in which direction it wasn't exactly clear.

"Come on!" Calum said, laughing. "Those who know my sister will know she's not usually this shy!" he joked.

Those standing about Amelia offered up their congratulations, all pointing excitedly to the stage in an effort to coax her up there. Eventually, after what seemed like forever, she started to move with the enthusiasm of an inmate walking the Green Mile, smiling like she had a severe bout of trapped wind.

"The Laxey Coffee Morning Crew!" Calum said, greeting Amelia with a hearty embrace. Calum handed over the trophy, which was accepted as reluctantly as if it had been attached to a lit fuse.

"Ehm… thank you," Amelia said meekly, forcing a smile. She gripped the trophy, holding it out in front of her like she wanted to keep it as far away from her as possible, while a photographer crouched down, hopeful of a snap for his next edition.

Charlotte, watching from the sidelines with her own trophy, took absolutely no pleasure from seeing Amelia in this awkward sort of position. She thought she would, not that long ago at all. Heck, she'd dreamt about seeing Amelia squirming like this for one reason or another. But right now, as the current scene played out before her, Charlotte's only instinct was to walk over and give the poor woman a hug.

Charlotte looked over to Amelia's club members, who'd turned up for the occasion in force, hugging each other and savouring the moment they'd all toiled so very hard to achieve. As Charlotte had learned, they weren't a group of people under the spell of a tyrant who was beating them until they'd fulfilled their daily crafting quota. No, they were a happy lot, as was perfectly evident by looking at them, all of them there to enjoy the fruits of what they'd accomplished by working together as a team. Also present were twenty or so school-age children, who Charlotte suspected were keen on learning from Amelia just who among them had been successful in winning the coveted PlayStation game system. But regardless of why they were there, they were there, of their own volition, on a Saturday afternoon. Amelia had managed to coax a group of teenagers into participating in a crafting competition, learning skills that would remain with them long after the gaming console was (heaven forbid) tossed in the bin. This, in itself, was no mean feat, in Charlotte's opinion, and something Amelia ought to be commended for.

A speech was naturally expected, and so Amelia cleared her throat, taking hold of the microphone from her brother. "This trophy means a great deal," Amelia said earnestly, looking over to her group, all smiling up at her. "To see you all here today warms my heart. And I don't just mean the members of my club, but all of you, everyone here," she said, looking out into the wider audience. "It's a testament to the community spirit of the island's residents, and demonstrates your generous attitude and charitable nature. You should all be rightly very proud of your participation, and what you've achieved."

Amelia lowered her head for a moment, taking a fleeting glance at the trophy she'd set down on the table before her. "Sadly, I can't accept this," she said softly, although not many beyond the front row could hear her just then, as she had allowed the microphone to drift away from her face. "I'm sorry," she said, lifting her head, and holding the microphone back up to her mouth. "Sadly, I can't accept this," Amelia repeated. "I don't deserve this, and I'm afraid I cannot accept it," she said, the strain in her voice evident.

There were a handful of confused but polite laughs in response, with people likely assuming this was a bit of simple humility on Amelia's part, or perhaps the lead-in to some sort of joke or other.

Amelia placed a single hand on the award, and then shifted the trophy a little off to one side. "My conduct has not been entirely honourable throughout this whole process," Amelia went on, a statement which brought a collective hush to the audience. "I was blinded by an overwhelming desire to win, which I'm ashamed to admit rather clouded my judgement."

Charlotte glanced over to Mollie with a grimace, covering her face with her hand. This was agony for her to watch.

"For what I've done," Amelia continued, "I shouldn't be stood here collecting this trophy, and for that reason, I'd like to—"

"Nonsense!" Charlotte called out, stopping Amelia before she could say anything more, and then stepping out of the crowd and making her way back to the stage. All eyes were now focussed on her, and while she didn't enjoy the attention, it was as if her legs were moving of their own accord, instinctively propelling her forward. Once up at the stage, Charlotte leaned in towards the microphone. "Amelia here is far, far too modest," she announced, which prompted another scattered round of confused, but this time slightly relieved, laughs from the audience.

"I am?" Amelia asked, rightly confused by the interruption.

"Sure you are," Charlotte replied, patting Amelia gently on the shoulder. "You see..." Charlotte continued, taking possession of the microphone, and all fears of being in the limelight apparently exorcised. "You see, what was worrying Amelia was that several of her group members also belonged to *our* crafting group," she said, speaking to everyone now and not just Amelia. "And being the silly sausage that she is, she worried that she'd gained an unfair advantage by counting the squares produced by another club's members in her own tally," she explained.

Charlotte waited a moment for the crowd to catch up with the unfolding drama. "She's just being daft, am I right?" Charlotte asked, cupping her ear to encourage a response from the audience. "Is she being daft?" Charlotte asked again, waking the masses from their confused state.

"Nothing at all to worry about!" shouted one person in answer. "Take the trophy!" urged another, and so on.

Charlotte picked up the trophy, holding it out for Amelia.

"I don't... I don't understand..." said Amelia, speaking directly to Charlotte and away from the microphone.

"Take it. You deserve it," Charlotte whispered to her. "Sure, you may not exactly be as pure as the driven snow, Amelia. But none of us are. And your heart was absolutely in the right place. So go ahead and take this trophy on behalf of your club members, who've all worked their bloody socks off for it."

"Okay," Amelia said, appearing slightly dazed. "Thank you," she added, taking the trophy, and holding it up in front of her. "Thank you," she said again, this time speaking directly into the microphone once again. "This is for you," she said, pointing it towards the members of her LAXEY COFFEE MORNING CREW. "I wouldn't be stood here without all of you amazing people. And a big thank you to everyone here as well. Cheers to you all!"

"Stanley!" Charlotte called out, trying unsuccessfully to grab his sleeve. "Will you give Beryl her walking stick back, please!"

But her request went unheeded, as Stanley continued riding the walking stick like a horse, struggling to see precisely where he was going on account of Larry's cowboy hat currently drowning his head.

"He's fine," Beryl offered, sat by the presentation tables with Joyce for company. "If I need to go anywhere, I'll lasso him with my scarf," she suggested, warming up her lassoing skills by swirling her hand in the air, above her head.

"Here you go, ladies," Bonnie said, placing paper plates down onto their table, beside them both. "The burger on the right has got the extra-hot chilli sauce, as requested," she reported.

"That's Joyce's," Beryl said, pushing the plate over to her friend. "And I wouldn't want to be sat next to her on the way home after she's eaten that," she added with a grimace.

I'll have you know my farts smell just like poo-pourri!" Joyce protested. "Always perfectly lovely!"

"Thought you'd appreciate this," Mollie said, arriving on scene with two ice-cold bottles in hand, offering Charlotte a selection of one beer and one cider from which to choose.

"Where'd you snaffle these from?" Charlotte asked, glancing about, and snatching up the bottle of cider quickly before it was possibly taken away from her. "And thank you."

"Some bloke's selling them from out of the back of his van," Mollie explained. "Not sure it's strictly legal, if he's got a licence to sell alcohol or if it's just some chancer who turned up hoping for a thirsty crowd, but hey, either way..." she added, raising up her own bottle in salute.

"Cheers," Charlotte replied, matching the glass-bottled salute, and then taking a grateful sip of her apple-derived nectar.

"I must say, Lotti," Mollie went on conversationally, "I wasn't really expecting an awful lot for today. Not really my idea of fun, you understand. Although no offence meant, because naturally it's always lovely to spend time with you. But, yeah, I've really enjoyed this afternoon, I have to tell you, and... and, uh..."

"Oi! Hello! Are you listening to me...?"

"What? Oh, sorry, Molls. Yeah, it *has* been fantastic, hasn't it?" Charlotte replied, though not giving Mollie her full concentration right at the present moment, as dear a friend as Mollie of course was.

Mollie turned to see where Charlotte's attention was currently being focussed. "Is that the lady who won the trophy for the most squares?" Mollie enquired. "Phyllis, I think it was? You're going to pounce on her. You are, aren't you?"

"Oh, yes!" Charlotte answered immediately, without the slightest of hesitation. "Only she's been talking to the vicar for bloody *ages*," Charlotte moaned. "The moment she's finished, then I'm right in there," she added, a CRAFTERNOON SEWCIAL CLUB application form already produced in her free hand, prepared to be thrust in an unsuspecting Phyllis Lyon's palm.

"You may need to wait a bit longer," Mollie suggested, looking across the mouth of her raised beer bottle towards the approaching Calum. "I'll leave you to it for a while," Mollie offered, and at which point she moved accommodatingly away in advance of their guest's imminent arrival.

"Something I said?" Calum asked, smiling as he watched Mollie wandering off.

"Oh, hi," Charlotte said. "No, not at all, just something about getting a burger," she assured him. "Anyway, well done up there, Calum. You sounded great over the microphone," she offered.

"I had fun," Calum replied, unable to contain his cheesy grin. "Listen," he said, lowering his voice, and moving a step closer. "I spoke with Amelia..."

"Oh?"

"Yes, as to why she was acting strangely. Or, well, weirder than usual, at any rate. And she told me all about... *you know.*"

"Ah, okay."

"Yes, and I just wanted to thank you. What she'd been thinking at the time is anyone's guess. Still, it would have been a shame to penalise her club members for a moment of complete stupidity on her part."

"*Several* moments of stupidity, in fact. But, agreed," Charlotte said, raising her bottle.

"So. About the theatre on Monday," Calum went on, moving the direction of the conversation away from Amelia. "I just wondered if, perhaps instead, you might fancy a few drinks and then a visit to my favourite Italian restaurant?"

Charlotte puffed out her cheeks, followed by an audible exhale and a sigh. "Well… I *do* adore the theatre" she began. "But, if you absolutely *insist* on a nice meal instead, then who am I to argue?"

"There was just one more thing I wanted to discuss, if possible?" Calum asked, glancing over his shoulder, and then back to Charlotte.

"Yes, of course," Charlotte replied, intrigued.

"Okay. You know that there's a cash prize for the winning team as well as the trophy?" he asked.

"Sure I do. It was very generous of you to sponsor it."

"Well, the thing is… Amelia has suggested that you might like to distribute the proceeds, rather than her?"

"I don't understand," Charlotte said. "Our group didn't win."

"I know. But Amelia thought you'd be better placed to allocate the funds, what with your extensive crafting background and all, and also given the, ehm, shall we say, somewhat awkward circumstances of her win."

"Ah. I understand," Charlotte replied. "That's very kind of her."

"After totalling up all the various sponsorships," Calum revealed, "the final cash amount comes to a little over six thousand pounds."

"Six thousand!" Charlotte responded, eyes nearly popping out of their sockets. "You mean I get to spend all of that money on crafting supplies for the local nursing homes?" she said, heart skipping a beat at the very prospect.

"If you'd like to?" Calum asked.

"Yes. Yes, I would. Very much so, in fact. I absolutely would. Did I say I would?"

"Wonderful," Calum said, sealing the deal with a handshake.

"Oh. I think I much preferred the kiss on the cheek, like earlier," Charlotte suggested, presenting her cheek to be pecked, although her mind was partially drifting away, thinking of the fortune she'd soon have available to spend in Joan's Wools and Crafts.

Calum did as instructed, one peck on each cheek, so the deal was completely sealed and with no going back. "Also…" he added, fidgeting like he wasn't sure how to go about saying whatever it was he wanted to say.

"Spit it out," Charlotte said with a laugh. "You've caught me at a good time."

"The issue as I see it," Calum ventured, "is that we need somebody to make sure these new supplies are to be put to best use, and utilised to maximum effect, as it were. Lessons, classes, and such."

"Yes, I'll be doing just that," Charlotte entered in, thinking this should have been completely obvious. "With my trusty assistants Stanley and Mollie likely chipping in, of course."

"I know," Calum replied. "But from what you've told me, you do all that purely on a volunteer basis. And you can't possibly pay your mortgage purely on good wishes, after all."

"Okay," Charlotte replied, not entirely sure where this might be going.

Calum shifted his weight between his feet, and then continued. "Charlotte, the thing is…" he said. "Well, the thing is, my company also offer several charitable grants each year."

"Okay?" Charlotte replied, still not entirely sure where this was going. Naturally, she could kind of guess. But the last thing she ever wanted was to appear in any way presumptuous, and so she allowed him to go on.

"So, I've seen first-hand the positive impact you've had on people. It's unbelievable to think about everything you've already achieved, helping so many in the community by volunteering so much of your time, when you could easily be doing other things. The question is, how much more amazing work could you do if you were paid to do it as a full-time job?"

"Ooh, lots," Charlotte replied, happily imagining the possibilities.

"Wonderful. So it's agreed?"

"What is?" Charlotte asked — although she wasn't daft, harbouring more than a sneaking suspicion about what it was that Calum was suggesting. Daring to believe it was another matter, however.

Calum smiled as he clarified. "For the next three years, you'll receive funding to roll out a programme of crafting classes," he said. "Now, I know you already do this at some of the nursing homes. But this should allow you to extend your reach to all of them. Assuming you'd like to, that is?"

"Are you saying you'll *pay* me to teach crafting?" Charlotte asked, squirming like she was about to pee herself.

"Yes!" Calum was happy to report. "You do need to understand that this is not solely my decision, however. That is, we have an independent charity committee that votes on such things. All I did was merely suggest you and your work to them, and they're the ones that rubber-stamped the final decision. But this is good, because bear in mind what that also means is that if we go on a date, and you think I'm the most oversized boring oaf on earth and never want to clap eyes on me again… Well, I'll be devastated, of course. But our relationship status, good, bad, or even non-existent, would have no bearing whatsoever on our committee's decision. Their focus is purely based on your charitable work and nothing else."

"I'll need to think about this," Charlotte said, eyes wide as saucers.

"Of course, yes. Take all the time you need to consider all of—"

"I'm joking!" Charlotte said, gently cutting across, and jumping up and down on her invisible pogo stick. "I would absolutely, positively, like to take you up on your offer."

"Do we need to seal the deal again?" Calum enquired.

"Yes, we do," Charlotte said, presenting her cheeks once more, each one in turn, which were both duly pecked, as prescribed. "Oh, wait until I tell Stanley," she added, looking around for a small person wearing an oversized cowboy hat. "This isn't a dream?"

Charlotte asked. "I've not fallen asleep somewhere?"

"No dream," Calum was pleased to inform her. "This is just what you deserve for being one of the most talented, selfless, and generous people that I've ever had the pleasure to meet," he said. "That is, even if you *did* lie to me about liking the theatre," he added with a wink.

"What?" Charlotte protested, before quickly giving up on presenting any form of defence. "Mollie told you?" she asked with a shrug.

"Yes, she did."

"That little..." Charlotte began to say, just as Stanley rode up towards them. "Stanley!" Charlotte said, reaching out for him just as he was about to gallop on by. "Stanley, come over here for a moment," she said, beaming with delight.

"What is it, Mum?" Stanley asked, dismounting his trusty steed and then drawing near.

"I've got some exciting news to share with you," she said. "And I think you're going to really like it."

CHAPTER TWENTY-SEVEN

"What the devil is that?" Beryl asked, hurriedly reaching for the spectacles that were hanging around her neck on a red cord strap.

"It's just like Cinderella's carriage," Joyce suggested. "Oh, my. How lovely," she added with a titter.

"Blimey O'Reilly, an *actual* horse and carriage?" Beryl said, now that she could see further than the length of her nose. "They certainly do things a bit differently than when I was a girl!" she remarked, shaking her head in wonderment as the magnificent mode of transport in question approached.

"Never mind *that* one. Clap your eyes on the mechanical beast coming after it!" Larry offered, drawing their collective attention to the bubble-gum pink Lamborghini easing its way up the drive following soon after, growling its arrival, and practically shaking the foundations of the surrounding buildings. "Holy guacamole, that's a thing of beauty," Larry observed, impressed further when, after coming to a stop, the car's gull-wing doors opened vertically to allow its occupants to disembark.

The Villa Marina, a sprawling entertainment complex situated in the island's capital of Douglas, was home to a splendid ballroom, and perfect for hosting the day's event, the annual school prom. The tarmac drive from the roadway to the main carpark was, presently, like something from an episode of *Top Gear*. Waiting patiently for clearance to proceed, an expensive array of vehicles, many of them rented out especially for the gala affair, were waiting to deliver their respective VIP passengers. Then, after said passengers' audacious arrival, it was a short walk up the sumptuous red carpet for them, past the waiting friends and family all there to witness them in their school prom finery.

The air was thick with the scent of both expensive perfume and exhaust fumes, a heady mix. Shimmering diamantes sewn into exquisite ballgowns reflected dazzling sunlight directly into the eyes of those watching on appreciatively.

"Is that them?" Stanley asked, each and every time another car pulled up in front of the red carpet.

"No," Charlotte had replied in response (on autopilot), each and every time as well. "Oh, wait," she said, raising her hand to shield the last of the evening's sunlight from her eyes in regard to this very latest in the series of Stanley's queries. "Hang on. Yes. Yes, it is."

Larry, Beryl, Joyce, Charlotte, Stanley, and Mollie all huddled behind the mob of camera-wielding folk. Like them, the others waiting patiently were there to photograph their loved ones stepping out of the various chariots appropriated for the evening, dressed to the nines. However, no matter where Charlotte & company stood, it was difficult to obtain a perfectly clear view due to the sheer numbers in attendance.

"Oh, fiddlesticks," Charlotte said, struggling to get anywhere near to the front as the chauffeur got out and made his way round to open the door of Bonnie's long black limousine. "Excuse me," Charlotte said politely, raising her camera to indicate her intention. But her pleas were promptly ignored by those standing their ground, eager to remain in whatever prime location they'd secured for themselves.

"Shift it!" Joyce barked, dispensing with the cordialities. "Two minutes is all we need, and then we'll be out of your way!" she added, forging a path through the crowd with her elbows, using her old age to her advantage, as it would have been terribly impolite to interfere with someone of such advanced years and mature standing.

Charlotte avoided awkward eye contact with those stepping to one side, making sure to keep close to the ever-advancing Joyce, using her as a human snowplough. "Well done, Joyce," Charlotte whispered once they were positioned near the front, readying her camera to take an action shot of Bonnie stepping from the car, and then doing just that as Bonnie did so.

"Doesn't she look absolutely divine?" Beryl said, following in just behind.

"She's like a princess," Joyce replied, dabbing at her eyes with her white handkerchief.

At the foot of the red carpet, Bonnie was soon flanked by her dad on one side and Sue on the other, both of whom had travelled with Bonnie in the limo, as Bonnie's date would be meeting her there, and Benjamin and Sue decided that a good limo ride shouldn't go to waste. It was evident from the reddening around Benjamin's eyes that the journey had been an emotional one for him. Fortunately, Bonnie's carefully applied makeup appeared to have survived intact, however, with her not succumbing to quite so much emotion as to mar it.

"Oh, Charlotte, would you look at that," Mollie said, stood there beside the others, and captivated by the understated beauty of Bonnie's scarlet ballgown. "That dress is simply stunning."

"Isn't it, though?" Charlotte happily agreed. "And it's so nice for Bonnie, as well, knowing that her mum and dad both had a hand in making it." It was also a fitting tribute, thought Charlotte, that Sue — being her mum's best friend — was on hand to help escort Bonnie up the red carpet along with her dad.

It was never lost on Charlotte just how personal some crafting items could be and also the comfort they often brought to people. And so whether it was a bunny rabbit made from an old school uniform, a memory cushion crafted from a loved one's shirt, or even a ballgown that she'd helped somebody finish, Charlotte invested the same amount of passion as if each item were her own.

"That's so special," Charlotte said, clicking away and capturing the moment for Bonnie and her dad to view later, as well as anyone else in the group who might wish to enjoy the images. It certainly pulled on Charlotte's heartstrings, observing the sheer devotion in Benjamin's eyes as he stood beside his precious daughter. They'd been through so much as a family, and to see them happy and smiling here now was an absolute pleasure.

With photographs taken and mission accomplished, Charlotte

and the crew turned to make their way back and thus clear a space for others to use. A few moments later, however, it was evident that Stanley was not among them.

"Now where's that boy gone…?" Charlotte wondered aloud.

"Charlotte, I think someone's inherited their father's eye for the ladies," Mollie suggested, one eyebrow raised, looking back to where the group had stood before. Young Stanley hadn't moved, and was still rooted to the spot as a steady procession of pretty girls paraded along the red carpet directly in front of him, one after another. "Come on, kiddo," Mollie said, after going back to fetch him, tapping him on the shoulder and snapping him out of his reverie. "Plenty of time for all that in a few years," she advised with a chuckle.

"Right, then. Do we stay any longer?" Charlotte enquired, looking around at the rest of the group for answers once they were all back together again. "We've seen Bonnie, and I've managed to get some lovely photos, which I'll share with anyone who wants them. So, maybe leave them to it?"

"I'm sure the ice cream shop is still open," Stanley chipped in, hope etched on his face.

"I could go for an ice cream," Larry said, rubbing his tum.

"Oh, look, there she is with her friends," Beryl pointed out, watching on as Bonnie, further up the red carpet now, was twirling like a ballerina showcasing her dress. "Bonnie!" Beryl called out, along with a vigorous wave.

"Leave her be," Joyce suggested. "We just saw her, after all, and I'm sure she doesn't want to be bothered with old duffers like us anyway."

However, Bonnie looked over, returning the cheery wave. She said something to her friends, and it appeared she *was* bothered about the old duffers, as she was now heading right in their direction, with three of her equally elegant girlfriends happily in tow. "These are my crafting buddies I told you about," Bonnie proudly announced to her girlfriends upon arrival, dispensing a round of generous hugs to Beryl, Joyce, and the lot.

"Bonnie…" Larry said, taking a step back to fully appreciate the wondrous vision stood before him. "Bonnie, you look absolutely radiant, young lady. And it's my opinion that any suitor who has his name on your dance card this evening is the luckiest chap on the Isle of Man."

"Aww, Larry. That's so lovely, thank you," Bonnie replied graciously.

"Oi, earth to Stanley," Charlotte said, prodding her son's arm. But he wasn't for distracting, captivated once again by the lovely young ladies before him. He looked up at them all, which was no surprise, really, as Bonnie and her three friends were roughly two feet taller than him, and possibly more, considering the height of their heels.

"We were hoping to come along to Crafternoon," one of the girls said brightly. "Bonnie's told us all about it."

"I'd love to be able to knit a bobble hat," said another of the girls.

"Not a problem," Joyce offered. "Get yourselves along, and we'll get you knitting in no time."

"How about a quick group photograph, of all of us?" Charlotte suggested, now that Benjamin and Sue had joined them also.

Charlotte commandeered the services of a passing couple to act as their photographers, so that she could get placed into the shot as well. "Snuggle in," Charlotte said, wrapping her arms around both Beryl and Joyce as they stood amongst the others, and with Stanley down in front.

"Smile," their willing photographer instructed, raising a thumb to indicate she was poised and ready. "Okay, say cheese."

"The Crafternooners!" Bonnie said instead, improvising with a broad smile.

"The Crafternooners!" the rest cheerfully repeated.

After that, Bonnie offered up her goodbyes, glancing down to the new watch her dad had bought her to complement the dress. "We'd better go," she said, noticing some of the others were now making their way into the main building.

"Oh! I just realised I've brought my camera along but haven't taken any pictures," Joyce said, raising her hand. "Bonnie, how about I take a quick photo of just you and your dad?" she proposed.

"Yes, please," Benjamin said, finding this to be a perfectly splendid idea, and smiling as he moved in and placed his arm around Bonnie's waist.

"Ooh, good idea. I'll take one too!" Charlotte chimed in, strategically positioning herself for another shot as well.

Joyce reached into her handbag, rummaging around for the digital camera that was somewhere amidst the darkest recesses within. "Ah, here we are," she said, upon finally locating the device, pulling it out with a flourish. "Beautiful!" Joyce declared, as she took aim, and then held her finger down — a little too long, judging by the audible, protracted series of clicks.

"I'm fairly certain you've just taken about sixty pictures there," Beryl suggested, shaking her head with a laugh.

"Well, thank you all for coming," Bonnie said, blowing a kiss to the group as she headed toward the Villa Marina with her friends now that the business of picture-taking had been sorted.

"You look stunning!" Benjamin replied, catching the kiss before anyone else could, and then returning one of his own.

The CRAFTERNOON SEWCIAL CLUB gang watched on for a few more moments until Bonnie and her friends were safely inside.

"Come on," Charlotte suggested, taking hold of Stanley's hand. "Should we get going?"

"Hang on, what the blue bloody blazes...?" Beryl said, delaying their departure for just a moment longer. She crouched down near to where they were standing, running her hand through the grass.

"Everything okay, Beryl?" Larry said, walking over. "Can I help?" he asked, ever the gentleman.

Beryl picked up the thing that'd taken her attention, there on the grass. "Joyce, I think this must have fallen out of your bag when you grabbed your camera," Beryl said with a smirk, standing upright now and holding up what she'd found for all to see.

Charlotte moved in for a closer inspection. She knew what she *thought* it was, but her brain told her it couldn't possibly be what she was thinking. "Is that not a...?" she said.

"It looks like a...." Mollie added, tilting her head. "It is. That's a leopardskin thong."

"Yes!" Beryl was happy to confirm. "And I'd dare to venture it's the very same leopardskin thong that our friendly neighbourhood male stripper was looking for."

Joyce shrugged her shoulders in response, appearing decidedly unsurprised and unperturbed by the discovery. "Oh, they landed by my feet when he was gyrating," she explained casually. "And somehow or other they must have accidentally ended up in my bag, although I honestly can't say how," she added, with a devious grin.

"Bollocks!" Beryl shot back. "You nicked them as a souvenir, you saucy old devil!"

"Well it's hardly my fault, is it?" Joyce replied, in her defence. "I'd had three large gins and tonic and didn't know what I was doing, now did I?"

Stanley tugged on his mum's sleeve, eager to get involved in this conversation it would appear. "Mum," he said, attempting to get his mother's attention. "Mum, what's a gyrating stripper, and why would he throw his underpants at Joyce?"

"Come on," Charlotte replied, looking down and acknowledging her wee one. "Let's go and get that ice cream," she advised, using the tried-and-true, universally accepted way of distracting one's child.

"With a Flake?" Stanley countered, like he knew just what he was doing in this negotiation.

"Yes, you can have a Flake."

"Can I have a Flake, too?" Larry asked, with puppy-dog eyes.

"Only if you've been a very good boy," Charlotte suggested.

"Marvellous!" Larry announced. "Good friends and ice cream. It certainly doesn't get any better than that!" he declared, leading the way.

The End (for now!)

If you'd like to find out what the Crafternooners get up to next, v 2, *The Crafternoon Sewcial Club: Sewing Bee* is available now! You can find all of the details and order via the author's website at:
www.authorjcwilliams.com/the-crafternoon-sewcial-club-2

And if you'd like to learn more about the Isle of Man's real-life Crafternooners who inspired this book, please visit:
www.makeitsewiom.com

Also by the Author

If you've enjoyed this book, the author would be grateful if you would be so kind as to leave feedback on Amazon. You can subscribe for updates and news on new releases at: www.authorjcwilliams.com

Also, if you've enjoyed this book, then please check out the author's other offerings!

The *Frank 'n' Stan's Bucket List* series:

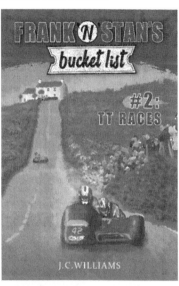

The Lonely Heart Attack Club series!

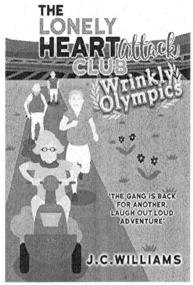

The Seaside Detective Agency series, and also *The Flip of a Coin* and *The Bookshop by the Beach*:

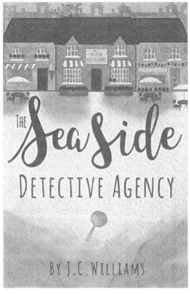

CABBAGE VON DAGEL

J. C. WILLIAMS

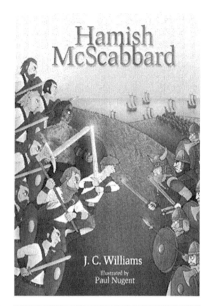

Hamish McScabbard

J. C. Williams

Illustrated by
Paul Nugent

LUKE 'N' CONORS

HUNDRED-TO-ONE CLUB

ONLINE IS FINE... BUT CAN IT COMPARE TO FRESH AIR?

J.C. WILLIAMS

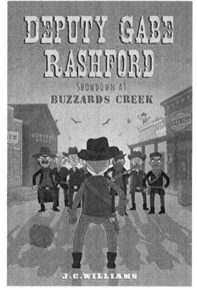

DEPUTY GABE RASHFORD

SHOWDOWN AT
BUZZARDS CREEK

J.C. WILLIAMS

Printed in Great Britain
by Amazon

32755352R00193